FIRST LESSON

Sir Nicholas's smile was mocking. "You've never even been kissed, have you?"

Emma was defensive. "Several gentlemen have *tried* to kiss me."

"I'm not surprised," he said softly as he twined a lock of her blond hair about his finger. "I think that you were very wise to wait until you had someone—hm, shall we say experienced—to introduce you."

"I . . . don't understand what you mean."

"I think you do." He touched the line of her throat as she swallowed convulsively. "Surely you are not afraid?

"Someone might come along."

He laughed, and bent and kissed her, a kiss nicely calculated to arouse yet not frighten her. When he drew back he had to steady her with a hand on her arm. "Let that be a lesson to you, Miss Berryman . . . and a standard. . . ."

Elizabeth Walker, who also writes as Laura Matthews, was born and raised in Pittsburgh, Pennsylvania, but after attending Brown University she moved to San Francisco, where she lives with her husband, Paul, who is an architect. Ms. Walker's favorite pursuits are traveling and scrounging in old bookstores for research material.

THE LOVING SEASONS

Elizabeth Walker

A SIGNET BOOK
NEW AMERICAN LIBRARY

SIGNET TRADEMARK REG. U.S. PAT. OFF. AND FOREIGN COUNTRIES
REGISTERED TRADEMARK—MARCA REGISTRADA
HECHO EN DRESDEN, TN, USA

SIGNET, SIGNET CLASSIC, MENTOR, ONYX, PLUME, MERIDIAN and NAL BOOKS are published by NAL PENGUIN INC., 1633 Broadway, New York, New York 10019

First Signet Printing, April, 1989

1 2 3 4 5 6 7 8 9

PRINTED IN THE UNITED STATES OF AMERICA

PROLOGUE

Everything had seemed so simple then. Emma perused the last invitation, wistfully remembering how orderly she and Anne and Maggie had thought life would be when they left school and burst on the London season. They had expected the stacks of pasteboard invitation cards, including them in masquerades and rout parties, balls and soirees. Wasn't life to be a whirl of carriage drives, picnics, strolls in the park, visits to the theater?

For three young ladies with the proper backgrounds, the best schooling, adequate dowries, life in London's exhilarating social clime was to be the greatest adventure thus far embarked upon. They had spent hours discussing fashion plates and members of the ton, most of whom they would not have recognized had they come face to face. But their visions were peopled with handsome gentlemen of rank, ballrooms bedecked with spring flowers, sparkling sunlight pouring down on them as they walked in the parks. For who could escape their own shining freshness: Emma's exotic coloring, Maggie's fine eyes, Anne's glorious hair? Girls fresh from the schoolroom, eager for what life had to offer them. What gentleman could be so insensitive as to pass them by?

But they *were* girls, when all was said and done: girls with more eagerness than knowledge, more enthusiasm than prudence. Emma could look back and see that now. Their dreams of how their lives would progress when they walked out the doors of Windrush House had not a shred of practicality. Things had started to go wrong even before they left school. Reality had intruded on their make-believe world and they had been powerless to handle even that first crisis. Emma had thought herself stronger than the others, but she had found herself no more effective then than she had been later in solving her own dilemmas.

As she placed the last invitation with the others in the stack, Emma sighed. Another season, and she was not at all sure she could face it. She smoothed out the skirt of the gray Circassian cloth dress, amused at its lutestring roses and modest bodice. Nor exactly the sort of dress she had expected to be wearing! Though, come to think of it, probably it was more in keeping with the school dresses they had all worn that day two years ago.

FIRST SEASON

CHAPTER ONE

Windrush House stood off the main road to Kensington and travelers unfamiliar with its purpose, that of educating young ladies of the first families to their future role in society, were more likely to think it the country seat of a minor aristocrat or a prosperous member of parliament. The village of Kensington was not far distant, and from the upper stories of the elegant Palladian mansion one could catch a glimpse of the roofs of shops in the High Street. Windrush House was a superior establishment, not merely providing the usual lessons in conduct and needlework, but including in its curriculum a smattering of drawing, dancing, music, French, Italian, arithmetic, and astronomy. The brochure for the academy pointed out that these fine arts were not extras, as one would find in the majority of schools, but included in the modest sum of forty pounds a year. Even tea and sugar were included, though there *were* extras (mentioned in smaller print) for letters, mending, washing, and tips. *However,* out of the fee each girl was allowed a shilling a week for pocket money, which most of the girls used to supplement the rather spartan diet with gingerbread in the village.

When not otherwise occupied, the young ladies frequently sat at the windows on the second floor, which looked out over lush lawns to the toll road beyond, and wove tales about the young blades who traveled the road in their dashing equipages. On this particular day, when spring was beginning to show signs of arriving at last, there were an exceptional number of modish vehicles plying the road but the three girls who sat in the parlor never once glanced out the window. One, a slight, pale miss, sat clutching a boldly penned letter in her hand and feeling as though the world had taken a violent turn quite beyond her comprehension. She lifted gray eyes to her companions who were anxiously watching her.

"My father has arranged a marriage for me."

"How very archaic!" protested the taller of the others, a striking blonde whose vivacious personality had made her the acknowledged leader of the little group ever since her arrival at Windrush House some years previously. Emma Berryman had not only a quickness of mind, but an aura of worldly knowledge (imbibed from her notorious aunt, Lady Bradwell) that never failed to attract the notice of her companions. She it was who always knew the latest on dits, who planned the most amusing pranks, who had an air of elegance and spirit that none of the others could ever hope to duplicate, though several tried, only to fall into the most ignoble scrapes. "Well, Maggie, don't leave us to expire of curiosity. Who is he?"

The name was unfamiliar to Margaret Somervale, which only made the matter worse. She had to consult the letter. "Lord Greenwood."

There was a sharp intake of breath from the third girl. "But, Maggie, he's a *rake*. My brother William has said so often enough. I couldn't be wrong about the name for it always reminded me of Robin Hood. Will had him to Parkhurst once when I wasn't home and Papa suggested that he leave after a week because of his . . . attentions to the maids."

"Oh, ho!" Emma cried, delighted to have some fix on the fellow. "I remember now. My aunt devoted almost an entire letter to him last winter, calling him a 'droll dog' and a 'sadly dissipated rascal.'" At Maggie's horrified gaze, she laughed. "Don't misunderstand, Maggie. Those are words of high praise from my aunt. She said she was forever amused in his company, though he was an impudent puppy with a love of riot and an ambition to be a buck. Let me think, now. What was it he'd done? Aside from making a set at her, that is. And you must know that my aunt is given to a certain amount of exaggeration about her conquests and amours. Hmm, I'll have to find the letter; I keep them for just such an occasion."

The third member of their group, Lady Anne Parsons, took Maggie's hand and pressed it, with a frowning glance at Emma. "Don't be alarmed by Emma's tales from Lady Bradwell, or my wretched memory, my dear. After all, Lord Greenwood is a friend of Will's, so he cannot be entirely lost to all sense of propriety."

This comment, meant to be encouraging, provided little relief to Maggie, who thought Lord William Parsons a terrifying being with his hearty laugh and rough good humor. Not for the world would she have said so to Lady Anne, of course, but she was a shy, retiring girl and boisterous men alarmed her out of all proportion to their intent. Perhaps it stemmed from her fear of her father, whose booming voice and frequent rages had, in her youth, sent her scurrying to her room to hide under the bed. Sir Robert was quick-tempered and held to a primitive theory of justice that had occasioned his striking his only child for misdemeanors when young, and though he was as quick to forget the punishments, Maggie was not. Her father had no clear idea of how to raise a daughter deprived of her mother at a tender age, nor had he any conception of how painful were the blows a sporting man could deliver to a child. His was not a cruel nature but neither was it tender. In his household he expected obedience, and Maggie had soon learned to give it, so much so that he found her too retiring and insipid to be of the least interest, and he sent her off to school, for which action she was extremely grateful to him. And now to find that he had arranged for her to marry a man such as her friends suggested Lord Greenwood to be! Her spirits flagged.

Lady Anne, who shared with Maggie a more serious turn of mind than Emma, attempted to restore some hope to the distressed girl. "Perhaps your father doesn't actually mean that he has arranged a marriage, but that he has spoken with Lord Greenwood about you. After all, Sir Robert is not likely to have contracted a settlement when you and his lordship have never even met."

"Papa is to bring him here tomorrow and we are to be married quietly next week. That is exactly what his letter says."

Whether she was more indignant with Sir Robert for his high-handedness, or his daughter for her lack of spirit, Emma announced, "Well, I would just tell him I have no intention of complying with his wishes, Maggie! You cannot mean to sit back and do nothing. Why, you will not even have a chance for a season in London. Don't you remember that you and Anne and I were going to set the town afire come next month? Just tell your father you will require time to get to know Lord Greenwood, and that a season is the perfect way."

Maggie folded the letter with a sigh. "No one tells Papa anything, Emma. He tells everyone else what to do . . . and they do it."

"Nonsense. This is your whole life you're talking about," protested Emma. "If our parents were willing to have matches arranged for them, we certainly are not of the same persuasion. Besides, I find it difficult to believe that someone of Lord Greenwood's reputation would so meekly agree to marrying a lady he's never seen. How do you account for that?"

In her misery Maggie had given no thought to that angle, but Lady Anne had been turning it over in her head without the least success. Certainly it seemed wondrous to her that Sir Robert could arrange such a match. Lord Greenwood was the owner of a handsome estate near High Wycombe and surely not in need of money. Anne's brother William had told her he was an open-handed man of fortune, so he could not possibly find himself in need of Maggie's considerable dowry. Of course, no man would reject such good fortune—but the fellow hadn't even met his bride-to-be!

With a worried wrinkling of her brow, Maggie said fervently, "I hope Papa hasn't told him I'm pretty. That would be too, too bad of him. There was a miniature done of me, but it's hardly like at all. Papa insisted that the artist give me more coloring and round out my features. I don't know why he bothered in the first place." She compared her own straight black brows with Lady Anne's delicately arched brown ones. Her own hair was a coal black while Anne's was a chestnut brown, which had the felicity of appearing to change color in various lights. And where her coloring was uncommonly pale, her friend's had a peachlike tone that gave her face an animation even when almost expressionless. There were too few curves in either of them to alleviate the trim, almost boyish figures, but Anne didn't suffer from a thin nose and high, prominent cheekbones, which Maggie thought, quite unfairly, gave her a rather pinched appearance.

Emma watched Maggie make the comparison and offered helpfully, "Anne and I will have you looking your best tomorrow, my dear. Mrs. Childswick cannot complain, considering the occasion. I have some fashion plates from *The Ladies' Magazine* which will inspire the most elegant hairstyle for you, and you may borrow my new walking dress, which will suit you to perfection. Have I shown it to you? It's a figured silk my aunt brought me last month, and it's the first stare, I promise you."

"Thank you, Emma, but I couldn't borrow your dress. I'm sure I must have several costumes of sufficient respectability to be presented to Lord Greenwood." Maggie rose stiffly and offered a brief, nervous smile to her friends. "You'll excuse me if I go to our room, won't you? I need a moment to compose myself."

"Of course you do," Lady Anne agreed, with more heartiness than she felt, and watched sadly as Maggie wended her way down the long gallery beyond the parlor. She saw the girl pause briefly before a portrait she had once mentioned bore a resemblance to her mother, before continuing dejectedly toward the girls' room. "Poor dear."

"Yes, but I ask you, Anne, would you accept such a decree from your father?" Emma insisted.

"My father wouldn't do such a thing." Lady Anne went to stand at the window, but she paid no heed to the high-perch phaeton passing on the road. "You've met Sir Robert. He's just the sort of country squire one most avoids—blustering, autocratic, interested only in his own comfort. I daresay he's done this simply because Maggie would be leaving school soon, and he didn't want to be bothered with keeping track of her. What a lonely life she's had!"

Though Emma's own life had not been filled with a loving family such as Lady Anne's, she was not one to allow others to pity her, especially since she intended to lead quite a different existence once she entered the social whirl of London in a matter of weeks. Emma hadn't had either parent since she was eight and had been shuffled between relations until she was sent to school. But her Aunt Amelia had taken a definite interest in her as she had developed into an elegant young lady, sharing far more of her exploits than an inexperienced girl not even out yet should perhaps have been an auditor to. There *was* a Lord Bradwell, but no one had seen him for years and Lady Bradwell cut a dashing figure in London entirely on her own. Emma had every intention of plunging into the high life with her.

"I don't need to consult the letter after all," she said now, "for I have just recalled exactly what it was poor Maggie's rake had done. Aunt Amelia was enchanted, and it was an instance she gave of how very charming he is. There is an actress, everyone apparently calls her the Jewel, who is in the keeping of a wealthy gentleman from Lincolnshire. I don't remember his name, but the story Aunt Amelia had heard was that he was not often in town and that Lord Greenwood sent the Jewel a draft for a hundred pounds, begging her for an interview. The lady sent back his draft with a note saying, 'The shoe is on the other foot, my lord. Call at three.' Which does say something for him, you must agree," Emma suggested with dancing eyes.

"For God's sake, don't tell Maggie. It is not the least likely to cheer her. I daresay she'd be a great deal more comfortable with a clergyman than with someone of Lord Greenwood's cut. What can her father be thinking of to arrange such an unlikely match?"

"I'm far more intrigued with *how* he managed it," Emma confessed.

* * *

Adam Robert Greenwood, sixth Baron Greenwood, was considering the same question over a bottle of port in his London town house. For the past two days he had done little else but mull the matter over and consider whether there was any conceivable avenue of escape, short of the dishonorable course of fleeing the country. Not that he had ever seen Margaret Somervale, but he had a hazy hypothesis on the subject, which was that children frequently took after their parents in looks, and if the chit bore the least resemblance to the rough, red-faced Sir Robert, he would rather die than wed her. This was more than a whim with Lord Greenwood; according to his own theory, weren't his children of her likely to resemble the florid country squire? Of course, he was somewhat solaced by the fact that his sister took after their mother, while he bore a strong likeness to his father, so if Lady Somervale had possessed some modicum of looks everything might be well. (On the other hand, if she had, why had she married Sir Robert?) But since that lady was long dead, there was not the least chance of finding out what she had looked like.

Dammit, who cared what she looked like? If she were a diamond of the first water it would make very little difference to him. He had not the least intention of marrying . . . that is, he hadn't until he had run across Sir Robert. For all the man's gruff, hearty nature, Lord Greenwood suspected, now that it was too late, that he was hardheaded and a rather close observer of his fellowman. Which, unfortunately, put Lord Greenwood at a decided disadvantage. His lordship found practically everyone he met to be good-humored, civil, honest, generous, agreeable, sensible, and open. It was his personal goal to be rational and composed while yet lively and entertaining. He certainly excelled in the latter two virtues, but whether he would ever achieve the former, not even his best friend would hazard a guess. While he could admire a man of constancy and reserve, he could not always enjoy his company to a high degree, and thus lacked the resolution to transform himself from the flighty fellow he acknowledged himself to be into a more genteel character. Life was very amusing just as he was living it, and he had the most lowering feeling that a more elevated existence would be a dead bore.

When Captain Midford was announced, Lord Greenwood was slumped dejectedly in a spoon-back chair contemplating his glass of port with a baleful eye. His lordship's perpetual grin was missing, which made the decidedly patrician nose look more at home than it usually did with his merry blue eyes and open countenance. The slight build was graced by impeccably tailored coat and pantaloons, though his lordship gave little attention to his attire and depended on his valet to turn him out in style. No hint of his flamboyant and frequently whimsical nature was to be detected in his dress, and only in country clothes did it become apparent that he was a notably agile and athletic man.

The captain cut a far more dashing figure, and had in addition a military carriage and aura of heroism that he fostered, though he had, at the conclusion of the war, gone on half-pay status when his regiment was broken up. Without invitation, being a frequent visitor to the house in Half Moon Street, he lowered himself into a chair and said, "I talked to Dunn about it. He said you were a fool and deserved to suffer for your indiscretions."

"A fine help he is, and surely not one to talk."

"Oh, I don't know. He does precisely what he wants, but he never seems to get in any scrapes. He couldn't see any way out of your marrying the girl, and said you'd best accept it with a good grace if you want to maintain your dignity, if you have any."

"You needn't repeat every word he said, Stephen," Lord Greenwood grumbled. "I know he thinks I'm a loose screw, though for the life of me I don't see why. I don't do anything he hasn't done any number of times over the last ten years."

"You haven't his style," the captain retorted, offended for his brother's reputation. "He says without a doubt Sir Robert tricked you, but quite legitimately, taking advantage of your hey-go-mad way of life. He says it might as easily have been me Sir Robert chose for his clever game, but for my lack of title and independent fortune."

"Dunn does admit it was clever, then?" Lord Greenwood asked eagerly.

"Not a trap in which he would himself have been caught, he assures me, but just what he might have known would happen to you . . . or me. He thought you arrogant to believe Sir Robert so simple as to make a foolish wager."

"Arrogant!" Stunned at first by such an epithet, Lord Greenwood after a moment's consideration grinned sheepishly. "I thought he was dicked in the nob, to be perfectly frank. To bet that a message could not be carried fifty miles in an hour! Of course, no postboy could have done it with any number of horse changes, but everyone knew Queensberry had proved it could be done years ago."

"Which is precisely why Sir Robert was sure you'd take the bait. Dunn says we should have smelled a rat the moment the old man suggested his terms. His five hundred guineas against your marrying his daughter, sight unseen! He had little to lose, compared with you. But we were so sure of ourselves!"

"Old Q had hired a team of twenty cricketers to toss the message about in a circle in a cricket ball. They went the fifty miles well within the time and it didn't seem so difficult to accomplish the task again. I simply assumed Sir Robert had never heard the tale. How was I to know it would be so damned difficult to find twenty capable men at this time of year?"

"Dunn says you were careless, that you could have assembled the necessary talent if you'd tried hard enough."

"I didn't have the time. Sir Robert only gave me three days."

"Dunn says you should never have allowed that stipulation in the wager."

"Oh, your brother can go to the devil! I'm not interested in what he says."

"Well, you told me to ask him."

Lord Greenwood thumped an impatient hand on his knee. "Yes, and what use was he? Calls me a fool and an arrogant fellow, and tells me to take my medicine like a good boy."

"Not exactly," Captain Midford retorted, thoughtfully stroking his sandy mustache. "Your only hope, according to my brother, is that the young lady won't accept you. The wager certainly said you were to marry her if you lost, but it would be impossible for you to do so if the girl won't have you. So Dunn suggested—though he said he would not himself do it on any pretext, but he thought you probably might—that you make yourself as disagreeable to the girl as possible. Not rude, or anything like that, just sullen and as though you were not entering into the contract with any enthusiasm. That might put her off or make her angry enough not to agree to the arrangement. After all, her father is hardly likely to tell her the true circumstances."

Though Lord Greenwood's eyes had lit at the possibility, he frowned and asked, "And why wouldn't your brother do such a thing?"

"Because he don't think it's honorable, that's why. Actually, though, I think it's because, for himself, he wouldn't want to look bad. Old Dunn can charm the ducks out of a pond; everyone says so. If he sets his mind to a lady, all he has to do is give her one of those looks of his and she's eating out of his hand. It would be repugnant to him deliberately to set out to discourage a lady, unless she'd been forward or presumptuous or something."

There was silence for some time while Lord Greenwood considered the problem. "Why would Sir Robert have gone to the trouble at all if the girl were presentable? And if she ain't, what in the devil's name am I to do with her as a wife?"

"Just what everyone else does, I imagine," the captain answered practically. "Leave her in the country and go about your business in town. She's in a school, isn't she?"

Greenwood groaned. "Don't remind me. I'm to go to Kensington with Sir Robert tomorrow to meet her. A schoolroom miss, for God's sake! You know all my involvements have been with older women!"

"I thought the Jewel was only five and twenty," the captain suggested mischievously.

"Well, that's a hell of a lot older than seventeen, and several years older than I am! And what will Cynthia say?"

"Haven't you told your sister? You really should, Adam. She'll be upset if you marry without telling her."

"I will tell her . . . if I have to. Dammit, Stephen, the man expects me to wed the girl within the week! If I can't get out of it, I'll have Cynthia and Morton to the ceremony of course."

"So you're going to try to discourage the girl?"

His lordship stomped one elegantly booted foot on the Turkey carpet. "Oh, Lord, I don't know."

CHAPTER TWO

Lady Anne received Mrs. Childswick's permission for the three young ladies to absent themselves from their lessons the next morning by the simple expedient of telling her that Sir Robert was calling with a suitor of Miss Somervale's. Since the schoolmistress's unstated aim was to prepare her girls for making eligible matches, she acknowledged the wisdom of the two friends providing encouragement, and she hoped a modish toilette, for the shy Margaret, whom she was more than a little convinced would be unable to open her mouth in the presence of a distinguished gentleman. Not that she had anything of which to complain in Miss Somervale's attention to her studies or her grasp of each of the subjects on the curriculum, but the girl was as timid as could stare when even the dancing master was in her presence.

It had taken a great deal of effort on Emma's part to talk Maggie into wearing the figured silk of green leaves on a gray ground. She stood back, her head to one side to study the effect. "You look charming, Maggie. I knew it would suit you, especially the full collar. You really should let us do up your hair into braids on the crown of your head. It's all the rage."

"The ringlets are quite enough. I've never worn them so profusely about my face," she confessed, glancing nervously in the mirror. "You don't think they make me look more pale?"

Lady Anne smiled reassuringly. "Not at all. They emphasize your bone structure. I think you're wise to wear the simpler hat. Have you a fan?"

As Maggie nodded, there was a tap at the door and Sir Robert's arrival was announced. The girl's face drained of color and Emma pinched her cheeks to restore it, saying heartily, "Your father will scarce know you, all rigged out in fashion. I daresay he's not seen you in aught but schoolgirl clothes. Take heart, my dear, you look splendid!"

Numbly Maggie walked down the long gallery and through the parlor to the head of the stairs. Visitors ordinarily waited in the ground floor drawing room, but she could see her father standing in the hall below, impatiently tapping his walking stick against his leg. At the sound of her step on the stair, he glanced upward, frowned momentarily, and then nodded. "I'm glad to see you've had the sense to dress for the occasion." His loud voice rumbled up to her. "I'll just have a word with you before you meet his lordship. Your lady scholar said we might use the study for a few minutes. It shouldn't take long."

"As you wish, Papa," she whispered, unable to keep her frightened eyes from wandering to the closed drawing-room door. For one hopeful moment she had thought she was to be saved the ordeal, and now she followed the stocky Sir Robert with greater despair than before.

He neglected to close the door after them, but knowing the penetrating violence of his speech, Maggie swiftly moved to do so. Her father did not suggest that she seat herself, so she stood rigidly by the desk while he paced about the room, punctuating his speech with an occasional thump of his stick.

"I have gone to a great deal of trouble to arrange this marriage for you. [thump] No young lady could ask for a more advantageous match: Lord Greenwood is young, handsome, well-heeled, and lively. His seat, Combe Lodge, is situated near High Wycombe, but he has several smaller properties in Hampshire and Somerset. I made it a point [thump] to check into his credentials, since men of his cut are given to raucous living, and I didn't wish to find that he had his estates mortgaged or his income pledged for the next five years. He first caught my attention at Tattersall's when I heard him discussing the merits of Hallander's gray. Make no mistake [thump], he is a fine judge of horseflesh and a splendid sportsman. I've talked to any number of my acquaintance in London about him, and other than a certain unsteadiness of character, which he will outgrow, he comes with the highest credentials."

"I see," Maggie said sadly. "Papa, don't you think it would be best if Lord Greenwood and I had a chance to get to know one another before we decided if we suited? I—"

"No! Haven't I just been telling you he is the perfect match? [thump, thump] Everything is settled! You're of marriageable age and it would do you not the least good to sit around Vale Hall to become a spinster."

"My friends are to have a season in London. I had written you—"

"Damnation, girl, you can't expect me to play duenna to you and pussyfoot all over town escorting you to overheated entertainments where everyone makes polite conversation and there's nothing decent to drink! A pretty picture I'd look. Don't think I'll not be generous with you; in addition to your mother's fortune, I'm making a liberal settlement on you. His lordship, I think, was rather surprised when I told him the arrangements in the carriage on the way here. Now you go in there and accept him like a good girl. [thump] There's plenty of time to get to know him after you're married."

As always, Maggie was unable to withstand her father's autocratic management of her affairs. He expected no opposition, and he would stand for none. Although it had been more common in the past for parents to arrange marriages for their children, the practice still existed in some measure, and even if it hadn't, Maggie had always considered her father a law unto himself, which one broke with dire consequence. She pressed her hands to her now-flushed cheeks and attempted to summon the courage to face Lord Greenwood.

Her father took hold of her elbow to usher her to the drawing room, and his grip, as usual, was not as gentle as he supposed it to be, making Maggie wince and hasten her pace to match his lengthy strides. Sir Robert had little social finesse. He shoved her before him into the room where a gentleman stood by the window watching the young ladies promenade in the garden and announced, "This is my daughter, Margaret. Speak to her." And then, to Maggie's horror, he left them alone.

Lord Greenwood took offense at this brusque treatment of himself. He was accustomed to receiving far more deferential and agreeable attention, and he watched the door close with unconcealed annoyance, remaining stubbornly rooted to the spot where he stood. If it had been possible for her to move, Maggie would gladly have advanced to meet him, in propitiation for her father's rudeness, but her legs felt paralyzed.

"Pray, sir, take no heed of my father's gruffness," she begged, but in a voice so soft that it did not reach his lordship.

"What's that you say?" he demanded, refusing to come forward.

Maggie made a supreme effort to walk toward him, but her legs refused her commands and she was forced to grip the back of a chair for support. In a voice scarcely louder than before, she repeated her apology.

Listening carefully, Lord Greenwood caught the message this time but his sensibilities were barely assuaged, and he took further umbrage that the girl had hidden herself behind a chair. What the devil possessed these Somervales? There was nothing especially noteworthy about the girl's face or figure, and he decided that she was passable, but a suspicion was growing in him that she was lame. Trust Sir Robert not to mention the circumstance! Well, he refused to display such uncouth manners as the distempered baronet. His face a polite blank, he came forward and assisted Maggie to a chair. "Miss Somervale, I beg you will allow me to introduce myself. Adam Greenwood, your obedient servant."

"Lord Greenwood! I . . . How do you do?" Poor Maggie could think of nothing further to say, search her mind as she would. If she thanked him for calling, it would sound grossly inappropriate, and he might think she was prompting him to get on with his offer. She felt an almost physical pain at her awkward situation, and her countenance betrayed her distress.

His lordship read this distress as a reaction to his own person. Whether or not he had decided to discourage the girl, he found now that he was stunned by her ready disapproval. In an effort to overcome her reluctance, he set himself to be charming, but his attempt was forced and even in his own ears sounded overly zealous, his voice too loud and his manner too spirited. "Well, then, Miss Somervale, are you an ardent horsewoman? Your father is quite a bruising rider, I hear."

"I . . . I don't like horses. They're so . . . big."

Lord Greenwood was shocked. "You don't know how to ride?"

"Yes, of course I do. My father insisted that I learn. I just don't like to. I'm sorry."

"Well, that's a fear I'm sure can be readily overcome." Her obvious dismay determined him to change the subject. "Do you like Windrush House? Your father said it's a very fine school."

"I suppose it is," Maggie conceded, trying to put some enthusiasm in her voice but feeling very timid before his jocular style. "I . . . have some very good friends here. Emma Berryman and Lady Anne Parsons. Anne said her brother knew you."

Lord Greenwood flushed. There had been a small misunderstanding when he had visited Lord William at Parkhurst. The marquess was a very fine man, thoroughly amiable and with a good heart, but he had taken exception to Lord Greenwood's attempt to seduce a parlor maid. And Lord Greenwood had been too much the gentleman to explain that the maid had been the one to promote the adventure. It was one of the more embarrassing moments of his life and one which he would just as soon have forgotten, that afternoon in the barn. The little hussy had stripped every last article of clothing from her body and teased him until there was no resisting her buxom charms. The Marquess of Barnfield had literally caught him with his pants down, and the interview he had been forced to endure later in the marquess's study had, for all that gentleman's kindly and paternal attitude, been the most painful of his life.

For Greenwood was not used to having anyone censor his behavior. His parents had been dead for some years, and had paid little attention to him when they were alive, other than to promote a magnificent sense of his own consequence in him. To have a man of Lord

Barnfield's stature quietly explain that he did not allow his staff to be taken advantage of by thoughtless hedonists was galling in the extreme. Greenwood was reminded that not infrequently a child was born of such a liaison, to the servant's perpetual shame. Just as though he had been sixteen years old! He knew where babies came from, for God's sake! It had not occurred to the young man that the marquess was not offering him a lesson in the facts of life, but in the responsibilities of privilege and licentiousness. Too disgruntled to face the family at the dinner table, he had excused himself from the house party and taken himself off without delay, back to London where no one cared a hoot whom he seduced.

If his lordship was remembering his last meeting with Lady Anne's brother, Maggie, inspired by his flush, had recalled the context of her friend's disclosure and turned her eyes away from his. This only served to make Greenwood more uncomfortable and he said roughly, "Lord William and I have been friends since Eton, but I've not met his sister Anne, so she could know very little of me."

"She didn't claim to know much of you," Maggie answered softly, her fingers tracing the design on the fan.

No, just enough to poison your delicate little ears, he thought belligerently. Well, there was no use beating about the bush any longer. If she intended to accept him, he might as well know now. He rose so abruptly from the chair he had taken that he startled her, and her fan fell to the floor. With a tsk of annoyance he swooped it up and replaced it in her cold hands. "Miss Somervale, your father has given me his permission to pay my addresses to you. I realize we are not really acquainted, but your father seems to think a match between us eminently suitable, and surely he more than anyone knows what is best for you. My parents are both dead, but I have a sister, Cynthia, married for some years now, with two children. Her husband, Captain Morton, is in the Guards. My seat is near High Wycombe and I think you would find it a pleasant place. It's a gray gabled manor house lying in a romantic old garden with acres of parkland about it. The countryside is pretty there and it's not far from London. I can make the journey from Combe Lodge to Hyde Park Corner in under two hours."

If this daunting speed was supposed to impress her, Maggie certainly reacted. Her face paled and she murmured, "Oh, dear God."

"That's with my curricle, you understand. With the traveling carriage it takes better than three hours."

"Do you . . . always travel at such a pace?"

"Of course. There's no use spending time on the road. But there's no need to worry. I haven't overset the carriage in two years." In order to be strictly honest, he added, "I have scraped it a few times, you understand, but nothing to signify. No need for a new painting or anything like that."

He appeared to expect some comment from her so she said, "Yes."

"Perhaps your father doesn't have a sporting vehicle," he suggested at such patent lack of enthusiasm. "They're all the rage, you know. Everyone is driving one. Why even . . . well, never mind." It would not do to tell her that the Jewel had taken to being her own whip in imitation of the foremost courtesans of the day, and Greenwood, for all his amusement, considered the roads a far more dangerous place than they had formerly been. It might be all for the best that Miss Somervale showed no inclination to aspire to such heights, but he thought it showed a want of spirit in her.

And then he remembered that she was lame (or so he supposed), and burst out, "But of course you won't want to drive one yourself! There's not the least need! I have a coachman at the Lodge to take you anywhere you wish in a very comfortable closed carriage. Is there anything else you would like to know?"

Most of all Maggie wanted to know why this elegant, if erratic, baron was willing to marry her, but she had not the courage (which she was sure her friend Emma would have) to ask him. And possibly it would be better not to know, anyway, since she did not feel strong enough to oppose her father and refuse him. He was not as terrifying as her father, but it was obvious that they were very poorly matched. One did not expect felicity in a marriage between a high-spirited aristocrat and a meek baronet's daughter.

Maggie moistened her lips. "Do you live mainly in London?"

"As it's such an easy drive, I come and go at will. I've a house in Half Moon Street which is not large, but has served me very well up to now. There's only a small staff and the place isn't very fancy. I think you would prefer the Lodge."

Some significance seemed to attach to his last pronouncement, and she studied his face with her large gray eyes, uncertain how to interpret him. Carefully, she asked, "So I could stay there when you came to London, if I wished?"

"Yes." Lord Greenwood found it difficult to meet her gaze and studied instead the statue of Plato that rested in the corner, with the hope of inspiring the young ladies in their studious pursuits.

"I see."

"Well, Miss Somervale, can I hope that you look with favor on my suit? Or would you like some time to consider?"

"No, no, Papa . . . That is, I am flattered, Lord Greenwood, and cannot express the honor you do me." She swallowed painfully and an agitated hand fluttered to her bosom. "I . . . would be pleased to . . . accept your offer."

She looked so thoroughly ill that he felt a twinge of sympathy for her, realizing for the first time that she was merely doing her father's bidding. But his sympathy for himself was greater, when all was taken into account. He, too, was being forced into the marriage, and he had no liking for Sir Robert and only resentment toward his daughter for being so weak-willed as to be unable to oppose her own father. Lord Greenwood's sister, Cynthia, had stood out against the opposition of both her parents to marry her captain, and Greenwood had admired her courage. In spite of himself, he could not resist saying coldly, "You realize that your father would like us to be married within the week."

Maggie regarded him with sorrowful eyes, almost unable to bear her role. "If that is inconvenient for you . . ."

"Oh, no, not at all." There was more than a trace of sarcasm in his voice. "I can easily enough procure a license and arrange for the ceremony to be performed at St. George's, Hanover Square, one week from today. I would like to have my sister and a few friends present to wish me well."

"Of course. I'm sure my father will want to arrange for some sort of wedding feast for all those who attend. I believe it's customary."

Since it was obvious to Lord Greenwood that Sir Robert was unlikely to know the first thing about how to arrange such an occasion, and his daughter, if capable, was in no position to do so, he relented and said almost kindly, "I beg you will allow my sister to attend to such matters. It would give her a great deal of satisfaction, I assure you."

"Thank you. Perhaps that would be best. I don't think Papa intends I should quit Windrush House until . . ."

"Yes, well, we'll consider it settled, then. Why don't I bring Cynthia out to meet you tomorrow or the next day, and you can arrange the details between you?"

"That would be fine. I shall be pleased to meet her, though I dislike giving her any bother."

There really was nothing more for them to say to each other and a gloomy silence fell, broken only by the sound, which neither had noticed previously, of Sir Robert pacing back and forth in his heavy boots. Maggie flushed for his lack of tact and Greenwood cast his eyes to the acanthus-strewn ceiling. Because Maggie had no faith that her father would not lose all patience and storm in on them, she rose and offered her hand to Greenwood. "I . . . I should tell Papa that everything is settled. Perhaps you would not mind waiting here?"

With her cold hand in his, he said firmly, "I think I should be the one to tell him. I'll have him come in." He did not notice her grateful smile as he strode to the door, and he would not have been surprised if Sir Robert had taken to listening at the keyhole and had fallen in at the opening, but the baronet was partway down the hall.

Sir Robert swung around at the sound and demanded, "Well?"

"If you will come into the drawing room, sir."

With a shrug the baronet followed him into the room, his eyes trained on Maggie's face, which offered no information. "Well?"

"Miss Somervale has kindly agreed to be my wife, Sir Robert."

"And the wedding? When is it to be?"

"A week from today. I'll make all the arrangements."

"Excellent!" His booming voice surely was not contained by the four walls, and Maggie winced as he pumped her hand in congratulating himself. "I felt sure you would have sense enough to accept his lordship, girl. You're my daughter after all! You've not thanked me, but there, it's no matter. I don't suppose this cursed school has anything worth drinking by way of a toast. Small beer with dinner!" he remembered, this item from the brochure having caught his attention, to his infinite disgust. "His lordship and I shall have a bumper on the road to celebrate. You run along now. We won't be needing you further."

If Maggie was surprised by this hasty dismissal, only the widened gray eyes gave any sign. She curtsied to her father, and then shyly to her fiancé without offering her hand again, and made her way from the room. Greenwood had meant to observe how bad her limp was this time, but Sir Robert immediately recalled his attention by announcing, "We'll go straight to my attorney and see that the settlement is properly drawn up. She'll want a decent allowance to keep up with your crowd, I daresay, but there's no problem in that. I've told you her mother's fortune comes to her on marriage and I'll add my own share, but the bulk will come when I die, which I have no intention of doing for a good number of years, mind you. Still, Vale Hall is nothing to sneer at, with some of the most productive land in Kent."

While he talked he urged Greenwood from the drawing room into the hall and, without bothering to thank or take leave of Mrs. Childswick, out onto the gravel drive, where a groom was waiting with his lordship's curricle.

From the second-floor window two young ladies watched the men climb into the carriage and drive away. Lady Anne turned at the sound of footsteps climbing the stairs and held out her hands to Maggie, who barely had the strength to join them before dropping in a chair.

"How did it go, love? Shall I get my smelling salts?"

Maggie smiled faintly. "That won't be necessary. It was very strange really. Sometimes he was hostile, and every once in a while he was kind. I am to marry him a week from today."

Emma shook her head wonderingly. "My dear girl, didn't you even ask your papa for a little time?"

"He wouldn't hear of it. I did make the suggestion, but you don't know Papa when he has his mind set on something. Nothing dissuades him. Lord Greenwood seemed almost as resigned as I." Lady Anne and Emma exchanged a glance that Maggie couldn't fail to see, and she responded in a quiet voice. "Oh, I know it is curious for him to be in such a position. When I was with him I almost considered asking him; I knew Emma would. But I'm not at all sure I want to know, since there is no changing the situation."

"We saw him from the window," Emma told her. "He's quite handsome, and he took the turn into the road with scarce a pause. It's an elegant carriage and the grays appeared, from this distance at least, to be perfectly matched."

"Apparently he's proud of his driving ability. Tomorrow or the next day he is to drive his sister out to meet me. He said she would arrange for some sort of wedding feast." Suddenly her poise deserted her, and she raised pleading eyes to her friends. "You will both come to the wedding, won't you? I would so hate to be there alone."

"Of course we will," Lady Anne assured her.

Relieved, Maggie hastened to her feet. "I should get out of your dress, Emma. The last thing I want is to crush it beyond repair."

"Did your papa make some arrangement for your bridal clothes?" Emma asked curiously.

"Oh, dear, I didn't think to ask him. There's really not time, anyhow."

Appalled at such a cavalier attitude, Emma said dryly, "I'm sure he'll be happy to do anything to speed you on your way, my dear. Send him a note suggesting that he have Madame Minotier come to you tomorrow. She can at least take your measurements and get started on a bridal gown and some necessary evening clothes. You have enough morning dresses, though God knows they're bland enough, and you can be a great deal more festive once you're married." Her cheery prognosis failed to raise Maggie's spirits, and touched by her friend's plight, and although she dearly loved the gown, she said, "You are to keep this silk, love. I've never seen anything that became you more, and it shall be my wedding present to you."

Maggie managed to gulp "Thank you!" before she fled the room.

Emma sadly watched her exodus. "I wish she had the courage to stand up to her father. *I* would. You know, Anne, we are hardly schoolgirls anymore. We're grown women and should be able to direct our own fates. After all, she's going to have to spend the rest of her life with Lord Greenwood, and the least she could insist on is that she have a chance to get to know him."

"You should give her credit for trying, Emma. I'm sure it took a great deal of courage for her even to ask her father."

"But that's not enough. You have to be strong enough to *insist*."

Anne regarded her with sympathy. "Emma dear, you have rather a glorified view of what a female can accomplish in our society. She is tied to her father until she marries, and then she is tied to her husband. Every woman is. The most you can hope for is a considerate parent, and then a considerate mate."

"You are too pessimistic, love. Women wield a very special power of their own," Emma replied with an air of superior knowledge. "Just see how my aunt has managed to have her own way. I have no intention of letting any man run roughshod over *me*! And if Maggie cannot stand up to her father, she must at least set the tone for her husband. Aunt Amelia says it is relatively simple to influence a man to your point of view, so long as you go about it the right way."

"And how is that?" Anne asked, amused.

"Well, I shall have to ask her. She hasn't precisely told me yet."

Her friend choked down a chuckle. "Let me know when you find out."

"I shall. And I shall let Maggie know, too, as she is most likely to need the information. You and I," she concluded breezily, "won't need it for at least another month!" Whereupon she retrieved her sketchpad and pencil from the table and became engrossed in the drawing of Sir Robert she had started.

CHAPTER THREE

A note in unfamiliar handwriting was delivered to Maggie the next morning, and she found it as difficult to decipher the message as the signature. Obviously it was from Greenwood, but his heedless scrawl was almost unreadable and she was forced to seek Emma's aid in making out the entire contents.

Her friend puzzled over it for several minutes before declaring, "He must mean half after ten; the word is too short to be twelve, though God knows it might be anything. 'Presents his compliments' looks more like 'peasants for continents' and he 'lopes' you will be able to receive 'leim' and 'lissiter' though it is certainly him and his sister. Goodness, how dare they say *ladies* have poor handwriting? Surely his sister's name isn't Mrs. Mutton!"

Maggie giggled. "No, it's Mrs. Morton, actually."

"And you will note that he has abbreviated 'humble and obedient servant' so obscurely that it appears to be 'hando savant.' And his signature! I dare anyone who had no knowledge of him to work it out, everything jumbled up on itself that way. Looks like a child's exercise in circles."

"The poor fellow is probably going round in circles," Maggie suggested.

Emma eyed her sharply. "Nonsense. More fool he if he is, my dear. He has yet to learn what a treasure he's marrying, but give him time. A few words in the drawing room with your father pacing in the hall is hardly a propitious time to get acquainted. I think it's a very good sign that he's bringing his sister, don't you? And so soon." There was the possibility, of course, that Mrs. Morton would storm in to identify the hussy who had snapped up her brother without warning, but Emma had no intention of alarming Maggie with such a thought.

Since the engagement was now a fait accompli, she would do her utmost to see that Maggie entered holy matrimony with a stout heart, and no one was quite as successful as Emma in showing the bright side to a faltering friend. Her allegiance to Maggie and Lady Anne was unquestionable, and her buoyant spirits infected them with a vitality not wholly alien to their natures, but not nearly so pronounced as in hers. Under her tutelage the most sanguine young lady found herself fascinated and amused by the rigid world at Windrush House that had formerly bored or oppressed her. It was Emma who pointed out that Mrs. Childswick's voluminous gowns never failed to conceal a large pocket in which was kept a small but framed portrait not of her deceased husband, whose staid countenance glared down on one when forced to endure an interview in the headmistress's study, but of another man, a dashing fellow in a Guards uniform.

This portrait was occasionally withdrawn from her pocket when she thought herself alone, and perused with tender eyes, which led to all sorts of speculation amongst her charges. It was Emma's thesis that the fellow was the object of her unrequited love, but Clara Marshfield, who was only fifteen and consequently knew little of the world, insisted that it was Mrs. Childswick's brother! In any case, the discovery had made it easier for some of the residents at Windrush House to tolerate Mrs. Childswick's haughty and oppressive attitude and her unfortunate insistence on strict discipline. No one, from the daughter of a marquess to that of a prosperous mill owner in the Midlands, escaped a smack across the hands if judged impertinent or indolent. And if Lady Anne was always willing to listen to the complaints of the younger girls, and Maggie to console them, Emma was the one who made them laugh and forget any disagreeable incident.

With dancing eyes she now grasped Maggie's hand to draw her over to the wardrobe where she kept, in a small and ludicrous sarcophagus her aunt had given her, the most valued of her possessions. "Come, my dear, we must look out some dashing ornament that will catch your hando savant's eye. I think an emerald green sash will do wonders for your chemise gown. White is all very well for schoolgirls, but you are a lady engaged to be married. Aunt Amelia sent me something . . ." She dug amongst the carefully wrapped pieces in the sarcophagus, unwrapping them just enough to see what each was, and at length came up with gleaming eyes. "Here. Isn't it splendid?"

Certainly the ornament was charming but Maggie was not at all sure she would look quite the thing with it pinned to her bosom. A very realistic miniature canary perched on a sprig with enameled leaves and a red rose. It was whimsical, delightful . . . and not at all what Maggie would have chosen to wear. "I . . . I think it would be a bit heavy for my bodice, Emma, don't you?"

"For your bodice? Lord, yes. Maggie dear, it's a clip for your hair, to be perched right at the edge of your cap, as though the canary had settled there to make his home. Aunt Amelia gave it me because she said one of those picture hats with a ship in full rig or a basket of fruit would be far too elaborate, but that this was simple and endearing without being pretentious." Emma considered her friend's piquant face, with its wide gray eyes and delicate features. "I think it's just the sort of ornament for you, to enhance your look of wide-eyed innocence and country freshness. Do you think it's too much? With your hair dressed as yesterday, and a *chapeau* it will just sort of peek out."

Reluctantly Maggie agreed to give it a trial, feeling that on Emma it would look a great deal more in keeping than on herself. Emma always managed to look almost exotic despite her English-rose complexion, her blond hair, and unusually dark blue eyes. There was a fullness to her lips, a languidness to her eyes despite their mischievousness, which gave her an indefinable air. That is, to Maggie it was indefinable; gentlemen had no difficulty whatsoever defining Emma's intoxicating appeal. One had told Lady Bradwell, who had related the story to her niece (though she shouldn't have) that Emma was "the most alluring, tantalizing, provocative creature" he had met in years. The compliment, if truth were told, rather turned Emma's head. On that particular evening, when Lady Bradwell had taken her from school to the theater for a treat, Emma had been attempting an imitation of her aunt's notoriously seductive air, and to find that she had succeeded was heady stuff indeed. It gave her, perhaps, too inflated an idea of her own powers when combined with the sophisticated lessons on amour with which her aunt frequently indoctrinated her. But her flair for costume was seldom at fault, and when Lady Anne came in to judge of the finished product, they were all agreed: Maggie looked enchanting.

Even Greenwood was a little taken aback when she entered the school drawing room, but whether the canary, the emerald sash, or her amusement accounted for this, Maggie could not be sure. She had been escorted right to the door by her friends, and at the last moment Emma had whispered, "Be sure to give our best to the Hando Savant!" before gently pushing her into the room. Actually, though Maggie could not possibly know it, the fact that she walked quite naturally was what first attracted Greenwood's attention, but the sash and canary and the faint grin did not escape his attention.

After one brief, exasperated glance at her brother, Cynthia Morton came forward with outstretched hands. "I'm so pleased to meet you, Miss Somervale." Her brother had come to the Mortons' Portland Place house (rented for the season) the previous afternoon while she was embroidering her husband's initial on a fine lawn handkerchief. His gravity had immediately raised her suspicions and she had lifted a questioning brow. "What's amiss, Adam?"

Though two years older than her brother, Cynthia bore a striking resemblance to him with her merry blue eyes and generous mouth. Fortunately in her the patrician nose had been softened somewhat, and her springy brown curls further alleviated any impression of severity that might have marred the cheerful countenance. She wore a high-waisted dress of sprigged muslin that only partially concealed the fact that she was increasing for the third time. In deference to her interesting condition he had said, "You'd best sit down, my dear. I have rather weighty news."

"You haven't been playing too deep, have you?"

"That's one way of putting it, I suppose," he had murmured as he swung around a chair so he could straddle it backward. "I'm going to be married."

Her needle arrested in mid-stitch, Cynthia regarded him incredulously. "But you've said nothing! Not the Penhall girl, surely. You told me she was only a flirt."

"It's very difficult to explain, my dear, but I think you should know the whole story—not that you are to spread it abroad, mind you. Do you know Sir Robert Somervale?" When his sister shook her head, Lord Greenwood sighed. "I wish I didn't. A few weeks ago I met him at Tattersall's, a jovial country-squire type more interested in the stables than the drawing room. Well, we got to talking and he offered me a chance to have a look at Grantley's pair of bays before they were actually turned over to Tattersall for selling. They're legendary, Cynthia! And not over three years old, with the sweetest dispositions imaginable. I'd have been a fool not to take the opportunity, and I got them for a song."

"But you already have a pair," his sister protested.

"Yes, but I'd intended to give them . . . That is, a very particular friend of mine had been wanting such a pair."

"Oh, for God's sake, Adam, not a present to that flamboyant peacock in Clarges Street. Haven't you any pride? Where do you think she gets all those jewels? Not from the dustbin, you may be sure. She has dozens of admirers and you are simply one of the train." Cynthia had a most unnerving thought, and her eyes widened in horror. "Dear Lord, don't tell me you intend to marry her!"

"Of course not! Don't be ridiculous," he snapped, entirely discomposed. "One doesn't marry women like that. Will you let me get on with my story?"

Meekly, she said, "Excuse me. Pray continue."

"Well, anyhow, I bought the horses and gave them to the Jewel with a very handsome little carriage, but I was grateful to Sir Robert for putting me on to them, you know, and so I invited him round to a little dinner party I was having. He drank everyone else under the table; I've never seen the like of it. Stutton and Norwood were literally on the floor, but Thresham and Midford were still in their seats, mostly by luck, I suppose, when he started to talk about how long it took to send a message to someone in the country. He huffed and puffed a lot about the mail coaches not maintaining their ten to twelve miles an hour, and said a private messenger wasn't much better. 'I'd give a great deal to see a message carried fifteen miles an hour,' he declared, all pompous. Well, years ago Old Q, when he was Lord March, had made a bet that he could have a message sent fifty miles in an hour, and he won. Thresham was about to slip under the table, but he nudged me when he heard Sir Robert and whispered so loud I was sure the old fellow had heard, 'Remember March!' I hadn't the slightest idea what he was talking about until Midford kicked me in the shin and winked slyly. 'Cricketers,' he mumbled."

Greenwood pursed his lips thoughtfully. "I suppose it was all a setup, as Dunn says, and I know it wasn't right of me to try to take advantage of him when he'd done me a favor, but I was half gone and I thought I was very clever to make him the wager. Magnanimously, I offered him terms that I could send a message fifty miles in an hour and he slapped his hand on the table and swore that it couldn't be done, but that by God he liked my pluck. 'Tell you what,' he says, 'if you can do it you'll win yourself five hundred pounds.' So I said, 'You're on. And if I can't, you shall have a thousand.' 'No, no,' says he, 'ye shall have my daughter for your bride; there's a consolation prize for you!' "

"Oh, Adam," Cynthia cried despairingly, "you didn't."

"It never occurred to me that I wouldn't win. Old Q's team had no difficulty, but I had only three days to assemble the men, and I couldn't find many good cricketers in that time." He groaned. "You should have seen the ragged scamps. Every two minutes someone dropped the ball with the message in it, and one fellow let it roll halfway down a hill before he retrieved it. We didn't even come close."

"So you are going to marry his daughter?"

"There's no way I can get out of it, Cynthia. A gentleman can't welsh on such a bet, no matter how harebrained it is. I met the girl today and offered for her. She's a little mouse, and lame to boot, but she wouldn't go against her father. We're to be married a week from today."

Cynthia had set aside the handkerchief and sat studying his face with something akin to horror. "A week from today? You can't be serious. There would hardly be time to prepare a wedding dress, let alone her bridal clothes."

"I don't think her father has even thought of that. I told her you'd see to the wedding feast, Cynthia. I hope you don't mind, for she's stuck out in a school in Kensington and wouldn't be able to manage. If you can, I'd like to take you to meet her tomorrow or the next day."

"She's a schoolgirl?"

"I imagine she's seventeen or eighteen, about to come out. Oh, and she's a friend of Lady Anne Parsons."

Cynthia had never been advised of her brother's misadventure at Parkhurst, but she was aware of his friendship with Lord William. "I'm glad to hear it, for it may give us an opportunity to bring this off with some degree of propriety. For heaven's sake, Adam, make sure that none of your cronies brute the truth about, or your poor bride will be an object of the most inhuman jokes."

"What about me?" he demanded, stung.

"You have no one but yourself to blame."

"She didn't have to accept me. You would never have let Papa push you into such a harum-scarum marriage."

"So you were depending on her to get you out of your scrape, were you?"

Seldom had Greenwood seen her eyes so cold or heard her voice so icy. "You really are a thoughtless nodcock, Adam. I can offer you no sympathy whatsoever, but I feel a great deal of concern for the girl. Of course she had to accept you. Anyone as heartless as Sir Robert was in making the wager is not a man whom a child can oppose. Why did he do it? Is she dowerless?"

"Far from it. She comes with a handsome fortune from her mother, and he intends to supplement it. I can only guess that he didn't want to be bothered with her any longer and chose me because I'm titled and well-heeled."

"And stupid enough to fall in with his scheme," she concluded with asperity. "Oh, Adam, I thought you were learning a little decorum and sense this last year. You know I dearly love you, but you came of age a year ago and should long since have left off your youthful spirits for a little dignity. No, no, I won't scold you. I can see you're feeling wretched enough without my aspersions. Come, we'll make the best of this pickle if you will only accept your responsibilities. You don't mind her being lame, do you?"

"No, of course not."

"What's her Christian name?"

He shook his head. "I don't remember. Now don't be irate with me, Cynthia. I'm sure if I heard it I was far too distracted to remember."

"Never mind. We'll find out tomorrow. Why don't you call for me at ten? And not in your curricle, please. I don't wish to meet your fiancée with my coiffure looking as though I'd tried to ascend in a balloon."

He rose when she did. "Will you bring James?"

"No, I think not. If she's shy, it will be better to introduce one family member at a time. Promise me you'll try to make the best of it, Adam."

The grin he offered her was crooked and did not light his eyes. "I'll try, my dear."

So it was with some surprise that Cynthia watched Maggie walk toward them, smiling, her wide gray eyes filled with pleasure at seeing his lordship's sister welcome her with apparent warmth. Cynthia would willingly have consigned her brother to the devil just then for his lack of insight and empathy with this lonely child. She took possession of Maggie's hand and tucked it under her arm. "We have a thousand things to discuss about the wedding, but it seems a pity to stay inside on such a day. Could we stroll about the grounds?"

"Why, certainly." She turned shyly to Greenwood to ask, "Would that suit you, sir?"

Momentarily forgetting the occasion and thinking of all the cloistered young ladies awaiting his inspection, he said with suspicious alacrity, "Of all things!"

Gratified by his ready assent, Maggie relaxed somewhat and led them out a side door into the grounds, where graveled walks led off in three directions. One of these was a sheltered stroll for cooler days near the house, but the other two were the ends of a wide circuit through the flower beds, hedges, and a little grove of horse chestnut trees. Gallantly Greenwood placed the ladies' arms through his and immediately headed in the direction that seemed most promising, that is, the one where he could see several girls walking on the path ahead and playing hopscotch to the left.

"Have you finished your lessons for the day already?" his lordship asked curiously. "There seem to be any number of girls wandering about."

"We have a little free time in the mornings about now, then several more classes before dinner. In nice weather most everyone goes outdoors, because if you stay in Mrs. Childswick is sure to set you at your needlework."

Cynthia smiled reminiscently. "It was much the same where I went to school in Bath. When I think of those hours spent over ridiculous homilies which no one's parents would contemplate hanging in even the most obscure rooms of their homes."

"Mrs. Childswick has a favorite, Corneille's 'Do your duty, and leave the rest to heaven,' which she uses as a punishment for anyone so careless as to fall into habits of Impertinence, Indolence, or Ignorance," Maggie told her. "She makes the offender embroider it on a velvet cloth, which the girl must purchase out of her own pocket money."

Adam grunted. "I should think you're well out of here."

Maggie's eyes dropped and Cynthia pinched her brother for such a thoughtlessly ungallant comment. Surprised, he stared at her a moment but she refused to enlighten him, talking instead of her old school at Bath until they had overtaken the first girls on the path.

"May I introduce you to my friends?" Maggie addressed her

question to Mrs. Morton, since she could not for the moment meet Greenwood's eyes.

When Cynthia nodded her agreement, Maggie called to Lady Anne and Emma, who, though aware that the trio was behind them, were steadfastly proceeding so as not to interfere. They turned around at Maggie's voice and waited for the party to join them. Like two spring flowers in their yellow and blue gowns, they bobbed curtsies to Lord Greenwood and his sister, their eyes full of curiosity and their lips formed into polite smiles. Reminded of his little problem at Parkhurst, and Lady Anne's probable opinion of him, Adam set himself to win her approval while Cynthia chatted with Emma and Maggie about the upcoming season.

"Lord William hasn't come to town yet, has he?" Adam asked politely.

"No, he's been with Papa into Cornwall for the last month or so. Mama wrote that she would come to town with Jack next week, and Papa and Will would follow when they return."

"Do you join them in Grosvenor Square?"

"Yes, in a while. I want to stay here until Emma leaves, too. She's Lady Bradwell's niece, and will spend the season with her."

"Is she?" Adam glanced at the girl with renewed interest, wondering what it would be like to be chaperoned by the dashing matron who supplied more on dits per season than any half dozen other ladies. He could not recall ever having met Lord Bradwell, though he had himself been on the town for four years. There had been a time, in fact, when he had thought to make up to the lady; at twenty anything had seemed possible. But Lady Bradwell did not encourage puppies and she had gently but firmly repulsed his advances. It had been rumored that season that she was having a fling with Sir Nicholas Dyrham, but no one could actually accuse Lady Bradwell of being indiscreet.

Undoubtedly that was why she was perpetually the talk of London. She pursued a course of unadulterated pleasure, and yet there was no gentleman who had ever breathed so much as a word of having been her lover. No fashionable fribble ever issued from her front door in the morning still dressed in his evening clothes. No daring blade escorted her home of a night who was not seen to issue forth within a very few minutes of depositing her. No crim. con. cases arrived in court naming Lady Bradwell as corespondent. Quite a remarkable career she was having, when one thought about it! And Adam was thinking about it as he observed Emma in animated conversation with his sister. A fetching girl, almost a parody of her aunt's older, more voluptuous charms.

His attention had wandered seriously and Adam was recalled to Lady Anne by a movement on her part to join the other ladies. "A thousand pardons! I was wondering on which side Miss Berryman is related to Lady Bradwell. For the life of me I cannot recall her family."

Lady Anne had a better understanding of what he had really been thinking than he could possibly guess, and it was one of the things that worried her—that men would look on Emma as fair game because of her aunt. Anne's frown called forth Adam's most charming smile, rather endearingly crooked in his embarrassment, and she relented. "Emma's parents are dead, but her father was Lady Bradwell's brother."

"I see." It seemed wisest to change the subject. "Are you to come out this spring?"

"Yes, Maggie and Emma and I have been planning for over a year what we would do this season, how we would support one another and, of course, take the town by storm," she confessed with a laugh that made the luminous brown eyes dance.

"I'm sure you will." Although he delivered this statement with due gravity, there was just enough amusement on the handsome face to show he was quizzing her.

"Well, with Maggie married, it will be different than we'd planned."

Abruptly recalled to his imminent marriage, Adam cast a hasty look at his bride-to-be, who was cheerfully immersed in conversation with Cynthia, and said stoically, "Better, I should think. As Lady Greenwood, she will be able to chaperon you. Not many young ladies could wish for more than to have a friend their own age as chaperon, rather than an older woman who might not see eye to eye with them."

"I . . . hadn't thought of that. Won't you be taking a wedding trip?"

"We haven't discussed it," Adam replied stiffly. "The season is about to begin."

Lady Anne felt a momentary flicker of anger, which did not escape her eyes, but she said pleasantly enough, "Of course," and turned to the others to suggest that she and Emma should be returning to the school. Readily agreeing, Emma strolled off with her arm in arm and

Maggie watched them go with a sigh. For a few minutes she had felt protected, and now she must once more face two people she had never even heard of a few days previously.

To banish the melancholy expression from the girl's face, Cynthia stepped into the awkward silence to say how pleased she was to meet Miss Somervale's friends and to express her approval of the modiste chosen to provide some wedding clothes. "Madame Minotier is not so well known as some, because those who discover her won't breathe a word for fear she will be too busy to handle their needs. I'm so glad Miss Berryman knew of her."

"Papa sent a note saying she had agreed to come directly considering the very limited time. I was surprised he could convince her."

Cynthia wasn't the least surprised. No modiste could ask for more than to have her fashions displayed (to how few she was unlikely to know) at the first wedding of consequence this spring, and to have them paraded about during the season by the new Lady Greenwood. A triumph indeed, and at that it wouldn't come cheap. Making a mental note to warn Adam of the expense, in case the unsophisticated Sir Robert balked at the reckoning, Cynthia let the matter drop. If the modiste was likely to arrive any moment, Cynthia wished to settle the details of the wedding celebration and leave the couple alone for a chance to get acquainted. Each of her suggestions was received equably by Maggie, who was apparently too stunned still to have any ideas of her own, and indifferently by Adam, for which she would dearly have loved to kick him.

From across the lawns they saw a chaise drive up to Windrush House, which, considering the quantities of fabric hauled out by a young assistant, and the elegant toilette of the older woman, could only be the modiste arriving. Cynthia firmly took charge, saying, "I will go ahead and see that everything is brought up to your room. It always takes them a while to set up for measuring and such, my dear, so don't you and Adam be in a hurry, please."

Instinctively, Maggie moved forward as Cynthia hastily left them, but Adam tightened his grip on her arm and insisted, "Let her go. We have several matters to discuss, and once a modiste gets her hands on you, there is no freeing yourself for hours. Did you expect us to take a wedding trip?"

The question startled her. Poor Maggie didn't *expect* anything, and she was not at all sure she liked the tone in which the question was asked; it had the bullying ring to it that she was familiar with, but would never become accustomed to, in her father. "I had given no thought to the matter."

"No? Well, your friends obviously have. I should think you would like to be in town for the season, and I know I would, but I am willing to take you to Combe Lodge for a week or two after the wedding."

Maggie studied the tips of her toes, which showed beneath her gown. "How very kind of you."

Although he could identify no trace of sarcasm in the dull tone, the words themselves disgruntled him. "You should see my seat, and there's hardly time to plan a longer excursion if we are to be here when most of the festivities get under way. Everyone will wish to meet the new Lady Greenwood."

The thought appalled Maggie, all those curious eyes observing her, wondering how such a pallid little thing had snared a baron, making snide remarks on her lack of polish, and speculating on her background. She was incapable of finding anything to reply.

"Well, does that suit you?"

"Yes."

Adam eyed her with disfavor, though he was really more disgusted with his own lack of forethought and ingenuity than with her meek response. "I could take you somewhere else later, in the summer or the autumn. To Paris, perhaps, or Naples. Spring isn't all that good a time to travel because of the rain, you know. The roads are often knee-deep in mud, and carriages are forever getting bogged down. Summer is much better, and even early autumn." When she said nothing, he struggled on. "I realize it's hot then, and the roads are dusty, but the channel crossing is a great deal more pleasant. Do you get seasick?"

"I don't know. I've never been on a boat."

He regarded her as though she were some sort of oddity beyond the limits of his comprehension. Most of his friends had at least been on the packet to France or sailing on the Thames. Gloomily, he remarked, "You'll probably be sick as a dog."

"We needn't go," she said softly.

"Of course we'll go."

"There is plenty of time to discuss it later."

"I said we would go. You may tell your friends so."

His scowl was intimidating and Maggie abruptly withdrew her arm from his. "If you wish."

Adam felt a churlish fool, making such a fuss over nothing. His custom was to spend the summer months at his seat, often having friends to stay with him for long periods of time, but since that would be out, there was no reason not to travel. Lady Anne had seemed to think it strange that they weren't to have a wedding trip, and he had only wanted to straighten out the situation, not to frighten the little mouse beside him. Maggie had started walking toward Windrush House and he set his pace to hers, though he made no attempt to regain her arm. "Miss Somervale, you must realize that I'm unfamiliar with what is expected of a bridegroom. Very few of my close friends are married, and I don't recall whether or not they took wedding trips. Cynthia didn't, but then Captain Morton had to leave almost immediately for duty. I don't mean to slight you in any way, I promise you."

This handsome apology was delivered with a smile that Adam knew to be particularly winning; seldom did it fail to gain him favor. But Maggie had not looked at him since the scowl unnerved her and she was currently in the process of adjusting the little canary in her hair where it had toppled in an unexpected gust of wind. "Thank you, Lord Greenwood. You are very obliging."

Exasperated, he watched her unsuccessful attempt to untangle the ornament. Was the girl totally helpless? "Here, let me. It's caught in your hair and you're twisting it the wrong way." He extracted the little bird with deft fingers and held it in the palm of his hand for a moment to examine it before replacing it near the edge of her cap. "A very charming piece. Are you fond of canaries?"

"Why, yes, but it isn't mine. Emma lent it to me," she confessed, embarrassed.

Adam was beginning to think there was nothing he could possibly say to her that would not in some way lead to an uncomfortable situation. Fortunately, they had arrived back at Windrush House, and it was obvious that she was impatient to be off to the dressmaker. Actually, Maggie thought it rude to keep anyone waiting, no matter what his or her position, and her fiancé showed no disposition to make her linger.

"Tell Cynthia I'll be in the village when she's ready to depart. I'll leave my coachman here for her and they can pick me up."

"Very well. Thank you for coming, and for bringing your sister," Maggie said with the formality of the schoolgirl she was. Her hesitant smile was answered by a nod, and she fled up the stairs while he, with a long sigh, strode purposefully toward the village of Kensington.

CHAPTER FOUR

Emma listened with interest to the list of dresses Maggie had ordered from the modiste, nodding her head in approval from time to time. So as not to interrupt the flow of her friend's discourse, she made notes on the back of the nearest sheet of foolscap, which happened to be an assignment in French translation she was supposed to turn in that afternoon. When Maggie finally concluded, breathless, Emma grinned. "I know it sounds a monstrous amount, my dear, but I've noted several items you will need to go along with all that. You mustn't forget shoes and reticules and bonnets. Madam Minotier won't be able to supply those. Do you suppose we could convince Mrs. Childswick to let us go into town? Considering the occasion, she would have to agree, wouldn't she?"

There was a decided snort from Anne. "Since when have you credited Mrs. Childswick with humanity, Emma? She's as likely to let us go into town as she is to fly. You are placing overmuch reliance on her good nature, which I admit tends to exhibit itself when there is a marriage in the offing, but she has already excused us from classes this morning and I have no doubt she expects us to attend this afternoon. Lord, I can just see her face if you were to ask her to allow us the carriage, and a maid to attend us, and the extra money we would need just for a few tolls and tea in London."

Ignoring these substantial objections, Emma was giving further consideration to the expedition. "I think we would wish to take Polly as our chaperon. She's much less starchy than the other maids. Or do you suppose Mrs. Childswick would insist on one of the mistresses?"

"*I* think you are all about in your head, Emma," Anne retorted.

Maggie looked more hopeful. "I really would like to go. Do you think you could actually arrange it, Emma? And if it has to be one of the mistresses, I would as soon have Miss Clements as any of the others."

"You're *both* crazy," was all Anne could say.

"I think you've solved our dilemma, Maggie." Emma's eyes were dancing with mischief. "Miss Clements would be the perfect chaperon, and besides, I think she would be very sympathetic to your cause. Do you mind if I approach her on your behalf?"

As Maggie nodded in bewilderment, Anne asked suspiciously, "You're going to approach Miss Clements *first*?"

"Why not? She took us to the theater, didn't she? I've always suspected that she was sympathetic to all of us locked in here as though it were a prison. Haven't you seen her gazing out the window when we're doing our work? It's just as much of a prison for them, you know. Mrs. Childswick gives them only a half day and Sunday off. Come to think of it, do either of you know when Miss Clements's half day is?"

"Of course, goose." Anne laughed. "She's off when the dancing master is here Thursday afternoons because she's the prettiest of the teachers and Mrs. Childswick doesn't want to take a chance on Monsieur Rovot falling in love with her."

"My dear Lady Anne," Emma opined in the arctic tones of Mrs. Childswick she so well imitated, "there is no other reason for Miss Clements having Thursday afternoon as her half day than that it is most convenient. And I think it would be convenient for us as well, don't you? Better tomorrow than today, that is. This way I shall have the opportunity to speak with her this afternoon to arrange it. We might have to have a glance at the Elgin marbles or some such edifying sight, and I for one would wish to treat Miss Clements to tea and perhaps a pair of lavender kid gloves for giving up her free time to us. I've saved a bit from what Aunt Amelia sent me. What do you say?"

"You never cease to astonish me, Emma," Anne admitted, convinced. "I do believe you can bring it off. I'll chip in for the gloves, but she may prefer tan. I have yet to see her wear anything so exotic as lavender."

Maggie surprised them by saying, "I have. One evening when I was downstairs looking for a book in the blue room she came in from her free afternoon. Did you know they have to be in by eight? Emma's right—it is as much a prison for them as it is for us! Well, anyhow, her dress was covered, so I couldn't see it, but she was wearing the most delightful lavender pelisse of that new silk called zephyrine. It had half sleeves of alternate folds of gros de Naples and zephyrine, and the skirt was trimmed at the bottom with a fullness of lavender-colored gauze intermixed with satin." Maggie looked apologetic. "I was so taken with it that I described it to Madame Minotier and asked that she make me something like it."

"Clever girl!" Emma congratulated her. "Did she have lavender gloves?"

"I don't remember. I was so taken with the pelisse that I didn't notice."

"Well, never mind. She shall have whatever color gloves she wishes, and we shall have a chance to complete Maggie's wardrobe. Her bridal clothes," Emma amended, smiling happily at her companions.

Neither of them doubted any longer that she could carry it off. Emma had a knack of accomplishing such hopeless feats, for which they were both grateful, since it had made their years at Windrush House a great deal more comfortable. They had left her alone with Miss Clements after class, and when she emerged to find them waiting in the hall, sure enough she was glowing with success. "She will speak with Mrs. C. about it right away and send us a message."

When the message arrived shortly before the dinner hour, Emma frowned. Her companions felt an unaccustomed disappointment until she said, "Ugh! It's to be the medical museum. Ah, well, we can survive looking at skeletons and various instruments of torture in a good cause, can't we?"

Since they were ostensibly headed for an educational experience, and one of the last they were likely to have while at Windrush House, Mrs. Childswick had grudgingly allowed them the use of the school carriage. It might look impressive in her brochure, she had once decided, if she were able to say that her girls made use of it on educational expeditions during the year. Could any other similar establishment make such a claim? She doubted it. It would be a first for Windrush House, and see if it didn't steal away some of the best families from the haughty Mrs. Wilson, whose school at Highgate was her main competition. Emma was astonished to find the headmistress there to send them off with a rather bombastic speech on the prowess of Windrush House education, its farsightedness and innovative philosophy. Her references to the carriage itself were almost ludicrous, since it was certainly no less than twenty years old and had been acquired at an auction when a previously wealthy family had been reduced to pauperism by the gambling mania of a succession of loose-living heirs.

Eventually Mrs. Childswick allowed them to depart, and the four ladies settled themselves back against the cracked squabs. Miss Clements directed her attention to Maggie with a kind smile. "So you are to be married, Miss Somervale. May I offer you my congratulations?"

"Thank you. You are kind, and especially so to come with us, ma'am."

"Miss Berryman is very persuasive," Miss Clements said with a rueful glance at her. "She was sure you would enter marriage with no more than the clothes on your back if you weren't allowed an expedition to town."

At Maggie's reproachful look, Emma grinned. "I did perhaps exaggerate the slightest bit, of course, but I knew Miss Clements would understand. And I admitted that Madame Minotier had been to school, though I did point out how devastating it would be to have all those lovely gowns and not a pair of shoes or a bonnet to go with them!"

Miss Clements patted Maggie's hand. "Don't fret on my account, dear. I promise you I relish the opportunity to observe a shopping spree. Who are you marrying, if you don't mind my being so presumptuous as to ask?"

"Lord Greenwood. My father arranged the match."

"No, no," Emma protested. "You aren't to tell people that! For God's sake, Maggie, let people believe that his lordship caught sight of you and fell desperately in love on the spot."

Maggie's lips trembled slightly. "No one will have to do more than catch sight of his face for them to know better than *that*."

"Emma is right, Maggie," Anne interposed. "Let people believe what they wish, but never tell them the truth. It is needlessly self-deprecating."

For some time Maggie stared at her hands and the others were silent as the carriage jolted along the road toward town. Eventually Emma broke their uncomfortable cogitations by suggesting, "I think you should simply tell them that your father introduced you to Lord Greenwood. You needn't say more than that, and it is perfectly true. After all, Maggie dear, there is nothing so exceptional in your marrying a handsome young lord. Your father is a baronet and you would be expected to marry well, with a good dowry. Now, Anne," Emma mused, grinning at her, "we shall all expect to marry a duke, at the very least, if not one of the doddering princes. With your father a marquess and your mother coming from a long line of earls, you would be foolish to throw yourself away on a mere baron or viscount. Even an earl may not be lofty enough, considering the size of your dowry."

Anne cast a hasty, apologetic glance at Miss Clements. "I promise you I have never so much as mentioned my dowry to her!"

Miss Clements gave her head an exasperated shake. "I think, as she mentioned previously, that Miss Berryman is prone to exaggerate, Lady Anne. No one could accuse you of exploiting your position or boasting of your family's wealth."

"Ah, but only a moron wouldn't know of both!" Emma protested. "Of the three of us, our Anne is destined to marry the best. And she deserves such good fortune, with her delightful modesty and genteel manners. I haven't a chance of competing with her! Alas"—she sighed dramatically—"I haven't the position of either Maggie or Anne. I shall have to content myself with some old man who leers at me, no doubt. My closest connection with the aristocracy is my aunt, and she only married into it. My family is really quite obscure and of no long-standing position in the ton. Not that my aunt has not drawn a certain amount of attention to us," she admitted with a roguish lift of one brow.

"You aren't dowerless," Anne said dryly, ignoring this reference to Lady Bradwell, "and your constant spirits are likely to turn every male head in sight when you make your bow in society. As to an old man for a husband, I think there's not the least likelihood. He wouldn't be able to catch up with you to offer."

Emma appeared to consider this. "Perhaps not. I shall have to gain sympathy from being an orphan, then. What a pity that my father did not die in battle. I might have gained the ear of some dashing young captain in the Guards with tales of his heroic deeds against the French brutes. Maggie, do you suppose Lord Greenwood numbers any such fellows amongst his acquaintance? He could introduce me."

"I wouldn't be at all surprised," Maggie said, in a burst of rueful candor. "He probably knows any number of them."

Emma laughed, and looked to Miss Clements. "You see how beneficial our jaunt is for Maggie?" But immediately she was back to her original hypothesis. "That is how it shall be, I imagine. Lord Greenwood will introduce me to a dashing cavalry officer in the moonlight at a masquerade. The captain will insist that I unmask so that he can identify me in future, having already been smitten with my dancing (à la Monsieur Rovot). When I take off my gilded mask he will be so overwhelmed that he will fall to his knees and declare himself on the spot."

With a mournful shake of her head Miss Clements said to the other two girls with a sigh, "I wish she would expend so much effort on her themes."

"I am saving my energies for the Real World," Emma declared magnificently.

"You will find, my dear," Miss Clements told her in all seriousness, "that in order to develop your potential, you will have to use your energies in all phases of your life, and not just the Real World, as you call it. You have invested society with a glamor you will eventually find superficial; someone of your caliber cannot fail to do so over a period of time. Most important are your friends and your mind. Cultivate both, Miss Berryman, and you will not find yourself lonely as you grow older."

At Emma's aggrieved expression, she continued, "I realize you think I'm lecturing you to no purpose on our holiday, but believe me, these are the truly vital elements of your life. I watch the girls leave school, with dreams of handsome men and lavish homes. A husband who will solve all their problems, present them with happiness. But happiness comes from within, not without. I am not saying that circumstances beyond our control do not influence grief or joy. Ultimately, though, your own attitudes and resources are what provide content or discontent."

That Emma thought such sentiments sprang from her unmarried state, Miss Clements could clearly discern by the girl's skeptically raised brows. She chuckled. "Oh, I'm not suggesting you don't marry! That friendship could be the most valuable of all, if you are willing to invest your energies in it. But not if you take it as a matter of course, as your right, your voucher to a place in society. And I don't subscribe to the theory that women are a mere ornament, to be worn with pride on a husband's cravat, or relegated to producing offspring. In either role you would soon expire of boredom, Miss Berryman. On the other hand, if you were to take an interest in the things that interest your husband, if you were to keep abreast of current affairs, if you felt you had some influence on those around you—that would give you satisfaction. Your mind is too active to settle for ignorance, your heart too generous to tolerate indifference. I won't say it is better to give than to receive, but the energies you expend on behalf of others make you feel more deserving of the rewards you reap. Otherwise the rewards are empty, meaningless baubles."

If Emma shifted a bit uncomfortably during this well-meant exposition, Maggie appeared to drink in every word with keen interest. "What if," she asked haltingly, "someone didn't want to take what you gave?"

"Then," Miss Clements said with a sad smile, "you would probably be giving to the wrong person. But I wouldn't worry overmuch about that. Very few people can resist a sincerely offered gift. I don't want you to misunderstand me. I am not speaking of a pair of cuff links or a handkerchief, but of yourself—your time, attention, thoughtfulness."

The carriage had stopped at the museum and Miss Clements cheerfully bustled them out into the street. "Only a half hour, I promise. You are not likely to find it elevating, I suppose, but I've always been fascinated and will be able to answer any of Mrs. Childswick's questions if necessary. And we will want to have a brochure!"

Amongst the skeletons and zoological exhibits, Emma regained her good humor, briefly dampened by what she thought of as Miss Clements's opinion that she was likely to behave giddily during her first season. There was really no other explanation for the lecture, except possibly to encourage Maggie, who, Emma had to admit, was looking thoughtful. Emma did not for a moment think that Maggie's interest was generated by scalpels, nor even by her own romantic tale. Without a doubt, Emma decided, Maggie had for the first time considered the possibility of winning Lord Greenwood's affections.

Lord Greenwood had been in no frame of mind to be alone the day after his second visit to Windrush House and he walked the short distance from Half Moon Street to Waverton Street. His destination, Waverton House, was a double-pile building of brick with Ionic pilasters and a stone pediment, every inch (and there were many thousands of them) the elegant gentleman's London residence. In size and grandeur there was no comparison between it and his own house in Half Moon Street. His town house could have fit in half of the building in front of which he halted.

When he was younger, he had thought it was the house itself that gave Viscount Dunn his superior air of refinement and grace, since to his untrained eyes there was little to choose otherwise between the viscount and his brother, Captain Midford. Both were men of darkly handsome looks, lively conversation, excellent understanding, even temper, and genteel manners. And there was no denying that Lord Dunn partook of the same daily round as every other gentleman of the time: a ride in the park in the morning, social calls until a light meal at midday, visits to art dealers or trying his hand at a translation of Horace, conducting business with his solicitor, displaying his conversational and epicurean prowess at dinner, dropping in at his clubs, and at length paying a visit to his mistress. Of course, the viscount did attend Parliament on occasion, and even delivered speeches from time to time, which were acclaimed for their ease and fluency, but he hadn't the reputation of a Fox or a Pitt. No one did these days. So it had seemed natural to assume that the house's grandeur added to the viscount's distinction and set him apart from his peers.

Over the years, however, Lord Greenwood had come to realize that wealth and the display of it had nothing to do with Dunn's eminence. Gentlemen did not gather at his table because of his superlative dinners, and ladies did not vie for his attention because they expected him to shower them with jewels. Dunn was a man of refinement, character, and charm, with a personal magnetism that drew people of every class and walk of life to him like so many metallic filings. And though Greenwood was far from impervious to the man's quality, he fervently hoped that the viscount would not be at home. When one had made a fool of oneself, one had no wish to display the fact to a being who, for all his involvement in every joyful pursuit, had never been known to disgrace or embarrass himself.

Not that Dunn would prose on or moralize about the matter. Other than matter-of-factly telling you you were a fool, he would allow the subject to drop. And besides, he already knew about the wager and the unfortunate necessity of Greenwood's having to marry Miss Somervale, because Greenwood himself had asked Captain Midford to sound his brother on any possible escape routes. Still, as he was shown into the library he was rather hoping that Dunn would be out and only the captain seated amidst the leather-bound volumes and leather chairs.

His luck was out, as it had been for some time now, apparently. Dunn's tall frame was disposed comfortably in one of the chairs, his long legs with their muscular calves stretched out on a hassock, and a book propped negligently on the chair arm. There was no mockery in the gray eyes, which looked up languidly to observe his entrance, and his greeting was perfectly cordial, though he made no attempt to rise. His brother, on the other hand, was immediately on his feet demanding, "Well, what happened?"

"I am to marry Miss Somervale a week from today."

At the announcement Dunn rose and offered his hand, while Captain Midford looked on in something like shock. "Congratulations, Adam. I'm sure, with the proper effort, you will make the young lady a good husband."

"Uh, thank you." The last thing Greenwood had expected was for anyone to congratulate him on the match, and he had given no thought at all to whether or not he was likely to prove a respectable mate. He was a great deal more concerned with whether Miss Somervale would make an acceptable wife.

Impatient, Midford thrust such considerations aside. "What's she like? Is she ugly?"

Though Dunn threw his hands up in a gesture of despair, Greenwood promptly answered, "She's a mouse and, though she's not ugly, she's certainly not pretty."

In a voice of quiet authority Dunn interrupted what were apparently to be further confidences in the same vein. "There is no chance of your succeeding in this marriage if you intend to disparage the girl, Adam. You could as easily, and with more propriety say she is shy and has a certain amount of countenance."

Before Greenwood could answer, the viscount excused himself, leaving the two to have an unadulterated discussion of Miss Somervale's faults, since Greenwood appeared too agitated to turn a blind eye to them. In the long run it might prove more beneficial for the young man to vent his frustration and annoyance to a friend, rather than keep it bottled up in him to explode in the poor bride's face one day.

When the door had closed behind him Greenwood heaved an expressive sigh of relief. "It's not that I don't like Dunn, you know; it's just that he don't understand. *He* don't have to marry the girl! I always thought to marry one day, of course, but I'd envisioned some lively, pert little thing who would blend in with my set. Miss Somervale is so timid I can't picture her even facing a tea party, let alone matching wits with my friends. She's terrified of her father, and I'm not so sure she isn't rather afraid of me, too. Imagine being afraid of me!"

Captain Midford laughed. "Even your worst enemy isn't afraid of you, Adam. Maybe it wasn't fear, but disapproval."

"Oh, there was that, too. Apparently Lady Anne Parsons is one of her friends and I told you the Marquess of Barnfield thought I had set out to seduce one of the housemaids at Parkhurst." Even to Stephen, Greenwood had not confessed the whole of that disastrous day. He sat with chin in hand, gazing glumly at the hearth. "I suppose she knows about the Jewel, too. What the devil am I going to do about Julia?"

"It would be a great pity to give her up now, when you've just provided her with that smashing rig," Midford commiserated. "You'll have to learn some discretion."

"Damn! This is taking all the joy out of everything. I don't like the idea of sneaking around. And what's the fun of having a mistress if you can't show her off?"

"I've always thought there was a great deal of fun in bed, myself," Midford teased him.

"Oh, you know what I mean. I was looking forward to Julia driving me through the park. She's not a bad whip, you know; not like some of them. Can't drive to the inch, precisely, but she'll not overturn the carriage either. Before all this I told her I'd take her to Vauxhall."

"Just pick a masquerade night and no one will be the wiser."

Greenwood eyed him with disgust. "Don't be a dunce. Of course they would. Who else would I be with? No, no, Stephen, what it amounts to is that my exchanges with Julia will dwindle to the scope of her house—quiet suppers there and having to leave without spending the whole night. Very likely skulking up to her back door so I won't be recognized in the street, with my hat pulled down over my eyes and a cadogan wig perched on my head. And you know what will happen then."

"What?"

"The Jewel will get bored just sitting at home. She'll find someone who can show her a lively time—take her to the pleasure gardens, to card parties, to masquerades and ridottos. You can't buy the loyalty of such a woman; just see how she's treated that protector of hers in Lincolnshire. He comes down every few months and she warns me away for a while." Greenwood frowned thoughtfully at a whimsical Staffordshire salt-glaze mounted figure that was probably meant to be King George II. "I wonder if he's coming to town for the season."

"Hasn't she said?"

"I don't think she knows, but fortunately he always sends word when he's expected. I've told her I'd take her entirely under my keeping if she'd get rid of him, and all she will do is smile and say that young men are volatile. This Osgodby must be fifty if he's a day, and apparently very attached to her. Perhaps she has a fondness for him, too, or maybe she simply likes the security. I don't know." He drew a hand over his brow in a gesture of defeat, grimacing at his friend. "I suppose I must tell her about my marriage. Lord, if I have to marry I wish it had been one of the other two!"

"Which other two?" the captain asked, bewildered.

"Lady Anne or Miss Berryman. Especially Miss Berryman. Just wait till you see her, Stephen. A regular flirt or I miss my guess. She's Lady Bradwell's niece," he explained with a meaningful roll of his eyes.

"You don't say! When can I meet her?"

"At my wedding, no doubt," Adam rejoined gloomily. "Oh, God, how could I have been so stupid as to make that wager?"

"I think, my dear fellow, that you were more than a little drunk, and Thresham and I were in no better condition. Sir Robert surely has the hardest head of any man I've ever met. Why, he must have drunk at least four bottles of canary by himself! Dunn says you should never try to outdrink someone who obviously has a hard head, and they don't come any harder than Sir Robert's!"

"Just once I'd like to see Dunn make a fool of himself," Greenwood growled.

CHAPTER FIVE

Emma was aware that Maggie slipped out of the school several times during the week to go into the village on an errand which she did not disclose to even her closest friends. Lord Greenwood and his sister or brother-in-law visited her, as did the modiste for hours of fittings, but it was not of these visits that Maggie confided in Emma: it was the visit her father made two days before the wedding.

"He came to inform me of the terms of the marriage settlement," she explained, her face drawn. "He has been very generous. I told him I could never use such a large allowance."

"Living in the ton, I daresay you'll think it barely sufficient two months from now." Emma laughed.

"That's what *he* said, more or less. And he gave me advice about spending it and not getting into debt and never lending money to my . . . husband. He said Lord Greenwood is reckless, especially when he's been drinking. That he's a careless gambler and I shouldn't encourage him by coming to his rescue."

"You will have to be the one to decide that, Maggie, not your father. I don't know anyone here who has a better mind for figures than you, and you'll soon know how best to deal with your finances. Don't worry about what Sir Robert said."

Maggie bit her lip and turned her head slightly away. "He said something else."

Conscious of her friend's need to tell her, and also her reluctance, Emma busied herself with sorting through her sarcophagus of treasures. "Did he, love?"

"He said . . . he said Lord Greenwood is currently 'playing footsie' with a pretty actress."

"Men often do, Maggie. He'll drop her when you're married."

"My father said he might not. That I might hear gossip about it and that I should ignore it. He said if I made a fuss, Lord Greenwood would take an aversion to me."

The lid of the sarcophagus snapped to with a bang as Emma rose to confront her friend. "*No one* could take an aversion to you, Maggie, ever! Aunt Amelia says men have mistresses after they're married only if they are neglected or unstable. I'm sure you won't neglect Lord Greenwood and he doesn't strike me as unstable."

"But Anne said he was a rake!"

"Which is only to say that he's been sowing his wild oats, just as one would expect of a healthy male, my love. He probably won't sit in your pocket after you're married, but he'll come to be as devoted to you as Anne and I are. Only in a different way, of course. Aunt Amelia says that the intimacy between husband and wife generates a unique affection."

A flush of color crept up Maggie's cheeks. "Emma, what if . . . if he doesn't like going to bed with me?"

"Why wouldn't he?" Emma asked, startled.

"I don't know. I haven't much bosom, you see. He'll probably think me skinny and unattractive."

"Goose! Of course he won't. Aunt Amelia says men hardly even notice whom they're in bed with once their passion is aroused. I think probably Lord Greenwood is a passionate man, don't you? Otherwise he would not have a reputation as a libertine."

"He hasn't shown the least passion."

Emma surveyed her companion's face carefully to assess whether Maggie found this comforting or upsetting. The mixture of wistfulness and alarm were so well blended that it was impossible to judge. "He will," she said confidently. "I don't think it has *quite* occurred to his lordship that along with the wedding there is a wedding night."

Not even to Emma could Maggie confide all the doubts that assailed her. When Sir Robert had stomped about the room blustering that he had gone to a great deal of trouble to see that she was well provided for, and that he expected her to do her part by making Greenwood a good wife, she had lifted her chin proudly and announced with dignity, "I shall certainly do my best." But in the nights, when her friends were asleep, she could not help but be less than optimistic. There was no drawing back; she had no intention of disgracing her father or her bridegroom. The thought of her father's wrath was horrifying, but when the day agreed upon arrived, when they were adjusting the white satin gown with its long train to her slender figure, she could almost not bear the heaviest burden of all. A white chip hat with one row of ribbons rested on her head and laylock slippers adorned her feet, the whole forming an image in the mirror that Maggie could not quite believe was real. Emma and Anne were chattering to her but no sense of their words seemed to filter through. Cynthia Morton stood watching the proceedings with a nostalgic smile.

Abruptly, Maggie grasped Anne's hand. "My dear, could you and Emma . . . ? That is, I should like a word alone with Mrs. Morton."

"Of course, love. We'll be in the hall."

Concerned, Cynthia stepped forward as the door closed behind the girls. "Is something the matter, dear?"

"I . . . If . . ." Maggie swallowed and moistened her lips. "How can I go through with this? I'm afraid of my father, but it's so unfair to ruin your brother's life. I know everyone has gone to a great deal of trouble and expense, but it might be better to see them all wasted than go forward with the ceremony."

"Poor Maggie. Are you afraid? May I tell you something? *Every* bride has doubts, to some degree. At the last moment one has second thoughts and they seem especially clear because in a short time there is no turning back. My mother was violently opposed to my marrying James. I cannot tell you the number of times she expressed her disapproval of my attachment to a captain in the Coldstream Guards with no pretension to title or fortune. She had married for both and had no intention of allowing me to throw myself away on such an unworthy object. Oh, Adam was impressed with the way I stoically bore all her rages and threats, with my calm assertion that we would simply wait until I came of age. But when I did, when I finally stood there at the altar, I was quaking in my shoes. I had fought so long for what I wanted that the fight had become almost more real than the love I felt for him. And I wondered if I, so young as I was, could possibly be right, and my mother wrong. I realize your situation is entirely different, but do you see what I'm saying? Even loving him as I did, I felt uncertain, alone facing an enormous change in my life."

"But you weren't alone, really. You had Captain Morton, and he loved you. Your brother—"

"Don't waste your pity on Adam," she said crisply. "I'm convinced marriage could be the making of him. Does that sound callous? I assure you I love him dearly and I do not envy you the straightening of him but—do you know, I think you are the perfect woman for him. On his own he would doubtless choose some flighty, exotic chit without the least sense, and then there would be no impetus to change his way of life."

"Papa said I would alienate him if I didn't just let him go his own way," Maggie protested, the gray eyes moist.

There was a look of surprise on Cynthia's face. "Did he? Well, that's true, of course, so far as it goes. I didn't mean you should nag at him, but that by your example you will be a calming influence. Adam has far too much money and freedom for his own good."

"Do you . . . know how he came to offer for me?"

"Yes, my dear," Cynthia said sympathetically, "but it's not an enlightening tale. If the time comes when you feel you *must* know, come to me, but don't fret yourself about it."

"Please, don't you think it would simply be best if I cried off now?"

"No, dear. If you don't marry Adam, your father will be very displeased, won't he?"

"He can't actually *force* me to marry."

"Well, not precisely. He can make your life miserable, I imagine." A gentle smile lit Cynthia's face. "Will you let me be your friend? I probably know Adam better than anyone else does and I assure you I would be honored for you to come to me with any problems. Adjusting to marriage is never easy, and when you hardly know your husband . . ."

Maggie reached out impulsively and clasped her hands. "You are very kind, and there's nothing I would more treasure than your friendship and your guidance. Have I thanked you for all you've done already? I must seem a woefully ungrateful child."

"Pooh. You thank me every time I turn around. Now, shall we have your friends back in to finish dressing you?"

Aware that Maggie's courage was fast deserting her, Emma and Anne were relieved to find on re-entering that she smiled at them with a degree of composure that saw her through the dressing, the drive to church, and even up the church stairs. But her nerves were so strung by that point that she began to shiver and feel a little faint. As though it were the most natural thing in the world for a bride to be in such a state, Cynthia cheerfully produced a vinaigrette from her purse and waved it slowly under Maggie's pinched nose. The effect was almost instantaneous, a clearing of her head and the stiffening of her body, but what put the proud tilt to her head was the sight of her father advancing on her.

His idea of dressing properly for the occasion was more somber perhaps than a wedding warranted, and she met with a smile the gleam of amusement in Emma's eyes. Still, she was determined not to disgrace him and she laid her hand on his arm to be escorted to Lord Greenwood, waiting at the altar in a coat of blue velvet and looking more distinguished than she had thought possible.

As they walked down the aisle Sir Robert observed, in a voice not suitably lowered, "Possibly the gown was not too dear after all. You look well enough in it."

From the corner of her eye Maggie saw Anne bite her lip, but she squeezed her father's arm and murmured, "Thank you, Papa."

The gauche remark froze Adam for a moment but he relaxed at his bride's calm handling of the situation. She did look rather attractive—young and fresh with no attempt made to appear more sophisticated or mature than her tender years. Adam was accustomed to experienced women and ladies of the highest polish, but when his bride's hand brushed his and he could feel how cold it was, a burst of protectiveness came over him and he smiled at her, a real smile, not the polite contortion of his features with which he was used to honor her.

No spoken vows could have moved Maggie as the kindly light in his eyes did. If you will just give me a chance, she promised silently, I will try to make you an acceptable wife, one you need not be ashamed of in front of your friends. Somehow it seemed a more appropriate vow than the one she repeated after the clergyman in a soft but steady voice.

Adam spoke his vows with a negligent confidence that caused Viscount Dunn to sigh, and Emma to lift an amused brow at Anne, who wasn't watching. In Adam's own opinion he had taken the whole catastrophe in very good grace. Who else would have held to such a wager, would actually have gone through with the ceremony as he was? He could name any number of fellows who would have shirked off—disappeared abroad or disputed the terms of the wager? After all, everyone had been drunk—with the possible exception of Sir Robert—and a small conspiracy might have been worked out with his friends to agree that a monetary figure had been set for the loser, and not marriage to Margaret. Well, he could certainly be congratulated on his forbearance and honorable conduct. Dunn could not possibly find anything amiss with his behavior. Adam, recalled to the service, placed a stunning ring on her finger, a sapphire set round with diamonds, and found to his dismay that it was by far too large for her long, thin fingers. His chagrin was so great that his bride could not keep her lips from twitching, and he responded with a lopsided, self-mocking grin.

"I now pronounce you man and wife."

Emma sighed as she watched Maggie return down the aisle with her husband, her eyes dropped before the curious gazes of her husband's friends. To Anne she said, "One down; two to go. Imagine having your life settled even before your first season. In some ways it seems a pity, but in others an advantage. Maggie will have a freedom denied to you and me."

"Oh, Emma, how can you think about such a thing when you know how miserable she is?" Anne protested in a whisper. "It's not as though she had any choice in the matter. Thank heaven she had Mrs.

Morton to talk to this morning, or I think she wouldn't have had the strength to go through with this wedding. Have you no sensibility?"

Not willing to show that she was stung by this rejoinder, Emma shrugged as she watched Maggie sign the register with a shaking hand. "I am simply being practical, Anne. Lord Greenwood is a handsome man, and charming when he wishes. I haven't the slightest doubt he will learn to value Maggie, and she him. There, see how avidly he is watching her sign the book."

"Humph. He's probably checking to make sure he remembers her name."

"My, how cynical you are today," Emma retorted, her eyes dancing. "Come, Mrs. Morton wants us to join her in the carriage."

The gathering in Portland Place was small, consisting only of Captain Midford and his brother, Viscount Dunn, and Adam's friends Stutton, Norwood, and Thresham. To Emma it was a joyous social occasion, to Anne an unnerving ritual. Emma blossomed under the attentions of the elegant gentlemen; Anne seemed oblivious to Captain Midford's gallantry on her behalf, so concerned was she for Maggie. The bride and groom sat at the head of the table, recipients of various toasts that Adam willingly drank, becoming more affable as the meal progressed. If his high spirits came more from the fact that the occasion had turned into a party than that he was satisfied with his bride, the end result was much the same. All the stiffness and formality of the past week were gone, and his merry blue eyes and laughing countenance settled often on his bride. His voice, it was true, grew louder as he drank, but Maggie herself was becoming a little light-headed and tended to giggle rather than quake at his boisterousness.

Emma watched, intrigued, as Greenwood reached over and laid his hand on Maggie's, a disturbing smile on his lips. His words, however, were mundane. "I've arranged for a closed carriage to take us to Combe Lodge from Half Moon Street, so you mustn't be alarmed if I'm not perfectly steady."

Maggie's wide gray eyes regarded him owlishly. "No, I . . . I won't be alarmed. I'm not completely in possession of my own faculties, actually."

"I know." He laughed and raised his hand to touch her cheek. "You have a most becoming flush from your indulgence."

Across the table Emma's eyes met Anne's with decided amusement. They had both witnessed the interchange, but it struck them differently. Anne had watched his lordship come and go all week, unsmiling and unbending in his wounded dignity, acting, to her mind, a martyr in marrying her friend. She was indignant that he had waited until this point to turn a little of his celebrated charm on his bride. Emma, on the other hand, considered it eminently practical for Lord Greenwood to do some overdue courting. After all, they were going to find themselves in bed in a short while, and lovemaking held a distinct fascination for Emma (on account of her aunt's lengthy career). Even Anne's exasperated grimace could not detract from her delight in seeing dear timid Maggie responding to his advances.

"Are you to leave school this year, Miss Berryman?" a well-modulated voice to her left asked politely.

Startled from her preoccupation, Emma turned to Viscount Dunn, who had previously been engaged by Sir Robert's enthusiastic tales of the previous winter's hunting. "Yes, I'm to come and live with my aunt, Lady Bradwell, in two weeks' time."

The faint raising of one dark brow was the only sign of his surprise. "I wasn't aware she had a niece, though come to think of it, I did once meet her brother, Gerald Berryman."

"He was my father. Do you know my aunt well, Lord Dunn?"

There was a stress to the "well" that Lord Dunn found as impertinent as her quizzing eyes. He was not accustomed to being the object of an impudent schoolgirl's curiosity, and he determined to set her firmly in her place. "I have known her for years and she's never so much as mentioned your existence."

"Ah, well, you could not expect her to put her friends to sleep with tales of her brother's child, now could you?" Emma replied, not in the least daunted by his haughty expression. "She's never mentioned you to me, either."

Her dancing eyes assured him that she believed she'd given as well as she'd gotten, and he was in no frame of mind to be upstaged by a precocious beauty, after patiently listening to Sir Robert's rambling and often boring stories of the chase. "When next I see Lady Bradwell I shall be sure to have her fill me in on the progress of your deportment lessons."

If he had meant to depress her forwardness, he had not expected to raise her ire. Bristling as can only a young lady whose inexperience has been used to taunt her, Emma set down her champagne glass very carefully (so as not to be tempted to dash its contents in his face) and said sweetly, "You are all graciousness, my lord. Fancy your taking so marked an interest in my welfare on such short acquaintance. Aunt Amelia will be duly appreciative, I'm sure, of your condescension." With a mocking flutter of her eyelashes, she simulated a blush of pure maidenly modesty. "I am wholly unworthy of your notice, sir, and can only hope you will not take it amiss if I beg that you desist in your very flattering attentions." And she turned her back on him to find Mr. Thresham watching her with something akin to awe. In a voice loud enough for his lordship to hear, she said archly, "You would never presume on a young lady's acquaintance, would you, Mr. Thresham?"

The poor fellow's eyes skidded past her to take in Lord Dunn's black scowl, and he cleared his throat. "Uh . . . no, ma'am, but I don't think . . . That is to say, I'm sure he never meant . . ."

Emma raised an imperious hand. "Please, the least said, the soonest mended. Or so I have been instructed. Mrs. Childswick once had me embroider it and made me promise to hang it in my room as an object lesson. Which I did, of course, but my skill with a needle is not remarkable and it was more pleasing to the eye upside down."

Slightly in his cups, Mr. Thresham could not contain what he thought to be a most appropriate sally, at the time. "I think your skill in needling is quite stunning, Miss Berryman." Even the grunt of annoyance from Lord Dunn did not serve to erase the wide grin from his face, and Emma beamed on him.

"Thank you, sir. You have no idea how pleasant it is to be addressed by a true gentleman. Even in the very best homes a lady cannot always escape someone whose ideas of gallantry are not right up to the mark, you know. I have myself experienced the occasional qualm at the hands of even a titled gentleman. You would hardly credit it."

"No," he agreed, studiously avoiding the viscount's steely gaze, "there is no understanding the ways of the aristocracy."

Adam would have enjoyed the interlude immeasurably, to see the Great Dunn handled so cavalierly by a miss from the schoolroom, but he was not privileged to overhear the conversation. Thinking it high time the newlyweds took themselves off, Cynthia had signaled to Maggie her intention of rising. The bride was aware that her husband was enjoying himself, and she rather shyly placed a hand on his arm to recall his attention. His hand immediately went to cover it and he turned to her with a smile. "Yes, my dear?"

"Mrs. Morton thinks it time we left."

"So soon? Well, she would know what's proper. Are you ready?"

As ready as she would ever be, Maggie nodded. Shortly they were surrounded by the entire party wishing them well, all totally eclipsed by Sir Robert's booming voice uttering his benediction. "Take care of the child, Greenwood. She's a good girl."

While Adam made the proper responses to her father, Maggie allowed Anne to hug her and assure her that they would meet again very soon. But it was Emma who put a sparkle in her eye by whispering, "I do believe he *is* a hando savant, my dear, and quite taken with you."

If Lord Dunn was looking for an opportunity to repay Emma's pertness, he did not find it in this kindly intentioned remark, on which he shamelessly eavesdropped. Though he could hardly have understood the significance of "hando savant," he was aware that the rest of the whispered confidence brought a warm glow to the bride, and he grudgingly admitted to himself that Miss Berryman had done her friend a good turn. He did not go so far as to believe she had done so other than thoughtlessly, but under the circumstances the words of encouragement were a much-needed boon for the poor bartered bride. Calculating his own tone to a nicety, he lifted Maggie's hand to kiss it, saying, "Lord Greenwood is a very lucky man, my dear. I wish you both every happiness."

In the carriage on the return to school Emma and Anne eyed one another rather warily. Their disagreement over Maggie's marriage put a rare strain on their friendship, and seemed senseless to them both, considering the concern they each felt for the new bride.

"How did you like Captain Midford?" Emma asked at length.

"I don't know. He was all right, I suppose."

"He seemed to like *you* very well."

"Mr. Thresham couldn't take his eyes off *you*." Anne toyed with the reticule in her lap, opening and closing the clasp. "Were you rude to Lord Dunn? He did nothing but scowl at you after you spoke with him."

"Hmm. I may have been the least bit pert to him."

"How could you, Emma?" Anne was genuinely concerned. "Don't you know who he is?"

"Oh, Aunt Amelia has mentioned him," Emma replied offhandedly, "but he was intent on treating me like a wayward schoolgirl, and you know how that sets up my back."

"Lord Dunn is a friend of my family's, and an acknowledged leader in society. Everyone knows him and all the men ape his style. Will talks as though he's a minor god; Jack goes into alt whenever he receives an invitation from him. If you wish to make an impression in society, my dear, it will not do to be rude to him."

"I didn't say I was rude, just pert. In fact, he was rather rude to me."

"Rude? Dunn? You must have misunderstood him, Emma. Or, oh Lord, you weren't impertinent, were you?"

Emma gave the matter a moment's consideration. "He must have thought I was, though I merely asked him if he knew Aunt Amelia well."

All along Anne had feared that Emma's connection with Lady Bradwell would do her more harm than good. Not that Anne had the least objection to her ladyship personally, but . . . well, one could not deny there were rampant rumors and speculation about the lady's private life. Asking a Corinthian if he knew Lady Bradwell *well* was tantamount to asking if he was a lover of hers! And knowing Emma, Anne wasn't at all sure her friend hadn't meant exactly that! Coupled with Emma's perpetually mischievous curiosity, Lord Dunn could not have failed to believe she was being impertinent.

"You don't ask a gentleman something like that," she groaned.

Emma was instantly defensive on her aunt's account. "Why not? I could ask him if he knew your mother well and he wouldn't think the least thing of it."

"Yes, of course, but . . . Your aunt's situation is different from . . . I beg you won't think I'm saying a thing against Lady Bradwell. It is just that . . ." Anne faltered to a halt, thankful for the darkness to hide her embarrassment.

"I know what you mean," Emma said gently. "And perhaps I *was* a bit out of line. I was only teasing, you know, what with the champagne and the excitement . . . and the way Lord Greenwood was looking at Maggie. But Lord Dunn was awfully quick to be critical. Mr. Thresham thought I answered him very neatly."

"I daresay, but Mr. Thresham is a rackety sort of fellow, isn't he? And he was foxed as well. Never mind, dear. I'm sure it's not important."

"I should think not!"

CHAPTER SIX

Long after Emma and Anne had fallen asleep in their room at Windrush House, Maggie lay awake in her husband's half-tester bed in Half Moon Street, alone. They had not gone to Combe Lodge after all because the coachman had liberally partaken of the brandy Adam had allowed his household in celebration of the wedding. Everything else had gone a little wrong, too. Maggie had refused, in a gentle way, to allow Greenwood to drive them in his curricle, which had been his rash suggestion on learning of the coachman's indisposition, and when she had joined him in his library after changing, his setter had barked, causing him to spill on his new coat a fair quantity of the brandy he had been sipping.

It was then that she had tried to offer him his wedding present, and he had stared at the silver-papered package as though it might bite him. Maggie had gone to a great deal of trouble to secure the fine leather driving gloves, since the only shop in Kensington that stocked such supplies carried a mediocre stock. She had been forced to talk the proprietor into having some merchandise of superior quality sent out to him for her inspection. With infinite patience she had gone through stacks of gloves to choose a pair that were well-tanned, of consistent coloration, and flawless.

And they fit him. Not that she hadn't wanted them to, but considering her ring, which hung loosely about her knuckle, it might have been better if they hadn't. Greenwood had been appalled that he'd forgotten a gift for her and blurted that hers hadn't been delivered as yet. She knew it wasn't the truth, and protested, "But you have given me my ring." It was too late; he had already intimated that a gift was coming, and he would have to see that one did. Despite his secrecy in sending a note off to Captain Midford, Maggie was aware that he had done so, since almost every member of the household was a trifle bosky except Mrs. Phipps, the housekeeper. It was difficult to avoid hearing Greenwood's wavering valet try to find a footman sober enough to deliver the message.

As Greenwood's embarrassment had eclipsed his pleasure in the gift, he had been too talkative at the hastily organized dinner. Throughout the evening, during a game of chess and her performance on the pianoforte, Maggie knew his ear was tuned to an arrival. Sipping absently at his brandy, his fingers tapping impatiently on the arm of his chair, he had watched her, at first almost unconsciously, but after a while with more interest. Her gown was cut to emphasize the swell of her youthful breasts, and she almost knew the moment when it had occurred to him that he could take her to bed. He had looked stunned.

Finishing a piece on the pianoforte, she had lifted her eyes inquiringly. "Shall I play another?"

He had put down the glass unsteadily and said huskily, "No, thank you, my dear. I've enjoyed it but the hour is late. We should retire." As he had walked her to the door, his arm possessively about her waist, the strange, impelling light was in his eyes again. "You look charming, Margaret." And suddenly his lips were on hers, demanding, his hands straying about her body. Shocked, she had stood perfectly still, unresponding, and after a moment he had seemed to realize the infelicity of his tactics. He said nothing, but placed his hands on her shoulders and kissed her gently. As her panic abated she returned the tender pressure of his lips and found herself released from his hold. His smile was almost sedate as he said, "Good. You change for bed. I'll be along in a few minutes."

But he hadn't been along in a few minutes. There had come a knock at the door and then for a very long time she had heard nothing. She lay rigid with tension, expecting him to come at any moment, bearing a wedding gift for her to assuage his conscience. At last the sound of raised voices in the hall and the banging of the front door reached her where she lay in bed. Her head had begun to ache and her fears to grow in proportion to the duration of her wait. Now she fully expected the silence of the house to be broken by the sound of footsteps on the stairs and the rustlings of her husband changing in his dressing room, but there was nothing. For another ten minutes she waited and then, in desperation, she gave a tentative tug to the bell pull. If no one had answered, she would not have had the courage to do so again, but shortly there was a tap at the hall door.

Mrs. Phipps entered, her face a mask. With a sinking heart, Maggie asked, "Could you tell Lord Greenwood that I . . . would like a word with him?"

"I'm sorry, my lady. Lord Greenwood has gone out."

"Out?" In the dim light of the one candle, Maggie could not read the woman's expression. Her aching head was now joined with a sickness to her stomach. "In that case, Mrs. Phipps, would you bring me a few drops of laudanum in water?"

"Right away, my lady."

When Maggie had downed the draught, she calmly bid the housekeeper good night and snuffed the candle. For a few minutes, before the drug offered her blessed sleep, she stared dry-eyed at the ornamental ceiling.

Convinced that he had behaved with great understanding, Adam had returned to the drawing room when Maggie disappeared up the stairs. She was shy, after all, and he had startled her at first, but when he had moderated the eagerness of his caresses, she had accepted them very well. He poured himself another glass of brandy, thinking that he would be wise to give her sufficient time to compose herself in bed. As he mentally ticked off the minutes and sipped at his drink, Adam considered his wife's situation, that is, that she was a total innocent and would need his consideration in being indoctrinated into the rites of love. Not that such a role should prove at all difficult to him. He was a man of the world, experienced, knowledgeable.

From his sixteenth birthday, when he had first indulged a hearty sexual appetite, he had never had the least problem finding women who were more than pleased to give themselves to him. And if they were usually older women, well, that was an indication of his own sexual prowess, his ability to satisfy a sexually mature woman. As a matter of personal honor, Adam had never taken a girl's innocence. The encounter with the parlor maid at Parkhurst that had caused such a fuss would have been no such thing. No virgin would have acted like that hussy!

The knock at the front door that he had been expecting the whole of the evening finally came, and he was too immersed in his meditations even to realize it until the porter showed a harassed Captain Midford into the drawing room. Adam regarded him blankly. "What the hell are you doing here?"

"I just got your note, Adam, and I thought it must be some emergency."

"For God's sake, I told you it was just a matter of buying a present for my wife."

Stephen threw his hands up in a gesture of disgust. "How was I to know? You wrote in such haste I couldn't make out one word in four. The very fact that you were still in town made me think there must be some problem."

"There isn't. Go away."

"Why are you still here? I thought you were going to Combe Lodge."

"The coachman was drunk. We're going in the morning. Go away."

Such subtle hints fazed the good captain not one whit. He had come dashing to his friend's aid, at great physical strain to himself, as he had continued celebrating since leaving the wedding reception in Portland Place and he had been in no condition to respond to the summons, only doing so at the promptings of a highly charged sense of friendship. Stephen did not intend to leave until he had gotten to the bottom of the matter.

"Why the hell would you write me about buying a present for your wife?" he asked as he poured himself some brandy in the empty glass Maggie had refused, and sat down.

Adam's brows lowered ominously. "At any other time I would be more than happy to enlighten you on the whole, Stephen, but not now. Go away."

"Nonsense. You said you were leaving in the morning, and if the matter was urgent when you sent the note, it must be so still." Stephen refilled his friend's glass without asking.

Since it was apparent that the captain had no intention of leaving until the story was unfolded to him, Adam made an effort to still the rising desire to have him tossed out. "Margaret gave me a wedding present, a very handsome pair of driving gloves. The nuisance of it is that I hadn't thought to get her anything."

"You gave her a ring. I was with you when you chose it."

"Yes," Adam admitted impatiently, "but that is not the same thing. And besides, the ring didn't fit. She said it was all right, my giving her only the ring, but by then I'd sort of suggested that I'd gotten her something and it just hadn't arrived yet. So I wrote asking you to find something nice for her and have it sent round." Adam had been carelessly sipping at the brandy, forgetting how far gone he already was.

"Well, do you want me to do it or not? I should think the poor little thing would be rather hurt that you didn't think enough of her to get her something."

"She didn't act the least offended, but I felt a fool. I never thought of it, Stephen. This whole marriage has been a ramshackle affair from start to finish. First I forgot about a wedding trip, and now forgetting a gift on top of it, I really thought I ought to do something about it." He finished the brandy in his glass and Stephen poured him another one.

"It's too late to get her something tonight. I can look around in the morning and send what I find off to you at the Lodge. What sort of thing did you have in mind?"

"Jewelry, I suppose. A necklace or a bracelet or something."

"But you've already given her a ring."

"Yes, but ladies *like* expensive trinkets."

"The ring cost you a fortune, and besides, you don't want to show up her gift. Gloves would look shabby against some costly bauble." Stephen rested his chin in his hand, since it had become difficult to think with his head buzzing so. "You know, Adam, that was very thoughtful of her. Could have given you a stickpin or a snuffbox, but she gave you something you'd use."

"I *know* it was thoughtful of her. That's why I'm so anxious to get her a gift she'll like." Adam's eyes were becoming a little blurry and his speech was not altogether clear.

"Tell you what, old fellow. Shouldn't give her jewelry. Give her something *personal*."

"Like what, for God's sake? She's just acquired a new wardrobe and I haven't the slightest idea what she'd think was special."

The two men sat silent for some time, sipping at their brandy and making a pretense of hard concentration on the problem at hand. They were both very drunk by now and suggestions of candlesticks and vases were offered only by way of breaking the oppressive silence. Adam had long since forgotten that his wife was awaiting him in his bed; the urgency of getting her a gift that had gripped him earlier in the day once again had the ascendency. After another glass of brandy, he had an inspiration.

"Canaries!"

Stephen looked at him sadly. "You've lost your way, old man."

"No, listen. I was talking with her one day and I distinctly remember her telling me she liked canaries. It's just the thing,

Stephen. Special, don't you see. It would show I'd given a lot of thought to her present."

"It would show you'd lost your reason," his friend responded pungently.

"No, why? I'll have them in a little golden cage, like Mrs. Harland does."

"Mrs. Harland says they're a goddamn nuisance and she wishes she'd never laid eyes on them."

A glow of pure delight sparkled in Adam's eyes. "Really? Do you think she'd like to be rid of them?"

"Definitely."

Adam lurched to his feet. "Then we'll go there directly and I shall bring them back for Margaret."

"You can't go there at this time of night!" the captain protested.

"Why not?" Adam waved a slightly unsteady hand. "It's an emergency. Mrs. Harland has a heart of pure gold; I've heard Dunn say so."

"I don't think that's what he meant, and she probably won't be home."

"We'll wait for her." Once determined on a course of action, Adam was not to be so lightly dissuaded. "She holds her card parties several times a week. What day is this?"

"Tuesday."

"There, you see! I'm sure Tuesday is one of her days."

Stephen was struck with the coincidence of this and struggled to his feet. "Well, then, what are we waiting for? You can have the canaries back here within the hour."

Mrs. Harland kept a discreet gaming house in Arlington Street that was frequented by gentlemen of the ton and frowned upon by the magistrates, but the latter had as yet made no move to close it down, though there were rumblings from that direction. The company was always select, and cards were sent to announce on which days she would receive company to her little "parties." Adam and Stephen had been there on any number of occasions, dropping a little of the ready, but never enough to cause suspicion of unfair play. Mrs. Harland was a shrewd woman, and she knew that echoes of large losses would more surely than anything else bring down the arm of the law upon her profitable premises.

On this particular evening she had allowed herself to be entreated into a game of piquet tête-à-tête with Sir Nicholas Dyrham and when the two bosky gentlemen arrived at her establishment they were admitted readily enough (no one was more likely to lose money at a game of chance than a man in his cups), but they were not allowed to approach and interrupt her game in the far corner of the room. Instead they were directed to a table of rouge et noir to await an audience with her, where, it was to be hoped, they would lay out a substantial sum in the meantime. Because his attention was directed toward the corner and grasping the first opportunity to speak with his hostess, Adam made only a desultory attempt to pay heed to the game, consequently finding himself twenty pounds the poorer within minutes. Not that this distressed him, for he had caught sight of the gold cage with its two canaries standing near the windows, and he was relieved to see that Mrs. Harland had not disposed of them already, if she truly detested them as much as the captain had intimated.

The instant Adam saw Mrs. Harland arise from her seat, he abandoned the rouge et noir table and appeared at her side, begging for a moment of her time. If she was surprised, she gave no indication, merely commenting with a teasing smile, "You know your credit is always good here, Greenwood."

"It's not that! I don't need to write a chit. I want to buy the canaries."

"My dear little pets? Whatever would you do with a couple of canaries, Greenwood?"

Obviously she didn't believe him, but assumed some prank was afoot, and he hastened to explain, to this lovely woman with her heart of gold, that he needed them as a wedding gift for his bride.

"I had no idea you'd married." Mrs. Harland regarded him calculatingly. "Is the Lady Greenwood so very fond of canaries, then?"

"Yes, well, I don't really know, but I think she may be. Midford said you find them a nuisance and I thought you wouldn't mind parting with them, since I'm in a bit of a hurry to get her something."

The canaries in question were perched drowsily on little pegs in the gilded cage, the tasseled cage cover hanging from the stand. Mrs. Harland spoke to them with great affection. "How are my little darlings today? Will you give us a song? It's all these noisy men and their nasty smoke, isn't it?" She turned with a sigh to Adam. "I know it's not the proper setting for them, but I would find it difficult to part with my dear feathered friends. Such a delightful sound, their song. It quite melts the heart."

Not hers, obviously, Adam thought unhappily. "I would be willing to give you ten pounds for the whole setup, right now," he offered with necessary generosity.

"Ten pounds? For my little carolers? I'm sure I could never part with them for ten pounds. The cage alone must be worth that."

"Come now, it's only gilded. I could buy the same thing in a shop for a great deal less."

Mrs. Harland smiled sweetly at him. "Then you should do so, my lord."

"Oh, very well. How much?"

One painted fingernail poked at a fluffed-up canary in an attempt to spark it to some kind of life as a negotiating point, but the bird refused to budge from his perch. "They don't sing at night. If you were to hear them during the day, you would think twenty pounds a more than reasonable price."

"Twenty pounds!" Adam yelped. "That's nonsense! I could get the whole setup at that shop in the Strand for ten."

"I thought you were in rather a hurry, my lord. And you must take into consideration my great affection for dear . . . Carol and Clyde. I would not so much as contemplate parting with them were it not for your obvious anxiety to have them as a gift for your wife."

Adam knew he had set the trap for himself, but he was loath to leave without the stupid birds now that he had so nearly accomplished his mission. Still, there was a stubborn streak in his character, and he did not like being taken any more than the next person. "Well, I would go to fifteen. Otherwise I may as well just visit that shop tomorrow and get a brand-new cage and some healthier-looking birds. These seem singularly placid."

Since Mrs. Harland had hoped for no more than twelve, she smiled benignly on him. "We shall call the difference my little wedding gift to you and your bride, Greenwood."

Her smug countenance did not improve his temper, but Adam thanked her with as little sarcasm as possible, wrapped the cover about the cage, and handed over the necessary sum. He was in the process of gathering up Stephen and lugging the awkward stand with its precariously balanced cage to the door when Viscount Dunn entered. Under the newcomer's incredulous stare he felt like a schoolboy caught out in some lark.

CHAPTER SEVEN

His voice carefully controlled to reach no one but Adam, Dunn asked coldly, "What the devil are you doing here, Greenwood?"

Adam had come of age several years before, and he had a title, position, and wealth of his own, but the force of habit was strong, and he was in the habit of answering to his friend's brother on certain matters of conduct in which Dunn had proved his mentor after the death of his father. Besides, under the haughty gaze he felt impelled to make some explanation for the ridiculous picture he made.

"I came to buy the birds for Margaret," seemed the simplest answer.

"Am I to understand that Lady Greenwood sent you to a gambling den in the late hours of the night to procure a couple of canaries?"

"She didn't *send* me. I wanted to get her a wedding present and I thought she'd like them for pets."

Dunn smiled at an acquaintance but joined his arm with Adam's and walked with him, his brother, Stephen, nervously following, back through the door and out into the hall. "Do you mean to tell me," he asked ominously, "that you have left your bride on your wedding night? Alone? So that you could come out on some harebrained scheme to acquire a cage and birds?"

Usually Dunn was reasonably patient with his brother's and Adam's little peccadilloes, tolerance being one of his most notable virtues where they were concerned. Adam had never seen him so blackly angry, and he strove valiantly to exonerate himself. "She gave me some driving gloves, Dunn. I'd forgotten to get her anything, in the rush and all, and I didn't want to disappoint her."

"And you thought she wouldn't be hurt when you told her you were going out?"

"I didn't tell her."

For a fraction of a second Adam thought Dunn was going to strike him, so fierce was the light that flared in his eyes, but the viscount never moved a muscle, save one that tightened in his jaw. "Of all the stupid, asinine, childish pranks you have played, none can compare with this. If it weren't for that poor child you married this morning, I swear I would wash my hands of you forever. How could you be so cruel as to leave her alone on your wedding night? Have you any idea how insulted she must feel? It makes no difference that you were forced to marry her; that was entirely your own idiotic fault. Were you not the least moved by the brave face she put on for a marriage which could be no more agreeable to her than to you? Is there no drop of compassion in you at all, Adam? No, I don't want to hear about how you are even now on an errand to buy canaries for her," he said disdainfully. "That is only an example of your own conceit—trying to save face. It would have been more honorable for you to have welshed on your bet with Sir Robert than to treat his daughter as you have tonight."

Adam was horrified by the virulence of Dunn's tongue-lashing. Not in the whole of his life had anyone so thoroughly chastised him for his conduct, and the worst of it was that, as his head began to clear, he could see that there was some justification for it. He felt, with a touch of bravado, that Dunn was not giving enough consideration to the effort he had made to obtain a gift for his bride that would especially please her. But he could see that poor Margaret must have wondered why he didn't come up to her as he had said he would.

His eyes returned to Dunn's from their inspection of the detested bird cage and he said stiffly, "I mean to treat Margaret with all the respect due her as my wife. There was no intent on my part to insult her this evening by going out to get her a present. Perhaps if I had not had so much to drink, I would have realized the . . . inadvisability of such a course, but I didn't think it would take so long."

"Will you accept a word of advice from me?" Dunn asked, his voice restored to its usual calm.

"Of course."

Dunn rubbed his forehead thoughtfully and turned to his brother. "Wait down at the door for Adam, if you please, Stephen. This is a private matter."

More than ready to obey, Stephen swiftly made his departure, relieved to escape so lightly for his part in the escapade. Still Dunn did not speak. Frowning slightly and tapping restless fingers on the head of his cane, he seemed perplexed as how best to put his suggestion.

"God knows this is no business of mine, Adam, but I would hate to see you carelessly throw away any chance you may have of building a solid marriage on the tottering foundations you have laid so far. Give your wife time to gain some confidence in you. When you want to, you can be exceedingly captivating to ladies, and you shouldn't think that just because you've married Lady Greenwood, she is not worthy of at least your ordinary effort to win her affection. If you . . . rush her now, you may never recover the lost ground."

"You mean I shouldn't sleep with her tonight?" Adam asked bluntly.

"I can see delicacy is wasted on you," his mentor grumbled with a pained expression. "You would be wise to woo her a bit, as you were at the wedding feast. She is, after all, very young."

"Oh, I had realized that she needed the proper encouragement," Adam responded somewhat loftily. "You may trust me to see she is handled with the greatest delicacy."

Nothing in Adam's prior behavior had given Dunn reason to trust anything of the sort, but he said only, "You reassure me. I hope you will pardon my interference."

"I know you only meant it for the best," Adam replied magnanimously, taking a firm grip on the stand and starting for the stair. "We leave for the Lodge in the morning. I think my wife will like it there."

With a negligent wave of his hand, he began the descent, hampered by the bird cage and stand, but undaunted. Dunn watched his retreat with a frown, then sighed and re-entered the gambling rooms. He had said far too much already to the young gudgeon, and it was likely to have no effect at all. There were lessons that could be instilled only through experience, and he very much doubted that Adam was a quick learner in the school of human relations. Given to believe from a young age that he was some sort of god, it would take more than Dunn's words to convince him that he had a very mortal path to tread.

Adam had shucked off the lecture instantly. It was mortifying, at his age, to be raked over the coals, whether he was deserving of the rebuke or not, and he felt that he had reclaimed a little ground by being able to say truthfully that he was aware of Margaret's innocence and the necessity of handling it with finesse. His head was a great deal clearer now, and the cold night air served to sober him almost entirely as he trudged along with Stephen, relating the bargaining for the bird cage. His friend was appalled at the price paid and expostulated almost to Adam's door in Half Moon Street, where he was dismissed with a friendly thanks for his assistance—only half in jest.

The porter was there to let him in, as usual, but it was out of the ordinary for him to find Mrs. Phipps still up at that hour. She came from the dining saloon where she had sat on a chair by the door listening for his return.

"Good evening, Lord Greenwood. I thought you would wish to know that the coachman is feeling better and will surely be fit to convey you and Lady Greenwood to the Lodge in the morning." Her eyes never once met his but seemed unable to detach themselves from the bird cage he carried.

"Yes, well, he'll be looking for another place if he isn't," Adam said curtly. He had no intention of explaining the bird cage.

"Lady Greenwood was not feeling well and took a few drops of laudanum before retiring."

A stab of remorse caused him to wince but he made no comment other than to bid her good night and march toward the stairs. One did not explain one's behavior to one's servants. He could feel her eyes on him as he lugged the cage and stand up to the first floor and down the hall to his dressing room. It would be just his luck if the damn canaries had died from their exposure to the cold night air, he decided morbidly as he poked his snoring valet in the ribs. Perkins rose magnificently to the occasion, giving a piercing yelp and then settling in to rid his lordship of his clothes and offer his night attire.

"I can put on my own damn nightshirt," Adam snorted. "Get to bed and be ready to leave for the Lodge early in the morning."

Eventually he crept into his bedchamber in total darkness, his consideration going so far as to suggest he not carry a candle, which might awaken his wife. But he still had the bird cage with him, and in the dark he tripped over a hassock as he looked for a suitable place to put it. The resulting clatter—the bird cage and stand bounced against the wardrobe and Adam landed on his face—apparently did not disturb his wife's sleep, for there was no movement from the bed. A horrid idea occurred to him and he left the birds to fend for themselves while he advanced to the bed and reached out to touch the sleeping girl. Her flesh felt warm and she appeared to be breathing quite naturally. Reassured, he returned to set the birds right, shushing their angry twittering and telling them to go to sleep. Finally he crawled into his bed, exhausted, and immediately fell asleep.

One of the things Adam especially liked about the Jewel was that she always awoke in the mood for love. When he spent the night at her house in Clarges Street he would feel her body next to his when he was half asleep and the first light was pressing its way through the draperies of her bedroom. As though in a pleasant dream he would allow his hands to wander over her where she lay nestled away from him, tracing the curves of her thighs and the firmness of her buttocks. He would press himself up against her, already hard with desire, and lay an arm over hers to reach the sensuous fullness of her breast. The luxury of caressing her in that soporific state had almost as much merit as the driving energy of the night before, when his passion, raised to a fine pitch, would satisfy itself in a more vigorous manner.

No, the morning was every bit as delicious, when he could bury his face in her hair and kiss the nape of her neck without even bothering to exert so much effort as to open his eyes, or speak a word of endearment. His hand inside her nightdress touching the soft flesh, calling forth a response, and the hardness of her nipple making his own desire too strong to bother controlling. Sometimes he would take her that way, simply rolling the nightdress up over her hips; at others he would pull her toward him and slide onto her . . .

"What the hell!" The dream was rudely shattered when he found himself unable to enter and his eyes flew open to behold not Julia but Margaret beneath him, staring with enormous gray eyes at his astonished face. There was nothing for it but to brazen it out. He had gone too far to draw back. But her maidenhood was firmly intact and the pleasant fantasy had become a laborious reality. Adam could see that she was frightened and that his thrusting caused her pain, but the only thing he could think of to whisper was, "There now, my dear, it will take but a moment." After the shock he had received he needed all his concentration to achieve his goal and his estimate of time was sadly off. His wife bore with stoical silence the callous and lengthy destruction of her virginity but a tear slid down her cheek which did not escape his notice, once he had succeeded and lay panting on her, his weight crushing her small body.

"You mustn't think it will hurt another time," he said consolingly, kissing away the tear.

Maggie said nothing. To come partially out of her drugged sleep and find his hands caressing her had not been entirely unpleasant, but his thoughtless consummation of their marriage had been even worse than she had envisioned. Neither passion nor tenderness accompanied it, merely brute strength and an expressed wish to get it over with quickly. She refused to shed further tears but gently nudged him off her so she could pull down her nightdress and climb out of bed. If she had not been so shattered, she would probably have remained there until he left her. As it was, all she wanted to do was get away from him and be alone for a while.

"Where are you going?" Adam had not meant for his voice to sound cross, but he knew he had botched the defloration and his vanity was involved.

Picking up her dressing gown from a chair, Maggie proceeded to push her arms through the sleeves and wrap it about her. "To wash myself and get dressed."

"It's hardly light yet. No one will be up to help you."

"That's better, I think. I don't want to see anyone just now." Before he could say anything further, she let herself out into the hall. The darkness there was a welcome cover to her as she made her way to the room at the back. No sounds of stirring reached her and she found the room blessedly deserted. Unfortunately, it was too early for a can of hot water to have been brought to the basin, but there was a fresh towel, too good to ruin, really, but she had little choice. She discarded her nightdress, tidied herself as best she could, and then pulled the cover off a chair to seat herself and doze off and on until the household awoke.

When Jennie brought a can of water, she was startled to find Lady Greenwood already in the room, and even more surprised to be dismissed before she could assist her ladyship with her dressing. Maggie's modesty was not ordinarily so great that she found it distasteful to be assisted at her toilette; she had had a servant to do so for most of her life. But not today! Not when she came from her husband's bed feeling embarrassed and somehow shamed, as though that one thing she had always considered her own, her body, could never again be hers. Which left her with only her thoughts sacred, and she vowed that they would remain untouched, unobserved even, by her husband or anyone else. If they were all she could call her own, then they must be treasured.

In the early dawn hours Adam slept fitfully, disturbed at what had happened and yet convinced that he was not really to blame. His wife did not return to the room, nor did he expect that she would. Hell, he'd *meant* to do it right and he could hardly be blamed for causing her pain. She would learn in time that there was no need for tears. Really, it was a great pity women had maidenheads to begin with, making their introduction to lovemaking such a painful business. Adam contented himself with the thought that his wife was fortunate to have such an experienced lover to guide her in the Paphian garden.

A sharp twittering awoke him from a sound sleep and he remembered the canaries. They were alive at least. How he could have forgotten to tell Margaret that they were here . . . Well, he would inform her at breakfast. Better yet, he would have them taken to the breakfast parlor to surprise her. Subconsciously he acknowledged that she would need something to cheer her low spirits; she had not left him in a particularly propitious mood.

Maggie was sipping at her third cup of tea when a footman brought the bird cage on its stand into the room. She felt it incumbent on her to be there when her husband came in for his repast, but she was up so long before him that it was a considerable wait. When Adam soon followed his present into the room, he was in flowing spirits, sure that now he had made restitution for any small oversights of which he might have been guilty. Like a conjuror he whipped the cover off the cage and declared, "Your wedding present, my dear."

The birds, restored to light, greeted the first signs of morning by hopping about, pecking hopefully at the floor of the cage. But the mishap of the previous night had tossed the bird seed on his lordship's bedchamber floor, and there was none to be had. Maggie rose from her seat and came to stand by them, at a loss for words. Not that she was speechless with gratification but rather mystified as to why he would have chosen such a gift. She lifted a piece of cold toast from the sideboard and crumbled it for them as she tried to invest her voice with enthusiasm. "How very thoughtful of you, Greenwood. Do they sing?"

"They're supposed to, but I don't know whether one can trust . . . That is, if they don't we can get ones that do. Remember you said the other day that you liked canaries?"

The hair pin! Trust him to take her answer to his casual question so literally. Maggie tried to summon up a real appreciation, tried to believe that he had actually given the gift serious consideration, but she failed. Everything in her felt flat and dry, emotionless, drained. One of the birds began to trill, the notes soaring and falling, skimming about the sunny room as though to fill it with joy. Maggie smiled faintly. "How pretty. Thank you, Greenwood."

Her response was not all that he'd hoped for. Perhaps he'd thought she would throw her arms about his neck and kiss him, as the Jewel had done when he'd presented her with the phaeton and pair. Not that he could really picture Margaret doing that, but the previous day she had been shyly accepting of him, pleased by his little attentions, ready to make an effort to earn his approbation. Now she was cool and remote, strangely unapproachable. Far too late he remembered Dunn's urging him to give Margaret time to trust him.

But that was nonsense. There was no reason she shouldn't trust him, after all. He pressed a kiss on her forehead and said confidently, "We'll take them with us to Combe Lodge. You'll like it there."

CHAPTER EIGHT

Emma settled back in the carriage beside Anne and declared, "I shall never set foot inside that place again!"

Anne's brother, Will, who was seated opposite them, grinned. "No wonder. To hear Mrs. Childswick you would think you were going out into a world full of depraved ogres and ferocious dragons ready to destroy your souls. Anne had told me what she was like but I thought she exaggerated. Mrs. Childswick seems to think Windrush House is the only port in a very stormy sea."

"More like a cloistered nunnery in a pleasure garden," retorted Emma, who had just been informed by her erstwhile preceptress that her frivolity, levity, and penchant for mischief would lead her into sorry scrapes if she did not learn to lead a more constant and elevated existence. There had been a hint, too, that Lady Bradwell was hardly the person to have charge of a volatile young miss such as herself, to which Emma had taken exception, though not out loud. Personally, she couldn't think of anyone she would rather have as her chaperon than the ever-cheerful Lady Bradwell. To her mind it was her aunt's perpetual good humor and optimistic outlook on life that inspired the jealousy underlying the gossip about her. Not that the gossip had no foundation, mind you, but it was the envious matrons, with nothing to do but order their own lives and those over whom they had control into the stuffiest and most boring of channels, who gave rise to the criticism, and not their lack of ambition to lead such a carefree existence.

Lady Bradwell was cautious in her choice of cicisbeos, never flaunting her power over a married man to pique his wife or enrage his children. In all likelihood she could count any number of married men amongst her train, Emma mused, but they were not visible at assemblies and card parties as her attendants. To be plucked from the sterile atmosphere of Windrush House and dropped in the swirling gaiety of London social life had been Emma's goal for so long that she could hardly believe that it was at last coming true. She did not bother to catch a farewell glimpse of the school, as Anne did, but set herself to questioning Lord William about the upcoming season. Did he frequent Vauxhall and Drury Lane? Did he prefer balls to card parties? Did he know any other young ladies who would be making their appearance this season? Did he know her aunt?

"Lady Bradwell? Of course. Everyone knows Lady Bradwell. She's been so kind as to invite me to entertainments at her house several times. To my mind she's the most vivacious hostess in town. You can always be sure of enjoying yourself there—plenty of food, drink, and good company. And her affairs are never littered with encroaching Italian sopranos or insipid pianoforte performances by untalented young ladies." When his sister gave him a reproachful glance he mumbled, "Beg your pardon! I'm sure I never meant your own performance."

Emma laughed. "Aunt Amelia knows better than to call on me, I hope! Though I don't mind accompanying if the men want to sing, mind you. There is nothing quite so lovely as to hear really fine male voices singing, is there? I could sit by the hour—and have at my aunt's—especially since the men are not generally accompanied. And I will play for dancing, since no one is particular about the music then, but in the ordinary way I don't like to perform. Now Anne is another matter altogether. She plays astonishingly well."

A gleam of brotherly pride sparked in his eyes. "Mama says she could perform professionally, she's that good. And, though I do say so myself, I think we all sing rather well together."

Anne shook her head mournfully. "You will have Emma thinking us quite vain, Will. I'm sure there's nothing out of the ordinary about any of our talents."

"If I had a special talent, I would not be so modest about it,"

Emma declared, her eyes dancing. "Mrs. Childswick is convinced that my only accomplishment lies in mischief-making."

Will grinned. "Then doubtless we will see you displaying your achievement during the season. No use hiding your light under a bushel, as you said. Things can get deadly dull and monotonous, even during the season. Never hurts to kick up a bit of a lark to liven things up."

"Will!" Anne protested, fearful that he would encourage her spirited friend into trouble, which was all too likely in any case, given Emma's temperament. With a close and solid family behind her, Anne had planned to include her friend in that very respectable circle, to counteract any stigma that might attach to her for being under Lady Bradwell's chaperonage. Though her ladyship was not denied entry anywhere, her reputation was not entirely intact, since she served as the subject of gossip from one year's end to the next. Anne knew that her own mother found Lady Bradwell a delightful enigma, and no word of censure ever passed her lips, but not everyone in the haut ton was so indulgent as the Marchioness of Barnfield. Anne said repressively, "I'm sure Emma and I are not likely to find our first season boring. You forget that all London's entertainments aren't old hat to us."

"You'll be fagged to death in a week," he assured her.

Knowing that her brother had been off in Cornwall with her father, and therefore a bit out of touch with the goings-on in London, she turned to Emma with a conspiratorial smile and asked, "Have you heard from Lady Greenwood?"

Emma knew very well that Anne had also received a letter from Maggie, but she was not averse to teasing Lord William. "Yes, they'll be back in town in a few days."

"Lady Greenwood? Dear God, never say Adam has married! When? Who did he marry? Surely not that little actress?" Will was more than a little appalled.

"He has married," his sister informed him stiffly, disliking the reference to Lord Greenwood's mistress, "our very dear friend Maggie Somervale."

"The devil you say! How did he meet her? I thought they kept you behind barred doors there at Windrush House."

Anne was slightly discomposed by his questions and Emma stepped into the breach. "Through her father, Sir Robert. It was quite a whirlwind courtship. Your sister and I attended the wedding, almost two weeks ago. They've been at Combe Lodge, but are returning for the season."

"What's she like—your friend?"

"Oh, she's very sweet, but quiet."

"Doesn't sound at all the sort of girl Adam's usually attracted to," Will said, suspicious. "Are you quizzing me?"

"Not at all," his sister assured him firmly. "You'll like her, Will, and I hope you'll be very kind to her. She's unfamiliar with society and as a married lady will be expected to know a great deal more than she does." Anne's eyes were gravely serious when she reached across to squeeze her brother's hand. "I'm counting on you to help her, Will."

"Well, of course I shall," he murmured stoutly, "but she's really Adam's responsibility."

"Lord Greenwood strikes me as a shade loose about his responsibilities."

"You're thinking about the parlor maid! Hang it, Anne, there was nothing in that. Turns out the girl's been . . . courted by half a dozen strapping lads in the neighborhood and Papa's gotten her married off to the best of the lot, since there's a child due. And it's not Adam's! The wench was just trying for a little after-the-fact support."

Anne sighed with exasperation and Emma shared an amused glance with Lord William, who was immediately captivated by her sparkling blue eyes. Of course Will was perennially being captivated by some pretty girl or other, so this was nothing new, but it boded well for the season, he decided, to know that the lively Emma Berryman would be on hand to add a little spice to the irksome round of formal dos.

When the carriage stopped before Lady Bradwell's door to deposit Emma, Lord William gladly supervised the removal of the trunk and valise into the house. Emma hurriedly arranged with Anne to meet the following day for a long-awaited shopping expedition. Anne hastened to suggest that her mother accompany them, to which Emma agreed, though she suspected her friend thought Lady Bradwell's advice on gowns might tend to the flamboyant or revealing. Actually, Emma knew her aunt's taste to be impeccable, suggestive but not obvious, as many a more reserved lady had been known to succumb to under the pressure of an influential French modiste. Not that Lady Barnfield could be counted in that number. The one time Emma had seen her at Windrush House she had been dressed with such exquisite good taste that the younger girls had gawked (until Mrs. Childswick had thrown them a threatening glance that scattered them like chickens).

As Lord William assisted Emma from the carriage, he expressed the hope that they would be seeing a great deal of each other. "That would be delightful," she returned cheerfully, allowing him to carry her hand to his lips. "I know very few people in town as yet, but with two such friends as your sister and Maggie I daresay that makes little difference. And my aunt seems to be acquainted with almost everyone! Thank you for your escort from school, Lord William. And may that be the last time I need ever mention Windrush House," she said with a laugh.

With a gay wave of her hand she left him and skipped up the stairs, greeting Lady Bradwell's butler with a query on his health. She removed the simple bonnet and shook out her golden curls as North informed her that her ladyship was to be found in the drawing room. "Oh, good, she's in." Emma caught her reflection in the glass and made a perfunctory effort to smooth her hair.

"She's expecting you, Miss Berryman. If you will follow me . . ."

It had not seemed necessary to don a special gown for the drive to London, and Emma thought nothing of her schoolgirl dress until she found herself in a room with not only Lady Bradwell but three elegantly dressed gentlemen. One she had seen before and she felt chagrined to be surveyed, critically, through his quizzing glass from the moment she stepped into the room until he was introduced to her.

"Lord Dunn and I have met, Aunt Amelia." Emma dropped a stiff curtsy and nodded to him before turning to the second gentleman. Sir Nicholas Dyrham was a little older than the other two, close to forty, Emma judged, and striking-looking in a rugged sort of way. His craggy brows over intent black eyes gave him a slightly devilish air that was enhanced by a firmly set chin and hollows in his cheeks. Her curtsy to him was in marked contrast to that with which she had honored Lord Dunn, a graceful flourish, only slightly marred by the impish light in her eyes as she said, "I have heard a great deal about you, Sir Nicholas."

"Have you now?" he asked, amused. "You surprise me, Miss Berryman. I had no idea my fame was so great."

"Your notoriety, one might more accurately say," Emma responded with a grin. "Aunt Amelia seldom sets pen to paper when there is not some adventure or other to be noted."

Not the least disconcerted, Lady Bradwell regarded her niece indulgently. "You will give him a puffed-up notion of himself, my dear, to believe himself the object of everyone's letters. But I must admit that Sir Nicholas provides more interesting tales than anyone else of my acquaintance."

Emma furrowed a brow in thought. "Let me see. There was the race where he rode his horse backward, and the evening he serenaded the princess, and the wager he made regarding the ducks . . ."

"Geese," he said, the black eyes studying her with interest.

If Emma had intended to continue the catalogue, she was given no opportunity, as her aunt begged to present her to Mr. Camblesforth, the third gentleman who was patiently waiting to make her acquaintance. A very mild-mannered fellow, Emma decided as she made her curtsy. He had neither the self-possession nor the address of the other two, and could not compare with them in looks (for she had to admit that Lord Dunn, if haughty, was well enough to gaze upon), but there was a gentleness about him that elicited her kindness. The pale hair and eyes, the almost studious look about him, as though he were perpetually startled to find himself in company, made her response quite different from the coolness she had shown Lord Dunn or the teasing of Sir Nicholas.

"I'm pleased to meet you, Mr. Camblesforth." She seated herself closest to him and offered to pour out another cup of tea since his was nearly empty. "Aunt Amelia always has the loveliest tea, hasn't she? Sometimes I thought they mixed ours at school with bark, it was so bitter. Do you take cream?"

"Yes, please. You're at school, are you?" It was the only thing he could think to ask her. Mr. Camblesforth was not ordinarily so tongue-tied; on the other hand, he was not ordinarily singled out by stunning young ladies, especially when the likes of Dunn and Dyrham were in the same room.

"Fortunately," replied Emma, dimpling, "as of today I have done with all that. My aunt is to bring me out this season."

Though Lord Dunn studiously avoided listening to the ensuing conversation by engaging his hostess, Sir Nicholas was not so scrupulous. He made no pretense of doing other than he did—which was to sit observing Miss Berryman describe to Mr. Camblesforth the hazards of life in a female educational institution—but neither did he enter into their exchange. Seldom had he seen, in the many years he had been on the town, a young lady walk out of the schoolroom and into the drawing room with more assurance. Her beauty, too, was not negligible and he turned his gaze speculatively to Lady Bradwell for a moment while considering what her motives might be in offering to sponsor the girl. There was no denying that Amelia at eight and thirty was still amazingly well preserved. No, that hardly did her credit. She was lovely, and showed no sign of aging beyond a mature voluptuousness that was uncannily linked with the most charming disposition. The girl had a freshness, of course, and a spirit that her aunt had never had, as witnessed by those sparkling eyes and frequently appearing dimples.

Sir Nicholas decided that Amelia had no other purpose than to give the child a chance to marry well, though he questioned the wisdom of setting the vivacious Miss Berryman against her own singularly languid charms. He would be surprised if Amelia could bestir herself enough to show her niece the full round of entertainment London had to offer; she was selective in her own party-going, choosing only such activities as suited her experienced taste.

Emma's revelation to Mr. Camblesforth of her friendship with Lady Anne Parsons and the new Lady Greenwood, however, indicated to Sir Nicholas that the girl would not be at a loss for chaperonage to any occasion she wished, so long as the invitations could be procured, and he had no doubt but that Emma herself would generate a sufficient number. Abruptly he entered their discourse to ask, "Has Lord William come to town?"

Though Emma was aware that he had been listening, she turned with mock surprise. "Why, yes, he brought Anne and me from school just now."

"And his older brother, Lord Maplegate. Is he here too?"

"I don't believe he was mentioned. Certainly the rest of the family is at the London house; the marquess came yesterday with Lord William." Emma regarded him with interest. "Are you well acquainted with them, sir?"

"Jack and Will are members of the Catch Club and their absence from town has been sorely regretted. We've had to depend on the lesser voices—like Dunn's," he said, with a wicked grin in the viscount's direction.

If Lord Dunn had thought to pretend he had not heard the jest, Lady Bradwell made it difficult. She tapped his wrist with her fan, smiling, and said, "You mustn't let him get away with that, Dunn. He may have the better singing voice, but I swear your speaking voice is not to be matched by the likes of Sir Nicholas."

"Any bird can sing," Dunn retorted, laughing. "Sir Nicholas comes by his voice quite naturally."

"You naughty man." Lady Bradwell waited expectantly for a riposte from the baronet, and she was not disappointed.

"And any huckster can speak. Unfortunately, with the speaking voice it is not how it is said, but what is said that is important. Ah, but with music it is quite the opposite. The trained voice has no need of a message; the melody is in itself the reward." He turned to Emma, his eyes mischievous, and asked, "Don't you think so, Miss Berryman?" Sir Nicholas missed little, and he had not failed to note the coolness between his lordship and the young lady.

"Oh, definitely. I have heard gentlemen with the most charming voices say the most disagreeable things." Her gaze fell briefly on the viscount, but returned to Mr. Camblesforth. "Do you sing, sir?"

Flustered by the full impact of her attentive blue eyes, he stammered, "Ah, no, no, I . . . That is, of course I sing now and again but I have no special talent."

"Hmm, talent," she said thoughtfully, as though she had forgotten those about her. "A really fine singing voice is a gift, I realize, but only through application does one realize its full potential. Perhaps, with practice, Lord Dunn could improve his voice," she suggested innocently. "I would be interested in the progress of his lessons."

Her repetition of his jibe at the wedding feast was not lost on Lord Dunn, but before he could make any response (which he evidently intended to do, considering the furiously sparking eyes) Sir Nicholas interjected, "It would be of no use, Miss Berryman, I'm afraid. The poor fellow hasn't The Gift, you know."

"I see. Well, it's a great pity since my aunt thinks he has such a fine speaking voice. I hadn't noticed it, myself, but my ear is sadly out, I suppose."

"Your ear, if I may say so, is the more perceptive . . . and adorable in addition," Sir Nicholas proclaimed.

He had gone too far, and Emma flushed. Mr. Camblesforth frowned, Aunt Amelia shook her head . . . and Lord Dunn offered her a coldly sardonic stare that made her wish to excuse herself. Instead she met the baronet's eyes, her own confused and hurt.

Considering the years he had spent in polite company, Sir Nicholas should have known better. In fact, he did know better, but he had been tempted to see how far he could push the game, and more, how far he could play the girl. She was a taking thing, but forward, and he was desirous of learning her limits. Not very great, he decided with a lamentable shrug. "I do beg your pardon, Miss Berryman. Sometimes it is difficult for one of my nature to resist such an opening. Come, say you'll forgive me."

"Certainly, Sir Nicholas." She smiled a little uneasily. "I'm sure you meant no harm."

"None whatsoever."

There was an almost audible sigh from her aunt, who took any disagreement as a reflection on her role as hostess, but who also considered an apology in the realm of magic. At once it blotted out any untoward comment. Lady Bradwell was of a most accommodating disposition. Her guests were willing enough to overlook the incident, but soon took their leave, much to Emma's relief. Not that she could not have held her own, she assured herself, but coming as it did on top of the excitement of leaving school she was just as happy to find herself alone with her aunt.

CHAPTER NINE

Comfortably pouring out more cups of tea for them, Lady Bradwell remarked, "One never knows what to expect of Sir Nicholas. He is given to doing and saying precisely what he wishes, and as often as not getting away with it. I have often thought that rakes are much maligned."

Emma giggled. "Have you, Aunt Amelia? How so?"

"Well, who is a rake, when you come right down to it? Usually he is so endowed with charm that everyone fawns over him, which is why his career is so successful. Now, if you were to take a man like Mr. Holwell—I will *not* call him a gentleman, for he isn't—there is a distinct lack of humor, and people don't call him a rake, they call him a debauchee. Perfectly true. He has no claim to honor and none of the little graces which are so evident in your real rake. Mr. Holwell drinks too much, cheats when he gambles, and soils innocent girls. A disgusting man, and there's no fear you will meet him, my dear, for he's not accepted anywhere."

"I should hope not."

"No, well there are others who shouldn't be but are. Never mind that now. We were discussing rakes." Lady Bradwell relaxed in her chair, ready for a good coze. "Generally they are men given to their own pleasure, and are condemned for that. But the truth of the matter is that everyone is in pursuit of pleasure; rakes are simply more honest about it. Society has engendered a sort of lip service to the proprieties, which does not mean that they are truly adhered to, but only that an appearance is given of doing so. Now you must admit that such a situation is highly hypocritical."

"Yes, but necessary to maintain some order," Emma pointed out as she poured herself another cup of tea.

Her aunt pursed her full lips. "Do you think so? Religion is used in the same fashion. One would think that there could be no morality without church attendance and the irrational clinging to outmoded dogmas. But there, I don't mean to stray from the subject. If Sir Nicholas gads about town with his current ladybird on his arm, he is called a rake. In my day the Duke of Devonshire had his mistress living in the same house with his duchess and he was merely considered eccentric."

"Did he?" Emma asked, wide-eyed.

"Of course he did," her aunt snorted. "And what was worse, the two ladies were the greatest friends. People say *my* life is irregular—pooh! Though I admit that I am one of those who pay lip service to society's demands, *I* do so because it keeps me acceptable, and *my* pleasure is to be invited where I will have the most enjoyment. Part of the problem for gentlemen is that they don't really enjoy the same things ladies do, and society is basically set to the tune of the ladies."

"How can you say that?" Emma cried indignantly. "Women haven't nearly the same freedoms as men! If I were to do what a man did, I would be a social outcast!"

"Just so, my love. Nonetheless, what I say is true." She sipped meditatively at her tea. "You will find, as you meet more men, that they take little pleasure in doing the pretty. Do you think, given a choice, that a gentleman would adorn a tea party rather than have a run on his horse? That he would dance a stately minuet in preference to a similar period of time in bed with a comely maid? That he prefers the stilted dinner conversation of a lavish entertainment to a rowdy repast with his friends, where he can speak freely?"

"No, but . . . but surely they must take *some* pleasure from the more civilized activities."

Lady Bradwell munched thoughtfully on a piece of shortbread. "I wonder. My dear child, you must consider my ramblings as naught. I shouldn't clutter your head with my useless observations."

Emma set down her cup and regarded her aunt with puzzled eyes. "No, please. What is it you are trying to tell me, Aunt Amelia?"

"That a silent, insidious bargain has been struck. The ladies have agreed to give their men the upper hand in exchange for a set of rules of the ladies' making. The men may do as they wish on the sly, but in company they are constrained to act 'civilized.' Of course, some men are content with the simpering platitudes of the social setup, but others are not. Take wigs, for instance. When I was a child, men wore wigs. Now where was the sense in that? Imagine your own blond curls shaved off to be covered by a bland white wig of someone else's hair. Is there anything more ridiculous? And consider, Emma, if a man lost his nightcap during the night! Bald or with a fuzz of hair no longer than the tip of your finger. Their heads look like eggs," she muttered with an involuntary shudder. "I remember seeing my father once.

"So why did men go to such hideous lengths? Because it was the *mode*, and the mode is set by the ladies. And the only reason they stopped wearing wigs was in rebellion against the powder tax. I tell you, Emma, men are virtual prisoners to fashions—in dress, behavior, activities, everything—which women have set."

"I can't feel a great deal of pity for them, my dear aunt," Emma said dryly. "They hold the purse strings." She swung her tiny shell-shaped reticule by its strap in demonstration.

"Yes," her aunt declared, triumphant, "that is the other side of the coin. I think it would be difficult to say which came first. It is rather a union of misery, is it not? The men are stronger, and see a superiority in themselves. They are made to rule! But just who is the ruler when they must kowtow to every whim of feminine fancy? No one is satisfied, but no one will give any ground. Which brings me back to the rakes, just when you probably thought I had forgotten them."

"Ah, yes, where do the rakes fit in?"

Lady Bradwell's eyes were dreamy. "They are the free spirits skirting on the edge of the acceptable. They do what they wish, with just enough regard for the rest of society to keep it in sight. A minimum of adherence to convention, a maximum of independence. Now, heed me well, Emma. Few men have the courage to skate on such thin ice and even fewer can do so with impunity. The secret is personal charm. To stray so far from the norm, one must have that special ingredient or one loses acceptance. But those who succeed—ah, they are the admirable men, the men one may trust to make life worthwhile."

"But one could not trust them to allow a woman a like degree of freedom," Emma protested.

Her aunt sighed. "No, I suppose not, my love, but that is more the fault of the other side of the bargain, the ladies' rules. I have been lucky in my situation, there is no doubt of that. Lord Bradwell hasn't the least interest in what I do in town, and I go very much my own way. I visit him twice a year for a month at a time and I promise you he is as glad to see my heels as I am to show them to him. And do you know why? Because when I am with him I remind him of all the social inhibitions which he can ignore in my absence. I give teas for the local gentry, and dinner parties and occasionally a ball of sorts. Poor Felix must leave off his country clothes and don satin breeches, give up his field sports (you must know I always make one of the visits in winter), and bring out his rusty social patter. On the other hand, once I've left he has the satisfaction of knowing he has done his duty for another year, or half year, and he can feel quite free to pursue his own pleasures again."

"And he allows you to expend what you wish in London?"

He would rather I spent it here than there. Felix is not a mean man; he's very openhanded, in fact, and I brought a sizable dowry when we wed. His country living is not vastly expensive, and since the estate will go to a nephew, he's in no mind to expand his holdings."

"Could you not have . . . children?" Emma asked hesitantly.

Lady Bradwell made an awkward gesture with her hand. "There was one—stillborn. It was a difficult labor and the doctor said I was unlikely to have others. He has proved to be correct. A heavy price to pay for my freedom."

A shadow of sadness passed over her aunt's face and Emma sat perfectly still, not wishing to intrude on her reminiscences, but convinced that Amelia had more to tell her.

The teacup trembled slightly in her aunt's hand and was set down carefully on the fret-bordered top of the stand beside her chair. After gazing for some while at the empty hearth she said softly, "I wanted to have babies, and of course Felix wanted an heir. The child would have been a girl, and she looked so very perfect, but she wouldn't breathe. I don't know what happened to me then—the doctor called it a nervous disorder. For months I ate very little and slept poorly, hardly got out of my bed. It's strange, but I don't remember how Felix took it all. I know how I expected him to take the loss of the child and the impossibility of having others, but I'm not sure that I didn't read into his long silences what I thought he was feeling, and not what he really felt. Perhaps his concern was for me and not for the end of his line, but he was inexpert at expressing himself.

"When I recovered sufficiently, the doctor suggested Bath as a place of recuperation. Felix did not come with me, which hurt me deeply. There may have been reasons for his staying at Thorpe Arch. If there were, he did not inform me of them. I felt very alone, and wretchedly unwanted, useless. Bath was very gay then and I was not quite twenty years of age. Probably I was still a bit unhinged from the lying-in. There was a very attractive gentleman there who was extraordinarily kind and sympathetic to me. I was so vulnerable . . ."

Lady Bradwell glanced at her niece, briefly, and smiled. "You see, my dear, therein lies a woman's only real freedom. I could not have children. To me, a few months previously, it had been a disaster. Presumably it was the same for my husband. And now, it meant that I really had nothing to fear if I had an affair. No illegitimate child to bring shame on me; no fears for the life such a child would be forced to live. And I thought, too, that I would give Felix an opportunity to divorce me, if he wished, so that he could remarry and have an heir. He was not such a stickler as to be alarmed by bringing an action before the Ecclesiastical Court and a petition before the Upper Assembly. You've heard of them: So and so being of a loose and abandoned disposition, and being wholly unmindful of her conjugal vow et cetera, did contract and carry on a lewd and adulterous conversation with such and such. And it was not as if he didn't know about it; his sister was in Bath at the time and sent off periodic expresses to Felix."

"But he didn't do anything?" Emma asked, fascinated.

"He wrote one letter, asking me to be more discreet." Lady Bradwell's eyes sparked momentarily with anger, and then she let out a little breath of exasperation. "Dear Felix. He suggested that any man of honor would gladly give his word not to breathe a whisper of the affair, and might be relied on to adhere to it, no mattter what the provocation. His advice has served me well."

"And when you met him again? Didn't he say anything then?"

"No, nothing. He acted as though the whole episode did not exist. We resumed our marital relations and the following spring when I broached the possibility of our going to London, he said I should go and enjoy myself. And that is how it has been ever since, more or less. I have always been discreet, and any tales you will hear of me are undoubtedly exaggerations. Though I have any number of gentleman friends, I am not entirely 'loose and abandoned.' My first friend and two others over the last eighteen years are the only ones who have been lovers, the rest are enjoyable companions—and camouflage. Do I shock you by being so blunt, Emma?"

Her niece had flushed slightly but vigorously shook her head. "Of course not. I'm not missish. What you do is your own affair."

"Pray remember that, my dear. Don't try to fight battles for me, or explain me to your friends. What I have told you is in confidence and not to be shared with anyone else. I think," she said, musing, "that I have told you all this because you will need to know, Emma. You are more spirited than I and you are like to wish to go against convention. I don't want you to think that I would encourage such behavior. Your position is entirely different from mine. Fortunately you are not likely to be intimidated by the old tabbies who will try to make you blush for my reputation. But you must see that any outrageous conduct will give them ammunition, and if you have a wish to settle well in life, you will have to keep a clean face to the world. All these roistering young men want virgins for brides."

"How nice for them," Emma said ruefully. "And are there gentlemen of your acquaintance, Aunt Amelia, who would like a young lady with some spirit?"

"I'll have to think about it." Her aunt smiled. "Run along and freshen up, my dear. I want to discuss your wardrobe before dinner."

The instruction Anne received from her mother was rather different from that Emma received from her aunt. Lady Barnfield was one of the best-liked society matrons in London, and her circle of friends was wide and eclectic. Despite her glamorous position, she was not haughty or exclusive, never acted the role of grande dame as some of the patronesses of Almack's were known to do. Above all she was kind and amiable, practical and intelligent. Her children loved and respected her, as they did their father. Jack and Will and Anne were so accustomed to their tight-knit family that they scarcely gave it a thought. Anne's return from school was the occasion for a private family celebration, a sumptuous meal from which the marchioness eventually led Anne to the drawing room, leaving the men to their port.

After a moment of studying her daughter, Lady Barnfield smiled. "You are going to make me very proud, Anne. And please don't think I refer to your beauty, which is certainly admirable. It is the combination of your looks and your conversation and your thoughtfulness which will see you well established. Not that I am in any hurry to get you married off! I am hoping you will enjoy yourself and give yourself an opportunity to choose wisely. But your charm does not rely on youth alone, and I envision more than a little interest the moment you appear in society."

"You flatter me, Mama," Anne protested, laughing. "I haven't nearly the beauty of my friend Emma, nor her vivacity. Will is already captivated."

Lady Barnfield's eyes danced. "Excellent. It won't do the least harm for him to have an interest which will keep him in town for the season. But you aren't to compare yourself with your friends, my dear. Each of you is unique and has something original to offer, I'm sure. There are men who are intimidated by too great a beauty or intelligence, just as there are men who will not so much as glance at a young lady who does not possess a striking loveliness. A reasonable man will consider a number of factors: countenance, companionability, position, dowry, intelligence, attitude. But in the long run, my dearest Anne, his heart will sway his head every time, because the heart speaks a language that is wholly one's own."

"You believe that one should marry for love, don't you, Mama?"

"Oh, definitely. But love is a deeper, more abiding sentiment than most people recognize. Infatuations such as those Will continually suffers are commonly thought to be love, but they bear only the faintest resemblance to the real thing. No one has ever adequately described love, but I am convinced that you will know it when you experience it. If you are filled with doubts while experiencing a euphoria, I am inclined to believe you are feeling only the pangs of infatuation. For there to be a lasting love, there must be a respect which cancels the doubts."

Anne met her mother's eyes steadily. "Did you never feel any doubts with Papa?"

The marchioness laughed. "Only of my own worthiness, love. He was and is such a sterling figure that I could not bring myself to believe that I deserved him. I should tell you frankly, Anne, that there are not all that many gentlemen who come near his standard. You will learn to distinguish between those with merit and those aimless souls with no substance. I would willingly wager that you will form no long-standing affection for one of the latter. I don't say that you may not be attracted for a moment by some consummate charmer who sets his mind to wooing you, but in the end you will have the sense to see him for what he is. I have enormous faith in your perception of worthiness."

"Mama, will they all know how large my dowry is?"

A rueful nod answered her blunt question. "I'm afraid so, my dear. Not that any of us would speak of it, of course, but these matters are somehow common knowledge. There will be fortune-hunters, and there will be aristocrats fallen on hard times. Don't let them disturb you. Just as your situation is known, so will theirs be. And it is not necessary that the fortunes of husband and wife be perfectly equal in any case."

"Did men pursue you for your dowry?" Anne asked, curious.

"Certainly." The marchioness smiled reminiscently. "Some very charming men who were vastly amusing. I remember one fellow who could make me laugh just by opening his mouth. He was intrepid enough, too, to jest about the difference in our fortunes, but my brother, all unconscious of my interest, I think, mentioned that this particular fellow was addicted to gambling. Very few things are as ruinous to one's life. Not just to one's fortune, either. Such an addiction eats away at the bond between husband and wife as surely as wood rot. One cannot be certain of one's financial position from day to day, nor of one's standing in the other's affections. The gambling addict is devoted to play, not to his wife. His lack of constancy generates a lack of trust on her part. It is a never-ending spiral of despair."

Fascinated, Anne asked, "But how can you tell someone who is addicted from someone who simply gambles for the entertainment? Almost everyone gambles."

Her mother shrugged. "True. It is a matter of degree. Some people develop a compulsion to gamble, but you aren't always aware of it. Nor is it the only addiction of which you must beware. Almost any compulsion—to drink, to associate with low company, to cheat—is ultimately destructive. Lord, I seem to be stressing all the unacceptable types of behavior. Truly, my dear, you are not likely to meet all that many gentlemen with such appalling habits!"

But in the days that followed she met a remarkable number of men, nonetheless. She went shopping with Emma and Lady Bradwell or her mother most mornings, but in the afternoons and evenings there were small entertainments to which she accompanied her family, and "morning" calls, which she almost came to dread.

A typical morning call made to the house in Grosvenor Square consisted of some aristocratic lady with her son in tow, coming expressly to make Anne's acquaintance. The correctly attired gentleman would cast a hasty glance at her, and then not infrequently withdraw his quizzing glass for a more thorough inspection, as though she were on display. Then he would address her in hearty tones, saying something remarkably witty such as, "So you are out of school now, are you, Lady Anne?" or "My, but you've grown since last I saw you when you were knee-high to a grasshopper!"

Such deadly starts to conversation were almost invariably overlooked by Anne. She learned immediately to turn the topic to one of general interest to the group—a new play at Drury Lane or the current unrest in the Midlands. Almost always she found that the gentlemen would tolerate this general discussion for only a while before they managed to draw her into private discourse. Their topics then were her own charms or their own prowess in whatever activity currently held their interest.

There was Sir Arthur Moresby, who fancied himself quite as good a boxer as Gentleman Jackson, and who sported his fives at number 13 Bond Street regularly. There was Lord Langham, who had a racehorse that was the envy of all the other owners, or so he said. There was Lord Brackenbury, who had more than a passing interest in the most outrageous men's fashions, and wore them with a notable lack of finesse. And there was Captain Midford, who regretted the end of the hunting season with something akin to depression.

"You must understand, Lady Anne," he said earnestly, "that I don't at all mind doing the pretty in town during the season. Dunn keeps the most splendid beasts in his stables here as well as at Knowle Park. But a ride in town, or even in the surrounding countryside, cannot compare with the excitement of the chase. It's a great pity the hunting season is so short! I've only time to stay with one friend each for rides with the Quorn, the Pytchley, the Cottesmore, and the

Belvoir. And sometimes the weather turns so rotten that you miss a day's hunt."

"Quite regrettable," Anne murmured. "My brother Will has lamented the same disappointments."

"Then you understand!" His relief was apparent. "I assure you it's not at all common to find a lady who does. Why, at the house parties, they sit around all day just waiting for us to return, and they expect us to take the greatest interest in their card games and dances in the evenings! I'm sure you know that the evenings are the times when we have a chance to go over each run to consider its merits. There's hardly the opportunity when you're out! I've known the fellows to outsit the ladies just so they could relax over a good glass of brandy and discuss the day's sport in peace."

"What do you think the ladies should be doing while you're out hunting?" Anne asked, trying to sound neutral.

Captain Midford looked surprised, as though he'd never considered the matter. "Well, I don't know. Doing embroidery, I suppose, or writing letters."

"And if there were no dances or card games in the evenings, I suppose they could write letters about the progress of their embroidery," she teased. "Since they are not encouraged to hunt with you, they could not describe the runs. Since you would have the men congregated together to discuss their sport, they could not write of their impressions of the company. Perhaps you think the ladies would do better not to attend the house parties at all."

The good captain flushed. "Nothing of the sort, Lady Anne! I'm sure they're quite welcome! They look very pretty and they laugh at all the stories, if one is careful of which stories one tells. And when the weather is unfit for hunting, they always think of some amusement for the whole company—charades or an impromptu performance."

"It's good to know that they're useful," Anne retorted. "And if luck is with them, they may even derive some pleasure from the gatherings, provided that it freezes over or the men condescend to honor them with their company."

Not sure quite how to respond to her sarcasm, Captain Midford actually said something pertinent. "The older fellows seem to like being with them more than the younger ones. Dunn don't mind at all sitting and talking with the ladies for hours, but then he's as interested in books and paintings as he is in sports. I'm not saying he's a pedant! Promise you he isn't! He just thinks about a lot more things than most of the sporting fellows. Always travels with some book he's reading, but I daresay there was a time, when he was younger, when he was more interested in hunting and shooting and cockfights and such."

"Do you think you'll get so old one day that you'll carry a book with you, Captain Midford?" Anne asked, her eyes laughing.

He offered her a look of mock horror. "Heaven forbid! Actually, I carry one now, just in case, but I don't tell anyone. Nothing educational, you understand. Just a novel by one of the writers Dunn suggests. They're usually very readable," he admitted judiciously.

Anne found that his observation was more or less correct. The younger men were still sowing their wild oats, while the older men had settled into a more diverse set of interests. She could see the difference even between her brothers Will and Jack, and though she found it difficult to envision Will ever attaining Jack's more serious turn of mind, she felt that a few additional years in a gentleman did not come amiss. Before five and twenty, she decided, they were distinctly more interested in adventure than domesticity. And there were those who never seemed to achieve any maturity at all, age notwithstanding. Anne was beginning to find the study of her fellow man quite intriguing.

CHAPTER TEN

Bright spring sunshine flooded into the drawing room of Lord Greenwood's town house and fell on Maggie's face as her visitors were announced. The canaries hopped about their cage in a corner of the room, one of them occasionally trilling or bursting into a short song. Lit by the sun and her pleasure in seeing them again, Maggie's face wore a gentle smile, but neither of her visitors could help noticing a difference. And it was not the stylishly dressed hair or any change in her coloring wrought by artificial means. The smile was as welcoming as ever, but the eyes, those large gray eyes, were not the same. Anne and Emma shared a quick glance.

"You look enchanting, my lady," Emma proclaimed, with a deep, humorous curtsy. What has he done to her? "You can see right off that I intend to toady to you, Maggie."

"I hope not," her ladyship retorted with mock horror. "Do sit down and tell me what you've been doing. Did Mrs. Childswick shed tears when you left?"

Anne chuckled. "Only if they were tears of joy, I suspect. And the only thing we've done so far since we left school is shop! Evening dresses, walking dresses, morning dresses, carriage dresses—with the odd bonnet and gloves and half boots. Emma got a lovely gray velvet pelisse lined with white sarcenet and I got a gypsy hat with a full plume of ostrich feathers. But we didn't come to speak of us! We want to know all about Combe Lodge and your husband. I trust he's well."

"Oh, yes. He's off to see Captain Midford just now. Greenwood purchased a new hack from a neighboring squire and wished to have the captain's opinion of him."

Pressed for details of her new country home, Maggie spoke enthusiastically of the lovely old stone building with its paneled rooms, the walled gardens, stableyard, dovecote, Home Wood, and the Gothic folly by the lake. She spoke of visits from the neighbors and a dinner party at the Lodge, of the kind housekeeper and the pretty village. But she said nothing further of her husband.

"Did you ride with Lord Greenwood?" Emma asked.

"A few times," Maggie said vaguely, her eyes lighting on the bird cage. "Greenwood gave me the canaries for a wedding present."

Anne was amused by the gift. "How delightful! Who would have thought of giving canaries? Do they sing like that all the time?"

"Mostly in the morning and evening. At night I put the cover over the cage and you don't hear a peep until you remove it. It's very cheering to hear the singing when you're writing a letter or reading a book."

"The Hando Savant strikes again!" Emma suggested, curious to see the reaction.

Maggie regarded her blankly, then offered a faint smile. "Yes, it was . . . thoughtful of him."

When Anne asked who the Hando Savant was, Emma, not Maggie, explained and Anne frowned. "You shouldn't tease Maggie's husband behind his back, Emma."

"Oh, Anne, it's but a joke. *You* don't mind, do you, Maggie?"

The eyes that met Emma's were strangely unreadable. "No, why should I? Greenwood has nicknamed me Intrepid. He said it would have been Courageous, but he already had a horse named that."

While Emma digested this bit of information in silence, Anne asked, "What did you do to earn such a formidable nickname?"

"I had the mare jump a rasper which he had just jumped." Maggie shrugged. "I thought he expected me to follow. Otherwise I would have had to go a good half mile out of the way to catch him up."

Emma's expression was grim. "Is he not aware of your dislike of riding?"

"Yes, but he considers it a girlish fancy, easily overcome by the bonds of matrimony, and a patient husband."

The flat tone in which this statement was delivered puzzled Anne, and made Emma irate. "Don't let him intimidate you into doing anything you don't wish, Maggie. Not everyone is at home on a horse, as his lordship must well know. It is unfair of him to expect you to suffer terrors at his whim."

"I'm afraid Greenwood doesn't know the meaning of terror," his wife replied calmly. "He chose the mare for her bidability, and indeed she proved astonishingly responsive. My father's style of horsemanship does not always leave a horse with the most tender mouth."

Dissatisfied with this skirting of the issue, Emma was about to press the matter when Anne spoke, bantering. "So we are like to see you riding in the park one of these days?"

"I'm sure Greenwood would be pleased if I did." Her eyes met Emma's indignant ones and she looked away. "He would never insist, of course."

"How very thoughtful of him," Emma murmured.

"Well, of course he wouldn't," Anne retorted in an effort to be reassuring. "Don't make a mountain out of a molehill, Emma. It is just as well that Maggie become more comfortable with horses, after all, if she is to spend much time in the country. One cannot walk everywhere."

Obviously this sentiment did not appease Emma, whose eyes still flashed with annoyance, but she allowed the subject to drop, realizing that it only made Maggie uncomfortable. Their talk turned to mantua-makers and silk warehouses, assemblies and card parties. But even this subject was fraught with dangers, for Maggie admitted that Lord Greenwood had requested that she plan a ball for the middle of May.

"But surely you will still be working on the house!" Emma protested. "You wrote that you intended to have several rooms done over. And what do you know of giving a ball? Dear Lord, you haven't even been to one yet!"

"Greenwood's sister will help, he says, and Mrs. Phipps, the housekeeper, is versed in such matters. And certainly I shall have been to several before that time."

Seeing the martial light in Emma's eye, Anne hastened to intervene. "*I* shall be happy to help you, if I may. Since the wedding was so very small, it is only fitting that you should entertain the ton fairly soon; I quite see Lord Greenwood's point. Mama is having my ball week after next and I shall pay a great deal of attention to how everything is organized. *I* think it will be fun for you, Maggie. A challenge."

Maggie smiled slightly and nodded, but said only, "Will the two of you help me to choose something special to wear for the occasion? Greenwood will expect me to be dressed like a plate from *The Ladies' Magazine*."

So their conversation was once again directed into harmless channels and kept there until the two visitors departed. As they climbed into the waiting carriage, Anne turned to Emma, a worried look on her face.

"I know you are as concerned about Maggie as I am, Emma, but what you were doing is not going to help her. Mama says no one should ever interfere in a domestic problem, other than giving encouragement. Finding fault with Greenwood won't help Maggie, whatever her problem is. Dear Maggie obviously has quite enough to handle without thinking that you don't like her husband."

"I'm not the one who has gone on about Lord Greenwood all this time," Emma pointed out.

"No. Very true. I'm sorry." Anne smiled apologetically, rubbing her temples to soothe away the tension. "But you see, love, now that she is married, there is nothing to be done but help her adjust. There isn't really anything singular in his wanting her to ride or give a ball. Oh, I know it is asking a great deal of *Maggie,* but it is the sort of thing a gentleman might expect."

"Anne, Maggie has always been shy, but never reserved and withdrawn as she was this morning. If you and I can see that, surely her husband should be able to and not make extra demands until she's accustomed herself. Say your husband fancied snakes and tried, during the first two weeks of your marriage, to get you to handle them . . ."

"That's absurd, and not at all the same."

"Not for you or me, perhaps, but Maggie has been pushed about so by her father that it must be torture to have her husband force her onto horseback, too."

"He doesn't force her; you heard what she said. She did it to please him."

Emma snorted. "And of course he counted on that. If she's not careful, he'll ride roughshod over her just as her father did."

"She's only trying to be accommodating, Emma. You cannot lay that at his lordship's door."

"Can't I? Perhaps not. But if she's being so accommodating, why isn't she happy?"

Anne shook her head and looked out the window at the passing shops. "I don't know, Emma. I'm not saying it isn't Lord Greenwood's fault, but just that it won't do Maggie any good for us to point out any problems. You may be sure she knows them well enough. Marriage is so frightfully permanent. Let her work out a comfortable arrangement with her husband. I imagine it takes time."

"Yes, and a willingness on the part of both parties." The carriage had stopped at Lady Bradwell's house in Bruton Street, and Emma pressed her friend's hand. "Don't be angry with me, my dear. I am only annoyed with Lord Greenwood for not doing his share. We know Maggie is trying; she wouldn't know how not to! You may count on my addressing invitations, or sampling lobster patties at the caterers, or whatever is necessary to help with Maggie's ball."

As Anne watched Emma gather up her skirts and skip up the steps to the large black door with its sparkling brass knocker, she felt a momentary stab of . . . what? Compassion? Emma seemed to think there was a solution to everything, that life was destined to be good to her. Perhaps it would. Certainly she would never fall into a loveless marriage like Maggie's, unless she did it for reasons of her own. Anne wondered if what Emma was looking for was love, or a comfortable position in society, or a degree of independence most ladies didn't have. Probably even Emma didn't know, but her expectations were high and Anne feared that the reality could not possibly live up to them. Emma didn't seem to understand that problems were forever cropping up in a person's life, sometimes very disturbing problems, and they didn't go away by wishing them gone. They weren't always solved by a clever-sounding solution, either, but by patience and time and effort.

The carriage moved forward toward Grosvenor Square and Anne sighed. Emma would like to solve Maggie's problem by placing the blame on Lord Greenwood and telling Maggie to hold him accountable for it. Very straightforward, but hardly likely to happen, or to be successful if it did. Emma had yet to find out that gentlemen didn't take kindly to being corrected. Anne knew; she had two brothers. And one of them, she thought ruefully, was going to make a fool of himself over Emma for the next few weeks, just as all the other young gudgeons would. You could tell by the way they stopped in the street and tried to obtain an introduction to her through Lady Barnfield or Lady Bradwell. Perhaps I'm jealous of her, Anne thought, startled. She's so exotically lovely and has such tearing spirits that no one who comes within her sphere can resist her. Everything is an adventure, an occasion. I could not possibly live at such a fever pitch, Anne mused, and somehow I can't work up the least enthusiasm for the frippery young men who hang around her. Which includes Will, she reminded herself, and my only admirer is quite as bad. Captain Midford had called three times and made her promise him a set at her ball. Ah, well, there is a whole season before us, and heaven knows what will happen before its end.

When she entered the house in Bruton Street, Emma was informed that her aunt was out, but that a gentleman was awaiting Lady Bradwell in the drawing room. "I shall join him," she announced, to the butler's obvious consternation. "Oh, is it one of the disreputable ones?"

North was at a loss as to how to answer. "It is Sir Nicholas Dyrham, Miss Berryman."

"Ah, in that case I shall leave the door open." Her eyes danced as she passed into the drawing room.

Sir Nicholas was lounging on a dainty Sheraton chair that looked entirely too insubstantial for him, but in a moment he was on his feet to greet her. "Miss Berryman. What a pleasure to see you."

"How do you do, Sir Nicholas? My aunt should be back shortly, and I thought you might make do with my company for a few minutes, if you wouldn't mind."

He cast a sardonic glance at the open door and assured her that it would be his pleasure. When she had seated herself, he did likewise, noting that the dress she wore was a great deal more stylish than the schoolgirl outfit she had worn on their previous encounter. "I see Lady Bradwell has had you out shopping."

"Endlessly. I love it, but I think I see an end in sight for the time being. Didn't you like my school dress?"

"My parlor maid wears more attractive clothes," he told her succinctly.

With a great air of innocence Emma asked, "Do you supply them to her?"

"No, I don't!" But he realized almost immediately that she was quizzing him and shook his head in mock despair. "I can see Lady Bradwell is going to have quite a time with you. I hope she will consent to my escorting you both to the Barnfield ball."

"You will have to ask her, Sir Nicholas. I don't know if she's made any other arrangement, though Lord William did mention that he would be happy to take us."

"Rattlepate! He'll have to be there in the receiving line."

Emma grinned. "He tends to forget details like that when he visits my aunt."

"Visits you, more like." Sir Nicholas studied her for any sign of serious starry-eyed attachment to Lord William, but Miss Berryman's eyes were always alight and it was impossible to tell. "Lord William has an unnerving reputation for switching his allegiance every month. I believe his record in devotion is five weeks."

"And what is yours?"

Sir Nicholas was tempted to give her a blighting set-down but her impudence was refreshing, a heady mixture of high spirits and assumed sophistication. There was little doubt she would cause quite a stir with her exotic looks and hasty tongue. Someone should have a talk with her—but it certainly wasn't going to be him! Sir Nicholas would find the season all the more intriguing for watching her bounce from folly to folly. Not so much as a quiver of remorse did he feel on behalf of Lady Bradwell, either. She had decided, being of sound mind and body, to act as Miss Berryman's chaperon, and one interview with the girl should be enough to alert any sane individual to her mischievous penchants. Lady Anne would have been impressed by how devout an adherent to noninterference Sir Nicholas was. And if the cause was that the affairs of others provided him a great source of amusement, well, the end result was much the same.

"Alas, I haven't any record. I've never been devoted to anyone."

"That could be considered a challenge," Emma informed him pertly.

His dark eyes regarded her with intentional mockery. "Could it?

You are easily challenged, Miss Berryman. But I beg you will save your energies for a worthier goal. Your humble servant is no match for a lady of your charms, nor a fit object for her devotion. I have quite a different reputation from Lord William."

"Yes, I know. Aunt Amelia told me she thinks rakes are much maligned." Emma laughed at his startled expression. "Is Lord Greenwood a rake?"

"Good God, no! You'll give the standing a bad name if you include nodcocks like Greenwood! He's no more than a rackety young man with a mistress." He knew immediately he had said more than he should.

"Will he keep his mistress now he's married?"

"How should I know?" And his shrug indicated his supreme indifference. Sir Nicholas discovered that one gleaming Hessian had a smudge on the toe and he concentrated his attention on it as though he could banish the spot with the power of his mind alone.

Emma wouldn't have been surprised if he could. The sound of a carriage arriving at the front door heralded Lady Bradwell's arrival, but the discussion of rakes, and with it any possible information on Lord Greenwood, had already been concluded. Sir Nicholas was perfectly content to banter words with her, but he had no intention of divulging his own, or anyone else's, secrets. Emma excused herself after Lady Bradwell joined them.

When her visitors had left, Maggie sighed and climbed the stairs to the first floor, where workmen were papering the room she had chosen for herself. There had been some disagreement as to whether she should take the room next to Greenwood's but it was a poky hole, looking straight into the bedchamber of the gentleman who lived next door, and Adam had reluctantly agreed that the room at the back would be more suitable. His sister, Cynthia, had learned Maggie's requirements and had the work started while they were away. Maggie paused at the door, watching with a detached interest as a section of the gold and white paper was expertly glued to the wall, and then turned to tread carefully past the pots of glue and rolls of paper in the hall.

The poky hole was her temporary bedchamber with a massive bed looking ridiculous in the half-light: heavy carved posts and a valance-draped tester, a squat, ornate headboard with projections of carved fruit on which Greenwood had carelessly grazed his head the previous evening to an accompaniment of muttered oaths. Last night, as every night since their wedding, he had arrived at her room, his eyes luminous with desire in the candlelight, his lips curved in a smile of laughing invitation that he apparently believed was welcome to her, his hands eager to caress her slender body.

And sometimes, when he murmured soft endearments and kissed her tenderly, as he had last night, she could feel a desire rise in her own body. But nothing ever came of it. That warm glow that suffused her was never fanned to fruition, never nurtured into an open flame that would consume her and satisfy the longing she felt. When Adam lay languorously spent, Maggie could still feel the tension in herself, and she resented the arm thrown casually across her waist—but she said nothing. He was her husband, with the right to enjoy her body when he chose. And he did seem to enjoy it, or at least to value the convenience of having a woman readily accessible to him each night. Maggie did not delude herself that he had any particular regard for her own meager charms. Now they were back in town she had to face the possibility that he would start seeing his mistress again, and she wasn't even sure she cared any longer.

With a shrug she turned from her moody contemplation of the mammoth bed to look for the book she had been reading the previous evening when her husband had entered the room. He had taken it from her, smiling, as he said, "You won't be needing that, my dear." Where had he set it? Not on the stand by the bed, or on the mantelpiece. Could he have simply dropped it to the floor and kicked it under the bed in his unthinking haste to be about his evening's sport? Maggie fell to her knees and pushed aside the damask spread that hung to the Axminster carpet, but there was nothing under the bed—not even dust, owing to Mrs. Phipps's careful surveillance of her domain. As Maggie attempted to withdraw her head she was startled by her husband's voice exclaiming, "What the devil are you doing?"

In her hurry to extract herself from such an undignified position she failed to notice that the fichu that alone kept her new gown from being provocatively low was caught on a splinter of the bed frame and dislodged from her bodice as she rose. Cheeks flushed, she turned to face him. "I didn't hear you enter, Greenwood. I was looking for my book."

"Do you usually keep it under the bed?" he teased.

"Certainly not!" Indignation served very well to cover her

embarrassment, and she continued defiantly, "It was you who took it from me, and now I cannot find it."

Adam produced a slender volume from behind his back. "Perhaps this is it. My valet found it in my dressing-gown pocket and I was just coming to return it. You had visitors when I came in and I didn't wish to disturb you." His eyes traveled to the expanse of bosom uncovered and the fichu, which hung uselessly about her neck, and he made no attempt to hand her the book.

His pointed interest was enough to alert her to the problem, and she gave a tsk of annoyance as she attempted to tuck the ends back into her bodice with hands made nervous by his steady gaze.

"Allow me," he suggested smoothly, once again absently disposing of the book by tossing it on a chair. Before his determined look Maggie warily allowed her hands to drop to her sides. Instead of proceeding to arrange the three cornered scarf as it had been, he slowly undid the knot, tracing with a finger the line of her gown across her breasts. There was little enough left unexposed but his gently exploring hands released the whole, pushing the gown down beneath her breasts with a murmur of appreciation.

"Greenwood!" she protested, attempting to rearrange her gown. "The draperies are open, for heaven's sake! And a maid could come in at any moment to . . . to clean or something."

He grinned and touched a finger to her lips. "Easily remedied, my dear." First he moved to the draperies and flung them closed with a jaunty wave at the opposite window, where fortunately no one was to be observed, and then he threw the bolts on each of the two doors to the room. "Now we won't be disturbed, Margaret. Have you any idea how desirable you look? No, don't try to cover yourself. I'm going to undress you."

"But . . ."

"I doubt you have anything pressing to do if you were looking for your book." He was already behind her, working on the fastenings of her gown. "Have you?"

"No . . . but there are people about . . . workmen down the hall . . ."

"They'll never know, my dear."

"If . . . if someone should try the door . . ." Maggie shuddered as the bodice and chemise fell to the carpet.

Adam laughed. "It doesn't matter, goose. To hear you talk, you'd think we weren't married."

Her skirt was loosened around her and his hands caressed her slender legs as he worked it down to her ankles. In a daze she stepped out of it, leaving the petticoats in a jumble on the bright carpet, allowing herself to be turned by his guiding hands to face him.

Unable to meet his eyes, she stared at the brass buttons on his coat and asked irrelevantly, "Wasn't Captain Midford at home?"

"No, he'd gone somewhere with Dunn. Sit on the edge of the bed, Margaret."

Obediently she perched where he could remove the buckled shoes and white silk stocking. "He . . . he might come looking for you."

"If he does, he can wait," Adam said gruffly. Impatient, he attempted to struggle out of the tight-fitting coat that had taken his valet some time to ease onto his shoulders. "Will you help me with this, Margaret?"

Startled, her downcast eyes flew to where he stood before her, hopelessly entangled in his own coat. A gurgle of laughter escaped her as she rose to assist him.

"I had no intention of amusing you," he grumbled as Maggie inched the coat over his shoulders and down the long arms. When his hands were free he caught her to him and kissed the tip of her nose. "But I like to hear you laugh. You don't do it very often, you know. Come to think of it, you don't smile much either. Aren't you happy, Margaret?"

Held there in his arms, naked, seeing his brow puckered with concern, Maggie had no idea how to answer him. The question itself seemed inappropriate, but his concern was apparently real, if momentary. Nonetheless, she knew he wouldn't understand how an insignificant little creature such as herself wouldn't be satisfied with the position she had achieved, content with the luxuries she could command, even delighted with him for a husband. Not that he was offensively vain. His high opinion of himself was as ingrained as his good humor, as much a part of him as his merry blue eyes.

When she made no reply he held her at arm's length and studied her face. "Is there something the matter? Did you want to stay at Combe Lodge? Or is Mrs. Phipps making things difficult for you?"

"No, of course not. Everything is fine." When he was boyishly eager to please her, she could not very well tell him that his own careless attitude to her was the source of her unhappiness. In a few minutes his concern, his interest in her, would be forgotten, and anything she said on the matter would be regarded with incredulity.

Had he not provided her with everything a woman could wish? Surely she didn't expect him to live in her pocket? Could she possibly have forgotten that he had given her those charming canaries as a wedding present? She dropped her eyes from his gaze and said again, "Everything is fine."

She had expected him to accept her words, to say, "Good," and let the matter rest. To her surprise he continued to frown slightly as he unbuttoned his waistcoat and shirt. Maggie turned away when he absently began to remove his pantaloons, so she was startled when he came up behind her and gently stroked her arms. She could feel the soft touch of his lips as he kissed the top of her head, murmuring, "You're not afraid of me, are you? In bed, I mean?"

"No . . ."

Moving closer, he pressed his body against hers. "No, I didn't think you were, but you haven't . . . been satisfied, have you?"

"I'm perfectly satisfied," she said stiffly.

"That's not what I mean." For a moment he was silent, allowing his hands to play over her hips and buttocks. "I haven't brought you to a point of . . . release, have I?"

"I don't think so."

"You would know," he said with a soft laugh, not unkindly. "I become irritable if I don't find that release. Perhaps you become unhappy."

The breath caught in her throat as his hands touched her breasts. "I . . . I don't think women are the same. I mean, they don't need . . ."

"Hmm." Other times he had been aware of her response to his touch, but vaguely; now he smiled at the back of her bent head. "Perhaps not, if their desire hasn't been aroused, but once it has . . ."

Maggie gave a muffled cry as he lifted her and carried her to the bed. There was a tap at the door.

"What is it?" Adam asked impatiently.

The valet, Perkins, spoke deferentially through the door. "Captain Midford has called, my lord."

"Tell him I'll meet him at White's in an hour or so."

"Very good, my lord."

Maggie shifted uneasily on the bed and whispered, "He knows why you're here."

"Perkins? My dear girl, who cares? He's not likely to announce it to the whole household, and there's absolutely nothing wrong with my being here." Adam shook his head ruefully and climbed onto the bed beside her. "Does it seem wrong to you for us to be in bed at this time of day, Margaret? Are the black stretches of the night the only appropriate time for such 'goings-on'?"

Convinced he was mocking her, she said coldly, "I had never given it any thought, Greenwood."

Her head was turned away from him but he could see the proud set of her jaw and he repented taunting her. The slender body lay rigid and he cautiously extended a hand to trace the line of her neck, allowing his fingers gradually to descend until they touched the firm, small breasts. For some time he fondled her, patiently waiting until she relaxed enough to respond to his touch, to his reassuring murmurs. When he kissed her he could feel the uncertain trembling of her lips, the quickening of her breathing. His hands roamed down her body, exploring, stroking, heightening her desire.

She regarded him with wide, bemused eyes. "Should . . . should you do that?" she whispered.

"Yes, my dear." He lifted a quizzing brow. "Don't you like it?"

"I . . . I like it very much."

"Hmm, yes, I thought you did. Please don't turn away! Your eyes are beautiful all moist with desire . . . And your lips so soft and eager. Are you. . . ? That's my girl, just enjoy it." He was too preoccupied for a while to speak, but he could not fail to notice the passionate manner in which she clung to him, the cry of release or the gray eyes glazed with wonder. Purposely he stayed with her for some time, stroking her hair, whispering tender if incoherent words of pleasure. Then his irrepressible grin appeared and he said, "*Now* you know."

A shy smile illuminated her ordinarily mild countenance. "Yes. It hasn't happened before."

He disengaged himself and rolled over on one elbow. "It will happen again, my dear; I will see that it does. After all, we don't want you getting in the crotchets, do we?"

Some of the glow remained and Maggie surprised herself by responding to his teasing. "I can see why *you* are never in low spirits."

"Hussy!" he laughed, touching the tip of her nose. "You've learned my secret, by Jupiter, and I will expect you to do everything in your power to see that I don't succumb to the megrims from now on . . . day or night. You won't mind, will you?"

Maggie blushed. "No, so long as you don't announce your intention to the whole household."

"I wouldn't think of it! It's much more fun waylaying you on the spur of the moment." He glanced at the clock on the mantelshelf and swung his legs over the side of the bed. "I have to go, my sweet. Midford will be waiting for me."

Unembarrassed, she watched as he drew on his drawers and hastily grabbed up the rest of his clothing. Before leaving the room, he bent and kissed her. "Shall I send your maid?"

"No, thank you. I'll manage for myself."

"As you wish. I'm dining with Thresham, but I'll be back about ten to take you to the Camerton ball."

"B-But you hadn't mentioned we were going out."

"Hadn't I? No matter. It will be an opportunity for you to meet some of the ton. I daresay half of them don't even know I've married." With a careless smile he vanished through the interconnecting door.

CHAPTER ELEVEN

Lady Anne had kept her promise to observe the preparations for her ball, but it became more difficult as she herself began attending all the functions and festivities London had to offer that spring. Her mind was awhirl with names, costumes, menus, and decorations, though she attempted also to concentrate on introducing Maggie and Emma to the numerous friends and acquaintances she had acquired during her excursions to London with her family.

Dear Maggie, she thought as her maid arranged two curls low on her shoulders the evening of her ball. Though the reserve remained, Maggie was making a valiant attempt to fill the position she held as Greenwood's bride, and it couldn't be easy for her. Shyness was not something Anne had ever suffered from—and certainly Emma didn't!—but Anne watched Maggie's anxious eyes and noted the effort she made to speak more than monosyllables to the countless matrons who believed in their hearts, and took little trouble to hide it, that Greenwood would have been better off with their daughters. And the dowager Lady Redwick had gone so far as to intimate to Maggie that Greenwood had been promised to her granddaughter. Anne had heard Lord Dunn tell Greenwood to "save your wife from old Lady Redwick or there's bound to be a scene. I've watched that woman reduce a well-established matron to tears in three minutes flat."

And that was one of the times Greenwood had fortunately been with her. As often as not he sent her off with Anne and Emma, determined, Anne felt, not to allow his newly married state to hamper him in any way. Occasionally he would drop in on the entertainment where she was, seldom staying long, and only rarely dancing with his wife. Very much in keeping with the times, of course, but a horrid strain on poor Maggie, who would have preferred to stay at home for all the enjoyment she got from the constant procession of curious ladies and gentlemen.

Lady Barnfield peeked round the door to ask, "May I come in, love?"

"Of course. I'm almost ready."

"Are you nervous, dear? You don't look it." Lady Barnfield settled herself companionably on the chair closest to the dressing table.

"Not particularly." Anne stood up to model the white crepe lace dress over a white satin slip. The bodice of emerald satin was made tight and cut to display an appropriate amount of decolletage, with a row of blond lace set to fall over it, and from the short slashed sleeves of emerald satin and white lace. Her headdress, a *toque de Ninon*, was settled on the chestnut curls as she watched in the mirror, but as she stretched out her hand for the pearl necklace, Lady Barnfield stopped her hand.

"No, love. Papa and I have a present for you." From the folds of her skirt where she had concealed it, Lady Barnfield withdrew a wide, flat jewelers box and presented it to her daughter.

A necklace and earrings of emeralds in a modern gold setting rested on the plush satin. "Oh, Mama, they're beautiful! How can I ever thank you and Papa?"

Her mother, dismissing the maid, fastened them and smiled contentedly. "By enjoying yourself this evening, Anne. I almost swayed toward the other gown we saw," she teased, "so that you could wear the sapphires."

The sapphires were a family joke. Their antiquity could not redeem them from the heavy, outrageous piece they were. "Not even a statuesque goddess could carry them off," Anne moaned, "though it did just pass through my mind that Emma might, with her exotic beauty. Perhaps Will is looking for someone on whom to bestow them."

Lady Barnfield met her daughter's laughing eyes with a rueful shake of her head. "Poor Will! What a dance she would lead *him*! But there's not a chance of his infatuation lasting, so I think there's nothing to worry about."

Anne's brow wrinkled into a frown. "Don't you like Emma?"

"I think she's delightful," Lady Barnfield asserted, "but you surely cannot believe Will is a suitable match for her. She would annihilate him. Will needs some demure miss he can think he dominates, though she had best have a great deal of character so she keeps a good steady pressure on the reins. Your friend Maggie will be like that, when she's had a chance to get her feet."

"Maggie isn't the least bit managing," Anne protested.

"You misunderstand me, love. I'm talking about a good, solid woman who won't be swayed by her husband's excesses or flights of fancy. One who will steer a straight path in spite of the starts and stops her husband is prone to."

"I hope you're right. I worry about Maggie a great deal."

"I know you do, love, and I'm proud that you're so loyal to your friends. There, you look magnificent. We should go down."

The guest list had included as many unknown names as familiar ones for Anne, but she found no terror in meeting new people, especially surrounded by her close-knit family. Her brother Will had contributed the names of every ramshackle young man in town, but her brother Jack was of a different nature altogether. His only addition to an already overflowing list was a gentleman he had met the previous year and to whom he took an instant liking. As the solemn butler intoned the names of Miss Helena Rogers and Mr. Harold Rogers, Jack murmured, "This is the fellow I mentioned, Anne. I think you'll like his sister."

Helena Rogers, at the age of twenty, had stark white hair, which she made no attempt to disguise in any way. Clear hazel eyes met Anne's with a peculiar frankness that told her Jack was right: she was going to like Miss Rogers. "I'm so pleased to meet you."

"And I you. Lord Maplegate has spoken of you often and I've

longed to meet you." Her eyes twinkled with merriment. "I didn't even mind missing the lecture on metaphysics to come tonight!"

Anne laughed. "I'm flattered." Her gaze turned to the gentleman who stood beside Miss Rogers. He was obviously considerably older, not much under thirty, Anne guessed, and of a tall, slender build. His straight sandy hair and high cheekbones combined with a firm chin to give him a rather austere appearance, but the same clear hazel eyes, with a similar humorous light, gazed down on her. Anne's sole thought was, "Oh, Lord!"

If she missed the introduction entirely, she was sure she must have replied automatically, for he seemed not the least alarmed, asking if there was any chance of securing a dance with her during the evening. "The second cotillion. I'd be honored."

With a smile he passed on down the line, shaking hands enthusiastically with Jack, and Anne forced her attention back to the continuing press of newcomers. Lady Bradwell, dressed as elegantly as the marchioness, was accompanied by Emma and Sir Nicholas Dyrham. Emma, resplendent in a crepe lisse gown of Haitian blue whose narrow notched tucker and folds stretched across her bosom in a most beguiling manner, squeezed Anne's hand, whispering, "Everything is perfect, my dear. Especially you. You look stunning." Emma glanced down the receiving line to where Lord William was impatiently waiting to greet her. "Yesterday your brother insisted on my standing up with him for the first dance, but Aunt Amelia thinks that might not be wise on such an occasion. I would like to, you understand. It's flattering to have him so attentive."

"You should enjoy it while you may," Anne laughed. "He's notoriously fickle."

"Ah, so I have heard. Sir Nicholas told me his limit is five weeks and I am determined he shall set a new record in devotion. Say, five and a half weeks. I'm not overly ambitious, you see!"

"If you make it six weeks, we will see him through the major part of the season. Mama would be grateful. Otherwise he'll probably run off to Newmarket."

Emma squared her shoulders in mock determination. "Trust me to do my very best, dear Anne."

Lord William wore a wide grin. "You promised me the first dance," he reminded her.

"Yes," she sighed, eyes demurely lowered, "but Aunt Amelia

thinks it might be wisest if I didn't dance with you so early in the evening. There are probably family obligations you should see to."

"What's this?" Lord William yelped. "Nonsense! M'mother hasn't asked me to step out for the first one with even one of my scraggly cousins! Told her I was promised to you for it and she just smiled."

"Poor Lady Barnfield! Very well, Lord William. I promise you I had no wish to go back on my word." Emma raised languid eyes to his triumphant ones. "I'm sure you know what is best."

"Certainly I do!" He swelled visibly with pride and smiled down on her with a rather fatuous expression. "I trust you'll go in to supper with me, too."

"Why, thank you, Lord William. How very kind of you." The line was backing up behind her and she offered him one quick, brilliant smile before hurrying on. Lord William shook out his shirt cuffs self-consciously while his brother, Jack, caught Anne's eye and shrugged.

Despite the number of guests still pouring up the stairs, the marchioness decided that the dancing had best begin and Lady Anne was led out for the first set by her father while William eagerly sought Emma. She was surrounded by a bevy of attentive gentlemen, but Lady Bradwell capitulated with good-humored tolerance, commenting to Sir Nicholas, "It will do her no harm to have Lord William doting on her; he is known for his unerring eye for a beauty."

"And he's unlikely to frighten anyone off, since his reputation for picking them is no better known than his reputation for forgetting them," her escort responded with notable dryness, his eyes, nonetheless, following the couple with interest. Lord William was a reasonably accomplished dancer, but next to his partner, who moved with a stately grace, he did not appear to advantage. Sir Nicholas wondered idly if Miss Berryman had purposely chosen her gown for the fascinating way it clung to her.

Lord and Lady Greenwood arrived when the first set was just concluding. Maggie bit back her chagrin at not seeing Anne in her moment of glory, but she was simply grateful that her husband had accompanied her. Really, for him, they were quite early at the Barnfield festivities. Anne saw them immediately as she and her father left the floor and, after stopping briefly to speak to a distant relative, directed him to them. Adam was so impressed with the emeralds that he determined on the spot to get some for his wife. Having thus mentally provided her with such a splendid gift, he proceeded to forget that she was not as yet provided with a partner . . . and asked Lady Anne for her hand in the set that was forming. Anne would have liked to pinch him; instead she allowed him to lead her into the dance.

Catching the astonished expression on the marquess's countenance, Maggie summoned up a laugh and said, "He means well."

"He has a great deal to learn," Lord Barnfield murmured as he held out his hand. "May I?"

"There's no need." Maggie looked about hastily. "I have friends . . ."

"So have I," the marquess retorted with an amused twinkle in his eyes, "but I have no intention of joining them until you've stood up with me. If you will?"

Maggie blushed for her rudeness, but one could not feel uncomfortable long in the marquess's presence. Here, she decided as he guided her through the steps of the dance while carrying on a reasonable conversation, was a gentleman on whom her husband might well pattern himself. A man of good sense, good humor, and yet of the first fashion, and though of the greatest consequence, a kind and considerate man. Of course, he was older, Maggie reminded herself severely, and married to the woman of his choice, with three agreeable children. Still, she could not believe that Lord Barnfield had been anything like her husband as a young man. He might have been like Lord Dunn, she decided judiciously, but *not* like Greenwood.

In his own fashion, Adam was trying to please his wife. Margaret had become remote again after that one lighthearted afternoon and he had come to believe, following his own erratic logic, that her friends were influencing her against him. Not Miss Berryman, he thought indulgently. Miss Berryman was far too lively to waste her time denigrating *anyone*. But perhaps Lady Anne felt he paid her insufficient attention, and it seemed that if he could win her to his side, his wife would come to see that he was not such a bad fellow after all. For one of Adam's incorrigibly open and whimsical nature, there was just the least bit of discomfort in having a wife who treated one as a rather undistinguished stranger!

Right off, though, Adam realized it was a mistake to have led Anne out. Her elder brother had expected the honor and regarded him with unnerving astonishment, while his best friend, Captain Midford, glared during the whole of the set. Lady Anne was pleasant, but slightly distracted, as one might expect of a young lady at her come-out ball, and the Marquess of Barnfield had an expression similar to the one he had worn that day at Parkhurst when Adam had very nearly succumbed to the parlor maid. All in all it was a disquieting interval and he escaped to the card room at the first opportunity.

Before supper Anne managed to dance with both her brothers, Captain Midford, Lord Langham, Mr. Thresham, Sir Arthur Moresby, Lord Brackenbury . . . and Mr. Rogers. Before the second cotillion she had made time to speak with Miss Helena Rogers, who sat out several of the dances, whether by choice or not, Anne could not be sure. Taking no chances, however, she asked her mother if she would pay particular attention to introducing Miss Rogers to gentlemen, and the marchioness nodded her understanding.

Coming as Anne did from dancing with a series of gentlemen who flattered her, Mr. Rogers was a refreshing change. He did not compare her gown with Aphrodite's robes, nor did he find any similarity between her teeth and Lady Hertford's pearls. When he spoke of the theater, it was in serious speculation about the quality of the performances and the merits of the drama. His interests were eclectic: the state of unrest amongst the factory workers, housing in London, the merits of watercolors, the progress of the Brighton Pavilion, the novels of Scott, the deficiencies of Parliament.

Asked her opinion of Ackermann's Art Library, Anne had to confess that she had never been there. "I should like to go sometime," she hastened to add.

"You'd enjoy it, I think. Helena cozens me into taking her at least once a month. My sister has real artistic talent. Mostly she works in watercolors, but I've been trying to convince her to try oils. Perhaps you'd like to join us the next time we go to Ackermann's."

"Yes, thank you, I would. And I would like to see some of Miss Rogers's work as well." Anne had intended to say more, but was separated from him for a while and when they were rejoined he spoke of her brother Jack and how they had met. As the music faded and the murmur of voices rose to replace it, she felt a sense of regret. Mr. Rogers made no effort to acquire her as a supper partner, whether because he assumed she was already spoken for, or because he had no wish to take her in, she could not know. And in fact Lord Dunn was waiting with her mother at the side of the floor to claim her, so she smiled as Mr. Rogers thanked her for the set, and watched him stride purposefully toward his sister.

In the supper room Dunn surveyed the company and asked, "Shall we sit with the Greenwoods?"

He could not have chosen a more appropriate table. In addition to Greenwood and his supper partner, Miss Penhall, there were Sir Nicholas Dyrham and Lady Bradwell, Emma and Lord William, Maggie and Mr. Thresham, and Adam's sister and her husband, Captain Morton. Anne thought it the perfect location and said as much. Every one of the others was well known to her, and if Cynthia Morton was annoyed with her brother for choosing his previous flirt as a supper partner, she didn't show it.

Liveried footmen served the sumptuous meal and refilled wineglasses with an almost alarming promptitude. Though she was seated at the opposite end across the table from her brother, Anne knew that his euphoria came only partly from his proximity to Emma. Unthinking, he downed glass after glass of the wine as he parried Sir Nicholas's waggish thrusts, at the same time attempting to impress Emma with his tales of personal glory in the sporting field. Unfortunately, Sir Nicholas was by far his superior in riding, hunting, shooting, and almost every other endeavor poor William brought forth as evidence of his prowess; in addition, Sir Nicholas was adept at a smiling, inoffensive mockery.

"What Lord William means to tell you, Miss Berryman," the baronet explained after one particularly moving description of a long run after the fox, "is that he was only once dislodged into a gorse cover. Why, I daresay half the field fared a great deal worse! And I assure you it is much more comfortable to land in gorse than in a stream."

Lord William was incensed. "I didn't land in a gorse cover on that run! You're thinking of the run through Wilton Woods! This was a week later and I had a perfect run."

Emma's lips twitched but she said only, "I can't imagine how anyone keeps his seat during such a headlong dash."

"There's nothing to it," Lord William assured her. "Give the horse his head and when he jumps . . ."

Since he was illustrating his words with the hand that held his wineglass, there was every reason to expect the accident that followed. Emma's attention had been momentarily distracted, however, by a footman inquiring if she wished a serving of the veal sweetbreads with mushrooms, and she was *not* expecting the large quantity of wine that splashed in her face and dribbled down onto her gown. Even a society matron might have been excused for uttering an exclamation in such a situation, and Emma, taken by surprise, let out a decided squeal.

There followed a certain amount of confusion—Lord William apologizing profusely, Lady Bradwell hastening to her niece's aid with a large napkin, the footman attempting to dispose of the Sevres bowl of sweetbreads so he could remove Emma's wine-sprinkled plate. The confusion was not completely understood by those at the far end of the table, as they had not been witnesses to the catastrophe. Greenwood was merely relieved that it was not his wife causing the commotion, and Anne decided that her assistance would only add to the bedlam. Miss Penhall was above regarding the scene at all, while Cynthia Morton shared a rueful glance with her husband. Lord Dunn raised his quizzing glass.

When Emma had finished mopping her face with her aunt's napkin, she returned it and, with a quick glance to see that she had Sir Nicholas's attention, turned to Lord William with a straight face and a sigh. "I believe *I* would have preferred the gorse cover to the stream."

There was a low rumble of laughter from Sir Nicholas and even Lady Bradwell could not contain a gurgle of mirth. "By Jove, you're a sport!" Lord William declared proudly, beaming on her. And Emma, pleased with her finesse in changing the awkward accident into a jest, smiled happily on the rest of the table. Her composure was greeted by approbation from all save Dunn, who continued to wield his quizzing glass. Impetuously she grasped Lord William's quizzing glass, which dangled on a long black ribbon, and placed it to her eye. She stared through it at Dunn until he dropped his, and then she declared in a voice loud enough for him to hear, "Someone must pass the word to Lord Dunn that our performance is complete and he may go on with his meal."

Maggie gasped at her friend's temerity, but Anne bit her lip to stifle a smile. Though Dunn nodded coolly to Emma, Anne could see that his jaw was clenched and the hand that held his quizzing glass remained tensely motionless. Torn between an admiration of Emma's calm and effective action, and a long-standing regard for Dunn, Anne could not resist asking, "Depressing her pretensions, were you, my lord?"

Dunn forced himself to take a leisurely sip of wine. "Someone should. Obviously I am not the one to curb her impudence."

"Oh, I don't think it's impudence, you know. She's just high-spirited. It was Will's fault, spilling the wine on her and bringing her to everyone's attention."

"Miss Berryman enjoys being the center of attention."

Anne observed him through carefully lowered lashes. "Has she done something to incur your displeasure?" But she distinctly remembered Emma's confession on the ride back to school from Maggie's wedding.

"You are mistaken, Lady Anne. I have only the smallest acquaintance with Miss Berryman. For Lady Bradwell's sake alone am I concerned about her niece's behavior, as I would be for any friend presenting an unruly child."

"But Emma is charming! Sometimes I wish I had the courage to thumb my nose at all the stuffy conventions. Do you think she puts herself forward? Really, it would be totally out of character for her to blend in with all the insipid debutantes. She was meant to stand out in any assembly, and it would be a great piece of nonsense for her to behave as some of the meeker mouses . . . ah, mice."

"A young lady can retain her individuality and yet maintain a proper reserve in company."

Anne laughed. "Only because most of them have no wish to be noticed in a crowd."

"Miss Berryman would be desolate if she weren't," he retorted.

"Yes, but what of it? It does no harm, and she is vastly entertaining. Have you noticed that she doesn't toadeat the aristocracy, or give her attention only to the most attractive men? I've seen her accept dances with men so shy they could hardly stammer out the invitation! She has a good heart, Lord Dunn."

"Which won't keep her from getting into mischief, Lady Anne. The trouble with Miss Berryman is that she believes herself possessed of a sophistication which she cannot begin to fulfill in actuality. Because Lady Bradwell is a seasoned matron, and has, I fear, shared more anecdotes with her niece than is wise, Miss Berryman acts as though she has her aunt's experience . . . and position. If you value your friend's credit with the ton, it would be wise to caution her that her 'high spirits' are no substitute for discretion."

Anne could not entirely disagree with his assessment of the situation; had she not worried about much the same problem even before they left school? "Such a homily would not come well from me, I fear. After all, Emma and I are of an age. Besides, I think you exaggerate her failings, and Lady Bradwell is not a lenient chaperon."

"Not lenient, but rather trusting. Like so many good-natured people she believes others are of a similar disposition." Dunn made a languid gesture of dismissal. "I am becoming a bore on this topic. Greenwood and my brother have the same effect on me. I feel like a veritable ancient: at times I am hard pressed to even remember what it was like to be their age! I couldn't possibly have behaved like those two gudgeons."

"But Jack once told me you—"

"Please." He lifted an admonitory hand, laughing. "Let me admit to some youthful indiscretions and beg you not to repeat them to me. Nothing is more lowering than having your self-consequence shattered by reminders of your own past."

A mischievous smile played about her lips. "Very well, Lord Dunn, but I think in that case you must do a favor for me."

His eyes became wary. "I can tell before you ask that it is going to be distasteful. Well, ma'am, what would you have me do?"

"Ask Emma Berryman to stand up with you."

"Why?"

"Because I think you haven't given her a chance. You are being very censorious and yet you admit to some youthful folly of your own."

"You drive a hard bargain, Lady Anne. I am not at all sure I would not prefer hearing of my . . . ah . . . misdeeds." His thoughtful gaze traveled to where Emma sat raptly listening to Sir Nicholas while Lord William impatiently attempted to get a word in edgewise. "Very likely she wouldn't accept."

"Which simply indicates how hard you've been on her," Anne pointed out.

"Perhaps I have. Not that I have bested her in any confrontation, you understand. As I recall, she has always had the last word, since she doesn't care a fig for my opinion."

"Ah, there is the crux of the matter, isn't it? She really should have the good sense to care for your opinion." Anne was quizzing him, but they both knew she had put her finger on the source of his annoyance.

"If you're not careful, my dear young lady, you're going to be even more awesome than your mother," he grumbled.

"You'll ask Emma?"

"I will, but you cannot hold me to blame if she refuses."

"I shan't."

* * *

Truth to tell, it was rather unusual for Lord Dunn to approach any lady for a dance expecting to be refused, and it was not an experience he would have cared to undergo regularly. After supper he stood up with Lady Anne and Lady Greenwood, and was promised a dance with Mrs. Morton later in the evening, but he did not find himself in Miss Berryman's vicinity and chose next to honor a Miss Rufforth and then a Miss Wilmington as partners. If he had not caught Anne's questioning look across the room, Dunn would then have adjourned for a brief spell to the card room. Instead he surveyed the thinning company and had no trouble locating Miss Berryman returning to her aunt with Sir Nicholas. With a mental shrug Dunn approached her.

His request so surprised Emma, who had, if not repented, at least regretted her pert words at the table (which had caused her aunt to frown most grievously), that she looked rather helplessly at him, stammering, "I—I think I have promised this set to Mr. Chamblesforth. Or was it Mr. Thresham. Yes, Mr. Thresham. But I—I don't see him."

Sir Nicholas intervened smoothly. "Norwood sent word that Thresham was indisposed, and forced to leave the festivities rather earlier than he had planned."

"Oh. Then I would be most happy to accept your kind offer, Lord Dunn."

As they took their places in the set, she said stiffly, "My aunt thought I was rude to you at supper."

"Very rude."

"You were not particularly polite to stare at me that way through your quizzing glass."

"No, I wasn't. I ask your pardon."

Emma blinked at him in surprise. "You do? That's very handsome of you. And I am sorry I spoke so . . ."

As she was at a loss for the proper word, he supplied it. "Impertinently."

"I hadn't in mind such a strong term, but I suppose it will do." She laughed as the Scotch reel separated them.

Dunn watched her glide through the dance, smiling, speaking with each of the gentlemen she met, enjoying herself. And the gentlemen were enjoying her. Not only for her vivacity, he thought, but for the way her gown clung so provocatively. Yet there were any number of gowns of a similar cut and fit that excited not the least interest. It was the girl's own awareness of her sensuality that made the difference, that added the spice to the package. An almost smug realization of her magnetism, he decided, disturbed.

Noting the direction of his gaze, Emma rewarded him with her most alluring smile. "It is fortunate, is it not, Lord Dunn, that the wine was white and not red?"

"Yes," he said shortly. But he had a good mind to shake the child. How dare she try to play off her wiles on him? On anyone, for that matter, at her age and in her position? Did she think herself invincible? London society, he trusted, would soon teach her otherwise. For if it did not . . .

Emma was disappointed by his reaction. Used to the admiring gazes of the infatuated Lord William, and the almost alarmingly knowledgeable half smile of Sir Nicholas, Lord Dunn's impassive countenance was an insult. Caught up in the first flush of her power over men, she determined to bring him to heel.

"I understand you are a notable whip," she remarked when next they faced each other. "I suppose you disapprove of ladies learning how to handle the ribbons."

"Very few excel at such a demanding pursuit."

"I would." Her eyes flashed a challenge. "Sir Nicholas is giving me pointers on riding and Lord William is instructing me about sailing vessels—he keeps one on the Thames. I want to learn about everything, do everything! You can't imagine how restricted it was at school! I should like to shoot a flintlock gun and visit the races at Newmarket. There are dozens of things I've never done, any number of places I've never been, books to read that Mrs. Childswick would not allow within the premises of Windrush House."

She was gone again and Dunn watched her with perplexed eyes. His attention was recalled by Miss Rowland, her patrician face unsmiling, looking far too high in the instep to be stomping through a Scotch reel. He swung her around, realizing as he did so what an impossible task it would be to engender the least enthusiasm in her for anything. When his arm was linked once more with Miss Berryman's he said warily, "I don't disapprove of ladies learning to drive a pair, so long as they don't endanger themselves or passersby, or the horses. You must realize, however, that it takes a deal of concentration to master the finer elements."

"So that what one needs is a notable whip for an instructor?" Emma asked, all mocking innocence.

"Precisely, Miss Berryman."

As the music wound to a halt, she smiled. "Would you teach me?"

Of course it was the question she had been angling toward through most of the dance and Dunn knew it. He had, in fact, prepared a very civil rejection, one that would show his amusement at her impertinence, and yet his innate courtesy, his surprise at the immaturity of the request, and yet his unblemished good humor. Unfortunately, in addition to the mocking gleam, there was also a light of eager anticipation in her eyes and he realized, almost with a start, that she really did wish to learn.

"Very well, Miss Berryman." Because he was annoyed with himself for giving in to her, there was no trace of enthusiasm in his voice as he led her toward her aunt.

"Thank you. Tomorrow, perhaps?" Emma suggested.

"That won't be possible," he replied dampingly. "I will send a message round in a few days to set a time."

Emma said nothing.

CHAPTER TWELVE

Even Lady Bradwell was surprised by the stir her niece was causing, and Emma herself was radiant. Never before had Emma had so much admiration, attention, and the sheer opportunity to indulge herself thoroughly in every pleasurable pursuit. Success is heady stuff and Emma had not the self-discipline to deny herself any pleasure that offered. Nor had she the experience to realize that novelty was at least a part of her good fortune. Gentlemen were captivated by her ready interest in their sporting ventures: what other lady was willing to listen (with true eagerness) to descriptions of sailing vessels and bouts of fisticuffs? Emma prided herself on giving each person who addressed her the undivided attention to which he (or she) was entitled.

In the bustle of her social activities she did not neglect her friends. Her efforts on behalf of the Greenwood ball were unstinting, her thought for her aunt's comfort becoming, her singing at musical evenings delightful. But in spite of her goodness to those about her, Emma was developing a rather high-flown opinion of herself. Inevitable, perhaps, in one so courted and petted by society, but nonetheless an alarming circumstance.

When Lord Dunn did not fulfull his word to write her within the next few days Emma smiled and thought to herself, *he is only trying to prove he isn't captivated.* Lady Bradwell was wise enough not to mention the matter at all, nor that he had called one afternoon when Emma was out riding with Sir Nicholas. Despite her frequent references to her niece, he had merely nodded and progressed to other topics as though her comments had been of some disorderly housemaid and called for no remark. A note did arrive, precisely two weeks after the ball, indicating that he could be free either of the next two afternoons if Emma should like to be instructed in driving. Emma chose to delay her answer until the morning of the first day, suggesting that he come around that afternoon. He failed to show, but there was a note later in the evening, when she returned from a very late party, politely explaining that he had not received her message until the dinner hour. He did not offer to come the next afternoon.

"I have just heard from Lord High and Mighty," she exclaimed, tossing the note on the floor after crumpling it satisfactorily, "and he makes no mention of another appointment to teach me to drive!"

"He did offer, my love, and you carelessly delayed answering him. Dunn is not to be toyed with, you know. If you were perhaps to write, apologizing for your tardiness, I feel sure he would suggest another opportunity."

"I'd rather not learn than apologize to him!"

"As you wish, Emma. Knowing how to drive will do you very little good, in any case, as I have no sporting vehicle." And Lady Bradwell continued on her way up the stairs.

Such a rational viewpoint did not recommend itself to Emma but she said nothing further. The hour was late and she trod wearily to her bedchamber, where the green-and-white check curtains of the tent bed had been drawn back and her nightclothes laid out. Preoccupied, she allowed her maid to undress her and slip the nightdress over her head, trying to decide whether she really cared if Lord Dunn taught her to drive or not. When she had dismissed the maid, her eye was caught by the cylinder desk near the window, already open because she had been too rushed earlier in the evening to finish the letter she had begun to Maggie with a final list of suggested food items for the ball menu.

Really, she should send it round first thing in the morning; the date of the Greenwood ball was drawing close.

In her finest copperplate hand she copied the names of dishes from the list she had researched, noting which she felt essential and which were optional. The candle flame flickered and she glanced up with a puzzled frown. No hint of a breeze stirred the curtains and her door was shut tight, but she could hear the vague whisper of footsteps in the hall. Probably one of the servants still abroad, she speculated. Still, it was more than half an hour since their return and generally the household was motionless by this time. Curious, she picked up the candlestick and moved to the door, opening it soundlessly and protecting the light of the candle with a hand.

The hall was in darkness save a brief gleam of light from her aunt's room that penetrated the gloom before the door shut. Emma had been too late to receive more than an impression, but she could have sworn that the figure of a man disappeared into the room. Strangely enough, in her preoccupation with her own social activities and the men who courted her, she had given no thought whatsoever to her aunt's reputation and, indeed, confession. At first, perhaps, she had wondered who her aunt's lover was, but she had seen no sign of their meetings, could not discern in the way Lady Bradwell treated her gentlemen friends any particularity that would distinguish one from the many.

Emma shielded the flame of her candle and trod soundlessly down the hall until she was opposite her aunt's door, where she paused to listen. Sure enough, there was a faint whisper of voices, blurred by the heavy door, but obviously two people in conversation. And though neither voice was recognizable, decidedly one was feminine and the other deeply masculine. Emma blew out her candle and waited.

After a while the tenor of the exchange seemed to alter, becoming softer and less frequent until finally there was almost no sound at all. Almost. Emma found herself feeling slightly giddy and she picked up the skirts of the nightdress and hastened back to her room, where she stood for some time leaning against the closed door, the echo of a most unnerving but somehow joyful cry ringing in her ears. With unsteady hands she set the candlestick on the nightstand and climbed into the welcoming bed. She would finish the letter to Maggie in the morning.

Two days passed before Emma happened to attend the same evening's entertainment as Lord Dunn. When he joined them there was no hint in his smiling countenance that any disagreement lay between them. His random remarks were directed at both her and her chaperon, he listened with interest to Emma's amusing comments on the company . . . and he asked Lady Bradwell to stand up with him. Since Mr. Thresham stood at her elbow only waiting an opportunity to make his own request, there was nothing rude or remarkable in this, but it rankled. Emma decided during the cotillion that when she returned from the dance and he asked *her*, she would tell him she had no unclaimed dances for the rest of the evening. She need not have bothered planning; he did not ask her.

Of course there was no lack of partners. Lord William was almost as assiduous as ever, but Emma, as propriety required, agreed to only two dances with any one gentleman. Already, however, she was finding the younger men a trifle immature and consequently rather boring. When one compared them with Sir Nicholas Dyrham . . . Well, there *was* no comparison. And yet the baronet was not so remarkably handsome. His height was only average and there was nothing especially notable in his features individually, but as a whole they emanated a rakish air of confident masculinity. Set beside him Lord William looked an eager puppy, straining at his leash to bounce exuberantly on anyone who took his fancy. Sir Nicholas had quite a different sort of aura about him, the aura of a passionate, even reckless man well able to control his intense emotions until he chose to let them loose. Sometimes Emma would unexpectedly catch his gaze on her, its blackness holding an almost scorching potency. Involuntarily she would look away, feeling shaken.

Miffed at Lord Dunn for his offhanded treatment of her, Emma turned to Sir Nicholas for the instant restoration of her self-esteem. His black eyes were faintly amused.

"It would seem that his lordship is immune to your charm, Miss Berryman. I shall have to revise my opinion as to his good taste."

"You have no high opinion of his singing voice, as I recall. Is he supposed to be a connoisseur of women?"

"I believe he is reckoned to be. You should ask your aunt. Ladies are more interested in gentlemen's reputations than are other gentlemen." He dismissed the matter with a wave of his hand. "Are you warm, Miss Berryman? You might benefit from a moment in the garden."

The offer was laced with a suggestion of challenge that he knew she would not refuse. She should not really be alone with him, but she prided herself on following her own dictates and not those of society. Emma felt perfectly capable of keeping Sir Nicholas in line and she took his arm.

Their host that evening had a mansion on the fringes of London that had more extensive grounds than those houses in the heart of the city. Other couples strolled on the gravel walks and sat in arbors covered with vines. As Sir Nicholas threaded his way through a bewildering maze of paths and hedges, Emma cheerfully recounted her morning's adventure in Bond Street when her reticule had almost been stolen. Although Sir Nicholas appeared intent on her story, he abruptly interrupted before she had quite finished.

"Do you approve of your aunt's way of life?"

"Why . . . of course." Emma regarded him with puzzled eyes.

"Come now, Miss Berryman, consider." His voice was lazy but with a touch of impatience. "Your aunt is married to a man who never accompanies her to town. While she is here, she is not faithful to him. You must know that. And you approve?"

She was disconcerted by his curiously intent regard. After moistening her lips, she said, "Well, there are reasons she does not . . . honor her marriage vows. I perfectly understand her situation."

"Do you?" A soft laugh drifted off on the night breeze. "And you understand how in the quiet late hours a man walks through her house, opens her bedroom door, and enters?"

Her face paled. "You?"

"No, certainly not," he said sternly. "I think . . . Well, that is no matter. Perhaps only one man over the years, but more likely two, three, four, have made that pilgrimage to her bed. And you approve?"

Emma could not answer him.

"They don't sing duets there, you know, Miss Berryman." He smiled. "Or, only in a manner of speaking. No, your aunt undoubtedly wears a nightdress which reveals her substantial charms and drives her lover to dispose of his own clothing as quickly as possible. And then he joins her in bed, Miss Berryman, and they . . ."

"Don't! You should not talk so. What they do . . . what my aunt does is none of my business . . . or yours." Shaken, she turned her back to him.

"I merely wished to ascertain whether you knew what you were talking about when you said you approved of her way of life. You are rather young to comprehend the entirety."

"Well, I do! I am not a child!"

"Aren't you?" Sir Nicholas placed his hands on her shoulders and turned her to face him. His smile in the dark was definitely mocking. "You've never even been kissed, have you?"

Since the answer was no, Emma gave instead what she considered a provocative look and murmured demurely, "I don't tell such secrets, sir."

As though she had admitted her purity, he replied, "No, I didn't think you had."

Emma was defensive. "Several gentlemen have tried to kiss me."

"I'm not surprised. I think," he said softly as he twined a lock of her blond hair about his finger, "that you were very wise to wait until you had someone—hm, shall we say experienced—to introduce you."

"I . . . I don't understand what you mean." His finger traced her chin, brushing her lips.

"I think you do, Miss Berryman. And I think it's high time you let someone taste those enticing lips you are so ready to pretend are available for the taking." He touched the line of her throat as she swallowed convulsively, and lifted one magnificent black brow. "Surely you are not afraid?"

"Someone might come along."

He laughed. "I doubt it, my dear." Before she could protest further he bent and kissed her, a long, lingering, seductive kiss nicely calculated to arouse and yet not totally frighten her. When he drew back he had to steady her with a hand on her arm. "Let that be a lesson to you, Miss Berryman . . . and a standard."

Emma refused to speak to him but hastened off in the direction she assumed must lead toward the house. In a moment he was at her side, correcting her confused senses by reversing her footsteps and keeping pace with her rapid if slightly unsteady progress. As they approached the building and passed several other groups, he murmured, "No one will know unless you act distracted, my dear. We have merely strolled around the grounds for a breath of fresh air."

With an effort Emma pulled herself up sharply and entered the ballroom as calmly as possible, only to have her aunt scold her for wandering off with Sir Nicholas.

"Dear Aunt Amelia, it was warm here and I am sure no harm could come to me in the earl's lovely gardens. I trust I haven't missed any of the sets."

"No, but you really shouldn't . . . Well, well, I shall speak with you later. Mr. Norwood is here to claim his dance."

Lady Bradwell was familiar enough with her niece to know that the high spots of color on her cheeks were not due solely to the heat of the ballroom. In the carriage on the way home she attempted to put into words her feeling of concern.

"I know that some of society's rules seem stuffy and antiquated to you, Emma, but you really must honor them if you wish to maintain your position. It is not the thing to wander off with a gentleman alone."

"Why not?" Emma asked, all innocence.

"Because, my dear, there are men who will take advantage of you."

"In an earl's garden? With dozens of other people about?"

Lady Bradwell sighed. "I realize it seems highly unlikely, does it not? But there, I'm sure it has happened in the past and will do so in the future. Not that I believe Sir Nicholas would behave improperly; he is decidedly a gentleman. But you must realize, my dear, that he is considerably older and accustomed to dealing with women who are more worldly-wise than you. And I think there is a rather perverse little devil in him which might just lead him to . . . to tempt you. You do rather invite attentions of that sort, Emma. Now don't take what I'm saying amiss! I can quite understand how you revel in your youth and your looks and your spirits, but you must be wary of where they can lead you, too. Because of your success, you have developed a sense of power, of invincibility, and you haven't the experience to handle it."

"What do you mean?"

Although Lady Bradwell was aware of the stiffness of her niece's deportment and the tightness of her voice, she plunged uncomfortably on, determined that her guidance was absolutely necessary. "You tend to . . . well, entice men, if you will. I have often been frank with you, Emma, and you should understand what I'm saying. No, I shall be blunt. You apparently attempt to raise a physical desire in men, a desire for them to bed you, and yet I presume you have no intention of satisfying that desire. You simply cannot do it until you're married, unless you wish to ruin your life. If you don't think of the poor men themselves, my love, you should think of your reputation. The way you disport yourself makes you appear *fast*."

"Why should I try to disguise my . . . my charms? You don't."

Emma stared out the window, but hardly noticed the passing linkboy with his torch.

Lady Bradwell was patient. "There is a vast difference between your situation and mine, Emma, and I don't think I have ever sunk to titillating men when I had no intention of giving in. A mild flirtation is expected of me. I am never indiscriminate, carefully choosing the gentleman for his situation. In your first flush of triumph, you seem intent on winning every man to your train, and you don't care how you do it. Using your sensuality is the easiest way, certainly, but it is the worst and the most dangerous.

"Because you are teasing the men, Emma, and some man will call you on your supposed offer. Have you not heard the story of Gertrude Tilson? Quite as gently born as you, my dear. She was Lady Kerry's daughter from her second marriage. Gertrude was a petite, precocious beauty who eventually eloped with Gilbreath Mahon. Her family didn't approve of him, and no wonder—he was no more than an adventurer. Mahon left her for Miss Russell five years later and Gertrude became a courtesan. They called her the Bird of Paradise. She acted at Covent Garden and drove her own phaeton, but what kind of life did she have, forever looking for a protector, haunting Feulliard's dancing rooms in Queen Street, Golden Square, and trying to decide which of the Bond Street loungers would be able to support her in style? I shudder to think of that happening to you."

"You may be sure it won't," Emma retorted. "I have no mind to lead such a life."

"But don't you see how it came about? Gertrude gloried in tempting all the men she encountered, and one was clever enough to call her on it. She was caught at her own game. Mahon built a similar desire in her, and she was willing to throw over her whole family to satisfy it. Don't think it couldn't happen to you, Emma, because it could."

The memory of Sir Nicholas's kiss was vivid in Emma's mind. She had indeed experienced something new then; its force was enough to shake her. It did not take much imagination to see how such a state of affairs could progress, but her aunt was proceeding to enlighten her.

"At first it is just a kiss. That seems simple enough, a kiss. But there are men who can easily excite you with a kiss, especially men who are appealing in themselves. And then comes a little snuggling and touching. You have no idea how vulnerable you are until a man starts to call forth your desire by touching you. From there it is only a very short hop into bed, Emma. I watch you every day doing precisely what you want, and I wonder if you would be able to resist if an unscrupulous man was determined on getting you there. Please don't think I'm scolding you! Some women with truly warm natures are unable to resist, especially when they're young and have never had the experience. There is a fascination, a curiosity, to partake of the ultimate physical excitement. And if you carelessly toss away your reputation by doing foolish things, you cannot expect a man to cling to his scruples and shield you from ruin. If a gentleman believes you well-bred and pure, he will have the strength to respect your virginity."

Lady Bradwell, in the darkness of the carriage, allowed herself a reminiscent smile but continued inexorably, "If you tease and act as though you have every intention of discarding morality, well, you are only asking for trouble."

"I see," Emma said softly.

"Of course, I am not one to be casting stones. My own life is hardly a model of virtue, but then I don't ask you to pattern yourself on me. Heaven forbid! Remember what I told you: Don't try to explain me or fight my battles for me. I want to do the best I can by you, my love, but if I feel that my unsavory reputation is damaging to you, or that you are attempting to imitate me in unbecoming ways, I will have to send you to one of your other relations. If my child had lived, I would want her to be like you, Emma, all full of high spirits and curiosity, ready to meet life head on and enjoy it. But I cannot and will not stand idly by while you court disaster."

The carriage halted in front of the house in Bruton Street and the flambeaux at the doorway cast a flickering light into the interior of the vehicle. Lady Bradwell was surprised to see the sign of a lone tear streak on Emma's cheek. As the footman leaped down and came around to let down the steps, Emma whispered, "I didn't understand, Aunt Amelia. Not truly. I'm sorry."

Her aunt patted her hand consolingly. "Well, of course you didn't, love. There's no reason to apologize. You must know that I only want you to be happy."

It was Sir Nicholas's habit to take Emma riding in Hyde Park, but on the morning after their encounter he was not surprised when Emma fobbed him off. His amusement grew as she continued to find excuses for not accompanying him—a necessary shopping expedition, a promised visit, a slight cold. Sir Nicholas, delighted—and perhaps urged on by that devil Lady Bradwell recognized in him—persisted.

Arriving one day when Emma was just ordering the carriage to go to Maggie's, he quickly interposed. "There's no need to have your aunt's carriage readied when mine is without. It would be my pleasure to convey you to the Greenwoods'."

Emma eyed him suspiciously. "That's kind of you, Sir Nicholas, but I shall be there some time and I could not possibly ask you to wait. Maggie won't be receiving; we are planning to organize the preparations for her ball."

To her surprise Lady Bradwell spoke in support of Sir Nicholas's proposal, declaring that she would send the carriage for Emma later in the afternoon. Emma studied her aunt's encouraging countenance. Then, with a mischievous twinkle, she nodded. "Very well. If you don't mind having your carriage treated as a hackney coach, Sir Nicholas, I would be grateful for your escort."

Placing a mulberry-colored velvet bonnet with plumes of white ostrich feathers on her blond ringlets, she tied it at a jaunty angle under her chin and allowed Sir Nicholas to escort her to his curricle. His groom had just returned from walking the horses to the corner, and as there was room for only the two of them on the seat, Sir Nicholas flipped him a coin and dismissed him. Emma laughed when he pressed her hand in helping her into the carriage.

"Do I amuse you, Miss Berryman?" he asked as he expertly gathered the reins.

"Occasionally," she admitted.

"Did it amuse you when I kissed you the other evening?"

"No." There was no trace of a blush on her cheeks and she met his quick glance at her as he set the horses in motion. "It was undoubtedly the most beneficial, and enjoyable, lesson I've received. But I can see why Mrs. Childswick has omitted it from her curriculum. It is also a rather dangerous lesson."

Sir Nicholas's brows drew up in surprise. "Nonsense. You have nothing to fear from me."

"I'm not at all sure that's true, Sir Nicholas. If I recall correctly, you took the opportunity to sound me on my . . . moral beliefs before you . . . Well, I may have left you with a misconception which I should like to correct." Despite the serious nature of the subject, her eyes danced. "I have not the least intention of straying from the path of virtue."

"And I have no intention of luring you from it, young lady! Did your aunt put such a notion in your head?"

Emma grinned. "Aunt Amelia said you were decidedly a gentleman and would not behave improperly, but that your perverse little devil might lead you to tempt me."

"And I did tempt you, didn't I?" he asked lazily.

"Oh, yes, I won't deny it. On the other hand, I won't offer you a chance to tempt me again. Nor act as though I wished you would." For the first time the color in her cheeks heightened.

"Ah, I see. Do you know you are extremely captivating when you blush, Miss Berryman?"

Emma demurely lowered her eyes, but not before the sparkle in them was evident. "Obviously I shall have to cultivate a more modest demeanor, Sir Nicholas, and go pink every time a man looks at me, like Miss Sherburn does."

"That widgeon! Do you know I heard her giggle when someone told her Mr. Hartcliffe had preached a most admirable sermon last Sunday? I beg you won't decide to represent yourself as an idiot!"

"Never," she assured him as she gazed with interest at the milling throngs along Bond Street. "What I don't know, I intend to learn, and what I don't learn I shan't let on. I have noticed that one can gain a great deal of information by simply listening to someone who has the mistaken impression that you know what they're talking about. And I'm sure you won't think me a bluestocking if I tell you that I make notes of names that are mentioned so that I may find out what I can about them at the lending library. Unfortunately," she confessed, turning to smile at him, "the fellow who helps me there has occasionally been shocked by my ignorance."

"I can picture it now," he admitted mournfully as he directed the horses into Piccadilly. "The poor fellow is captivated by you and would do anything in his power to please, but cannot disguise his alarm when you approach him under the impression that Samuel Johnson was an actor."

"Something like that. Mr. Edgars could not believe that I had never heard of Henry Fielding, but, you know, Mrs. Childswick could not really be expected to have works like *Tom Jones* or *Joseph Andrews* at Windrush House. And frankly I did not find *Tom Jones* all that edifying."

"No? I would have thought you might." His eyes shifted from the road to mock her.

"Mr. Fielding's conception of women is perhaps just what gentlemen like, but I found it annoying. His heroine is a pretty doll, languishing of an excess of sensibility or misunderstanding the simplest matter. With such a want of spirit it is inconceivable to me that Mr. Jones could have the least interest in her." Emma adjusted the mulberry pelisse she wore as they turned into Half Moon Street. "I should have thought a gentleman of Mr. Jones's temperament would look for something more lively in a wife, but there is no accounting for taste. Do you ever picture Mr. and Mrs. Jones five years later?"

The horses were neatly drawn to a halt before the Greenwoods' residence and Sir Nicholas sat with the reins held lightly, making no move to descend. "I confess I never gave Mr. and Mrs. Jones another thought after I closed the last volume."

"Well, I picture them surrounded by five children; they had two by the summary of their future lives in the last chapter. Sophia plays for her father and her husband and toadeats Squire Allworthy, no doubt. And Mr. Fielding says that Tom 'has also, by reflections on his past follies, acquired a discretion and prudence very uncommon in one of his lively parts.' Uncommon, indeed! But we are assured that any vice he may have had was corrected by conversing with Allworthy and his wife. To be sure, I can quite picture them lecturing him day in and day out on the rewards of proper conduct. What a merry life he must lead!"

Sir Nicholas laughed, touching a finger to her cheek. "I daresay you would have made a much more appropriate wife for him, Miss Berryman. Certainly you are every bit as lovely as the fair Sophia, and would have ridden to hounds with him as well!"

"If he'd allowed me," she retorted. "My impression is that gentlemen become filled with rectitude on the taking of their marriage vows. Not necessarily rectitude for themselves, but certainly for their possessions—such as their wives. If a man is unable to show a clean face to the world himself, he must surely have someone else do it for him. A very convenient arrangement."

"In that case," Sir Nicholas remarked as he climbed down and assisted her from the carriage, "you had best find a husband who will be the one to show the clean face in *your* marriage."

As before, Sir Nicholas pressed her hand and Emma frowned. "Then I shan't be surprised to hear that you have offered for Miss Rowland, sir."

"You should be vastly surprised to hear that I have offered for anyone, my dear. I haven't the constitution to take on an aura of holiness through matrimony or any other institution, I promise you."

The dark eyes were amused, and even perhaps slightly challenging, as they regarded her. Emma took a firm grip on her reticule as she turned to mount the steps, pausing only to say, "Thank you for conveying me here, Sir Nicholas. I daresay we will meet again soon."

"As soon as this evening, no doubt, but in the event we should miss one another at one of the entertainments, may I hope that you will ride with me tomorrow?"

Since she felt she had handled the situation reasonably well, she turned in the act of lifting the knocker and smiled at him. "That would be delightful, Sir Nicholas." As she allowed the knocker to drop, though, she had a moment's misgiving. Had not the porter responded instantly, she might have changed her mind. The door opened and she glanced back at the baronet, but he had already climbed into the curricle and tipped his hat to her as he drove off.

Emma was shown to the drawing room, where Maggie rose to greet her. Despite the valiant smile and the rush of words that flowed forth in welcome, Emma could not fail to note her friend's pallor. Maggie's large gray eyes seemed even larger in the drawn face and a woolen shawl was pulled close about her even on the warm spring day.

"You don't look at all well," Emma declared, concerned. "Are you feeling poorly?"

"Just a little off color," Maggie admitted as they seated themselves on the green-and-white striped sofa. "I'm sure it's nothing."

"You mean you haven't had the doctor come? You should have sent for him."

Maggie self-consciously studied a Dresden shepherdess on the table beside her. "It's not the sort of thing a doctor could help, Emma."

If this obscure hint was supposed to enlighten her friend, it didn't serve its purpose. "Well, I know doctors are of very little use most of the time," Emma agreed, "but occasionally you find one who can cure you."

Her friend's giggle surprised her. "You can't be cured of being enceinte, my dear Emma."

"You're going to have a baby? How splendid!" But Emma's initial excitement was quickly dampened by a renewed concern. "Really, Maggie, you cannot have been taking care of yourself! I don't believe it is normal to be looking so very haggard. Forgive me for being blunt, but your face is very nearly white and you look inordinately tired. I think you're working far too hard on the ball, and keeping late hours every night cannot be at all good for you."

"No, no. It's not uncommon to feel poorly at such a time. I've spoken with Cynthia—Mrs. Morton—and she said that she was prone to disagreeable bouts for the first few months with her first."

"And she wasn't concerned at how pale you are?" Emma demanded.

"Well . . ." Maggie fingered the fringe on a silk-covered pillow and refused to meet Emma's eyes. "She insisted that I rest more, and call a halt to any further remodeling."

"But what of the ball?"

Maggie's voice dropped to little more than a whisper. "I must have it for Greenwood, Emma. He wouldn't understand if I called it off now. The invitations have been sent. Cynthia thought perhaps we could delay it, but Greenwood said that was nonsense and that I could have as much help as I needed so there would be no strain on me."

"Confound the man!" Emma exclaimed imprudently. "Does he not realize that no matter how much help you have it will still be an intolerable burden?"

The wide gray eyes met hers implacably. "He has asked very little of me, Emma, and I really wish to do this much for him. He's very pleased about the baby."

With an effort Emma bit back the retort she longed to make. "I see. Well, we shall just have to make the best of it, then. But you will stop going out every evening, won't you? That much you could certainly do."

Uncomfortably, Maggie dropped her eyes to the hands that lay twisting in her lap. "There always seems a good reason to go. I didn't wish to miss Anne's ball, of course, and then there was the Rowlands'. Some evenings I tell Greenwood I don't feel well and he is all solicitude, but I cannot very well do it every night."

"Of course you can. You must."

"He wouldn't understand, Emma."

"For heaven's sake, who cares if he understands?" her friend asked impatiently. "If he were ill, he wouldn't go out."

"He's never ill."

"I daresay, but he isn't carrying a baby. I'll . . ." But Emma decided not to mention the possible solution that had occurred to her. She was not on particularly good terms with Lord Dunn just at the moment, and he might not be willing to do a favor for her. She forced a smile. "Well, stay home as often as you can. I'll plan to devote more time to helping with the ball, and you plan to lie in every morning till noon, my love."

"Thank you, Emma. You and Anne and Cynthia have been of enormous assistance. Greenwood is quite right, you know; there is hardly a thing for me to do."

Wholly unconvinced, Emma withdrew from her reticule some lists she had made and began to go over them with her friend.

CHAPTER THIRTEEN

> Miss Emma Berryman presents her compliments to Lord Dunn and begs his forgiveness of her negligent tardiness in responding to his kind invitation to take her driving. In lieu of this endeavor, which it was most kind of him to agree to after her great impertinence, she requests merely a word with him on another matter altogether, which is of some urgency. If it would be possible for him to call on her at Lady Bradwell's house one afternoon this week, she would be at home to receive him. Miss Berryman remains, as always, his lordship's most obedient servant.

To say that Lord Dunn was surprised to receive this submissive epistle would be a gross understatement. He was astonished, and very suspicious of Miss Berryman's motives. As he set it down on his desk he had half a mind to ignore it. Really, she should not be writing him at all except in reply to some letter of his own—an invitation or the like. Quite possibly she intended to play a hoax on him. Did she really think he would believe she would sit in every afternoon in hopes that he would call? Dunn retrieved the letter and reread it. Begged his forgiveness, did she? How likely was that? And to admit her great impertinence was certainly doing it much too brown. Dunn felt sure that Miss Berryman had not the first notion of how impertinent she had been, and would certainly not admit it if she did.

Nonetheless, the viscount found it difficult to ignore any plea for help, though it came from the most rag-mannered of villains. Not that he had ascribed such a lowly situation to Miss Berryman. As a man of lofty ideals and impeccable manners, he would never sink so low as to judge a green girl in her first season as anything worse than imprudent and foolhardy. Both of which, he decided impartially, Miss Berryman was. Dunn folded the note and placed it in his waistcoat pocket. He would go, but if he found she was trying to hoodwink him, he would personally see that she regretted the prank. In either case he had the strongest sentiment that her note should be framed; one was not likely to see such a penitent attitude expressed by Miss Berryman more than once in a lifetime.

When he arrived in Bruton Street the butler North showed him to a small writing room at the back of the house where Emma sat amongst a litter of notes. He had no way of knowing that her endeavor was in a good cause, or that they were not all billets-doux that she had bribed some maid to bring her without her aunt's knowledge. It seemed quite conceivable to Dunn that half a dozen young men of fashion would find it beyond their meager powers to resist sending declarations of love to the young lady who stood as he entered. In the blue figured silk round dress with its white crepe full ruff she looked both regal and vulnerable.

Emma was a little surprised to see him so soon. She had assumed that his annoyance with her would at least have caused him to delay his coming for a day or two. There was no triumph in her attitude, however, merely gratitude.

"Thank you for coming so promptly, Lord Dunn. Won't you have a seat?" It was necessary for her to clear the dainty chair of lists of fruited jellies and vanilla creams, ornamented tongue and garnished ham. "For Maggie's ball," she explained. "Lord Greenwood wants one of those ice sculptures, but the man who does them is out of town just now."

Dunn seated himself as Emma dropped wearily into her chair. "My chef's assistant has some experience in sculpting ice. He came to me from Gunthers. Would it help if I sent him to Lady Greenwood?"

"Why, that would be perfect! How kind of you to offer. You wouldn't mind?"

"It would be my pleasure." Dunn reached down to pick up a note left lying on the floor beside his chair. It was indeed a list of edibles and not a lover's note at all. He handed it to Emma and asked, "What was it you wished to speak about so urgently with me?"

Noting that the paper contained a list of the sweets, she placed it on the third stack before replying. "That has to do with Maggie and Lord Greenwood, too. I very much fear you will think that I am interfering, but I have noticed that Lord Greenwood pays some attention to your advice and guidance. So I thought you might help." She was not looking at him but was aware that he rose abruptly.

"I don't involve myself in other people's marriages, Miss Berryman. I think you must excuse me."

His voice was so cold and his eyes so angry when she glanced at him that for a moment, but just a moment, she felt stricken. In turn she leaped to her feet and planted herself in his path to the doorway. "I will *not* excuse you, my lord," she flared. "Maggie is one of my dearest friends and I am perfectly willing to accept Anne's dictum that one does not interfere with someone else's marriage, but we are discussing the urgent matter of Maggie's health!"

"Are we?" The viscount looked slightly discomposed. "You had not said so, Miss Berryman."

"Well, you hardly gave me the opportunity, did you? You may be sure you are the last person I would ask for a favor if it were not of the utmost importance. Could we sit down?" she asked more gently.

"Certainly."

When they had once again taken their respective chairs she studied him gravely. "Lord Dunn, Maggie is increasing. It's not precisely a secret; on the other hand I imagine very few people know. I believe I may trust to your discretion in not mentioning the matter. Yesterday when I visited her she did not look well at all. Obviously Mrs. Morton has counseled her to rest as much as possible, but Lord Greenwood . . . Well, I daresay you know his lordship well enough to realize that he would have no patience with a little indisposition. Maggie insists on proceeding with the ball because he has asked it of her, and because he has offered any help she may need."

"You consider that an unreasonable attitude?"

"Whose?"

"Lady Greenwood's." He crossed his long, elegantly clad legs before adding, "She strikes me as a lady who would attempt if at all possible to earn her husband's approbation."

"Of course she would." Emma felt he was being purposely obtuse, and perhaps hinting that she herself would be quite a different sort of wife. "No matter how much help Maggie has with the ball, a great share of the responsibility will fall on her. But that is not why I've asked you here, and if you wish to see it as an admirable instance of wifely obedience, enjoy yourself. I could not convince Maggie to postpone it, I feel sure, so I would like to see that be the only effort she has to expend."

She brought out the sarcasm in him. "How very considerate of you. And what does Adam have her doing otherwise—mopping the stairs and grooming the horses?"

This time Emma rose, and walked to the door. As she turned the brass handle she said over her shoulder, "Thank you for coming, Lord Dunn. I'm so sorry to have caused you such inconvenience for nothing." And before he had a chance to speak she slipped out the door and pulled it closed behind herself. The hallway was deserted and she knew she had only a moment to get out of sight, so she hastened across and through the green baize door that led into the domestic areas. The kitchens were below but the plate and silver and crystal were kept in a large closet off the dining room and Emma, feeling rather cowardly but self-righteous, stepped into it.

Dunn was furious. Left alone in the writing room, he stared unbelieving at the door as it closed with a snap. Miss Berryman had taken leave of her senses! Never in his life had he been treated to such a rare display of rudeness. If he had been guilty of a slight flippancy himself, it was nothing to compare with the girl's reaction. How dare she do such a thing to him? No matter what the provocation, she should have sat there politely and smiled at him, waited for him to make some move to leave. After all, she was the one who refused to come to the point. Granted, she had been explaining *why* she wanted him to help, but she had never even stated what she wanted him to do.

Unfortunately, Dunn was too familiar with Adam to believe that he could not possibly be at fault. Of course he wasn't requiring his wife to mop stairs or groom horses, but he was very likely demanding other things of her that would exhaust her in her worn-down state, if she were indeed as poorly as Miss Berryman suggested, a situation that Dunn would not necessarily accept as the whole truth. Young ladies were forever thinking someone was going into a decline.

Without consciously willing to move, Dunn found himself standing in the empty hallway. Had she had time to reach the front of the house? He doubted it. The green baize door opposite him was a swinging door, and even as he glanced at it he noted a whisper of movement as it finally swung completely to rest. Trust her to hide in the servants' area! Giving no thought to how ludicrous he would look if found there, he pushed open the door.

First he tried the door on the right but it gave onto nothing more useful than a storage closet for cleaning apparatus—mops, brooms, rags, pails, scrub brushes, and the like. Inside the door on the left he found Emma perched on the high stool where footmen sat while polishing silver with thumbs made wide by the chore. He had not thought what he would say to her and simply stood glaring down.

"You were supposed to leave," she said, blinking uncertainly.

"I didn't. You have yet to tell me what it is you wish me to do." He extended a hand to assist her from her perch, and with a little moue of annoyance, she accepted it.

She walked stiffly back to the writing room, then dropped unceremoniously into her chair and grumbled, "You showed no interest, my lord. I am perfectly serious in my request for your assistance, but you are intent on ignoring or turning it into some sort of haughty joke. Maggie is not feeling well and Lord Greenwood seems oblivious to the extent of her discomfort. He expects her to continue attending all sorts of evening entertainments which she is not up to doing. My sole purpose in requesting that you call was to ask you to speak to him. That is a slight interference in their marriage, I daresay, but his lordship enjoys such splendid health that he cannot recognize Maggie's very real problem."

Dunn had not seated himself this time but stood by the mantel surveying her with what he considered an impartial expression. "Is Lady Greenwood of a weak constitution, Miss Berryman?"

Impatient, Emma tapped her long fingers in a staccato rhythm against the desk. "No, Lord Dunn, she is not. I have been at school with her for several years and have known her to suffer no more than a slight cold in all that time. She is increasing, enceinte, pregnant! Do you know what that means?"

"Mind your tongue," he snapped. "Why is it you cannot so much as be civil with me, Miss Berryman?"

She sighed and met his blazing gaze across the room. "I honestly don't know. You keep wandering from the point and this is important to me. Will you speak with him or won't you?"

"I will assess the situation for myself, and if I feel there is cause to speak with Adam, I will do so."

"Thank you," she said, rising. "That is all I could ask. They will undoubtedly be at Almack's this evening. At least Maggie will. She is to go with Anne and me." At the stubborn set of his face she shook her head unhappily. "Lord Dunn, I am not trying to pressure you into seeing her there. I know you often go and I thought it would spare you a visit to Half Moon Street. Dear God, if *I* am uncivil, *you* persist in misunderstanding me!"

"Perhaps you're right, Miss Berryman, but if you're so concerned for Lady Greenwood's health, why are you taking her to Almack's with you?"

Emma clasped her hands tightly and forced herself to speak with infinite calm. "Maggie is going with us solely because she believes that she should go out. Lord Greenwood expects her to go out. Occasionally she pleads a headache to stay home but she does not feel she can do that regularly. I believe she should, in her sickly condition. She needs all the rest she can get. What is needed here is for Lord Greenwood to come to the understanding that during these early months of pregnancy his wife does not have the strength to carry out an active social life. I am hoping that you will be able to bring him to such an understanding."

Only with an effort did he bite back a query as to whether he should also attempt to interfere in the rigors of their private life. Her patent attempt to state her goal in terms a child could comprehend made him bristle with antagonism. Was he really being as dense as she indicated, or was she so wrapped up in her friend's problem that she had not clarified her position from the start? Perhaps a little of both, he decided with chagrin. And he should at least give her credit for her concern, which sprang from no more self-interested motive than the wish to see her friend happy and healthy. On the other hand, she was probably exaggerating; *he* had not noticed anything amiss with Lady Greenwood when he had last seen her at the Barnfield ball.

"If I don't see Lady Greenwood at Almack's this evening, I'll call on her tomorrow," he promised. As though it were an afterthought, he asked, "Would you like to have a driving lesson tomorrow afternoon?"

"Thank you, no. As I said in my note, Lord Dunn, I am asking this favor of you in lieu of that promise." She extended her hand in farewell, only the faintest, most formal smile on her lips.

Dunn shook her hand briefly. "Have you lost interest in learning to drive?"

"No, but I realize it was a mistake to cajole you into offering to teach me. One day I may find someone more willing. Good day, sir. I appreciate your coming."

There was nothing more to say. He certainly had no intention of pressing the issue; he had been no more than lukewarm from the start and see how she had treated his first attempt to set a date for the lesson. She had tried to manipulate him like one of her suitors. It was easy enough to forget that he had purposely waited a great deal longer than he should have to extend the invitation. With a stiff nod, he left her.

The door closed silently behind him and Emma stared blankly at the lists for several minutes. Why should it trouble her that she could not be with Dunn for even the least amount of time without squabbling with him? She acknowledged that she was largely at fault for continually baiting him. Well, they had gotten off to a bad start at Maggie's wedding and things had not substantially improved since. Absurd to think of trying to bring the haughty viscount into her train. What would she do with him if she had him? And probably she had antagonized Dunn from the beginning with what her aunt called "enticing."

Emma dipped a quill into the inkstand in a determination to get on with her work, but she found she was only doodling on the pad of foolscap before her, drawing interlocking boxes and circles across the sheet. Amusing men were the most profitable to cultivate in any case—men like Sir Nicholas. Granted, it would get her no closer to a solid match but it would prove the most enjoyable. Lord William and Thresham and Norwood were amusing, too, of course, but they lacked a challenge. Admiration was all very well, but as the start, middle, and end of every confrontation it began to pall. And Lord William was, as expected, coming out of his infatuation. Thresham and Norwood were beginning to make noises of a serious offer of marriage. Emma could not imagine being married to either of them. They were fashionable, likable . . . and interchangeable. She suddenly felt a decided lowness of spirits.

Tonight there would be Almack's, tomorrow the Whinchats', the next day the Cottingwiths'. She would likely not miss a dance, but to what purpose was all this entertainment? If it was to fill her hours, it served her well enough. If it was to provide her with a husband, well, she was no nearer to finding a suitable mate than she had been at the start of the season. And she had begun to question if she really wanted a marriage like that of the Greenwoods or so many she saw about her each day. Of course the Marquess and Marchioness of Barnfield had the ideal arrangement—devoted yet independent, based on a mutual affection and respect. Who among her admirers was Emma likely to respect?

Unbidden, the image of a man in a dark hall slipping into her aunt's bedchamber came to her mind. There had been no recurrence of that episode, at least none that Emma had witnessed. After a full evening's exercise of dancing and the excitement of bantering with innumerable gentlemen, Emma ordinarily fell asleep the instant she climbed into her bed. Not that she would consider spying on her aunt. Lady Bradwell had a right to her privacy. But the mysterious rituals that went on in the bedchamber intrigued her. Emma remembered the exotic sensations Sir Nicholas had aroused in her with his kiss. Small wonder she should link in her mind the ideas of marriage with that nighttime visit. There were, it seemed, some strong inducements for marriage after all.

With an impatient shake of her shoulders, Emma set herself to finalize the list of food for Maggie's ball, its placement on the table and the quantities of each item. Before she had finished she was summoned to the front drawing room to greet two callers, Captain Midford and Mr. Thresham. For the first time she went reluctantly, finding little enthusiasm for yet another half hour of flattery and talk of the betting book at White's.

As Lady Bradwell had other plans for the evening, the Marchioness of Barnfield took Anne, Emma, and Maggie to Almack's. Lord William accompanied them, and though he chatted animatedly with Emma, it was obvious that his infatuation had nearly run its course. His eyes no longer wore that dazed look when she spoke to him and he had lost his own incoherence of speech. Well, six weeks was probably a record, Emma thought ruefully, and shared an amused glance with Anne, who returned it willingly enough, though she could not conceal her concern for Maggie.

Lady Greenwood looked decidedly ill, in spite of the rouge that she had allowed her dresser to put sparingly on her cheeks. Anne had made some alarmed comment when Maggie joined them, but it was brushed aside with a faint smile. At the first opportunity Anne took Emma aside from the others and exclaimed, "She's not well! What can she be thinking of, going out in such a state?"

"She thinks Lord Greenwood expects it. We discussed it yesterday when I called on her." Emma looked about the crowded room for the familiar figure of Lord Dunn and located him in a set with Miss Rowland. "I hope you won't disapprove, my dear, but I spoke with Lord Dunn about the problem. Maggie is enceinte and having a bit of a rough time. I thought Lord Dunn might have a word with Greenwood about the necessity of her resting instead of wearing herself out with all these parties."

Anne raised a questioning brow. "I had no idea you were on such terms with Lord Dunn that you could ask a favor of him."

"Well, I had to exchange my driving lessons for it," Emma admitted, her eyes teasing. "Lord Dunn seems to have some influence with Greenwood, so I hoped . . . I thought it very important, Anne, or I wouldn't have done it, as I know how you feel about interfering."

"I'm glad you did. And Lord Dunn agreed?"

"More or less. He said he would speak to Greenwood if he could ascertain that what I said was true."

"If he gets within five feet of her he cannot fail to believe you," Anne assured her, pressing her hand. "Thank you, Emma. I was really worried about her when I saw her this evening."

Their chance to talk privately was ended by the advent of Mr. Norwood and Captain Midford soliciting the next set, and Anne had no further opportunity to speak alone with Emma for some time. She watched Dunn approach Maggie, but instead of joining the dancing they sat quietly talking as far from the musicians' balcony as they could manage. Anne felt sure that Dunn would be convinced of the necessity to speak with Greenwood, but Greenwood never put in an appearance. When the hour of eleven had come and gone, and no further gentlemen no matter how influential would be admitted, Maggie approached Lady Barnfield to tell her that Lord Dunn would escort her home, as she was not feeling quite the thing.

A set had just concluded and both Anne and Emma stood with the marchioness. Dunn nodded stiffly to Emma and spoke a pleasant word to Anne and her mother before taking Maggie's arm and guiding her through the crowd to the door. Anne pursed her lips thoughtfully.

"I gather you and Lord Dunn did not have an entirely agreeable discussion of Maggie's health," she whispered.

"We never have an entirely agreeable encounter, my dear," Emma retorted. "The gentleman is intent on finding fault with my every move. I cannot entirely blame him, you know. There have been several occasions on which I have not behaved at all well with him.

Don't look so concerned, Anne. I'm sure he has no intention of ruining my credit with the ton. Lord Dunn finds it sufficient merely to snub me."

"He didn't precisely snub you," Anne defended him, "but I will admit that he was odiously *formal*."

"It's of no importance," Emma said brightly. "I am convinced he will speak to Greenwood."

And Dunn indeed had every intention of speaking with Greenwood. As he drove home with Maggie in the carriage, the flambeaux shedding light on her face now and again as they passed through the streets, he marveled that she could keep her head so proudly erect. In her lap she clutched nervously at a handkerchief that she once or twice pressed despairingly against her lips. The motion of the carriage, in spite of its being marvelously well sprung, made her churning stomach heave at every bump and turn. The heat of the rooms and of her own nervous dread of appearing there without her husband had only exacerbated her indisposition. Frantic now at the taste of rising bile, she moaned, "My lord!"

Dunn instantly rapped on the roof of the carriage with his cane, crying, "Stop here!"

Before Maggie could even think what to do, he had lifted her bodily and climbed down from the carriage. Setting her on her feet, he put an arm around her shaking shoulders and held her head down as the waves of nausea washed over her. How mortifying to succumb to this wretched weakness when he had removed her from the rooms and talked so kindly to her! Tears of frustration welled in her eyes. At least he had acted quickly enough that she had not soiled his carriage.

Maggie groped in her reticule for the handkerchief that should have been there, but she had dropped it as he picked her up and he pressed one of his own into her hand. The fine linen only served to distress her further and she stood helplessly staring at it, unable to ruin the monogrammed square.

"Come, come, my dear," he said gently, taking it and dabbing first at her eyes and then her mouth. "There is nothing to be ashamed of. I have a dozen more handkerchiefs exactly like it. You mustn't worry that I think you have overindulged this evening. You're with child, aren't you? Adam should not have let you go out in your delicate condition. Do you think you can bear the carriage again or shall we walk the rest of the way? It's not far."

"If you wouldn't mind, I would prefer to walk," she admitted, her voice almost too faint to hear.

He nodded and gave instructions to his coachman to return the carriage to Waverton Street before taking her arm and adjusting his stride to hers. "The fresh air will clear your head. We're having an uncommonly fine spring, aren't we?"

"Yes, delightful," she murmured, trying not to sound too insincere.

Dunn chuckled. "I daresay it doesn't feel particularly fine to you, Lady Greenwood, just at this moment. I almost prefer London in the rain, though. When the sun is shining and I know life is being renewed all over the countryside, I frequently regret not being in Herefordshire. You spent some time at Combe Lodge, I believe. I've visited there on several occasions with my brother." And since he did not think she wished to do much of the talking herself, he proceeded to recall the occasions and entertain her with anecdotes of Adam as host, carefully expurgated to portray him in only a favorable light.

When they reached the town house in Half Moon Street, he accompanied her inside and instructed that the housekeeper be called to see to her needs. Mrs. Phipps, well aware of Maggie's condition, was waiting in her room for such a call and came immediately. Maggie thanked Lord Dunn for his thoughtfulness and wearily climbed the stairs, wondering if she should attempt to stay awake until her husband returned. It seemed pointless to try; her exhaustion was great . . . and he would doubtless wake her when he returned, as he always did.

The night porter was surprised to find that Lord Dunn had no intention of leaving once Lady Greenwood had vanished from sight. Instead he tossed his gloves in his chapeau bra and handed them with his cane to the porter, announcing, "I will wait in Greenwood's study for his return."

A decanter sat on the massive side table on a silver tray that also held several glasses. Dunn lifted the stopper and sniffed. Adam at least had reasonable taste in brandy, he decided as he poured himself a glass and seated himself at his leisure in the enormous red leather chair. He drummed his fingers thoughtfully on the chair arm, gazing unseeing at the sporting prints on the wall opposite him. There were several by Stubbs and Wolstenholme that ordinarily would have called for his closer scrutiny, but even the Pollard failed to gain his interest at the moment. So Miss Berryman had been perfectly correct, he mused as he sipped appreciatively at the brandy. How could Adam be so blind as not to see that his wife should not be out galivanting every night? A blind man could see—or sense it!

Not that this made Dunn feel any more in charity with Miss Berryman. Quite the contrary. Since she had been right, it now fell to him to speak with Adam, a task he did not relish. Greenwood was a grown man and should be able to manage his own affairs. Recollection of the wedding night when Greenwood had bought the canaries and Dunn had spoken to him brought not comfort but a sense of frustration. Dunn felt he had overstepped the boundaries of good taste that night, for all his worthy intentions. And it was unlikely that Adam had heeded his advice. Why should he?

A good two hours passed before sounds of entry alerted Dunn to the baron's arrival. Adam was astonished to be informed that a visitor awaited him in his own study, and alarmed to hear that it was Dunn. He did a hasty mental recapitulation of his possible sins as there seemed no reason for Dunn to wait for him at this hour of the night except on some mission of disfavor. True, Adam had not gotten to Almack's until it was too late to enter, but then his wife had been with the Marchioness of Barnfield, and he had not specifically promised to join them there. And he hadn't been gambling an unusual amount recently, nor done anything foolish in the way of shatterbrained bets—like Sir Robert and the cricketers. Adam was at a total loss—until it occurred to him that perhaps Captain Midford had met with some accident. He hastened his pace toward the library and swung the door open with an excess of energy, causing it to smack sharply against the paneling.

Dunn winced at the resultant crack and dent in the dark wood and rose to confront the younger man. Before he could say anything, Adam blurted, "Has Stephen met with some harm?"

"Stephen?" the viscount asked blankly. "Not that I know of. He looked perfectly fit at Almack's this evening."

His alarm abruptly eased, Adam felt almost cross with relief. "Then why are you here?"

"God knows!" Dunn indicated the decanter. "I've helped myself. Can I pour you a glass?"

Wary now, Adam grumbled, "You may as well."

When they were seated, Adam eyeing him rather belligerently, Dunn forced himself to get on with the matter. "I brought Lady Greenwood home from Almack's this evening. She was sick on the way here."

"Oh, God, she didn't throw up in your carriage, did she? It takes forever to get rid of the odor."

"You have the sensitivity of a snail, Adam. Don't you care that your wife was ill?"

"Well, of course I do, but she's ill all the time right now." Adam stared at a Reinagle engraving of ptarmigan shooting. "She's going to have a baby."

"So I understand. Adam, if Lady Greenwood is ill all the time, as you say, why do you let her go out every evening?"

Adam brought his startled gaze back to the viscount. "Mostly she's sick in the mornings, I suppose. Has a very difficult time keeping down any breakfast. Sometimes she has the headache and doesn't go out."

"Have you," Dunn asked, all interest, "noticed how pale and drawn she looks?"

"Margaret has fair skin, Dunn. She's always pale. And there's no need for her to look all wracked up. I've gotten her tons of help for the ball, and her friends come over almost every day to do what they can."

"There are some gentlemen," Dunn informed him, his eyes snapping, "who would take a little more interest in their wives. Lady Greenwood is decidedly not well. The very fact of her delicate condition should prompt you to take better care of her. She is, after all, carrying your child. If she were my wife, I would forbid her to exert herself in any way which would do her the least harm. As I recall, your own sister did not disport herself early on in her first pregnancy because of her indisposition. Just because she is enjoying perfect health this time around should not make you lose sight of the fact that women often do suffer discomfort. You do wish your wife to be delivered of a healthy child, do you not, Adam?"

"Certainly I do," Adam barked. "Margaret doesn't have to go out every night. I'm not forcing her. If she wishes to stay at home, there's no one stopping her. On several occasions I have myself carried her a cool cloth to lay on her forehead when she stayed in."

"How considerate of you." Dunn's sarcasm was so thick that Adam blanched. "Is it necessary for Lady Greenwood to point out to you each time she doesn't feel well? Had it not occurred to you that she may never at this stage feel completely healthy? She is a self-effacing woman, Adam, trying her best to please you, and I'm sure she does not wish to complain incessantly. Try to get it through your thick head that she constantly feels rotten. That she only goes out to please you. That she would far prefer to stay at home without having to explain why."

"She never said so," Adam complained. "How was I to know?"

Dunn had begun to pace the room. Perhaps there was no hope for Adam after all. He was too preoccupied with his own pleasures, his own comforts, to recognize the needs and desires of others except in so far as they related to himself. A pity. Dunn paused by the door and said coldly, "Obviously there was no way you could know, Adam. Her friends could see it, I could see it, but I accept that you could not see it. If you are interested in her health, I suggest you keep her at home. Good night, Adam."

Adam stared blankly at the door for some time after it closed softly behind the viscount. Although he was not a particularly sensitive man, he was stung by the import of Dunn's words. The marriage had not been to his liking in the first place, but Adam felt he had handled the whole thing quite successfully. He had not allowed it to hamper his way of life unduly, and his little mouse of a wife had been well received in society. On most occasions he had met her at some function during the evening, and when she had asked him to accompany her to Lady Anne's ball, he had willingly done so. The arrangement was working out a great deal better than he had expected.

Why in God's name should Dunn hold him up to ridicule because Margaret insisted on going out when she wasn't well? She could have stayed home; he wouldn't have objected. Possibly he had urged the wisdom of her attending several functions in the last week, but it was only because the hostesses were ones he thought she would not wish to offend by her last-minute absence. There was certainly no cause for her to go to Almack's if she didn't feel well. The patronesses were not likely even to notice whether she was there or not.

Adam set down his half-empty brandy glass with an impatient gesture and rose to his feet as the clock chimed two. He wasn't even that late. Of course Margaret would be asleep if she had come in some time ago feeling ill. The remodeling of her room at the rear had been completed and she had moved there a week previously. It wasn't as convenient for him but he had not complained, had he? She had stubbornly refused to have the massive bed moved from the smaller room and had chosen to retain the less substantial four-poster that had been there, pointing out that it was more suitable in the light, airy room she had planned. His sister, Cynthia, had agreed wholeheartedly, but Adam somehow felt that it indicated his wife's seclusion from him. She had withdrawn into her charming room where he felt a stranger, overwhelming in his masculinity and out of place.

For the sitting area she had brought a dainty secretary from the back drawing room and several delicate Chippendale chairs. The heavy Axminster carpet—perfectly usable, he thought—had been banished and the floors polished to a rich sheen and dabbed here and there with little bitty Oriental rugs. One night he had nearly broken his neck when he tripped on the one nearest the bed. And the portraits that had hung there had been moved to the hall so that some colorful landscapes could replace them. All in all it was not a room in which he felt comfortable. Each time he came he felt vaguely as though he were invading her private retreat.

Adam told the porter to lock up before climbing the stairs, hesitating at the head momentarily, and then walking toward his wife's room. There was a lamp burning low on the dressing table; Margaret always left it there for him. Adam walked silently to the bed and studied her face in the shadows. At night she slept with her hair tied back, giving the full effect of her slightly sharp features and the lashes that curved down onto her cheeks. She had been too exhausted to remove the rouge, and it stood out now against the whiteness of her face. One hand curled under her chin, the other was hidden beneath the bedclothes, and she lay close to the side of the bed, her side. She looked strangely unprotected.

The covers had slipped down on her shoulders and he gently tugged them back up around her. Even the slight disturbance must have alerted her to his presence and her eyes flickered open. Adam thought she regarded him almost fearfully, the gray eyes unnaturally wide for having so recently enjoyed slumber. Could she possibly be afraid of him?

"I understand you were ill this evening, Margaret. I'm sorry," he said softly, brushing back a strand of hair that fell across her face. Did she shrink ever so slightly from his touch?

"I shall be better tomorrow."

The note of supplication in her voice did not elude him, though it sat oddly with her words. Adam could not for a moment understand what it was she wanted of him. Her eyes never left his face but she lay rigid, almost as though she willed herself not to cry out if he made some movement. For God's sake, she didn't think he was going to make love to her when she was sick, did she? Adam became painfully aware that she did when she whispered, "If . . . if it is all right with you, I should like to rest tonight. The feeling of nausea has not entirely abated."

Dunn's sarcasm had stung Adam; Maggie's entreaty horrified him. She really believed him such a monster as to force himself on her when she wasn't well. How could she have acquired such an impression? She must surely be delirious?

"I was on my way to my room," he said stiffly. "I just stopped in to check on you."

Her eyes dropped, but not before he saw the relief in them. "That was kind of you, Greenwood. I'm sure I'll be better tomorrow."

"No, you won't," he retorted. When her eyes flew to his, stricken, he continued, "You are likely to feel ill for some time, Margaret, in your condition. I don't want you going out in the evenings anymore. You should stay at home and rest. There's the child to think of, you know."

Maggie turned her head away from him so he wouldn't see the traitorous tears that sprang up. "Yes, of course. Good night, Greenwood."

Now what had he done? He had at least planned to kiss her before he left. But if he approached her now he knew almost for a certainty that she would shrink from him. "Good night, Margaret." Abruptly he turned and extinguished the lamp before stomping from the room. There was no understanding women, no matter how patient you were with them, he decided, upset. When had he ever forced her to make love with him? Her enthusiasm for the sport, it was true, was not always equal to his own, but she had never complained or fobbed him off with some imaginary headache.

As he allowed his valet to remove his cravat and coat, he remembered that his sister, Cynthia, had not been at all easy to get on with when she was pregnant with her first child. That was it, of course, he thought with relief. Margaret's illogical fancies were caused by her delicate condition and would vanish with the advent of the child. Unfortunately that happy occasion was months away, he remembered as he climbed into bed and punched his pillow into submission.

CHAPTER FOURTEEN

Anne set down her book as her elder brother Jack entered the conservatory. He was a decided contrast to William, not only in looks but in personality. Where William was fair and only of average height, Jack was dark and tall. Anne often felt that she fell somewhere between them, though luckily she was wrong. If she thought her chestnut hair undecided, others wondered at its magically appearing to change color with the light. Her height was perhaps above average for a woman and she had a rather boyish figure, but her countenance was most decidedly feminine with delicately arched brows, luminous brown eyes, and a cream complexion. Jack towered above her as she remained in the wicker seat.

"Done in, are you?" he quizzed, pulling up a chair to join her.

"Not a bit, though I admit to treasuring a few peaceful moments."

"Would you rather be alone? Actually I'd come to ask if you'd like to call on the Rogerses with me. You and Miss Rogers seem to have rapidly developed a thorough regard for one another."

"We have, or at least I for her. Oh, do sit down, Jack; I'm not that desperate for peace," she assured him. This was her opportunity to do a little subtle investigation of her new friends, and she had no intention of allowing it to slip past. "Jack, Miss Rogers wasn't at Almack's last evening—I've never seen her there—and I was wondering . . . Well, I didn't like to ask her, but do you suppose she doesn't have vouchers?"

"I daresay she doesn't, Annie, but not because she couldn't get them. Harold and Lord Sefton know each other well, and *I* would be happy to secure them for her myself. I'm sure Harold knows that. They probably just don't want to go. Not everyone is enamored of stuffiness and stale cake, you know."

She nodded dubiously and placed the book on the table beside her chair. "Is there some reason they don't go about more in society, Jack?

I mean, I've never seen either of them at an entertainment, except my ball and once at the theater."

"They live quietly," he said, regarding her puzzled face. "You aren't worried that you shouldn't associate with them, are you, Annie? I thought I knew you better than that!"

"No, of course it's nothing of the sort!" Anne ran a finger along the arm of her chair and said carefully, "They're friends of yours. I suppose I take it for granted that if one is accepted into society, one goes about as we do. Well, it's almost expected of one, isn't it?"

"My dear sister, the advantage of being accepted in society is that you may do precisely as you wish, go where and when you wish. The Rogerses simply choose to limit their engagements to smaller circles. I've seen Harold and his sister at any number of dinner parties where there is some opportunity for intelligent discourse. Miss Rogers may not be at ease in large gatherings, but I promise you she holds her own in a lively discussion!"

"I'm sure she would." Anne smiled dolefully. "I can scarce keep up with her at times. But . . . Mr. Rogers. I mean, does he feel the same, or does he shun society in order to accommodate his sister?"

Jack shrugged. "Lord, I don't know, Anne. He doesn't actually shun society; he's as sociable as the next fellow, though a trifle more serious than most, perhaps. That's one of the reasons I like him. Do you want to come with me or not, my dear?" he asked as he rose.

"Let me grab a bonnet and wrap."

Mr. Rogers had a modest house in Argyll Street that Anne had visited on two occasions since her ball. Miss Rogers had once come to Grosvenor Square, but the carriage was not always available to her and Anne actually preferred the quiet of their time in Argyll Street. The house was never swarming with callers as her own often was, though on both previous occasions there had been numerous calling cards on the silver salver in the hall.

The dark-red brick of the facade was pierced by tall, many-paned windows which were gracefully arched but stood in uneven rows. There was no imposing entrance, not even a stair, because the house was set almost at the level of the pavement. The pediment over the door was an inverted V of spectacularly modest proportions, and it echoed the roof line with its short exposed beams under the eaves. Anne adored the house.

Inside the setting was just as unassuming, yet comfortable. Jack and Anne were led by a footman up the stairs to a drawing room overlooking the street. It also had a view of the house opposite, of course, which the present occupant had turned into a fencing studio. Miss Rogers had laughingly confessed to Anne that she spent hours watching the gentlemen learning the graceful but dying sport. "I use my opera glasses and sit back from the window. Do you think it terribly outré of me?" she had asked. Anne found Miss Rogers delightful.

Mr. and Miss Rogers were alone in the drawing room, which was furnished with a silk-covered Hepplewhite sofa of carved mahogany and several painted oval-back chairs. On the walls hung some landscapes done by Miss Rogers, professionally mounted and framed at her brother's insistence. Mr. Rogers did not embarrass her by pointing them out to visitors, but proudly admitted her talent when they were praised. In his own home he appeared slightly less austere than he had at Anne's ball, and the clear hazel eyes were more frequently lit with the humorous gleam she had detected that evening. On each occasion when she had called he had stayed with the two young ladies for a brief ten minutes before excusing himself. But always prior to leaving them he smiled at her, a smile so warm it made his eyes crinkle. Anne thought him charming.

In fact, she thought him more than charming. His presence seemed to affect her entire body in a way that she had never experienced before. She found herself slightly breathless when speaking to him, and noted a tension in her chest that was not altogether unpleasant. But these symptoms of heightened awareness frequently had the adverse effect of making her somewhat awkward. She would lose the train of the conversation and have to beg his pardon, or make Miss Rogers repeat herself. Her hands would become conspicuous (to her mind) so that she had to think of where to put them. She smiled too much to cover her confusion. And yet, for all this discomfort, she made no effort to avoid Mr. Rogers's company. She felt drawn to him, came especially alive in his presence.

And Miss Helena Rogers fascinated her. With her stark white hair, she might have been mistaken, from a distance, for a woman years older. A stranger was far more likely to take her for thirty than twenty, and thus automatically assign her the position of a spinster. Realizing it was unfair of her, and yet unable to block out the thought, Anne wondered why Helena did not resort to the simple expedient of dying her hair. Surely it would make life simpler, make her acceptance by her contemporaries easier. It was not as though she were disfigured in some uncorrectable way—with a squint or limp. A skilled hairdresser could dye the hair to a perfectly normal color and Miss Rogers would appear just as everyone else. It was not as though the young lady relished the difference in her appearance. Had it been Emma . . . Well, Emma would have made the most of a unique attribute, exploited it for the attention it drew. Miss Rogers made no attempt to flaunt or disguise it, but her unease amongst strangers pointed—did it not?—to an unhappy awareness of her difference. She might go about more in society with her brother if she looked more usual.

Lost in her thoughts, Anne was unaware that she had been questioned until her brother Jack tapped her wrist and asked, "Well, my dear, do you wish to go to Ackermann's Art Library? Harold says he promised to take you there one day."

Embarrassed, Anne hastened into speech. "Oh, yes. It's in the Strand, is it not? Papa has all twenty-four parts of the *Microcosm of London* which Ackermann published."

"Yes, I mentioned that," Jack replied patiently.

Helena Rogers smiled understandingly at Anne. "Harold thinks I'm the only lady in London whose mind wanders occasionally. Do you think he believes one's own thoughts could not possibly be as interesting as the conversation going on about one?"

Trying to recover lost ground, Anne gave a mock sigh. "I fear my thoughts are never as elevated as they might be. While those about me are discussing intriguing philosophical issues, I suddenly find myself wondering if I replied to an invitation I had set aside to consider. Mr. Rogers would be quite right in thinking my wool-gathering frightfully uninteresting."

Mr. Rogers smiled at her. "A mysterious thing, the working of the mind. How easily it accommodates both the sublime and the practical. Helena can make a most penetrating remark on the nature of ethics one moment, and the next apply it quite specifically to the running of a household." He gave his sister a fond look. "I admire such a facility."

As they descended the staircase Mr. Rogers spoke of Mr. Rudolph Ackermann, who was not only a bookseller and publisher but a successful coach designer who operated an art school, sold materials for artists, and had provided aid to refugees during Napoleon's oppression. No comment was necessary and Anne found herself staring at Miss Rogers's hair as she followed her friend. But Anne was not unconscious of Mr. Rogers handing her into the carriage and she almost missed Helena's question on a gentleman emerging from the house across the street.

"Do you know that man, Lady Anne? I've never met him anywhere, but you should see him fence! I daresay he doesn't come for lessons at all but for a mere sparring session with M. Persigny. He's incredibly graceful and astonishingly swift."

The gentleman in question was adjusting his beaver hat to a suitably sportive angle, and Anne had only a glimpse of his face before he turned and strode down the pavement, his malacca cane swinging cheerfully. He was dressed fashionably in a blue coat and tan pantaloons that set off his athletic figure. Even as he turned the corner his self-confident air was as unmistakable as his coal-black hair.

"I have the feeling that I've seen him," Anne mused as her brother and Mr. Rogers joined them in the carriage, "but I cannot remember where. Did you know that gentleman, Jack? The one who came out of the house across the street?"

"I didn't notice him, Annie. Sorry. Harold and I were discussing the merits of the bays. I'm afraid the off-leader is about due to be put out to pasture, and Harold said Brackenbury has a bay which might do admirably. I'll suggest that Father speak with him."

Anne grinned at Miss Rogers. "Trust the men to be more interested in horseflesh!"

But both Jack and Mr. Rogers were perfectly content to turn their attention to artworks when the party reached Ackermann's. Several men and women wandered about the gaslit room, where books lined the lower walls and paintings, busts, and statues hung or rested above them. Seated at the tables were further visitors pouring over open volumes, quietly remarking on the shading or detail of a beloved work. Anne found herself partnering Mr. Rogers while his sister explained to Jack that several of the paintings had been done by one of her drawing instructors.

Pausing before a statue of a Grecian lady holding a cup, Mr. Rogers studied her apparel with interest. "She might as easily be dressed for a ball in London in the spring of 1819, might she not? The problem is, I suppose, that the climate of Greece is a great deal milder than that of England."

For Anne it was exhilarating to find herself more or less alone with Mr. Rogers. She wanted to say something startlingly brilliant but found her mind blank of witticisms. "Oh, it's preposterous of us to disport ourselves in flimsy cotton gowns on windy spring days." Anne was grateful that she wore a pale-green wool round dress more in keeping with the weather.

Mr. Rogers cocked his head to one side. "You mustn't think I don't approve of the current styles, Lady Anne. On many woman they are most becoming."

He would not, apparently, go so far as to say they were so on her, she noted, disappointed. But there was a politely admiring light in his eyes. Anne wandered on to a Grecian urn and studied the frieze intently. At her elbow Mr. Rogers asked if she knew the myth it portrayed. "Why, no. Should I?"

"Of course. Everyone should," he mocked her, his eyes dancing. "This is Selene, who drove her milk-white horses across the night skies, allowing her moonbeams to fall on the earth below. The nymphs and satyrs dance to Pan's music, but Selene merely observes from her position above, making the enchantment possible and yet not really a part of it all."

"Oh, a goddess of the moon."

"Yes. She fell in love with Endymion, a handsome young shepherd asleep by his flock, and asked Zeus to give him eternal sleep. Her wish was granted and he smiled perpetually in his sleep, dreaming that he held the moon in his arms. Selene gave him fifty daughters."

"Fifty? Good heavens!" Anne met his quizzing gaze with sham astonishment. "Did poor Endymion despair for never getting a son?"

"Not that I've heard. After all, there were no estates to pass on."

Anne had always recognized the humorous light in his eyes, despite the apparent austerity of his face. Now she could see that the lines about his mouth were not those of asceticism but of frequent amusement. His grin was slightly crooked, to be sure, but absolutely captivating. She had to resist an impulse to move closer to him.

With an effort she pulled her attention back to his story. "Why did she ask for Endymion to be granted eternal sleep rather than eternal life?"

"Eternal life hadn't worked out so well for another such couple. Would you like me to lend you a book of Greek mythology? I have a very good one."

"I'd be fascinated, Mr. Rogers. Thank you." She determined to read every word of it so that she would have something intelligent to say to him. "I may not have a chance to read all of it just now, however. Lady Greenwood is a very dear friend of mine and Miss

Berryman and I are helping her to organize for their ball. Will you and Miss Rogers be attending?" Anne knew they had received an invitation because Maggie had included them on her list after meeting them at Anne's ball. Anne had, in fact, been the one actually to pen the invitation when she and Emma spent a long afternoon with Maggie assisting in the wearisome task.

Mr. Rogers turned his gaze thoughtfully to his sister, where she stood in animated conversation with Jack. "I believe we were previously engaged and were forced to send regrets. The ball is Friday, is it not?"

Experiencing an almost painful disappointment, Anne nodded. "How unfortunate. I know Lady Greenwood hoped to see your sister again . . . and you, of course. During the season there are so many entertainments, it's impossible to attend them all. Sometimes we go to several in an evening, but it's exhausting."

If she had meant to hint that he and his sister might squeeze in the Greenwood ball after some other occasion, Mr. Rogers gave no indication of comprehending. After all, he could not very well leave his own dinner party, though others might. It had been planned for some time with a group of friends who met regularly on the third Friday of the month for a relatively quiet evening of music and discussion, an oasis in the desert of formal entertainments consisting of frothy exchanges and fashion displays.

When Anne turned aside to contemplate a miniature on the leather-topped table, Mr. Rogers studied her unobserved. She dressed fashionably, conversed sensibly, listened with flattering attention—most of the time. Which made her the usual debutante, did it not? And were not her amiable disposition, her sweetness of manners, and her easy politeness precisely what one would expect of a girl of her birth? Wherein lay the difference he found in her?

For he did find her different. Perhaps it was her admiration of his sister, who was eccentric by any standards London society might set. Or again it might be that for all she was being spoiled and petted by the ton, she seemed genuinely unaffected by the attention. There was a laughing gleam in her eyes when she observed the pomposity of an aging dandy, a patient set to her face when she was forced to listen to the inanities of matronly gossip. Mr. Rogers had observed her closely at her ball—because she was Jack's sister, of course.

Anne glanced up to find him regarding her with a slight frown. Oh, dear, he thought her pushing for having suggested one might accommodate two entertainments in one evening. And she had tried so hard to make it sound a casual observation! She bit her lip and felt a momentary—and absurd!—desire to cry. There was no one she wished less to offend than Mr. Rogers, for some obscure reason. Perhaps because it appeared that his good opinion was not easily won.

To dispense with the awkward moment, she asked, "Has . . . has Miss Rogers ever tried her hand at miniatures?"

"No, Helena says she cannot achieve such detail in a small space. Patently untrue, you will agree, having seen her close studies of birds and plants. But I think her real objection is that she finds portraiture alarming. No bird can come up and say, 'It doesn't look the least like me' or a tree protest that its branches have been made to look a great deal thicker than they are." The hazel eyes invited her to share the whimsicality of such a concept.

Anne gladly laughed, as much because his frown was gone as because of his ridiculous examples. "My friend Emma—Miss Berryman—was good at capturing a likeness when we were at school. Alas, she has never spent the time to develop her ability. There were always too many other activities to divert her attention."

"If she couldn't find the time at school, I cannot imagine she will find it now she is out in society." He regarded her with interest. "The three of you—Lady Greenwood, Miss Berryman, and you—seem oddly assorted to have been such great friends in school."

"We are rather different, I suppose," Anne admitted as he led her toward the far wall hung with recent landscapes. "But adversity has a way of drawing people together. And proximity. I don't mean to indicate that Windrush House was such a trying time. I remember begging to be allowed to go there. Mama had intended that I have a governess, but my cousin had gone to Windrush House and told such fascinating tales of the other girls, the dancing master, and Mrs. Childswick that I felt certain it was just the place for me. I can't think why!"

"Because it was something new," he suggested, enchanted by her disclosures.

"Yes, but my own family was a great deal more stimulating—not to mention loving. Once I was there I felt I ought to make the best of the situation."

Indeed, Mr. Rogers thought, Lady Anne would always make the best of the situation. Perhaps that was one of the qualities that so appealed to him. In time, he decided, she would develop into a woman such as her mother, a remarkable combination of beauty, intelligence, and compassion, with a strong will to not only survive but to flourish.

Anne gazed up at him with a grimace. "I hated to be proved wrong, you see, and besides, I found Maggie and Emma were as delightful as any of our neighbors at home. Maggie is so practical and Emma can find humor in almost any circumstance—including Mrs. Childswick. I'm afraid we were a bit disrespectful, though not to her personally, of course."

"Occasionally that's the only way to see yourself through a difficult time." Mr. Rogers felt protective toward her, or so he convinced himself. He was not unaware of how lonely it could be for a child away at school, and his compassion was the impetus, no doubt, for his desire to stroke her glorious chestnut hair. Not that she needed his comforting now, when she was returned to her family, but with his singular ability to cut through the trappings of convention to the core of character, Mr. Rogers decided that a generosity of spirit lay thinly concealed by Lady Anne's social manners and he did not wish to see that rare gift trampled upon by society. He wanted to shield her from disappointments and see that her good nature was not taken advantage of by thoughtless nodcocks who would not realize her value.

He stopped in front of a painting and asked her, "Do you like this scene of Middlesex? I know precisely where it was taken, not too distant from Farthing Hill, my house near Enfield."

Anne studied the painting closely. She did not wish to appear ignorant or say something gauche or artificial. "It's rather flat, isn't it? Not like this one where the sky is alive with storm. And yet there's no feeling of bucolic laziness in the first, either. I don't mean that a landscape need be dramatic to catch an atmosphere!" Anne felt suddenly as untutored in painting as poor Catherine in *Northanger Abbey*—rejecting the whole of Bath as unworthy to make part of a landscape after Mr. Tilney's talk of foregrounds, distances and second distances, side-screens and perspectives, lights and shades. And yet there was no excuse for her hesitation; Anne had been nourished on a diet of some of the most notable paintings of modern and past times at Parkhurst. Why was she so nervous of sounding foolish to Mr. Rogers, who had been nothing but kind to her?

His face had become austere-looking again as he surveyed the painting, obviously attempting to find some justification for her censure, Anne thought uneasily. He seemed wrapped in his contemplation, almost unaware of her presence. At length he mused, "Perhaps it is my own partiality to Helena's work, but her landscape done at nearly the same location has a great deal more vibrancy, I think. Do you know the watercolor I mean?"

"No," Anne admitted, almost faint with relief, "I don't believe I've seen it."

"Hmm, it's in my study. I'll show it to you one day." And he turned from the painting to find her warm brown eyes rather anxiously surveying him. Until that moment he had quite easily believed his concern for her was as brotherly as any he could have felt for Helena. His vision abruptly cleared. Anne's chestnut hair shone in the sunlight streaming through the windows; her tall, slender figure leaned ever so slightly toward him, as though to catch not only his words but his feelings. His awareness of her physical presence was not in the least brotherly, he realized with a sense of shock. Almost as rapidly his mind thrust aside the thought. This was Lady Anne Parsons, daughter of a marquess, sister of his friend. Her family could expect to see her marry well, to have all the advantages of wealth and position. Such an alliance was practically a birthright. Mr. Rogers turned back to study the painting on the wall.

Strolling over to join them, Helena shook her head disparagingly at her brother. "It's the landscape again, is it? Harold can become a great bore about it, Lady Anne. Pay him no heed."

But her brother scoffed at this evidence of modesty and turned to Jack. "Come, you've seen Helena's landscape in my study. Don't you think hers is better than this?"

"You'll embarrass Lord Maplegate," Helena protested, but with no sign of a blush. Anne was continually astonished at her self-possession. It had no hint of bravado or self-conceit, simply a confidence beyond her years and single status.

After Jack expressed polite agreement with Harold, Helena pointed a long finger at the trees in the painting. "His technical perfection is far greater than mine, Lord Maplegate. See the subtleties of green? I had never thought to use such widely diverse shades until I saw his work, but of course," she confessed with a grin, "I shall do so in future. And you must bear in mind that they are entirely different in mood, as well. I fear mine has an almost whimsical quality, while this is far more sober. Harold is influenced by the fancifulness as well. To him everything about Farthing Hill and the county is invested with a kind of magic. The sun is always shining there."

"You exaggerate, my dear," Harold sighed. "Never mind. I don't mean to put you to the blush. Have you seen everything you wish, Lady Anne?"

"Oh, yes, thank you, as much as I can absorb in one afternoon." Now why did she have to put it that way? Anne could have pinched herself for making it sound as though she wished to be included in further expeditions to Ackermann's. Why was she so stupidly awkward with Mr. Rogers?

In the carriage she said little, merely listening as the others discussed works of art on which she felt unworthy of giving an opinion. Thinking that she wasn't feeling well, Jack refused with thanks the Rogerses' invitation to come in for tea. Anne heard with a twinge of regret their assurances of seeing one another the next evening at a quiet dinner party in Berkeley Square. *She* was going with her mother to a rout party in Piccadilly.

And what was worse, Mr. Rogers seemed rather formal in his leave-taking. The distress this caused Anne finally led her to acknowledge the state of her emotions. She was falling in love with this man. But was that wise?

CHAPTER FIFTEEN

"Everything looks splendid!" Emma declared as she surveyed the drawing rooms with enthusiasm. Despite the limited space at the Greenwood town house, she felt the three of them had achieved quite an air of openness with the doors pushed back between the rooms and the spring flower theme running through each of them. Her concern for Maggie was unabated, especially since Lady Greenwood looked, if possible, more pale than usual on the afternoon of the ball. Assuming that worry over the festivities was contributing to her distress, Emma was determined to set her mind at rest. "I've not been to a single ball since Anne's where the rooms looked so fine."

The three of them were gathered for last-minute preparations but had taken the time to relax with cups of steaming tea in a corner of the front drawing room. Emma kicked off her shoes, protesting that they were new and pinched her. As she surveyed her stretched toes in the fine silk stockings, she mused, "I wonder how many miles they've traveled in the last few weeks. When you think about it, the distance must be quite great. Not only walking about the shops and running up- and downstairs at Aunt Amelia's but the dances! Lord, think of traveling about on them for four or five hours an evening. No wonder they protest at being squeezed in such bitty shoes."

Maggie was slightly shocked to see Emma abandon her shoes in the drawing room but Anne merely laughed, saying, "You mustn't forget how many times they've been stepped on, either. I swear not an evening goes by that one of my partners doesn't clomp on my poor feet. It's a wonder all my shoes aren't ruined, and one's bills for stockings become quite outrageous. Mr. Thresham is particularly prone to forget which way to turn. You must have noticed it, Emma."

"Mr. Thresham is a nodcock!" Emma pronounced roundly, a suspicious twinkle in her eyes. "You'll never guess what he's done!"

Maggie startled them by suggesting, "He's offered for you."

"Why, yes. How did you know?" Emma felt the smallest bit deflated to have her news so easily uncovered.

"He has been so attentive," Maggie said softly, "and I really think he's fond of you. I hope you weren't unkind to him."

"I didn't accept, if that's what you mean. Really, he's not at all what I imagined by way of a husband. It's not just his dancing." Emma tucked her toes around the chair legs as though to protect them from marauding feet. "Mr. Thresham hasn't a thing to say for himself. He's not interested in sporting activities, or country living, or town living, for that matter. I rather think some of the other men put him up to it."

"Surely not," Maggie protested, aghast.

"Perhaps not, but I cannot see why he should have gone to the bother. Oh, Maggie dear, I didn't laugh at him or make a jest of the matter, you may be sure. I was decidedly regal in my refusal, telling him I thought we should not suit, and that he was a prince among men. Cross my heart! Still, I found it difficult to take him seriously."

Anne wondered whether it was her imagination, or whether Emma was a trifle less flamboyant than she used to be. Oh, it was perfectly normal for her to make an anecdote out of Mr. Thresham's proposal. Yet she had not capitalized on it the way she might have in the past, going into details that would have ridiculed the young man in a good-natured way. With his high shirt points and his multitude of rings and fobs, Mr. Thresham was a natural target for Emma's wit. Earlier in the season Anne had succumbed to a fit of giggles when Emma described Mr. Thresham's encounter with an amorous poodle in a fashionable lady's drawing room. On another occasion he had been described in conversation with the learned Mr. Camblesforth, and completely at a loss as to what that gentleman had been discussing, confusing two French words of such different meaning that Anne nearly choked on the biscuit she had been eating. And it was true that his proposal must have come as rather a surprise, since Emma had been careful to keep him at something of a distance despite his attentions. That was possibly the most unusual circumstance of them all, for Emma to show some reserve with a gentleman!

"Have you enjoyed the season, Emma?" Maggie asked when there was a lull in the conversation. Both Emma and Anne seemed lost in thought and she assumed her role as hostess was to provide some new conversational gambit, though it had never proved necessary in the past with her friends.

"I suppose so. Yes, of course I have. The entertainments have been lavish, the gentlemen attentive, the ladies accommodating. There is always more to do than one has time for, and yet . . . Well, when we were at school I imagined myself head over heels in love with a dashing blade by this time. I fancied some distinguished peer would glimpse me at the theater or waltz with me at a ball and fall down on his knees forthwith to declare his undying love. I haven't even *met* the sort of dashing blade I pictured!" Emma pursed her lips in self-mockery. "And if I did, I probably wouldn't be interested in him."

Anne eyed her curiously. "Why not?"

"Oh, because my vision had no substance. He was perfectly handsome, had the manners of a prince and the sporting skills of a nonpareil. But that was all he had. The kind of savoir faire I longed for comes with a gambler and a rake, which, by the by, my aunt considers a much-maligned breed. She thinks rakes are the freest of gentlemen, living to their own code to the fullest of their ability. I'm not sure I agree. Take Sir Nicholas . . ."

"Heaven forbid," Maggie murmured.

"No, really, he's not such a bad fellow," Anne interposed. "There *is* something missing from his makeup, however. His charm is taking life not quite seriously, but that is also his problem. I don't think he has any real feeling for other people."

"Exactly," Emma agreed, surprised that Anne should have seen so easily what it had taken her weeks of constant association to decipher. "Don't misunderstand me. I like Sir Nicholas. His conceit doesn't take the form of most of the gentlemen we've met: he's not high in the instep or particularly vain or conscious of his own consequence. He doesn't care much about other people, but what is harder to comprehend is that he doesn't care much about himself, either. That's not to say he doesn't spend all his time amusing himself, for he certainly does. As Anne says, though, he doesn't take himself seriously and there's something most unnerving about that."

"He's . . . rather old, isn't he?" Maggie asked.

"Aunt Amelia's age," Emma admitted, "which is eight and thirty. To me he makes the younger men look like puppies."

"Still, my dear," Anne suggested, "he's old enough to be your father, though I don't suppose many women look on Sir Nicholas in a paternal light."

The strange smile that flickered about Emma's lips gave both her companions cause for alarm. "Hardly," she agreed fervently.

Aware that she might be saying precisely the wrong thing, Maggie could not refrain from speaking. "It has always been my impression that Sir Nicholas is not a marrying man. You never hear stories of his having proposed to anyone, and that sort of gossip usually follows a man of his . . . reputation."

"I doubt if he's ever had the least inclination to marry," Emma said. "In fact, he told me he hadn't."

Anne laughed. "Was that in the nature of a warning?"

"I imagine it was, but he needn't have worried. Being married to Sir Nicholas would offer few advantages, though I can think of one or two." The memory of his kiss did not disappear, Emma found, somewhat to her disgruntlement. It seemed as good a time as any to turn the conversation. "And you, Anne? Have you enjoyed the season?"

"I confess that I like being out; it's a great deal more interesting than not. But it's been tiring, and I find it difficult to know how to handle the gentlemen. Lord Brackenbury is persistent and Sir Arthur Moresby keeps trying to get me alone in a corner, preferably a dark one. I daresay you wouldn't have any trouble with them, Emma, but I do."

"At least they're a trifle more respectable than Mr. Thresham and Mr. Norwood, love. And Mr. Stutton is not above holding one too close when waltzing. Usually I jab my elbow into his stomach."

Though Anne smiled briefly, a frown quickly replaced it. "My family protect me from the unruly ones, I suppose. No, what I mean is, how do you discourage them from becoming interested in you when you cannot return their regard?"

"How can you ask me?" Emma wiggled her toes back into the tight shoes. "I've just told you that Thresham actually offered for me and I assure you I'd done everything in my power to discourage him politely. They have such thick skins, haven't they? Not that Mr. Thresham truly expected me to accept him. He wore the most becoming air of fatality, such as one might when gambling on a sure loser. So you see, Anne, he *had* received the message, but did not choose to believe it. I'm sure Lord Brackenbury and Sir Arthur are aware of your reserve with them; it is their own high opinions of themselves which prevent them from believing you could have no interest in them. Which should quite free you from feeling sorry for them, my dear."

"I think Emma is right, Anne," Maggie agreed. "When you have done what you can to indicate your lack of enthusiasm for their attentions, you must not repine if they are too callous to refrain. I think for all their vaunted graces, men are appallingly insensitive!"

Her companions stared at her forceful expression of this opinion. Meek Maggie had not in the past so much as uttered a syllable on anyone else's faults. Seated in the low tub chair, her face pale but for two spots of agitated color, she clasped her hands tightly in her lap and did not meet their eyes. When neither of her friends spoke, she went on in a low voice, "I am reminded sometimes of what Miss Clements said to us that day we came into London from school. She told us to cultivate our friends and our minds. She said that happiness comes from within and that giving to others enriched your own rewards. I want you both to know how proud I am to have you as my friends . . . and how thankful."

Emma and Anne were as aware of what she left unspoken as what she said. They remembered her hesitant question: "What if someone didn't want to take what you gave?" Miss Clements had smiled sadly and said: "Then you would probably be giving to the wrong person." Was dear Maggie giving her time, attention, and thoughtfulness to the wrong man? How unfair that she, the kindest and gentlest of the three of them, should have her lovely gifts wasted on a man of Greenwood's unappreciating temperament! Their hearts ached for her.

In the silence that followed they heard a man's jaunty step in the hall and the murmur of voices before the door into the drawing room opened and Greenwood himself stood surveying their tea party.

"Oh, ho, I see the three of you are having a cozy chat. I told you there would be nothing left for you to do with all the help you had, Margaret. May I join you?"

Did he still call her Margaret, Emma wondered in amazement. After several months of marriage one would have thought he might have addressed her as her friends did. And how dare he insinuate that they had spent the afternoon lazing about when they had spent hours arranging flowers and directing the rearrangement of the furniture? As Maggie invited him to join them, Emma rose and said, "Anne and I were just leaving. We'll need time to dress properly for your ball. Don't get up, Maggie love. We know our way out."

There seemed no point in discussing Maggie's dilemma as the Barnfield carriage conveyed them to their homes. Nor did Emma feel inclined to impart any further confidences regarding Sir Nicholas. Anne was tempted to ask her for advice on how to gain the interest of a man who regarded you in a brotherly light, but she could not bring herself to speak. So they rode in silence, occasionally sharing a rather wistful smile, but mostly wrapped in their own thoughts, and they parted only to meet a few hours later headed once again for the Greenwoods'.

The rooms were already filling when they entered to find Maggie, her pale face looking more pinched than ever, standing at her husband's side and greeting guests with a smile they alone could tell was painfully forced. Spring flowers scented the air and added bursts of color about each room, but in time there were so many people that they could scarcely be seen. Maggie found that the smell was making her ill, along with the heat of the candles and the press of bodies. Why had he insisted that so many people be invited? They could not be at all comfortable so closely pressed together, so that when one moved one was bound to touch another.

And her husband made a rather unnerving host. He was not used to entertaining such a large or elegant party and he tended to leave the reception area to wander off with a friend. Maggie's nerves began to splinter as she was forced, again and again, to call: "Oh, Greenwood, here is Lord Langham," or "My lord, your sister and Captain Morton are arrived." Cynthia spoke to her brother, but he did not really understand the responsibilities of a host. He was accustomed to the role of guest, of enjoying himself, and presumed that one was expected to do much the same when the ton arrived at one's home. After all, if one weren't enjoying one's own party, would others?

This attitude did not meet with Lord Dunn's approbation. As Adam attempted to walk off with Captain Midford, Dunn gave him such a freezing stare that Adam hastily returned to his post. And since Dunn managed to remain in the reception area until the dancing began, Adam did not make the faux pas again. He might, or he might not, have realized that he was supposed to open the ball with his wife. In any case Dunn reminded him, in the most casual, most offhand manner possible. Adam wished he could have the viscount thrown out.

"The man is incorrigible," Anne muttered to Emma as they watched this charade from the first reception room. "I don't know how Lord Dunn can be so patient with him, or why he takes the trouble, but I'm grateful he does. Maggie looks terribly ill."

"No wonder. One would have to have an iron constitution to put up with Lord Greenwood's shenanigans. Fortunately, after the ball Maggie will be able to have a complete rest. Perhaps we should urge her to go to Combe Lodge for a while."

"What a splendid idea! The country air would do her a world of good. I hope she won't try to dance after this opening set."

Apparently Lord Dunn had the same idea, for he solicited Maggie's hand after the opening set and took her away from the dance floor to stand quietly where she could greet latecomers and speed departing guests. The trickle of departures could not compete with the stream of arrivals, however, and the rooms became more crowded with each passing hour. Emma found her attention wandering from her partners to where Maggie stood, sometimes with Dunn and sometimes with a gentleman he provided for her companionship. Because Dunn was often with her, Emma did not approach her until she saw Maggie double over. To her partner's surprise, she left him standing in the dance floor with only the briefest of excuses, and hastened through the mass of people standing on the fringes. She reached Maggie just as Dunn did.

"Show me where her room is," he ordered as he scooped Maggie up in his arms and started toward the stairs.

She nodded, frightened by Maggie's apparent unconsciousness, and scurried before him. As she reached the stairs, she stopped a passing footman and said, "Tell Lord Greenwood that his wife is indisposed and he should come immediately to her room. Please make no commotion about it. Oh, and send Mrs. Phipps to us."

And then she ran up the stairs, nearly tripping in her flight, and only glancing quickly behind her to make sure that Dunn followed. The upper hallway was bright with candles in every sconce, their flames lighting the portraits that Maggie had caused to be hung there. Generations of Greenwoods impassively viewed the hurried procession down the hall to where Emma flung open Maggie's door, only to find a young couple in each other's arms there.

"Get out . . . quickly," she demanded, not pausing to see that they did but going directly to the bed and throwing back the bedclothes.

Faces red with embarrassment, the couple (neither of whom Emma could remember afterward) allowed Dunn to carry his burden through the door before they fled. As Dunn lowered Maggie onto the bed, Emma dipped a handkerchief in the ewer of water, wrung it out, and placed it on Maggie's forehead.

Anne appeared in the doorway. "What's happened?"

Dunn had stepped back and turned to answer. "Lady Greenwood collapsed from the heat."

"Oh, Lord, it's worse than that," Emma whispered, her voice catching. "I think . . . Oh, Anne, I think she's losing her baby. Help me. Lord Dunn, please see that her doctor is summoned straight away."

"Can you manage?"

"We shall have to. Mrs. Phipps will know who he is. Please hurry."

The viscount gave a cursory nod and turned on his heels. As she turned back to Maggie, Emma could hear his voice in the hallway speaking to Mrs. Phipps. Maggie's eyes flickered open, wide and frightened. "I . . . I feel terrible, Emma. I can't possibly go back down to the guests."

"Hush, love. Of course you can't. Don't alarm yourself about it. I'm sure everything is well in hand and Lord Greenwood will be with you shortly." Emma continued to bathe her forehead with water. "Anne is here, too, and your doctor has been sent for."

Maggie looked from one to the other of them in confusion. Their sad, worried countenances brought the dawn of understanding. "The . . . baby?"

Before either could answer her, Mrs. Phipps bustled into the room, her round form exuding confidence and concern. "There now, what's this I hear of your indisposition, my lady? Dr. Botley should be along in no time for Lord Dunn has gone himself. Will you trust yourself to my care so your friends can be seeing to your guests?"

"Oh, yes, if they would," Maggie whispered, attempting a faint smile at them. "If you shouldn't mind, Emma. It would set my mind at ease."

Exchanging a helpless glance, the two nodded. "Certainly we will," Anne assured her stoutly. "Just send for us if you need anything."

In the hall they encountered Lord Greenwood, belatedly making his way to his wife's chamber, his brow puckered slightly, but whether in irritation or alarm they could not distinguish in the candlelight. He paused as they approached, asking, "Is Margaret better then? If she's resting, perhaps she won't want me to intrude."

"Mrs. Phipps is with her, Lord Greenwood, but I think you'd best go in," Anne replied. "Emma and I will be downstairs to see to your guests and Lord Dunn has gone for Dr. Botley."

"Dr. Botley? Whatever for? I thought . . ." He left the sentence unfinished as a pained cry was heard from the room. Without bothering to excuse himself, he bolted toward the door, opened it and went in, closing it softly behind him.

Anne paled at the cry. "Perhaps we should . . ."

"No," Emma said gently. "We would be in the way. Come, we'll be of more use downstairs."

Adam was appalled by the sight before him. Mrs. Phipps and Maggie were unaware that he had entered, and he saw his wife clinging to the housekeeper's arm as Mrs. Phipps crooned to her and attempted to work the beautiful ball gown up above her waist. A plain cotton nightdress lay waiting on the covers, but Maggie was too racked by pain to assist in the undressing. Resisting a craven impulse to desert the room, Adam moved forward and silently lifted Maggie as Mrs. Phipps methodically inched the stained gown over her head. It was the closest he had come in his entire life to fainting.

"Now, my lord, if you will just hold her while I slip on the nightdress," Mrs. Phipps instructed in a matter-of-fact voice, busying herself with towels and cloths as she spoke. "You'll be more comfortable, my dear," she told Maggie with a motherly smile.

Her kindness was lost on her mistress, who was regarding her husband with horror-stricken eyes. "No, you mustn't . . . I can manage to sit, I'm sure. Oh, Greenwood, your coat sleeve is soiled!" And she burst into tears.

"Hush, hush!" he said gruffly, stroking back her hair. "I have dozen of coats. Come, put your arms through the sleeves like a good girl. Now let me settle you properly." When she was at length disposed easily on the bed and Mrs. Phipps had discreetly picked up the ball gown and taken herself into the dressing room, he sat down beside her, taking her hand in his. "Can I get you something? A glass of wine, perhaps?"

"Thank you, no." She bit her lip to stem the tide of yet another wave of tears. "I'm so sorry, Greenwood, but I think I've lost the baby."

"Yes, well, it's not your fault, Margaret. I suppose the ball was too much for you after all," he murmured contritely, giving her hand an awkward pat.

"Oh, no! It wasn't that! I've had so much help. Ordinarily I'm quite strong. I can't think why this should have happened." Now a tear did escape her eye and her lips quivered uncontrollably. "I hope . . . I hope it doesn't mean I am unable to give you children!"

"I'm sure it doesn't! Pray don't give way to such thoughts, my dear. Is the pain very bad? Shall I have Mrs. Phipps give you a few drops of laudanum?"

"I would prefer to have my wits about me when the doctor comes. Hadn't you best go down to our guests, Greenwood?"

Adam had nearly forgotten that there was a party in progress, though the strains of music filtered through to her chamber. Because he couldn't think of anything more to say to her, he was tempted to leave her to Mrs. Phipps's more able ministrations, but her pale face held him mesmerized. He had always thought her looks only passable, and her ethereal beauty at the moment frightened him. Was she going to die? Was that why there was this special aura about her? Lord, she was only a child!

Her fingers gripped his hand as the pain contorted her body. Women did die in childbirth, and presumably they could die during a miscarriage. He observed the fear in her eyes and wondered if the thought had occurred to her as well.

"I'm going to stay with you until the doctor comes," he told her firmly. "Just rest and I will be here."

Maggie closed her eyes, a faint smile on her pale lips. "I'm glad you're going to stay."

Though he found it difficult to credit, Adam realized it was the first time she had acknowledged a desire for his presence. Was it only her illness, or was she coming to accept him? It was comforting for him to know that his being with her helped her to bear the pain. He didn't often feel of use to her, and her need gave him a unique feeling of strength.

He wouldn't let her die. She was his wife and he would see that she had the best care he could get for her. Surely her gentleness, her goodness, were not going to be snuffed out like some guttering candle. Adam had come to depend upon those essential qualities. Not once did it occur to him that he had not wanted to marry her, that if she died he would be free again. Margaret had become a part of his life, and he intended to have her remain there.

CHAPTER SIXTEEN

"I know you would like to be the one to go, dear Anne," Emma assured her as she nodded her satisfaction at the gown her abigail was holding up for her inspection, "but really only one of us can go, and you have your family to consider. The season isn't over yet and your mama has two more entertainments planned at which you really should be present. Aunt Amelia will go on just as well without me—probably better. I have the nagging feeling that I am cramping her style."

Anne accorded her friend's rueful grin a careless shrug. "Lady Bradwell has never been in better spirits, my dear. In fact, I think she will miss you. Has the doctor said when Maggie will be well enough to travel?"

"*Maggie* says she is ready right now, but the doctor and Greenwood insist we wait until Friday. We'll make the journey to Bath slowly, of course, traveling only a few hours at a stretch. Do you think I shall need the gold-striped gossamer for Bath? I cannot imagine we will be going about much in company with Maggie ailing."

"Take at least three formal gowns." Anne sorted through the wardrobe, holding up several dresses for inspection before choosing her favorites. "These are the most flattering to you and they should do for the warmer weather. Emma, really, won't you miss going to Brighton with your aunt?"

"Not at all," Emma told her airily. "There is bound to be a crush there this summer. Sir Nicholas told me the Prince Regent intends to spend a great deal of time at the Pavilion and you know that means all the ton will be in town. I understand that even if one is invited to dine at the Pavilion, it is most uncomfortable because of the heat the Prince insists on. Bath will be a deal more to my taste."

Anne laughed. "Yes, for I know you are enamored of goutish old men and snippy old ladies. It's very good of you, Emma. I know Maggie appreciates the sacrifice you're making."

"Don't make a martyr of me," Emma protested crossly. "Truly, I'm a bit tired of town and all the gadding about. Bath will seem a regular haven after this hive of activity. It's not as though I were missing a chance to bring some eligible young man up to scratch, as you are. No, don't bite me. You have Langham, Brackenbury, and Sir Arthur all eating out of your hand. I shall be fortunate to escape the attentions of Stutton and Norwood. Think of the trouble I'll be saved!"

Since the abigail had left the room to find another valise, Anne eyed Emma seriously. "And what of Sir Nicholas?"

"I don't deny I shall miss his company," Emma admitted as she set out a pair of tan chamois gloves. "But we are merely friends when all is said and done. I amuse him and he amuses me. Rather a convenient arrangement."

"For a flirtation. Not for a marriage."

"No, I suppose not." Emma was thoughtful for a moment. "Do you think, Anne, that marriage to Sir Nicholas would be better than no marriage at all?"

"Has he asked you?" Anne was astonished.

"No, no. I am merely hypothesizing."

A dangerous sort of pastime, Anne thought, and chose her words carefully. "Being married to Sir Nicholas would not, I fear, be particularly comfortable. I cannot imagine him leading any life other than that he does now. He's quite set in his habits, Emma. I think he would take little heed of a wife, if one could suppose that he would ever marry, not an altogether likely assumption. A woman has some need for her husband's affection, not just his name. There must be interests in common and a similar view of the world. There must be an attempt by both husband and wife to make life together satisfying. I am inclined to believe that anyone who married Sir Nicholas would find herself in a position of perpetually according him his will. Can you see him giving up his *chères amies*, his wanderlust, his pleasure-seeking?"

"Well, no, but I do think he would accord his wife a similar freedom, don't you?"

Although Anne was tempted to disagree, since in her opinion no husband should be so irresponsible, on reflection she assented, adding the proviso, "Which is only to point out that he really would not care a great deal about her, Emma, to let her go entirely her own way. And if that is the case, why should he seek a wife?"

"Why indeed?" Emma sighed.

Anne was tempted, for just a moment, to pose her own problem to Emma, to confess the attraction she felt for Mr. Rogers and her doubts about the wisdom of it. She decided that her position was far too tenuous to do any such thing, but her need to discuss the matter, if only in the abstract, was insistent. So she approached the matter as circumspectly as possible by remarking, "My mother says that people are prone to infatuations, such as my brother Will's for you, but that when such euphoria is accompanied by doubts, you can tell it's not a lasting love."

"Lord, Anne, I'm not talking about love," Emma protested, laughing. "I'm not even talking about infatuation, really. I'm only talking about marriage."

"Don't you want to marry for love, Emma?"

"Well, of course I do, but it is not an option open to all of us. Look at dear Maggie. Not that I am comparing my situation with hers. I simply don't want to remain unmarried forever."

Anne chuckled. "I think there's very little chance of that, Emma. But what if you fell in love with someone . . . oh . . . I don't know, someone who was not of your own rank in life. Perhaps he was a doctor or a solicitor. Would you marry him?"

"Hmm." Emma drew a comb through her blond curls as she considered. "I would have to be very certain that I loved him. The disadvantages are apparent and the advantages might be illusory. It is certainly the sort of alliance one would want to give a great deal of thought. Not that I wish to sound mercenary or snobbish! I am only trying to be realistic."

"Yes, I know," Anne said softly. "Do you think that you could gain control over your own emotions, force yourself not to love him?"

"I should think not," Emma replied after judicious thought. "On the other hand, I believe I would spend a great deal of time with more eligible men in the hopes that my attraction would diminish, that it might be replaced by a more appropriate gentleman. After all, it would be rather a shock to poor Aunt Amelia if I were to marry a man who was in one of the professions, and I should hate to disappoint her. I feel I have some responsibility to my family, such as it is."

"Yes, it's an important consideration," Anne agreed, her face serious.

"What would you do?" Emma turned from the mirror to ask, interested.

"Me? Oh, I suppose just the same sort of thing. A great deal is expected of each of us, and the decision is a permanent one. One would have to weigh one's priorities very carefully." Anne made a graceful gesture with her hand, smiling. "Fortunately, it's not likely to happen, is it? We are surrounded by the most alarmingly eligible gentlemen."

Emma gave a snort of disbelief. "Their credentials of wealth and rank may be adequate, but I haven't met so very many men with whom I would willingly spend the rest of my life. Which reminds me." Emma seated herself in a green velvet elbow chair at the foot of her bed. She was going to miss her room in Bruton Street. Not only had her Aunt Amelia redecorated it entirely to her taste, but whenever boredom overcame her here she could simply wander out into London, attended by a footman, and indulge in the pleasure of window-shopping and people-watching. Of course, Bath offered shops and people in profusion, but Emma's purpose in going there was to provide companionship for Maggie. Her freedom of movement would be severely restricted, by her own choice, but she was not sure being cooped up wouldn't get on her nerves in a very short period of time. She had completely forgotten what they were discussing and considerably startled Anne by asking, "You've become friends with Miss Rogers, haven't you?"

"Why, yes, I see her often." Anne was guarded in her speech. "I had thought, since you will be in Bath with Maggie, that I would invite her to spend some time with me at Parkhurst in the summer or autumn."

"You've mentioned that she draws exquisitely. But she won't allow her work to be exhibited, will she?"

Anne had no idea where the conversation was leading but felt relieved that it remained on *Miss* Rogers. She nodded.

"Do you think, Anne, that, were I to have a drawing master in Bath, I might achieve some degree of skill? I've always enjoyed portraiture and I thought it would give me a project on which to work while Maggie was resting."

"What a famous idea! I was telling Mr. Rogers that you had not kept up with your art since you left school and that it was a great pity, for you showed decided talent." Obviously, Anne surmised, Emma was more alarmed than she was prepared to admit about her seclusion in Bath. Sitting day after day in the house Lord Greenwood had caused to be let in the Royal Crescent would not appeal to one of Emma's lively disposition. Anne felt sure Maggie would insist on her friend taking the air and going out to what entertainments offered, if a suitable chaperon could be found, but she was not averse to promoting Emma's return to the study of painting. "Would you like me to have Miss Rogers search out the name of a suitable drawing master there? I'm sure she or her brother could come by the information with little trouble."

"If you would, my dear. I am persuaded I shall have the time and inclination to paint there. If it would not be asking too much, I should like the fellow to specialize in portraiture. I have a desire to paint Maggie."

"Nothing could be better! I shall send a note round to Helena this very afternoon."

Emma grinned. "There is just one thing, Anne, and you may not approve of it."

"And that is?"

"*If,* and I am not saying it is a certainty by any means, but *if* I should prove to be good at it—painting portraits of people, I mean—then I have no intention of hiding my light under a bushel. If I paint something worth being exhibited, I shall want to see it exhibited. I haven't Miss Rogers's modesty, I fear. But I shall not be the judge of my work, I promise you! I only tell you now so you will not be overset should such a thing come to pass!"

There was a decided twinkle in Anne's eyes. "I would expect nothing less of our flamboyant, generous, kindhearted Emma. If your work is good enough to show, I shall personally see that all of London has the opportunity to see it." Casually reintroducing Sir Nicholas into the conversation to ascertain exactly what Emma's feelings were in that quarter seemed impossible, and Anne felt that Emma had confirmed her own thoughts on the subject of Mr. Rogers (without exciting Emma's suspicions), so she soon took her leave, passing Sir Nicholas on the entry stairs.

When Emma was informed that this caller awaited her in the drawing room she scavenged amongst the notes and invitations on her escritoire to at length dislodge a plain pad of paper and a pencil which she carried with her when she joined him. Her mischievous expression alerted him but he made no comment. After they exchanged greetings and Sir Nicholas was informed that Lady

Bradwell would not be returning much before dinnertime, they seated themselves in facing chairs, Emma propping the pad on the arm of hers.

"Have you been with Lady Greenwood today?" he asked, disposing one leg elegantly over the other. "Does she continue to mend?"

"Anne and I called this morning and found Maggie in satisfactory health. In fact, she is to travel to Bath come Friday, for a course of the waters and a rest. When the doctors consider her well enough restored, she will take up residence at Combe Lodge." Emma began to sketch on the pad, a smile playing about her lips.

"I presume Greenwood accompanies her."

"Oh, yes. He has been very attentive, though I am not at all sure he will stay long with her once she's settled in the Royal Crescent."

Sir Nicholas had been watching with interest the progress of her drawing but his gaze sharpened at her words. "He can't very well leave her alone there."

"But he can, as I am to accompany them and stay to provide Maggie companionship."

"You're leaving London . . . before the season is ended? You astonish me." And if the words were mocking, the swiftly raised brows indicated that he spoke no more than the truth.

"I daresay you think it quite out of character for me to assist a friend in need," Emma quizzed him, undaunted.

"Not at all, but surely it would be more appropriate for Lady Anne to accompany her."

"Why so? We are all friends from school. Anne has pressing engagements in town with her family and I have none." She cocked her head, appraising him. "Shall you miss me, Sir Nicholas?"

"London will seem deadly dull without you," he responded automatically. His sincerity might have been questioned because of the rueful twist of his lips, but he continued, "Watching you cut a swathe through society is more enjoyable than Drury Lane, my dear. Doubtless your esteemed aunt could use the respite, though. When do you plan to return?"

"I have no idea. It will depend on Maggie's improvement, I should imagine. Is Bath dreadfully dull at this time of year?"

"It will be for you," he pronounced with confidence. "You already have London in your blood, Miss Berryman. Bath will seem horrendously flat." His curiosity as to her activity with pencil and pad got the better of him and he made a languid gesture toward them. "What are you doing?"

The mischievous twinkle reappeared. "Why, I'm sketching you, of course. I know few men who would make a better subject. While in Bath I intend to study portraiture and, if you are especially kind to me, I shall paint your likeness in absentia. Then when I return I shall have it hung in my bedchamber."

The baronet gave a snort of laughter. "You really are the most outrageous girl! Sometimes I've a mind to . . ."

Whatever he had a mind to do was never disclosed, as the butler, North, appeared at the open door to announce, "Viscount Dunn, ma'am."

Emma looked about her for a place to hide the pad and pencil, but there was no time to do so before the newcomer strode into the room. "Lord Dunn! Did North not tell you that my aunt is out? She won't return until almost dinnertime."

"I asked for you, Miss Berryman. Servant, Nick." Although Dunn noticed Emma's hasty movement to conceal the pad behind her back as she rose, he made no mention of it and waited patiently for Emma to suggest that they seat themselves.

"Shall I ring for refreshments?" she asked nervously. Why did he always make her feel like a naughty schoolgirl?

Aware of her discomfort, Sir Nicholas, with his most unholy smile, excused himself. In his considered opinion, it would do Miss Berryman not the least harm to sustain a visit tête-à-tête with her most recalcitrant acquaintance. He purposely pressed her hand as he took his leave, making sure that Dunn observed the familiarity, and murmured, quite loud enough for Dunn to hear, "I shall excessively like being in your bedchamber!"

"Wretch!" she groaned, casting a hasty glance at Dunn's impassive countenance. "I told you I wouldn't paint you at all if you were not especially kind!"

"My misfortune." He sighed, and pinched her cheek before striding jauntily from the room.

Emma could not decide where to look when he was gone. Dunn stood a few feet from her, apparently still waiting to be seated, but she could not recall whether he had requested refreshments or not. When she attempted to wave him to a chair, forgetting the pad of paper in her hand, she flushed with embarrassment and dropped her hand into the folds of her dress. "I'm sorry, Lord Dunn, I cannot recall whether you wished refreshments."

"If you please." His voice was entirely expressionless and still he stood.

Realizing he could not sit until she did, and that she had yet to pull the bell cord, Emma almost skipped to it and gave a hearty tug, sliding the pad and pencil into a drawer of the side table that stood nearby. She gave Dunn a perfunctory smile and dropped into her chair with a singular lack of grace. In a strained voice, and not even trying to meet his gaze, she said, "How kind of you to call."

"Balderdash! You wish me at the devil!"

Startled, Emma looked up to see that his eyes were twinkling. Twinkling, for God's sake! The man had seldom done anything other than frown at her and treat her with the coolest of civility and now he was amused with her. How mortifying! "I'm sure," she said stiffly, "I have no such wish."

"Don't you? You surprise me. But then you know Sir Nicholas well enough to . . ." He was interrupted by the advent of a footman who received the instruction for tea with no indication that he noted the strangled voice in which it was given. When the servant had vacated the open doorway, Dunn intended to continue his sentence, but was given no opportunity.

"If you will excuse my contradicting you, my lord, I must correct a mistaken impression you have received. I do not know Sir Nicholas *all that well*. He is a friend of my aunt's and mine, and I make no apologies for that friendship. However," Emma declared, sitting up as straight as possible and folding her hands in her lap, "I should perhaps explain."

"Please, Miss Berryman, there is no need. What I meant to say was that I don't doubt you are well enough acquainted with Sir Nicholas to know that he was deliberately attempting to put you in an awkward situation."

"Well, yes . . ."

"And I assure you I presumed no—ah—wrongdoing on your part. Sir Nicholas could not resist so blatant an opportunity to make a little mischief. As I recall, he did so at your very first meeting."

A flush stained Emma's cheeks, but his regard was not unkind and she said, with some hesitation, "Just as . . . I did on our own first meeting. I've never apologized. I don't think I meant to be rude." She smiled faintly and shrugged. "Perhaps you remember what it's like to leave school and think the world is at your feet, Lord Dunn."

"Very distinctly, though it was a long time ago. Lady Anne

reminded me once that I was not precisely an angel at that time." His gray eyes smiled at her. "Shall we confess to having gotten off on the wrong foot and start again, Miss Berryman?"

Despite her knowledge that he was famed for his charm, Emma had not previously been the object of it and found, to her infinite surprise, that she was not proof against it. If Sir Nicholas spoke with his eyes, the message was of his inner amusement or mocking desire. Not so Lord Dunn. He gave of himself in his smile and his eyes shared with her a feeling of intimacy that made her heart quicken. "I . . . I should like that extremely," she said somewhat breathlessly.

"Good." His lordship raised a quizzical brow. "And though I assured you there was no need for you to explain, I admit to being vastly curious as to what Sir Nicholas meant by saying he would like being in your bedchamber!"

Her lips twitched as she shook her head in exasperation. "Wicked man! I told him I would paint his portrait and hang it there—just as a joke you understand!"

He regarded her thoughtfully. "Was it a joke that you would hang it there or that you would paint it?"

"Oh, I intend to paint it, but I certainly shan't have it in my room! If all goes well, I shall take lessons in portraiture and practice on poor Maggie."

"Ah, Lady Greenwood. I am sorry your intervention did not serve, but I understand she's coming along nicely. Adam said he was taking her to Bath."

"Yes, we go on Friday."

"We?"

"Did he not mention that I am to be one of the party? But, no, it was only finally decided this morning. Maggie would have it that I could not possibly leave London before the season was over, and Anne insisted that she should be the one to accompany them. Such a fuss! As though it made the slightest difference to me! It is Anne who needs to be here for the parties her family has planned." At his slightly frowning look she protested, "I shan't interfere in their marriage, Lord Dunn."

"You mistake me, ma'am. I am merely disappointed that you are to be from town. My hope was that you would allow me to teach you to drive a pair in the coming weeks."

Really, this about-face was too much! All very well for him to suggest they make a fresh start without the bickering in which they had indulged, but to offer to teach her to drive! Obviously my lord Dunn had lost his reason, or had some underlying cause for so abrupt a change. "Why?" she asked suspiciously.

"My dear Miss Berryman, surely you remember that you expressed an interest in such lessons."

"No, no, that won't do!" she cried as the footman entered with a silver tray, which he set on a table near the sofa before departing. Emma was obliged to move her chair closer to Dunn's in order to pour out. "Sugar? Cream?"

When he had expressed his preference and sat back comfortably with his cup, Emma surveyed him with narrowed eyes. "Why this sudden interest in accommodating me, sir? I am ready, to be sure, to dispense with our mutual animosity, but this is doing it much too brown, I fear. I teased you into offering to teach me in the first place, and you have to admit you were not well pleased. I even used the lessons as an exchange to get you to do something you did not wish. And now out of the blue you offer again! What am I to think? Have you merely offered because you know I am to be out of town and cannot avail myself of your generous services? I would not have credited you with such a purposeless scheme."

To even the most casual observer it must have been clear that Lord Dunn was sternly controlling a rising temper. "Must I have some nefarious purpose to show a little attention to you, Miss Berryman? It was my understanding that half a dozen young swains did so on a regular basis."

Emma grinned. "Not gentlemen of your distinction, I promise you! Ramshackle, every one of them! Come, I never meant to set up your back. You must admit it is wondrous strange to see you so reformed in your attitude toward me. But then, I can see that if I persist you intend to revert, and I have no wish for such a step. Can you not be frank with me?"

In truth, the viscount was not at all sure what had precipitated his about-face. Oh, it was easy enough to tell himself that Miss Berryman's concern for her friend showed a merit with which he had heretofore not credited her. Or he could point to her improved behavior with her gentlemen friends—possibly excluding Sir Nicholas. Then again, it might be that judicious consideration had led him to think he had dealt too harshly with her in spite of her failings earlier in the season, and her lack of appreciation of his position. Surely he was not influenced by the memory of her horrified and helpless expression on realizing that Lady Greenwood was losing her baby, or the dignified composure with which he found her later in the evening dealing with the Greenwoods' guests at the ball. Before leaving that night, he had gone to find Adam to offer any assistance in his power; he had discovered Miss Berryman instead. She was standing outside her friend's door awaiting word on Lady Greenwood's condition, and in the candlelight he could see that a tear was coursing down her cheek.

At sight of him she had said, "Never mind me! I am the silliest goose alive," and hastily wiped away the offending moisture with the back of her hand. "Are you leaving? Should I be downstairs to see the guests off? I just came up for a moment to learn if there was any news."

His instinct at the time had been to press her head to his shoulder and murmur assurances that Lady Greenwood would be perfectly all right, but he was aware of the stiffness of her posture and the way she drew back from him, as though he were more likely to censure than comfort her. Momentarily he had been stunned by such a misreading of his character and noted that his response was, inexcusably, anger. Schooling his features, he had said quite calmly, "Yes, I'm leaving and wished to tell Greenwood that he has but to command me if any problem arises. I shouldn't think you are needed downstairs just now. Lady Anne and Adam's sister are seeing to the departing guests. If you will convey my message to Greenwood, I'll be on my way."

No, it was Dunn's considered opinion that he could not be frank with Miss Berryman, as she requested. He could hardly tell her that he had spent a restless hour in bed the night of the Greenwoods' ball thinking of how it would have felt to hold her in his arms. Nor could he admit that he wished to change the unfavorable view of him she certainly held. Why he should desire that she regard him more kindly, even with some of the affection she showed Sir Nicholas, he would not even consider himself.

"Being frank with young ladies," he told her lightly, "is not one of my strong points. Let me just say that I believe I have misjudged you, and feel that for your part you perhaps regard me in a rather unflattering light. I have the greatest aversion to being considered an ogre! Lady Bradwell is a friend of mine and for her sake I think we ought to be friends. I am sure our antagonism has been a cause of uneasiness to her."

"Very true," Emma agreed with ready solicitude. "For Aunt

Amelia's sake then and . . . and because I would be honored by your friendship."

What a surprising girl she was. For all his supposed address he would not have thought to say such a handsome, simple thing to her. Though he sat with her for another fifteen minutes, and spoke on any number of topics, he found himself unable to match that one example of easy graciousness. When he rose, he offered his hand, saying, "When you return to town I shall teach you to drive a pair, if you wish. I suppose you will be back in the autumn."

"Oh, I should think so, and I would be delighted to learn." His firm handshake, unlike Sir Nicholas's intimate pressure, was a model of propriety, and yet Emma was strangely moved by it. He had been out of sight only a moment when she hastened to the side table to retrieve the pad and pencil. Sitting at her aunt's desk in the corner she had no difficulty conjuring up his features and setting them down with bold strokes before they should fade from her memory. Because they showed not the least tendency to fade during the two days preceding her departure for Bath, she reminded herself sternly that Lord Dunn was a consummate charmer, that his decision not to be at outs with her merely illustrated the months he *had* been, and that Anne, if she had the least sense, would capitalize on his close friendship with her family to make him one of her admirers, and maybe more.

There wasn't the least reason to let him cut up her peace . . . and yet she seemed to have no choice in the matter. He would not be ousted in her thoughts by the more easygoing Sir Nicholas despite the latter's fulsome apologies for his naughty display, the posy he brought, and the ride he took her for in the park the last day before she left. Emma was heartily annoyed with herself for this contrary behavior. *Neither* of them could have the smallest place in her future, and she was determined to exhibit a more practical turn of mind when she returned to London in the autumn.

SECOND SEASON

CHAPTER SEVENTEEN

Lady Bradwell came forward with outstretched hands. "My dear Emma, how very well you look! It just shows what a healthy outdoor life can do for a woman. I've no patience myself with this fashion for white faces, though I confess that even in the country I am outdoors very little. Riding . . . Well, I never have cared for horses above half and long walks in the country can be tiring for one of my age."

"Your age! Pooh! I've never seen you in better looks, Aunt Amelia." Emma stripped off the beige traveling gloves and tossed them on a quartetto table near the door. "Lord, I'd almost forgotten how bustling London is."

Her aunt gave her a concerned look. "Have you missed the excitement, Emma? I never guessed when you went off with Lady Greenwood last spring that I'd not see you again until now. You never complained in your letters—in fact, sounded quite cheerful!—but I could not help thinking it deadly boring at Combe Lodge all these months. I had begun to think that you intended to miss the season, and I could not believe that possible. How does Lady Greenwood go on?"

"Very well. Her husband wanted her in town in plenty of time for her lying-in. But you mustn't believe I've pined for the high life while in the country. No such thing! Wait until you see what I've accomplished. And I *do* love riding, and walking, and having the neighbors in to tea. Maggie has such delightful neighbors."

The sparkle in her eyes caused Lady Bradwell to shake her head dolefully. "Trust our Emma to find entertainment in the wilds. I daresay you set up a flirtation with some eligible gentleman in the neighborhood."

"Two of them, actually," Emma admitted with an impish grin. She settled herself comfortably on the sofa and accepted the cup of tea her aunt handed her. "Nothing to signify, of course. Mr. Hill is wild to a fault and not yet of age, and Mr. Bampton is an aging widower with a sharp eye to someone who will take over the management of his obstreperous children. It shan't be me! Still, for various reasons, I found them both amusing, and Maggie was delighted that I should not fall into a decline from being out of town. Poor dear, Greenwood won't allow her to do a thing because of her losing the first baby, and she must sit in the house all day and do needlework or read."

"I needn't ask if he spent all his time in the country, since I've seen him in town myself." Lady Bradwell took a sip of the steaming tea and set it aside. "I trust there have been no complications this time with the pregnancy."

"None whatsoever. Maggie's in blooming health. Even the journey to town didn't tire her. Greenwood came down to escort us—though he didn't drive! And he did spend a certain amount of time there, off and on. Going back and forth to town for him is no more than an excursion. Sometimes he would bring one of his cronies, usually Captain Midford, and we had quite a lively time." Emma reached over to squeeze her aunt's hand. "But it's lovely to see you again, my dear, and I am grateful that you're willing to see me through another season. How is Lord Bradwell?"

Amelia smiled, a tender, whimsical light in her eyes. "Much as usual. Cross as a hornet to interrupt his sporting for a lot of entertainments, but pleased with himself to have done so. A bit of gout these days, too, which hampers him. Really, we were remarkably content when he had his legs all swathed in bandages for a week and I sat and read to him. I'd forgotten how droll he can be. His comments on the book I was reading—*Marriage*—were excessively amusing. He didn't at all like the doctor's orders to reduce his consumption of port! And growled when I set out to follow them to the letter. I'm sure he was delighted to see my heels." She expelled a small, wistful sigh, but immediately brightened. "Several gentlemen have called to see when you were returning. Mr. Stutton seemed especially eager to see you, and Sir Nicholas declares the little season in the autumn was decidedly flat with you away. I'm planning a small dinner party tomorrow night to welcome you back, with just a few of our closest friends."

"How kind of you." As casually as she could, Emma asked, "Who is coming?"

The list included Sir Nicholas but not Lord Dunn, and Emma hid a twinge of disappointment. She had thought a great deal about the viscount while she was in Bath and subsequently at Combe Lodge. Despite Maggie's protests that she would do very well, and that Emma should return to Lady Bradwell in the autumn, Emma knew that Lord Greenwood's frequent absences were hard on her friend. There was always the fear of another miscarriage, and the problem that Maggie at first knew few of her neighbors in High Wycombe.

And Emma was not ready to be distracted by the continual round of activity in London. She took her painting seriously from the first day Mr. Rodford, the drawing master, came for a lesson. In deference to her enthusiasm, Maggie had a studio prepared for her use at Combe Lodge when they removed from Bath. Emma's first endeavors were less than successful, but she was determined and had a great deal of native talent, and by the third time she had painted Maggie they both knew she had achieved something special. Not only were the coloring and features true to life, but she had captured the strong character about Maggie's face and the gentleness of her eyes.

Since this last attempt had only been finished toward the end of November, Emma had secreted it away in a closet before Lord Greenwood descended on his ancestral home for the Christmas season. He was aware, of course, of her previous efforts to paint his wife, and had so far exerted himself as to offer her his opinion as to her artistic faults, but he was allowed no sight of the final portrait until Christmas morning when Emma presented it to him. The painting was set on an easel in a corner of the green saloon, covered with a velvet drapery. Greenwood raised his brows in a mocking question and Maggie watched anxiously as he unveiled it. His complete astonishment made Emma laugh and Maggie blush with pleasure as he exclaimed, "By God, you've quite captured her, Miss Berryman! This is just how I think of her when we're apart!" Emma was surprised to learn that he thought of his wife at all when they were not together.

Settling into the pattern of life in Bruton Street presented no problems. Her aunt ran a rather casual household where butler, housekeeper, footmen, cook, gardener, and various housemaids went about their light duties with a good will generated by Lady Bradwell's generous heart. Emma found the male servants especially willing to assist her in any way, and with her aunt's permission she set up her studio in the minuscule conservatory to the rear of the house. From time to time Amelia had considered having it torn off and a ballroom built to replace it, but the expense would have eaten into the budget she allowed herself. As far as Lord Bradwell was concerned there were no limits put on her spending, but she had, out of an innate sense of fairness and honesty, devised a rather haphazard budget for herself to which she strictly adhered, despite her husband's lack of interest in reviewing her expenditures. She was delighted to see the conservatory put to some use, as she had never enjoyed the cloying atmosphere of the thick-leaved green plants and never took enough care of the area to see any actual blooms.

Given free rein with the area, Emma heartlessly disposed of the majority of sickly plants, placing them in Maggie's tender care to thrive once more in Half Moon Street. Large expanses of glass allowed the proper amount of light for her projects, though on sunless days the room was appallingly cold. Emma merely draped herself in shawls and often painted while wearing a pair of gloves too old to grace any public appearance.

On the evening of the dinner party she had only just begun her preparations in the conservatory, but she took Anne and Sir Nicholas to view his portrait where it leaned against the wall. It had been difficult, with him not posing, to remember every detail, despite the sketch she had made, but there was no denying, even at the briefest glance, that she had translated to canvas the rakish sophistication he exuded.

"My word!" Anne exclaimed, staring first at the portrait and then at Sir Nicholas himself. "Emma, when did you have time to do this? I had no idea Sir Nicholas had sat for you."

"I didn't," he retorted, shaking his head. "Miss Berryman made a quick sketch one day before she left for Bath. And I thought," he mused, his eyes sparkling, "that you had another location altogether planned for your work of art!"

Ignoring his attempt to fluster her, Emma smiled benignly on him. "You misunderstood, I presume. Now that you are here beside it, I can see that the coloring is slightly off. I believe I have improved on you." She laughed.

Vaguely disquieted by their familiar raillery, Anne interjected, "But it's famous, Emma! Do you intend to exhibit it?"

"Exhibit it!" Sir Nicholas bellowed, stunned. "Have you a mind to make me the laughingstock of society? Painted to look like the original sinner by a mere slip of a girl? Hung up on some gallery wall alongside glowering dowagers? I won't have it."

Emma was not the least concerned with his diatribe. "Come, Sir

Nicholas, no one would think any less of you." Her lips twitched at the double entendre of the statement and she shared a grin with Anne. "I promised Lady Anne I would not exhibit the paintings unless they were adjudged worthy. Whom shall we have appraise them, Anne? Not Sir Nicholas. I am convinced he hasn't an eye for such things and he is too nearly involved in any case. Your brother perhaps—Lord Maplegate, that is. Would you consider his decision adequate?"

"He's not in town just now," Anne informed her, hastening to add, "but I think Helena's brother, Mr. Rogers, would be more than willing. He takes such an interest in Helena's work and is undoubtedly the most knowledgeable gentleman I have met concerning modern works of art. Have you more than just this one?"

"Oh, yes. There is one I did of Maggie, but I gave it to Lord Greenwood. And I did one of Mr. Hill and another of Mr. Bampton when we were at Combe Lodge. I can't seem to get Lord Greenwood himself quite right yet, but I'm working on it." Somehow she found it impossible, in front of Sir Nicholas, to admit that her favorite was that of Lord Dunn, which was indeed in her bedchamber, though not hanging on the wall. She kept it there under a dustcover and hidden behind two boxes of hats so that no one would see it, but now and again when she was alone she brought it out and studied it. Sometimes she would think that it needed a different shade of brown for the hair, or a bit more firmness to the chin, but she found she could not change it.

Even once when she had brought it out a month after it was finished at Combe Lodge and actually set it on the easel and prepared her pallet with paints, she could not force herself to make the first stroke. It was finished—for good or ill. Her original perception of his character had not allowed her to show the traces of amusement that had temporarily exhibited themselves on the last occasion on which they had met. Somehow it was easier to portray him with his air of reserve tinged with disapproval than as a more human sort of being. There was a haughty lift to his brows, and a slight pursing of his lips, though his eyes—well, his eyes did hint, just the tiniest bit, that he was not entirely devoid of humor. Emma could go no farther than that.

Sir Nicholas, his indignation far from assuaged, was regarding Emma with narrowed eyes. "And you propose to exhibit me with two country bumpkins, do you? I say, Miss Berryman, it's downright cruel of you. You said you would place my portrait in your—"

"No, no, Sir Nicholas," she interrupted. "Pray spare Lady Anne my little jest. I tell you what I shall do. I shall have it hung in a frame without any indication of your identity. It will say, quite simply, 'The Rake' "

Not proof against her dancing eyes, he laughed. "Oh, very well, Miss Berryman! But allow me first option to buy it. The thought of that painting hanging in some cit's picture gallery as a fake relation makes my blood run cold. Nor would I fancy it in some old lady's book room being pointed out to her nieces and nephews as an example of what will become of them if they go astray, like one of Hogarth's gruesome Progresses."

"You may have first chance to buy it, but not until it's been shown. And I shall expect Mr. Rogers to set a price on it." She turned to Anne with a deprecating smile. "That is, if he thinks it's worthy of showing. Otherwise, I suppose I shall have to give it to Sir Nicholas. I can't think who else would want it."

Arrangements were made for Emma to call on Anne before the two of them adjourned to the Rogerses' house. Emma suspected that Anne wished to prepare her for the possibility of Mr. Rogers's not thinking the paintings quite well enough done actually to display to the discriminating London connoisseur. And maybe they weren't, Emma thought, worried. She had enjoyed every moment while she worked on them, and was personally pleased with the results, but she was, after all, an amateur, barely instructed in the art of portraiture. In Bath and at Combe Lodge she had studied the compositions and elements involved in the paintings that hung in houses she visited and the Greenwood gallery. And capturing a likeness was not at all the same as painting a successful portrait, she reminded herself as she assured the footman she could find the back drawing room in Grosvenor Square.

Lord William and Anne were standing by the open window, he with his quizzing glass to his eye and she tugging at his sleeve. "I swear one daren't let you out of doors at this time of year, Will," she protested, laughing. "What charmer has caught your attention now?"

Indignant, Will retorted, "You're one to talk, Anne. A fellow can't make his way through the hall without stumbling over one of your suitors once we're in town. Mercifully only a portion of them make their way to Parkhurst and spend most of their time unable to find the drawing room."

Emma's giggle made the two of them swing around, at first alarmed and then smiling, as she said, "So Anne is accumulating beaux like ribbons, is she? I've been out of London too long."

"Miss Berryman! How good to see you again." Will raised her hand to kiss with more speed than elegance and proceeded to elaborate on the preceding conversation. "One poor fellow was actually lost at Parkhurst until a party of footmen were dispatched to track him down. The experience so unnerved him that he never found the courage to declare himself. Which was all for the best! He would not have made Anne a particularly fitting life's partner."

"Hush, Will," Anne urged, but her brother paid no heed.

"Poor Langham took himself off in one devil of a hurry. Now Brackenbury! You won't credit this, Miss Berryman, but the man actually took a tumble from his horse when he was merely galloping across a field. Imagine! Not that it did him the least harm . . . Practically made it to the house before his horse got to the stable. And do you know why?"

Intrigued by his obvious annoyance with the dismounted earl, Emma encouraged him to continue. "Why?"

"He followed his nose! There never was a man who could tell so precisely when Cook had baked a batch of lemon tarts. Not one left by the time *I* got home."

"Ah, I see," Emma said as she took the chair Anne indicated.

"I can't stay," Will declared, heading for the door. "Must go round to White's. Promise me you'll save me a dance at the Alderley ball."

"With pleasure." Emma watched Anne shake her head ruefully as the young man disappeared. "Anne, may I ask you something?"

"Certainly."

"Have you decided to accept one of your suitors?"

Anne flushed. "Lord, Emma, you would think I had a whole army of them!"

"Your brother makes it sound as though there have been several. And yet you didn't write anything about them. I won't believe none of them has come up to scratch!"

"Unfortunately," Anne retorted, her eyes demurely downcast, "it has become fashionable to offer for me."

"Yes, that is indeed unfortunate," Emma agreed, sighing. "Can't you like any of these gallants?"

Anne cocked her head and played with the lace at her wrists. "Oh, I like some of them well enough as friends, Emma, but hardly for a husband. It's the very devil having a large dowry. You can't be sure when they look at you whether they're seeing your face or a bag of gold sovereigns. And some of them are half in love with Mama and simply see me as an available substitute."

Convinced that Anne was avoiding the issue with her light banter, Emma was disappointed but strove to conceal it. After all, Anne had a right to confide in whom she chose. Was it only a year ago they had been so close, sharing every girlish secret? Their secrets were not so girlish now, Emma realized, and there were some she would not choose to confess, either.

As though reading her mind, Anne regarded her seriously. "One is often silent in matters of the heart, isn't one? Sometimes, I suppose, it's pride, but I like to think it's the delicious treasuring of a delicate bud, which one is afraid a strong wind will blow away, or the glare of daylight will wither. You don't want all the world to know, for fear they will spoil it; you don't want even your closest friends to guess for fear you are mistaken."

"Yes," Emma agreed quietly, "I know."

"Have you brought your pictures in the carriage? I could have had Mr. Rogers come to Bruton Street."

"I preferred to take them there. Then I shall have the opportunity to see Miss Rogers's work as well."

Anne nodded, a small frown creasing her brow. "Emma, Mr. Rogers is very honest in his opinions and I have asked that he be quite frank with you. Perhaps I should not have done so, but . . ."

"Ah, my love, don't fear for my feelings. It was only after Greenwood's criticisms, ramshackle as they were, that I was able to do Maggie's portrait to my satisfaction. I'm sure Mr. Rogers's help will be vastly appreciated. I don't really need to show them, you know. Shall we go?"

Emma was charmed by the house in Argyll Street and encouraged by the welcome she received from Helena and Harold Rogers, though she had met them only once before, at Anne's ball. The friendship that had grown up between the two women had not included her, as yet, which was not to be wondered at when she had been out of London the greater part of the time since then. A footman carried in her wrapped paintings and set them carefully in the hall. Emma knew a moment of panic, almost wishing she had never decided on this course, but Helena caught her eye, smiling with understanding.

"We should get the moment of truth over with immediately"—she laughed—"and then we can all sit down and be cozy over a cup of tea. I'll have Phillips add a jot of brandy to yours, Miss Berryman, should you need it!"

The paintings were unwrapped right there in the hall, and Mr. Rogers directed they be placed on the mantel one at a time. By chance, the portraits of Mr. Hill and Mr. Bampton came first, and having no familiarity with the sitters, Mr. Rogers could judge them solely on their artistic and technical merit. He made few comments, and those of a slightly critical but constructive nature. Next came Sir Nicholas, at which Helena exclaimed, "Gracious, how absolutely perfect! Look, Anne, how she has conveyed so much by the devilish gleam in his eyes. I swear I've seen him look just so."

"You should have seen how he looked when he saw it," Anne laughed. "He said Emma had made him look like the original sinner."

Mr. Rogers had been standing, hand on hip, surveying the painting, but he turned now to smile at Anne. "Who can blame him? Miss Berryman has indeed invested him with a most uncanny roguish quality. What I find remarkable, though, is that she has suggested, in addition, his good humor and his air of fashion. There is nothing depraved about him despite the suggestion of rakishness. A difficult resolution to accomplish, I promise you."

As Emma murmured her thanks for his kind words, she watched nervously while the footman lifted the last canvas from its protective covering. No one had seen this portrait as yet, but she had been unable to leave it in the obscurity of her closet. By way of explanation, she hastened to say, "Both the painting of Sir Nicholas and this, of Lord Dunn, were done from sketches I made of them before I left town. Mr. Hill and Mr. Bampton sat for me, so it was easier to portray them more exactly. I . . . I don't know Lord Dunn so well as Sir Nicholas but I thought . . . Well, he does have rather interesting features and . . ." She stumbled off into silence, trying to observe her audience's reaction.

There was a stunned silence. Shock at her audacity? she wondered. Certainly none of them would believe that Dunn had given her permission to paint him. To suppress the flush that threatened to rise to her cheeks she reminded herself that she didn't have to have his permission. She could paint whomever she wished! It occurred to her that she might tell them that she was currently painting her aunt and working on the portrait of Greenwood, but she found she could not say anything at all.

As though they were one, her three companions stepped closer to the portrait, leaving her to stand alone by the canvases that had already been exhibited. Her heart sank as she heard one of them say, "Fascinating," the way one would when one couldn't think of any more appropriate comment. Anne slowly turned to face her.

"Why didn't you tell me you'd done this one?"

Emma shrugged. "Oh, I'd put it away. I haven't seen Lord Dunn since I've been back and had nothing to compare it against, as I did with Sir Nicholas. I just thought you might be interested in it because you know Lord Dunn."

"But, Emma, it's incredible! You don't seem to realize what you've accomplished." She laid a hand gently on Mr. Rogers's arm to gain his absorbed attention. "Don't you think so? The portrait absolutely breathes. I've seen one done of him a few years ago that he commissioned for his family portrait gallery and it can't hold a candle to this!"

Mr. Rogers grinned at Anne and placed a hand over her fingers. "Now don't be too hard on Carlson's painting, my dear Lady Anne. I suggested him to Dunn and he did very well. True, he hasn't caught quite the same essence as Miss Berryman has, but it was a perfectly adequate painting. You say his lordship didn't sit for you?"

"No," Emma admitted, "he didn't even know that I sketched him. The thing was that I had just sketched Sir Nicholas when he called, and the pad and pencil were there, and . . ."

"I see."

Emma had the odd sensation that Mr. Rogers did indeed see and lowered her eyes as she mumbled, "There weren't all that many subjects for me to work with, being out of London."

"No, of course not," Anne readily agreed. "And I should think he would like it, don't you, Helena?"

Her friend had been studying the portrait, a strand of her pure white hair twined round her finger. "Hmm, yes," she said absently, not shifting her eyes. "Harold, he looks quite a bit like my fencer, doesn't he?"

Surprised, her brother turned his skeptical attention once again to Lord Dunn's likeness and his brows lifted slightly. "Why, he does rather."

Emma's confusion was evident to Anne, who explained, "Helena has done a painting of a man who takes fencing lessons across the street. I'm sure I've seen him but I can't for the life of me place who he is. And he does rather look like Lord Dunn at that."

"Not Captain Midford?" Emma asked.

"Oh, no. Actually he looks more like Lord Dunn than Captain Midford does."

Emma turned to Helena. "May I see the painting?"

After a brief protest that she was new to this type of work, Helena allowed the painting to be brought to the hall and placed on the mantel, explaining her "absurd" habit of watching the fencers through opera glasses. Never having been privileged to see anyone fence, Emma was fascinated by the stance and the foils, but even more so by Helena's obvious skill . . . and by the face of the man.

"I've seen him," she declared, after offering fulsome praise for the work. "Give me a moment and I shall recall his name. Aunt Amelia introduced me to him once or twice last season. Now where . . . Oh, I remember. At the Hardwood ball, it was. He came very late and had time for only one dance, and he chose Aunt Amelia. Something to do with a hat, I believe. Ah, yes, Hatton. Mr. Hatton."

Anne shook her head in mock exasperation. "Something to do with a hat indeed! Is that how you remember names? My dear Emma, you never cease to amaze me."

"Mr. Hatton." Helena, who had observed her fencer off and on for better than two years, tried out his name for the first time. Then she laughed. "It suits him, you know. Each time when he leaves he sets his hat at a jaunty angle before striding off down the street. Come, the hall is drafty. Let's have tea in the drawing room and Harold can tell you whether he thinks your paintings should be exhibited." She linked her arm with Emma's and whispered, "*I* do."

Mr. Rogers, following with Anne, easily overheard this remark and smiled. "Not for the world would I have any other sister than Helena, but you must admit, Lady Anne, that she's an impish baggage. Opinionated, too. And to top it off she knows very well that I think the paintings are excellent. She just wants to get her oar in first."

Their progress up the stairs was halted when Emma swung around to stare at him. "You really do? You think they're good?"

"More than good, Miss Berryman. You have a real talent. I would caution you, though, that they are not perfect. You have a tendency to disregard the background, which can be distracting. Of course, I must remember that two of the gentlemen didn't sit for you and a setting was left to your imagination. However . . ."

Though Emma listened carefully to his strictures, and felt a vast relief that she was not deluding herself, another worry was beginning to nag at her. When they were settled over cups of tea, she asked hesitantly, "Do you think, if I wish to exhibit them, that I should . . . well, tell Lord Dunn first? I mean, he might be just the tiniest bit annoyed to have his portrait on display. Sir Nicholas didn't like the idea but he agreed."

"Just the tiniest bit annoyed!" exclaimed Anne, almost spilling her tea. "For God's sake, Emma, he would be livid! Of course you must tell him! And get his permission. I feel sure he would grant it, if you were to but ask. Dunn is . . . well, he's a proud man, but I'm sure he wouldn't stand in the way of your . . . your art."

"It does sound extravagant, doesn't it?" Emma asked cheerfully. "MY ART in capital letters, as though there were something sacred about it. I don't really feel the way I did before I started, you know. That was just whistling in the wind. Now that I've found what hard work it is, and what pleasure it gives me, it's enough to simply have done them, and to go on doing them. I suppose I wanted Mr. Rogers's opinion not because it might allow me to exhibit them but simply so that I would know whether I was living in a dream world. I have a very special feeling when I'm working, as though I were having a conversation with the subject, learning what sort of person he or she is. I'll take the paintings home and . . . and perhaps give them to the subjects."

"No," Mr. Rogers insisted. His three companions stared at the firmness of his tone. "I realize that Helena's modesty prevents her from exhibiting her watercolors, but I do not think Miss Berryman suffers from the same problem, and I would like very much to have her work exhibited at a gallery I am associated with in Bond Street. I refuse to have the myth perpetuated that half of our race has no observable creativity in the field of art. If Madame D'Arblay and Miss Edgeworth and Mrs. Radcliffe are willing to expose their writings to the public eye, there is no reason why Miss Berryman should not expose her paintings as well, with no apologies for her gender." With a rueful grin he cocked his head at Emma. "Am I wrong? Would you mind being the object of a little curiosity and perhaps even censure? My fellow art admirers may be a trifle critical just because you are a woman, but I would gladly stand behind you. We have the precedent of Angelica Kauffmann, of course, and one hopes more enlightened times. What do you say, Miss Berryman?"

Never able to resist a challenge, Emma nodded. "Put so forcefully, I could hardly decline. I promise you I am flattered, Mr. Rogers, and I would try not to be dejected by any untoward comments on my work or my person. But I have not the slightest idea how to go about anything, and frankly, I'm not very interested in making arrangements."

"I will see to everything. Just leave the paintings with me."

Emma caught Anne's eyes. "Very well, except that of Lord Dunn. I will take it home with me and speak with him before I make a decision on whether to exhibit it."

"I'm sure he'll agree," Anne told her confidently. She found Mr. Rogers's gaze on her, warm and approving. There had been no change in her affections, despite her continuous association with half a dozen eligible gentlemen. Her pulse still quickened when he permitted the full force of his intense eyes to rest on her. Her senses, which seemed only half awake when she was not near him, came alert in his presence. With her heightened awareness, she could see more clearly the faces around her, understand more thoroughly the philosophical discussions, even taste more precisely the subtle flavors of the unusual cakes Helena served for tea. Only her original awkwardness had disappeared.

Acknowledging that this euphoria she felt was similar to that of which her mother had spoken the previous year, Anne nevertheless recognized that her feelings for Mr. Rogers were not merely an infatuation. She did not disregard the difference in their social positions: though his was a perfectly acceptable place in society, he had no title and only a modest fortune by the standards of the ton. These drawbacks did not in the least deter Anne: she felt quite certain now that she knew her own heart. Her admiration of Mr. Rogers's finer qualities left no room for doubts about the disparity in their fortunes. Her love was not blind, but radiantly clear. He was a gentleman, above all: a fine, distinguished gentleman. But Anne did realize that Mr. Rogers's financial and social deficiencies might influence others, and especially Mr. Rogers himself.

As she and Emma left, Mr. Rogers took her hand, smiling, and carried it to his lips. He rarely did this, and when he did there was a quality about it that suggested he was doing it against his will, unable to refrain. But he pressed her hand before letting it go, saying calmly, "Thank you for bringing Miss Berryman, Lady Anne. Do come again soon and help me convince my sister to show at least one of her works at the same time."

Anne nodded, and suppressed a sigh.

CHAPTER EIGHTEEN

"If you would just turn your head a slight bit toward the right."

Lady Bradwell did as she was instructed, beaming on her niece, who stood across from her in an old sprigged muslin gown liberally spattered with paint. Two wisps of blond hair had escaped the knot at the back of her head and hung unnoticed on either side of her intent face. Emma delicately touched brush to canvas, remarking after a moment, "Yes, I think that will do for the present, Aunt Amelia. Are you frozen? The sun seems to have disappeared."

"Not at all, my love," Amelia assured her, rising to stretch her legs and shake out the skirt of her pearl-gray kerseymere gown. "May I have a look at it?"

"Certainly. You've been wonderfully patient, Aunt Amelia."

Emma could see the footman through the glass doors that led into the house and motioned him to enter. When he informed them that Viscount Dunn had been directed to the front drawing room, Emma took a deep breath, as though she had just been called to Mrs. Childwick's office at school. "You run along and join him, Aunt Amelia. I must speak with him, but I shall have to change first."

"Of course, dear."

It was ridiculous to feel so nervous, Emma scolded herself when her aunt had left her alone in the studio. What could he say but that he did not wish for her to exhibit the painting? When she had seen him the previous evening at a rout party, he had been gratifyingly attentive, had even grinned when she asked if he would come to call soon, as she had a matter she particularly wished to discuss with him. "Ah, your driving lessons," he had teased. "I see you are not to be put off now you are back in town. Your absence was a great deal longer than you led me to expect, Miss Berryman." And she had found herself, instead of correcting his misunderstanding, explaining how she had come to be away so long. She had not even told her aunt about his portrait. Returning with it from Argyll Street the previous day, she had had the footman stand it against the wall in the studio, still covered.

Anxiety gripped her and she strode over to nervously twitch back the sheet and hold the canvas out at arm's length. Was there anything in it that disclosed her emotions? Mr. Rogers had seemed somehow to guess the state of her mind, hadn't he? Or had he? Was it only her imagination? Perhaps his comments on background were specifically directed to this one portrait. Torn as to where to locate him, Emma had shown just the hint of a landscape with the richly orange and purple shades of a sunset. Oh, Lord, it was wretchedly romantic, wasn't it? She should paint it out and have him in a study, with dusty books on shelves at his back. Startled to hear the door open, she nearly fainted to find her aunt entering the room with Dunn.

"Oh, dear," Amelia murmured, stricken, "I felt sure you would have gone to change by now, Emma. And I so wanted to show Dunn the portrait you're painting of me. I know you don't think it's far enough along to show people, but . . . Where did that come from?" she asked, staring at the canvas Emma could find no way to hide.

"Well, I . . . That is, I wanted to speak about it with Lord Dunn. You see, I . . ." Emma had avoided his eyes until this point but forced herself to glance at him. He was regarding her, and the painting, incredulously. She licked her lips and tried to set the portrait on an easel so that it would not be evident that her hands were shaking. Why in heaven's name hadn't she asked Anne to do this for her? she wondered desperately. If she had only had a chance to explain before having him see it.

"I . . . I spent a great deal of time when I was out of town learning portrait painting, after a fashion. I did one of Maggie, and one of Sir Nicholas, and Mr. Hill and Mr. Bampton. And I'm working on one of Lord Greenwood, and of course Aunt Amelia. But . . . but there was a time, just after we left Bath, when I couldn't seem to capture Maggie quite right, and I didn't yet know Mr. Hill or Mr. Bampton, when I . . . I thought I might just do one of Lord Dunn. You see," she explained to her aunt, breathlessly, "I made a sketch of Sir Nicholas one day before I left, and then Lord Dunn called and . . . Well, I made one of him, too."

There was merely a grunt from Dunn.

"I didn't think it would do any harm," she protested, stiffening. "And Mr. Rogers, who is rather an art connoisseur, says that they are good enough to exhibit, and he is associated with a small gallery in Bond Street. Of course, I never meant to show this one until I spoke with Lord Dunn and . . . and that's why I asked him to call!"

"Well, dear," Amelia said, advancing slowly toward the painting, "I can see that it's very good, but I really think you should have asked Dunn's permission. It must be rather a shock for him to come upon it this way."

"He wasn't meant to come upon it this way," Emma retorted with some asperity. "I had intended to explain the whole situation to him before I brought him here to see it. In fact, if he seemed not to like the idea at all, I had intended just to pack it away without bothering him."

Dunn had come to stand beside Amelia in front of the painting. It was impossible, Emma decided, to discover what he was thinking from his expression; he had none. In moving farther away from them she happened to recall how she was dressed and glanced down at the sprigged muslin with a kind of horror. Thrusting the stray locks of hair back into the knot, she murmured, "If you will excuse me, I'll just go and change."

"One moment, Miss Berryman," Dunn commanded. With a pleasant smile he addressed Lady Bradwell, saying, "Perhaps I should have a word alone with your niece, ma'am, if you wouldn't mind."

Amelia looked questioningly at Emma. After all, the two of them had not gotten along at all well last spring, and it would be rather hard of her to leave Emma to have a peal rung over her head alone. Emma gave a helpless gesture with her hands but told her aunt that might be for the best. With several backward glances, Amelia made her exit.

The sun chose that moment to break from the clouds and send playful beams into the studio, highlighting the painting with a warm glow. Dunn stood with his hands loosely clasped behind his back, a puzzled frown now on his face. "I don't understand how you have managed to accomplish so much in less than a year, Miss Berryman."

"I've worked very hard, Lord Dunn. Contrary to popular opinion, even two women together cannot find something to talk of all the time. Maggie encouraged me to paint as much as I wanted. She even had a studio set up for me at Combe Lodge. I spent large portions of each day at work there. And she sat for me a lot. I had to start over twice before I felt I had gotten her right."

"And me? Did you 'do' me more than once?"

"No." Emma refused to meet the grave gray eyes. "I had only a sketch of you, if you will remember. Without you sitting for me, there wasn't the complication of comparing my work with the original, so to speak."

"I see. You've made me a little forbidding, don't you think?"

"You *are* a little forbidding, Lord Dunn."

"Am I?" He raised a quizzing dark brow. "Surely not to you, Miss Berryman."

"Alas, even to me," she sighed, attempting to match his light tone. "I've been all aquake about asking your permission to show the portrait. Anne assured me that I had only to ask and you would agree."

"Did she? Such faith in my good nature."

Emma, who had been avoiding his eyes, met them now and asked, "Will you let me show it?"

A moment passed when he did not speak but held her gaze with a curiously penetrating one of his own. "Yes, if you wish. I shall look forward to seeing the others. Why don't you go and change while I have a look at this one of Lady Bradwell you're working on? I thought we might go for a drive, if you've a mind. You could have your first lesson."

She smiled faintly. "Thank you! I won't be a moment."

His lordship's curricle was elegantly black with red trim and wheels, and a tiger was walking the matched grays when they came out of the house. Before handing her up, Dunn carefully explained the draft gear—center pole, swingletree, traces, neck collar, steel bars, and rein loops—so that she would understand wherein lay the control of the pair. The hood was up and Emma settled herself carefully so as not to disturb the wide-brimmed primrose bonnet she wore.

Sitting in a carriage with a gentleman had always seemed even more intimate to Emma than waltzing with him. In a curricle especially it was impossible not to be touching, to be aware of the strength in his gloved hands and the proximity of his closely clad legs and top-booted feet. Though Dunn spoke with her as he wended his way through the crowded London streets, she was less aware of his voice than of the tightening of his thighs and arms when he exerted pressure on the reins to draw in the spirited grays. His concentration on his driving kept his whole body alert despite the ostensibly relaxed posture. When a sporting vehicle guided by a brilliantly outfitted young buck made an erratic turn into his path, he averted an accident with calm skill, never breaking the flow of his discourse.

"Driving is harder than it looks, isn't it?" Emma asked, slightly unnerved.

He turned his head to grin at her. "Yes. And it requires strength as well as skill. You won't have any trouble with the grays because they were well trained, but you should not assume that every pair is as easily handled. Fortunately we have an hour before the park becomes crowded," he observed as he drove past the gates at Hyde Park Corner. "You will need to give your whole attention to the horses and not to some acquaintance who may be passing by."

Emma took this stricture in good part, especially when he added, "Remember, I'm putting my life in your hands!" Whereupon he proceeded to give over the reins, making sure that she held them properly and got a feel for their purpose before removing his own guiding hands. "If you intend to take driving seriously," he cautioned, sitting slightly back, "you will need to get yourself a pair of gauntlets. Your gloves aren't going to protect you from the leather digging into you when you have to take control physically."

Determined to prove to him her seriousness, Emma did precisely what he told her. The grays responded immediately to any movement of her hands on the reins and kept up a pace so brisk that it rather alarmed her. They seemed to be flying past the trees and bushes and were quickly bearing down on a solitary carriage when Dunn said, "Rein in slowly." His instruction would have given her plenty of time to do so, had not the other carriage stopped abruptly. Realizing there was no time to halt her own horses, she made them swing out to the right where there was barely enough space to pass. From the corner of her eye she saw Dunn start to reach for the reins and then drop his hands to his knees, murmuring, "A little harder on the right, Miss Berryman." They whizzed past with barely an inch to spare.

Once clear, Emma drew in the pair with shaking hands. "I'm sorry. I hadn't time to stop them."

"You managed extraordinarily well, Miss Berryman. One thing a driver continually has to bear in mind is that every other driver on the road, or even a pedestrian, might at any time do something foolish. Driving would be a great deal simpler if there were no obstructions, but that's not a condition one finds in the ordinary course of a day's drive." He called for his tiger to stand at the horses' heads and took Emma's hands in his. "Don't let the experience unnerve you. Your instincts were perfect. Usually a beginner has a tendency to overcompensate in an emergency, but you didn't."

Since he made no mention of the fact that he held her trembling hands, Emma attempted to ignore the contact but found it difficult. It was a gesture of reassurance, of comfort, she knew. There was no undue pressure, no sophisticated gleam in his eyes, just firmness and understanding. "I suppose," she suggested, gazing out over the Serpentine, "that it's like taking a spill from a horse. I must do it again before I lose my confidence."

"Yes." He motioned the tiger back on his perch. "And the sooner the better. In a few minutes there will be any number of carriages to contend with. Are you all right now?" When she nodded, he released her hands and smiled. "I knew you would be."

The rest of the lesson consisted of his teaching her to turn the carriage in a rather tight place. Before they had progressed halfway to the gate, the crush of carriages and equestrians had begun in earnest and Emma willingly allowed him to resume the driving. Dunn assumed he was giving Emma a chance to greet her friends and acquaintances in their smart carriages with bewigged coachman and powdered footmen; Emma assumed he had not enough faith in her skill to trust her in the mob, an opinion with which she agreed wholeheartedly. Her attention, however, stayed with the driving, watching how he maneuvered through the press of vehicles and horses, to the point where she almost failed to acknowledge Sir Nicholas on a stunning young bay she had not previously seen. Dunn drew in the grays.

"Miss Berryman, Dunn. Servant. What do you think of Watchman?" Sir Nicholas asked, indicating the bay. "I've just had him sent up from the country. A little nervous in town as yet, but adapting well."

"He's splendid," Emma said, her eyes running over the horse's points. "Was he sired by Lightning?"

Sir Nicholas smiled appreciatively. "You're becoming quite an expert on horses, my dear. He was indeed. I have a filly by Lightning and a different dam, Hazzard, which might interest you as a hack. She's a sweet goer if ever I saw one, but not quite up to my weight. If you're interested I'll have her brought up for your inspection."

"Let me think on it," Emma returned. "I already have Enigma, and I can't really use two horses in town."

"Certainly." He turned to Dunn. "Rumor has it that Miss Berryman has immortalized you, too, in oils. Has she caught that patrician brow and those steely eyes?"

If he was hoping for a rise from the viscount, he was not disappointed. "I would say she's accomplished a fair likeness. I shall look forward to seeing her portrait of *you*. Her eye for breeding, as you say, is excellent, and I don't doubt she is as competent to discern the lack of it." His eyes twinkled in the late-afternoon sun.

"Really, gentlemen," Emma scolded, "I see no need to trade insults. And I do not understand how you could have heard of Lord Dunn's portrait, Sir Nicholas. Very few people know of it."

"I stopped at your aunt's on my way to the park, thinking you might enjoy a ride." His skeptical glance ran over the grays and the curricle. "I was informed that Dunn had taken you out for a driving lesson, but I see he lost his nerve. There's no apparent damage to his vehicle."

Emma was indignant. "It is no such thing, Sir Nicholas! I drove the curricle for a good half hour, did I not, my lord? And though there was nearly an accident, I assure you I did not so much as graze the other carriage. Why, at least Lord Dunn is willing to take a chance on my driving. I remember distinctly that you once told me you had not and never would allow a woman to handle the ribbons of your shabbiest dog cart!"

"How ungallant of you," murmured Dunn, his shoulders shaking with suppressed laughter.

Ignoring him, Sir Nicholas leaned toward Emma with his devilish grin. "That is because I recognize a woman's limitations, Miss Berryman. Even you, whom I know to be quite . . . enthusiastic in your pleasures—that is, your interests—I would not trust to have control over your emotions. And believe me, Miss Berryman, though there are places where I find it perfectly acceptable for a woman to abandon herself, driving is not one of them!" Satisfied with her disconcerted expression, Sir Nicholas tipped his hat, winked, and spurred his horse down the path leading away from them.

Emma watched him disappear in aggrieved silence, unable even to glance at Dunn. No one else she knew had the ability to discompose her so thoroughly as Sir Nicholas, except the man at her side. And why Sir Nicholas should choose to do so continually in Dunn's presence she could not begin to fathom. His teasing always had a kernel of truth to it, which made it all the more difficult to shrug off. Emma clutched her hands tightly in her lap as Dunn directed the grays through the park gates and out into the London streets beyond.

"I've known Nick for years," Dunn remarked conversationally.

"Ever since I first came to town with my father at eighteen. He hasn't changed much in the twelve years, but I've never seen him on terms of such easy camaraderie as he is with you."

"I presume you mean he's too familiar with me."

"No, Miss Berryman, that is not what I am suggesting at all. Despite his penchant for baiting you in my presence, he seems to have a real regard for you. I'm sure he wouldn't take the trouble with someone else, but he can't resist putting the cat amongst the pigeons from time to time. You may be sure he noticed from the start that we were at loggerheads, and he continues to do everything in his power to keep us that way. I wonder why?"

His glance at her served only to make her grip her hands more tightly. When she said nothing, he mused, "I would consider it only sport with him, except that I've not noticed him do it with any other man. Does he?"

"No."

"I thought not. Well, perhaps it is merely an unconscious antagonism he feels toward me, though I cannot account for it. We've always been on the best of terms: no gambling losses to one another, no rankling dispute over other people, no envy or malice apparent. Why, we dined just the other evening in Waverton Street quite amicably. But the moment he sees you with me . . ."

"Please, Lord Dunn . . ." Emma swallowed with difficulty. "I know you are only joking but I . . . I'm afraid I cannot enter into the spirit. Perhaps my nerves are still a little overwrought from the near accident."

His expression, a compound of surprise, uncertainty, and possibly even a slight hurt, was quickly corrected to one of the utmost pleasantness. "Of course. I had already forgotten. I trust you won't dwell on that, Miss Berryman, and that it has not given you a dislike of driving. My hope was to take you out again on Thursday."

Emma could not understand why she was having such a difficult time being as light and casual with Dunn as she was with any other gentleman with whom she might chance to drive out. His implications of Sir Nicholas's interest, even perhaps of his own interest in her, left her feeling tense and awkward. Ridiculous, yes, but she did not seem to be able to control the conflicting emotions that raced through her, making her feel first hot and then cold, tingly and then shaken. Forcing a smile to her lips, she murmured, "Thank you. I'd like that, Lord Dunn."

CHAPTER NINETEEN

The months they had spent together in Bath and at the Greenwood estate had drawn Maggie and Emma even closer together than they had been at school. Despite the disparity in their personalities and situations, they had come to a deeper understanding of one another, and when Emma called on her friend the next morning it was to unburden herself of some of the confusion she had suffered the previous afternoon. She could not as easily confide in Anne these days, not only because of Anne's reluctance to do likewise, which she could appreciate, but because Anne's friendship with Miss Rogers seemed to have withdrawn her slightly from the charmed schoolgirl trio the three of them had originally made—Emma, Maggie, and Anne. It had been only a year since they had left Windrush House, but none of them bore much resemblance to the innocents they had been. Emma suffered a great deal of emotional discomfort when she remembered how she had thought herself so worldly, so knowledgeable, compared to her friends. How little any of them had known of the world that lay outside their school, and she least of all, for all her superficial sophistication imbibed at her aunt's dimpled elbow.

Maggie's health, which was of concern to all of them, seemed only to improve with the advancing of her second pregnancy. Her coloring was good and she was laughingly proud of the increase in her bust, which showed to advantage in the simple peach-colored cottage dress she wore. "I've just come in from a drive," she told Emma. "Fortunately, the doctor insists on my taking the air each morning and afternoon, so Greenwood drives me in the park—in a most stately fashion. You would think I was made of fine porcelain. I assure you it is not his standard driving method."

"I remember." Emma laughed, settling herself into a velvet-covered easy chair. "He took me driving at Combe Lodge and my heart was never in its proper place. If we weren't running an inch from a ditch, there were the most hair-raising curves in the road. I shall never understand why road builders found it necessary, in perfectly flat countryside, to zigzag about in such a fashion."

"They follow old footpaths, I daresay, and folks were not necessarily headed in the most direct route, having to skirt fences or whatnot. In the country at least you can hope to land in grass on the verges if you take a spill. In town you haven't that solace, so I'm grateful Greenwood is exceptionally careful."

"So am I." Emma reached over to pat her hand. "He really does wish to take good care of you, Maggie."

"Yes, but . . ." Maggie bit her lip and shrugged. "Yes, he does."

"My dear, we spent months together and you were not so shy of speaking with me. You know nothing you tell me will go any farther. If it will help you to talk about a problem, please feel free. I came intending to bend your ear about a problem of my own."

"Did you? Oh, dear, surely everyone could see how good the portraits were!"

"Sometimes you put things in perspective with astonishing speed, my love. Yes, I have been fortunate enough to meet with approval of them. Mr. Rogers is arranging for them to be exhibited at a small gallery in Bond Street. He warns me, though, that I must expect a certain amount of derogatory comment. Not only is everyone's taste different, but there may be some disinclination because of my sex."

"I see." Maggie gave a gentle tug on the bell rope. "Have you . . . have you finished the portrait of Greenwood?"

"I'm still working on it, from time to time." Emma frowned. "I don't know what it is, Maggie, but I can't seem to quite get him. You would think with all the times I've been with him that it wouldn't be so difficult, but I find him elusive. As a subject, that is."

A footman entered and was instructed to bring tea. When they were alone again, Maggie toyed with the satin ribbon at her wrist. "Do you suppose that's because you have two different impressions of him—yours and mine? What I mean is, you want to see him in the best light for my sake, but you can't force yourself to paint him that way because that's not how he really is?"

At first Emma intended to deny such a thought categorically. After pondering it for a moment, she sighed. "Possibly. He's not a bad man, Maggie. It's just . . . Well, he seems to shift about in my mind. There are times when I'm overwhelmed by his care for you, and others when I'm appalled at his . . . carelessness. I know he means well but the dichotomy makes it strangely unnerving to put him down on canvas."

Maggie released a long, tremulous breath. "I have come to believe that he does care for me, after his fashion. The problem is that his fashion is so erratic. I have a very logical mind and a tendency to act with consistency toward people. Greenwood behaves as the spirit moves him. He may be whimsical, tender, preoccupied, abrupt, all within the course of a day. At breakfast he may be solicitous of my condition, insisting that I drink a glass of milk or even buttering a muffin for me. But by mid-morning he may have forgotten that he suggested a drive and ask me to shop for a new table for his library. You know what those furniture warehouses are like, Emma."

"Exhausting."

Maggie nodded. "I do it, of course. Really, there is so little I can do for him." Her eyes became suspiciously shiny and she turned aside as the tea tray was brought in and set down in front of her on a low mahogany table. The smell of freshly baked cakes permeated the room and she motioned Emma to help herself as she poured them cups of tea.

Alone again, Emma said urgently, "But, Maggie, you are carrying his child."

"Oh, Emma, you can't possibly understand, not being married yet. There are things I can't discuss with you. Intimate things I've no right to tell anyone."

"He doesn't mistreat you in bed, does he?" Emma asked bluntly.

Aghast at having elicited such a shocking question, Maggie hastened to reassure her. "Oh, no! That's not what I mean at all! He . . . he asks nothing unusual of me." A tear slid down her cheek. "Oh, Emma, he doesn't ask anything of me at all anymore!"

"Well, for heaven's sake, Maggie, you're pregnant! He doesn't want to take any chances of your losing the child or harming you. Surely it's perfectly understandable if he doesn't . . . ask anything of you right now."

Maggie dabbed at her eyes with a fine lawn handkerchief. "I know. Oh, I do understand that he's being considerate, cautious, but . . . Emma . . . No, I mustn't . . . It would be improper for me to speak of it to an unmarried woman."

"Improper my eye!" Emma retorted, impatient. "You forget that I live with my aunt, who hasn't your sensibility about such topics, Maggie. I intend to be married one day, so I can see no purpose in beating about the bush. Is it that you miss . . . going to bed with him?"

Wide-eyed, Maggie stared at her. "You can really talk about it as easily as that? I haven't ever talked about it with anyone at all . . . except Greenwood once. It's such a private matter."

"I don't intend you should go into specifics, my dear," Emma agreed with a comforting smile. "It's just that I don't as yet understand your problem."

"Greenwood is very . . . That is, he seems to *need* to go to bed with a woman. And if he's not . . . going to bed with me, then he must be going to bed with someone else. I keep thinking of what my father told me about the mistress he had, and I have to assume that he's seeing her again, or someone else. It doesn't seem fair, Emma. Being available to him was the only thing I had to offer and now, because of the baby, or perhaps because I am so bloated and misshapen, I am not even called upon for that."

"The only thing you had to offer!" spluttered Emma, irate. "Where in heaven's name did you come by that? Surely you have more self-esteem than to say such a thing!"

"I shouldn't have phrased it quite that way. Believe me, I'm quite proud of myself for the way I've run the household and managed my finances. I've even been surprised at overcoming my shyness somewhat in society. I've improved my performance on the pianoforte and read a great deal. Really, I simply meant that *that*—the giving of my body—is the only thing Greenwood *appreciates*."

"You're wrong, you know." Emma was emphatic. "He appreciates your gentleness and your competence and the effort you've made to make him comfortable. He likes *you,* Maggie."

"Yes, I think he does—now. But he takes so much for granted. He *expects* me to be competent and make him comfortable, and never says a word about it. For some reason—I can't think why!—he sometimes thanks me when we . . ."

Emma giggled. "Does he? How sweet! Perhaps I shall be able to finish his portrait after all."

"When you do, I should like to purchase it, Emma. You gave Greenwood mine as a gift, which was very kind of you, but when you're satisfied with his, have Mr. Rogers appraise it and I shall buy it."

"I can see that it won't do at all to paint people's portraits," Emma grumbled. "Everyone thinks they must buy them when they're done."

"I never told anyone this, but right after we were married my father insisted that Greenwood and I have our portraits painted. I knew Greenwood would just hate the idea, so I put my father off. Imagine my doing that! I told him I would be the judge of when it was time to have them done and thanked him for his interest. He sputtered and stomped, but finally agreed. And I'm so pleased you were the one to do them in the end."

Emma regarded her wonderingly. "You really have developed the most amazing strength, my love. Probably you always had it. If Greenwood is seeing his mistress again, you'll be able to handle that. Things will change again once the baby is born."

"But it's so lonely in bed at night!" Maggie blurted. "He used to come every night and stay until morning. At first I resented it, having no privacy, depending on his whim for enough . . . attention to give me pleasure, having to tug the covers back from him when he wrapped them around himself in his sleep. But I've gotten used to having him there. Now I don't know whether he's even at home at night or not. I lie in bed and wonder if he's with her and it hurts, Emma. All very well to believe that he cares for me, in a way, but that doesn't seem to help at night when he's not there beside me, quizzing me and holding me. I've rather come to depend on the affection he shows me."

"Have you asked him to come?"

"Heavens, no! I couldn't do that. I don't want to interfere with his freedom. It's only because I have allowed him to do just as he wishes that he has finally accepted me as his wife."

"Maggie, dear, don't you think he has some responsibility to you, too? Don't you think he'd want to know that you're lonely? I'm afraid Greenwood is not so sensitive to people's feelings as to be aware without being told. Ask him to stay with you, Maggie. Not every night, but now and again. I'm sure he won't resent it."

Her cup tinkled faintly as Maggie set it on the table and offered a rueful smile. "You may be right, but I'm not sure I dare take the chance. If he has . . . made other plans, he'll be in an awkward position, and Greenwood doesn't handle that very well. I told you about the canaries."

"Maggie, why don't you call him Adam?"

Unprepared for the question, Maggie made an expressive gesture with her hands. "He's never asked me to. He calls me Margaret."

They sat in silence for a time, contemplating the complexities of relationships between men and women. Eventually, because it seemed pertinent, Maggie said, "You haven't told me about your problem."

"It's not a problem, exactly. It's more of a . . . a dilemma, I suppose. You see, I once let Sir Nicholas kiss me and he has a tendency to tease me about it, in a roundabout way, when I'm with Lord Dunn. He does it out of pure devilry, Maggie!"

"Are you with Lord Dunn much?" Maggie asked, surprised. "I thought the two of you were at daggers drawn."

"For a long time we were, but he's been kinder to me recently. He's teaching me to drive his curricle."

"And you want Sir Nicholas to cease embarrassing you in front of him?"

"With anyone else I wouldn't mind so much, but Lord Dunn . . ." Emma ran her finger around the rim of her teacup, considering how best to phrase her objection without exposing the attachment she was beginning to feel. As Anne had said, one is often silent in matters of the heart. "Lord Dunn realizes that Sir Nicholas is merely baiting me, of course, but I am loath to lose his better opinion of me, and I cannot help but fear I will if this continues. Or . . . or it will lead Lord Dunn to think that Sir Nicholas has a special interest in me—which he hasn't! At the very least, it must lead his lordship to surmise something untoward has happened. It was only a kiss, Maggie, but Lord Dunn is so very proper, and so easily persuaded that I've misbehaved."

"Hmm. It sounds very much to me like a small boy pulling the pigtails of the girl in front of him in school. Sir Nicholas's behavior, I mean. Are you sure he doesn't have a special interest in you?"

Emma stared at the silver tea tray, trying to evaluate more precisely how Sir Nicholas did feel about her. "Well, he's not interested in marrying me. He's not interested in marrying anyone, actually. And he is fully aware that I am not appropriate material for a mistress. Still, he may be attracted to me, a little, or he may simply be teaching me a lesson. He only does it with Lord Dunn, though, as if to prove to him that I'm not the sort of lady he might think me. Oh, I don't know, Maggie. It's very confusing. And it makes me feel awkward and nervous, because I really want Lord Dunn's good opinion. He's the sort of gentleman you don't want to think ill of you."

"I quite agree. I don't think I've met any gentleman I admire more than Lord Dunn, except possibly for Anne's father. And both have been so very kind to me. Let me think on it a while, Emma. There must be some way to persuade Sir Nicholas into silence, or if not persuade him, trick him."

Emma laughed as she rose. "I like the way your mind works, Maggie. I must be off. Please give my best to your husband."

"He told me he would join me for tea after our drive but I suppose he forgot," her friend said matter-of-factly. "Do come again soon. I don't visit much, in my condition, but I love company."

"I will."

Adam had not forgotten that he had promised his wife to join her for tea. He had, in fact, been coming down the stairs to do so when the footman carried the laden tea tray into the drawing room, the aroma of freshly baked cakes wafting up to him. As the door was open for a moment, he clearly caught the sound of Miss Berryman's voice and was reminded that he had set out an art book he planned to lend her. So instead of going directly into the drawing room, he wandered into the green room, vaguely recalling that he had set the book on a shelf there. The green room connected with the drawing room through sliding doors that were for some reason slightly ajar. (The downstairs maid was in a bit of a hurry that morning because she had been given the afternoon off to consult an apothecary on the rash that persistently reappeared on her hands.)

With not the slightest intention of eavesdropping, he heard Miss Berryman ask, "He doesn't mistreat you in bed, does he?" and stood rigid, straining to hear his wife's reply. He gave a snort of satisfaction (not loud enough to be heard in the drawing room) at her answer, but soon found himself feeling very uncomfortable as the discussion progressed. He *had* been seeing the Jewel again, regularly, when he was in town. It had never occurred to him that his wife might be lonely, and he had no reason to suspect that she knew about Julia. What the devil had her father meant by telling her? And the canaries! Who had told her about the canaries? Probably no one, he realized after a moment. Margaret was quite astute enough to have guessed what happened that night—their wedding night.

When the discussion ranged to Miss Berryman's problems with Sir Nicholas and Lord Dunn, Adam was not particularly interested—except for grinning when he heard that Miss Berryman had allowed Sir Nicholas to kiss her. What did catch his attention—in fact, stung him surprisingly—was his wife's comment: "I don't think I've met any gentleman I admire more than Lord Dunn, except possibly for Anne's father." It was conceivable that she meant to the exclusion of himself, but he really didn't think so. The possibility that his own wife, that poor little mouse he'd married, accorded him a lesser position in her estimation than Lord Dunn was a lowering thought. In truth, that "poor little mouse" he'd married had turned out to be nothing of the kind. Somehow she had become pretty and gracious and the central focus of his admittedly ramshackle life. When he was with Julia he thought of her, rather than the other way about. For God's sake, he was only trying to be considerate—and it was difficult for him. Didn't she realize that? He didn't mean to hurt her. Quite the opposite.

There was silence now in the drawing room and Adam replaced the book he had stood immobile holding. Not for the world did he wish his wife to know that he had overheard her conversation, and he quietly let himself out into the hall. The drawing room door was closed and he could easily have sneaked past it and out of the house, but he had indeed promised to join his wife for tea and though he knew she'd already had hers, he was not averse to having some, so long as she applied for more hot water for him. He knew she would; she always did when he was late.

Guiltily, he stepped into the room to find her thoughtfully gazing out the window into the street, her teacup empty and returned to the tray. The pale sunlight shone on her face, which was fuller now, softening the once-sharp features. Her hands rested on the mound that was their child, and she smiled gently at a movement there that he could see from across the room.

"The baby moved," he gasped, awestruck.

Maggie turned to smile at him. "Yes, all the time now. Would you like to feel it?"

"Could I?" It had not occurred to him that she would want him to touch her body at all, if he weren't going to make love to her.

"Certainly. You may have to wait for a few minutes. I'll ring for more hot water."

"No, let me." Adam hastened to tug the pull. "I'm sorry I'm late. You've already had yours."

"Emma came and I thought you wouldn't mind if we didn't wait for you."

No trace of reproach colored her voice, which did not prevent

Adam from feeling something of a fool. "I was looking out a book," he explained as he seated himself. "One for Miss Berryman on art."

"That was thoughtful of you. I'm sure she'll appreciate it." She gave instructions to the footman to bring hot water and another cup. "Mr. Rogers is arranging to have her paintings shown. She's still working on yours; she's not satisfied with it as yet. If you like it when it's finished, I thought we might purchase it from her."

How cautious she sounded—as though she had to tread carefully to avoid upsetting him. "Well, of course we shall purchase it! Even if it's not quite right. I daresay she's worked very hard on it, and she certainly did a wonderful job with yours. Margaret, I—"

"Quick. Put your hand here. The baby's moving again."

Adam did as he was instructed, a huge grin stretching across his face. "My word, how astonishing! We have a very active little fellow there!"

"Will you be disappointed if it's a girl?"

"Of course not," he declared stoutly. "Sometimes it's just the thing for a fellow to have an older sister."

Maggie nodded as the footman entered and Adam resettled himself in his chair. "You certainly are fortunate in your older sister. Cynthia has given me a complete list of the items we'll need for the baby and offered to lend us anything we wish." When the footman had departed she said earnestly, "Greenwood, I would prefer not to stay in town too long after the baby is born, if you don't mind. The air in the country seems so much healthier. And everything is quiet there, not the continual racket of London streets. I won't mind being alone there—with the baby," she hastened to assure him.

Was the baby to supplant him in her affections? Was he even in her affections? He had just heard her tell Miss Berryman that she was lonely at nights. Would she start to devote her life to the child, as he saw some women do, and forget that he needed her, too? It was a sobering thought.

"Margaret, I want you to do what you think is best, but I don't like to be away from you for any long period of time." He smiled hesitantly. "I get . . . restless when you're in the country and I'm in town. On the other hand, Combe Lodge is not exactly a stimulating spot so far as entertainment is concerned. The riding is fine, but the company is sparse. I'm not saying you're not excellent company! Don't mistake me, I beg you. My disposition is such, however," he admitted ruefully, "that I like to be surrounded by people. I seem to absorb their energy. Just as I absorb your tranquillity from time to time, and I need that quite as much. Margaret, do you like me a little?"

The question surprised her and made her throat ache. The smile she attempted went slightly astray. "Yes."

"More than a little?" he persisted anxiously.

"Yes."

Adam caught her hand and lifted it to his lips, but retained his firm pressure when he lowered it. "I suppose I've been too corkbrained to tell you how much I like you, haven't I? And I can't think how you should know if I don't tell you. I had no idea it would be so pleasant being married. I told Stephen—Captain Midford—just yesterday that he should think of getting hitched and he laughed. Said not everyone could find someone like you! Made me feel very proud, Margaret."

The ache in her throat had grown to such proportions that Maggie found herself unable to speak. Her lips trembled and her eyes filled. She was forced to turn her head aside so he would not see, but he placed his hands on either side of her head and gently turned it back to face him. In a peculiarly gruff voice he said, "I want to make you happy, my dear, if it's in my power. I know we aren't as well suited as we might be, but that doesn't seem to matter anymore, does it?"

Maggie bit her lip and shook her head.

"No, I didn't think so. Would you like me to come into the country with you after the baby's born?"

"Very much, but it will probably be before the season ends. Perhaps you could come after . . . and invite some friends to join us. I'll be rested by then."

He searched her face for any sign of hesitation but found none. Had she grown so used to compromising that it had become natural? Had he made any effort to accommodate her? When she had been at Combe Lodge, he had come regularly to visit, but that was because he found it impossible to stay away for long, not because he had particularly considered what *she* would want. Adam promised himself then and there that he would use his head a little more where his wife was concerned. After all, she had become his touchstone and his hearth: the standard by which he judged the worth of even the most trivial matter, the ever-present warmth of his home. There was no going back to those premarriage days . . . and he no longer wished to. He leaned over and kissed her gently.

"We'll see how things go, my dear. I, at least, will be with you."

Adam was not at all accustomed to being tactful, but he made a supreme effort. She must never learn that he had overheard their conversation. "Does the baby move much at night?"

"Oh, yes. More perhaps than during the day."

"Well, then." Adam cleared his throat. "Would you mind very much if I . . . ah . . . joined you at night? Not to . . . That is, just so that we could be together and I could feel the baby move now and then."

Maggie swallowed painfully. "Please do. I . . . I've missed you."

"Have you? By Jove, I've missed you, too." Despite the protrusion that was their growing child, he hugged her to him, murmuring, "I do treasure you, my love."

CHAPTER TWENTY

The buildings along Bond Street contained some of the most exclusive shops in London. Not every business, however, was patronized only by the wealthiest of the ton. There was a bow-windowed storefront between Clifford and Burlington that attracted quite an unusual assortment of ladies and gentlemen. On that particular Wednesday afternoon an observer might have witnessed the arrival (and eventual departure) of three very grand dames with their undistinguished companions, half a dozen cits, five respectably (perhaps, if the observer were not of a charitable disposition, they would have been described as dully) clad ladies ranging in age from their mid-twenties to their late sixties, and twenty or more individuals who could be classed only as gentlemen of the highest order—in their starched cravats and elegantly cut coats and pantaloons. The swish of tassels on Hessian boots would not have been noticed in the clamor of carriages passing back and forth, but the cat who sat lazily in the window eyed their motion with a fascination so profound that the owner of the shop, having no desire to be called to account for his pet's destruction of such delicious baubles, soon relegated the poor animal to the office at the rear.

"Do let me hold him," Anne urged when Mr. Wigginton made to set the cat on the floor beside her. As the animal folded up in a gray ball in her lap, she asked diffidently, "How does it seem to be going, Mr. Wigginton? Are they approving or disapproving?"

"Quite a varied response," the young man informed her, taking the opportunity to sip from a cup of cold coffee left sitting on his desk. "The very number of people who have come attests to the novelty of the show, but I cannot in good conscience say there is unilateral appreciation of Miss Berryman's work. The young gentlemen especially are prone to mock her efforts, though two of them have taken me aside to ask how one arranges for a sitting with her."

His ironic gaze rested on her briefly before he glanced through the glass window into the shop. "Ah, here is Mr. Rogers now. I'm delighted he was able at last to convince his sister to put one work in the show, though I regret it wasn't one of her delicate watercolors. 'The Fencer' has power and elegance, but her special forte is landscapes and the intricacies of plants and birds. I grant you 'The Fencer' is more appropriate to this particular exhibition, but I hope the two of you will continue to urge her to show more of her work. If you will excuse me."

With a slight bow he opened the door and stepped into the shop. Anne shifted in her chair so that she could just see the two of them meet in the center of the room, without herself being obvious to the other customers. The men held an earnest conversation and Mr. Rogers's eyes traveled momentarily to the room where she sat, but he gave no sign of recognition. Instead he wandered amongst the people standing in front of the various portraits and other works of art, obviously saying little but listening and storing what he heard. Anne stroked the cat absently and never took her eyes from Mr. Rogers, distinguishable in any gathering by his height. After a lengthy period of time he made his way deliberately to the office, closing the door after him with alarming firmness. He was frowning.

"You really shouldn't be here alone, Lady Anne. Not that any harm is likely to come to you, but I cannot believe your mother would be pleased to learn that you spent the afternoon in the office of an art gallery."

"I told Mama I was coming," she protested, patting the cat so vigorously that it leaped from her lap. "A footman came with me and I've sent him off on an errand. He'll be back shortly."

"After scavenging the Arcade for a nonexistent brand of hand cream, no doubt," he said, the frown beginning to crease his forehead.

"Really, I'm not that devious, Mr. Rogers." A grin peeked out from her impish eyes. "It was a very *long* list I gave him."

He shook his head sorrowfully but the frown disappeared. "Why did you want to be here so badly?"

"Because Emma and Helena really couldn't. I walked around the paintings and listened to people, just as you have. Mr. Wigginton says the reaction is mixed, which was the conclusion I reached, but I might observe that those who were critical were also the ones to scoff at a woman painting portraits. I couldn't stay out in the shop all afternoon, so Mr. Wigginton suggested I wait here for the footman. This way I can at least watch their faces."

Mr. Rogers seated himself casually in a chair opposite hers and thoughfully stroked the cat when it descended on his lap from a shelf where it had perched. "Have Sir Nicholas and Lord Dunn been in?"

"Yes, both of them. Dunn hadn't seen the other paintings and he was visibly impressed. He spoke to Mr. Wigginton for some time, but I couldn't hear what they said."

"You tried?" he asked, his eyes laughing.

"Of course I tried." But Anne had the grace to flush. "Emma said Sir Nicholas has asked for first option to buy his, but that Dunn had said nothing. I was curious to see if he wanted it."

"Hmm." Mr. Rogers continued to rub a finger between the cat's ears but his mind was obviously otherwise occupied. "Don't expect Wigginton to tell you what was discussed. He's a model of discretion."

"I'm sure he is. He made me a cup of coffee earlier."

"Which you haven't touched," he pointed out.

"I don't like coffee."

"You should have told him."

"I didn't see a tea caddy, so when he asked I accepted politely."

Mr. Rogers sighed. "Let me see you home now. Wigginton can send your footman after us."

Without the slightest demur, Anne rose. "Thank you. I'm afraid I'm a great bother."

"You know you aren't." But there was no smile to accompany his words.

There were perhaps half a dozen people in the gallery as they came out of the office, and all of them were congregated around Helena's picture, "The Fencer." Despite the numerous voices chattering at once, one voice could be heard above them all. A gentleman with his back to Anne was demanding of Mr. Wigginton, "I wish to know who painted this picture of me, my good fellow. Surely that is not asking too much."

"I'm afraid it is," Mr. Wigginton said apologetically. "The artist agreed to have the work exhibited only if done anonymously. As I am sure you can tell, it was not done by Miss Berryman or Mr. Hopethorn, the other two exhibiters."

"But I never posed for it! How the devil did anyone see me at Persigny's?"

Anne had stopped to listen to the confrontation and now turned to glance at Mr. Rogers with questioning eyes.

"What did Miss Berryman say his name was?" he asked.

"Um . . . Hatton."

"Wait here a moment, please." Mr. Rogers joined the party in front of "The Fencer" and introduced himself to the puzzled man with the utmost ease, mentioning Mr. Hatton's name and that they had mutual friends. "If you would care to come with me, I believe I can explain the painting to your satisfaction. Lady Anne Parsons and I are walking toward Grosvenor Square." When the man nodded agreement, Mr. Rogers passed on a message for the footman, took Anne's arm, and led the way out into Bond Street.

Up close, Anne decided, he did not look nearly so much like Dunn, though there was nothing inaccurate about the painting. He bowed politely to her when he was introduced and paid her no further attention. His curiosity was almost palpable, or perhaps it was annoyance. Anne couldn't tell.

"Now then," he began, directing his question at Mr. Rogers, "would you be so good as to tell me who painted the picture, and how I came to be the subject?"

"My sister and I live in Argyll Street, directly opposite M. Persigny's fencing studio. On duller days," he said with a rueful smile, "we are given to watching the performance across the street, and my sister especially admired your skill. She ordinarily does only watercolors—landscapes, flowers, birds—but I had urged her to try oils, and she told me that if she were going to use such expensive ingredients she needed a subject worthy of the endeavor. She chose you."

Mr. Hatton paused at the corner of Conduit Street to stare at him, patently unsure whether he was being ridiculed or not. His gaze traveled to Lady Anne, who could not resist the urge to add her own contribution to the discussion. "I beg you won't be offended, Mr. Hatton. Miss Rogers meant not the least harm. I don't suppose any of us thought for a moment that you would ever see it, or that you would recognize yourself as the subject. She might as easily have painted a stagecoachman at work, you see. Her fascination is with the skill involved, as Mr. Rogers said. No one else at M. Persigny's studio is nearly as talented as you are."

"Have you seen me, too?" he asked incredulously.

"Well, yes," she admitted, sneaking a glance at Mr. Rogers for encouragement. "Miss Rogers has a pair of opera glasses which we use on occasion."

"I don't believe this! For God's sake, we're not putting on a show for the amusement of the public! My fencing lessons are a private endeavor and not to be gawked at by a pair of schoolgirls."

Mr. Rogers was as imperturbably calm as ever. "Might I suggest that you mention to M. Persigny the possibility of curtains? On a gray day the attraction of the activity across the street is as appealing as attending a magic lantern show. Just as you might delight in watching a bout of fisticuffs for the skill and grace involved, so we, who rarely have a chance to see an exhibition of fencing, delight in watching M. Persigny's pupils. If you are indeed disturbed by having the painting exhibited, I will have it withdrawn from the show."

"Oh, no!" Anne protested, laying a hand urgently on his sleeve. "Please don't do that! Helena could change the features so that it was not recognizable as Mr. Hatton, but please don't have it removed. It is the first time she's agreed to have a work shown."

Mr. Hatton seemed quite as offended to think that his face would be wiped from his body as he had been at being the subject of prying eyes. He stared fiercely at Anne for a moment and then shifted his glowering eyes to Mr. Rogers. Mr. Rogers's lips were twitching and his shoulders shook slightly, though he managed otherwise to maintain a rigidly polite expression.

The longer Mr. Hatton stared at Mr. Rogers, the harder it was for him to sustain his own offended dignity. Despite his efforts, he ended by shaking his head and grinning. "Oh, what the devil! Begging your pardon, Lady Anne. Let her show the painting. No one is likely to recognize me, though I'm not saying it isn't good. In fact, I've a mind to go back and have another look at it. When you only have one achievement, which is almost as antiquated as jousting, it's rather flattering to be immortalized at it. Lady Anne, Mr. Rogers, your obedient servant."

And he strolled off with a cheerful wave, his walking stick swinging briskly from his fingers, much as Anne had seen him the first day Helena pointed him out. Astonished, Anne looked at Mr. Rogers suspiciously and asked, "How did you do that?"

"I did nothing, my dear Lady Anne. It was you who suggested his face might be so easily replaced. You could be rather hard on a man's self-esteem."

"Nonsense." They had crossed to the other side of the street and she felt him shorten his stride to match hers. "How could you tell that he had an ounce of humor in him when he was acting like the avenging furies?"

"Quite simply because I have observed him. Granted we didn't know his name until Miss Berryman informed us, but we've seen him fence, and we've seen him laugh with Persigny, and we've seen him walk down Argyll Street in charity with all the world. No man who behaves that way is as rigid as Mr. Hatton gave us to believe. He had only to have the humor of the situation . . . ah . . . pointed out to him."

"Can you really read people as simply as that?" Anne asked uneasily.

Mr. Rogers studied her averted face for a moment. "Not always. There are numerous indications of a man's—or a woman's—personality in every encounter. Does he perpetually frown? Does she blush for no apparent reason? If you're interested, you study people. Some are more fascinating than others."

He held her eyes with a steady gaze until she turned away to straighten her already-straight bonnet. "There is some truth to what Mr. Hatton said about privacy, however. We put a public face on when we expect to be observed. There is something unnerving about learning that you have been watched without your defenses in place. You, for instance, would not be best pleased, I imagine, if you went out for a solitary walk at Parkhurst, singing to yourself, poking into bird's nests, hopping over stiles, generally reveling in your freedom, and found later that someone had observed you the entire while."

Her eyes darted to his face, remembering a day only a few weeks ago . . . "Did you?" she whispered.

"Yes." He shrugged. "At first I intended to join you because Helena had decided not to drive with me to the village after all, but sit with your mother. You were some distance away when I spotted you, and seemed so . . . carefree, that after a moment I decided you would prefer to be alone. I sat on the hillock overlooking the lake and watched your progress. You needn't tell me I shouldn't have; I couldn't pass up the chance. It was the day before I brought Helena back to town with me."

Anne remembered the afternoon he spoke of quite vividly, because of what had happened in the morning. He had only stayed four days, and those at the urging of her brother Jack. Originally he had merely planned to stop overnight before bearing Helena off with him. And Anne knew he did not speak the entire truth when he said he had not joined her because he thought she preferred to be alone. The real reason was that he did not trust himself to join her, to take the chance of a repetition of the morning.

How she had hoped he would be by the lake before breakfast, as he had been the previous day, with the mist clinging to the water and eddying out into the stand of trees. And he was there, staring out over the ghostly scene, his hands in his pockets, his booted feet sinking slightly into the marshy ground.

Anne had intended to surprise him, walking silently along the overgrown path until she was no more than three yards behind him, but the heel of her stupid half boot had caught in a vine and she had tumbled ignominiously into the bushes with a muffled grunt. He was almost instantly beside her, reaching down to help her up, asking if she had hurt herself. How mortifying it had been! How stupid she must have seemed to him. In her embarrassment she wanted to crawl away and hide in the trees, angry with him, with herself, with the whole ridiculous expedition. And he had laughed. Just as he had now with Mr. Hatton, a silent, unerring amusement that was meant to be shared. But she had shrunk from him in her turmoil, refused the hand he held out to her.

Mr. Rogers had cocked his head to one side, eyeing her with those infuriatingly omniscient eyes of his, and said, "To think I have admired your gracefulness all these months!" And before she could think of a suitable reply, he had reached down and grasped her by the waist, lifting her to her feet with one effortless motion. She had still wanted to run away, but he continued to hold her and, to her profound confusion, bent and kissed her, softly, on the lips. Instantly the anger, the embarrassment, the chagrin, fled and she clung to him shyly until he firmly disengaged himself. "You'll want to change before breakfast," was all he had said before he pushed her gently in the direction of the house. She did not look back.

No, he didn't seek her out that afternoon, merely watched her. He never sought her out, really, and she found herself constantly seeking him, finding opportunities to be with him. Anne had known he would come to the gallery and she had made sure that she would be there until he did. The poor footman was probably still searching out the objects on her list, but she had known that when Mr. Rogers arrived, he would walk her home, and that was all she asked, to spend a little time in his company. Lady Anne Parsons, sought out by any number of eligible gentlemen of the aristocracy, chose to keep them at a distance, kindly but firmly. She felt, somewhere deep inside her, that Mr. Rogers returned her affection, whether or not he was willing to express it.

And he certainly was not willing to express it. That kiss had been the only lapse in his otherwise impeccable behavior. He was invariably kind, thoughtful, humorous, polite . . . and slightly withdrawn. His treatment of her differed from that of his sister, but not radically. He had never given the least indication that he aspired to be a suitor. Anne's assumption (made with the facility of the hopeful), that he considered his position not sufficiently grand to attempt to gain her hand, had never been confirmed nor denied. She counseled herself in patience, tried to control her impulse to thrust herself before his notice, and worried incessantly that she had misjudged the case, that she was indeed merely a friend of his sister's and not the object of his heart's desire. Heart's desire! Lord, what had happened to the supposedly high tone of her mind? She sounded like an infatuated schoolgirl.

Lost in her thoughts, she was not aware that Mr. Rogers expected some comment from her on his reprehensible spying activity until she chanced to look up at him. He had obviously observed her while her mind wandered, and a puzzled expression remained on his face. Anne strove desperately to achieve a light response.

"I don't mind your having watched me that afternoon, Mr. Rogers, but I would have preferred your company. After you and Helena left there was plenty of time for solitary walks before we came to town."

For a moment she thought he was going to say something personal, for there was that in his eyes that spoke to her, but instantly it was gone and he said, probably more flatly than he intended, "But you can see that Mr. Hatton might feel uncomfortable being watched without his knowledge. Privacy is an important right."

Mr. Hatton, so far as Anne was concerned, could go to the devil! What did he have to say to anything? "Of course privacy is essential," she admitted solemnly, mocking him with her eyes. "I have always said that privacy is essential. You may ask my brothers and my parents. Everyone will tell you that I have made it a point to express my opinion on the subject. Very few things are as important as privacy. Cleanliness, godliness . . . and privacy. My motto, I assure you."

He looked as though he wished to box her ears, but could not resist a chuckle. "I had no idea you felt so strongly about the matter, Lady Anne. Strange how we can deceive ourselves into thinking we know someone well, and learn that we have missed a vital element of their character."

"Did you think you knew me well, Mr. Rogers?" she taunted him. His eyes remained on hers, entreating her to—what? Retreat from this dangerous ground? But when he spoke, there was nothing but raillery in his voice.

"Did I say that? I should hope not. It would be very ungentlemanlike to declare one comprehended the character of a lady. Tantamount to expressing a knowledge of creation, I daresay, in its very outrageousness, to say nothing of being sacrilegious. A woman remains always mysterious, no matter how diligently a man endeavors to understand her. Whereas men, on the other hand, are an open book. One has but to look at them to realize the innermost workings of their minds."

"Or their hearts."

Mr. Rogers's lips tightened as he guided her across Davies Street. "As to what you should tell Miss Berryman regarding the exhibit," he remarked, as though continuing an ongoing discussion, "I am convinced that overall the reaction is favorable, despite the negative criticism. Do mention the rougher side, though, as it is impossible to predict that any newspaper fellow who took it in wouldn't be one of the ones who disparaged her work. I should hate for her to have the shock of seeing in print a scathing review when she had been led to believe there was universal acclaim. Wigginton is satisfied, and so am I, that the show will do well, even if"—he managed to grin—"the subjects are the only ones to buy the works."

"So Dunn did express an interest?"

"I didn't say that," he retorted.

"No, of course not." Anne smiled angelically at him. "If Emma had done a portrait of you, would you buy it?"

"Probably, if it was of the quality of her others. She would find me a dull subject, I daresay, with none of Sir Nicholas's roguery nor Lord Dunn's aristocracy."

"You wrong her in an attempt to underestimate yourself, Mr. Rogers," Anne said angrily. "The portraits of Mr. Hill and Mr. Bampton have neither, and yet are quite charming studies. I should know either of them anywhere, and have some idea of what they were like. Surely you did not arrange for her show simply because of the prominence of two of her subjects. That would be despicable!"

They were about to cross to the Square when he stopped, scowling at her. "You know that isn't so, Anne. And I was not making reference to their prominence but to the uniqueness she found in their countenances. My own is hopelessly ordinary by comparison. You cannot deny that."

"Oh, but I can, Harold," she whispered. They stood staring at each other, and she could feel the tension in his body. Slowly, as though attempting to break a spell, he shook his head.

"Now that's another thing I didn't know about you," he said grimly as he propelled her across the street, "that you are so fanciful as to allow yourself unrealistic daydreams. You have a position to maintain, Lady Anne. *Believe me, I never forget that.* I had thought you an eminently sensible young lady, not given to such nonsense. Doubtless this is an aberration which will pass. Let us hope so."

Anne said nothing until they stood before her door. "Won't you join my mother and me for tea? Jack may be in this afternoon as well."

"Thank you, no. I have some rather pressing engagements." When a footman opened the door to her, Mr. Rogers bowed, unsmiling, and left.

CHAPTER TWENTY-ONE

Emma had intended to work on the portrait of her aunt that afternoon but she found there was no pretending that the exhibition was of only cursory interest. Mr. Rogers had suggested she not come by, since she had been there the evening before to see how the pictures were displayed and it was inevitably awkward for the artist to be in the gallery when there were spectators around. Still, Emma found it impossible to concentrate on the nearly completed portrait of Lady Bradwell. She wandered out into the small garden, cursorily inspecting the spring plants as she hugged her shawl more closely about her. Technically winter might be over, but the chill in the air did nothing to prove it. She slumped on a bench, her chin cradled in her hands.

"Now don't eat me for springing on you unawares," a voice begged, as a hand on her shoulder prevented her from rising in alarm.

"I shall have to have a word with the servants," she grumbled. "It's their attitude toward my painting, you know. If I were dressed in rags to—oh, polish silver or something—you may be sure they wouldn't admit visitors."

Lord Dunn grinned down at her. "I should very much like to see you polishing silver, ma'am. I distinctly recollect a time when I saw you seated on a footman's stool where you might have done so."

"Yes, well, I never have. Does that make me unutterably spoiled?"

"Probably. May I sit down?"

Emma waved a gracious hand toward the seat beside her, which was littered with fallen leaves. "Help yourself, though I don't wish to be held accountable if you ruin your pantaloons. I never have to worry when I'm dressed to paint."

Dunn withdrew a handkerchief and efficiently disposed of the debris. "I went to the gallery this afternoon."

A half-eager, half-alarmed light sparked in her eyes. "And?"

"I admit to being immensely impressed, Miss Berryman. Mr.

Wigginton told me the reaction has been mixed, but on the whole favorable. There is never universal agreement on a new painter's works, you know."

"What about Miss Rogers's painting? Did you like it?"

"Very much. Someday I should like to see her watercolors."

A bird sang nearby and Emma smiled. "They're exquisite. I wish she had allowed some of them to be shown."

"Give her time. Some people like to get their toes wet first."

"Not me. I had much rather do it this way. My impatience, I suppose. I shouldn't like holding my breath over a long period of time." Unable to resist, she asked, "Were there many people?"

"Quite a few. The place wasn't packed by any means, but for word of mouth it was better than I expected."

She frowned slightly, rubbing at speckles of paint on her hand. "Curiosity, I imagine. Do you think it would have been better to have concealed my identity?"

"Better for whom? For the gallery, no. For the public, no. For yourself . . . I'm not sure. It really doesn't matter now, though. You will have to expect your name to be bandied about a bit. I shouldn't have thought you would mind," he teased.

"Oddly enough, I do . . . a little," she confessed. "Last year at this time I wouldn't have, but now . . ." Emma glanced hastily away from his interested gaze. "Silly of me. Mr. Rogers assumed that I of all people would have the courage to withstand any censure. And I shall," she declared firmly, straightening her shoulders.

To her surprise he reached for her hand, all paint-spattered as it was, and squeezed it. "I don't doubt it. Remember, you have numerous friends to stand by you. I hope you will count me in that number."

"Thank you! I don't want to be an embarrassment."

He regarded her seriously, still holding her hand. "There are, I'm sure, things you could do which would be an embarrassment but exhibiting good paintings is not one of them. Do I seem so very straightlaced to you?"

"No more than is in keeping with your position," she admitted, gently withdrawing her hand, "but that is quite enough! I am not, and never shall be, a model of propriety, as I am sure you are aware. You've heard Sir Nicholas. He seems intent on blackening my character, but . . . but he would not do so if I had not talked . . . and acted so freely with him."

"I'm not concerned with what Nick said, so far as your character is involved. I would be the first to acknowledge that you are a spirited young lady. What does . . . interest me is his apparent attachment to you. I wonder if he is considering a re-evaluation of his marital status?"

Emma resisted the desire to look away from his searching gray eyes. "I am certain he isn't! Everyone knows that Sir Nicholas will never marry. He has no need for a wife, would only find one a nuisance. And as to his attachment to me . . . Well, we are friends and have been since we met. I don't believe Sir Nicholas is capable of a deep and lasting affection for anyone."

"Hmm, possibly. That does not preclude the possibility of one's feeling a deep and lasting affection for *him*."

It was a question. Absolutely no doubt about it. His brows were raised and the hands that now rested on his knees were far from casually relaxed. Why did he want to know? Was it conceivable . . . Emma answered carefully. "I should think it would be very difficult to feel that way about Sir Nicholas. One could enjoy his company, be amused by his wit, marvel at his scandalous style of living, even feel a sort of kinship with the liberty he has achieved, but only a very green girl would find any substance on which to attach her affection. Sir Nicholas would surely be the first to discourage such a bond."

As though satisfied with her response, he nodded and his face relaxed. "You must be cold, Miss Berryman. I should hate to see you take a chill, as I am hoping to stand up with you at the Inglestone ball this evening. Would you save me a dance? Or perhaps two?"

Unique indeed for Dunn to request a dance in advance. To request two was coming very close to saying that he had a decided interest. Emma rose to cover the confusion, and hope, she felt. "The second waltz and the last cotillion?"

"Excellent. I shall look forward to this evening."

As with many anticipated treats, the evening did not live up to its promise. Emma had dressed particularly carefully, choosing a white crepe round dress over a white sarcenet slip cut low all round the bust, but not so low as to cause disapproval. The white crepe apron and the bottom of the skirt were ornamented with scarlet beads that matched the ribbons wound through her shining gold hair, and the armlet of gold set with rubies that she had inherited from her mother. Before she left her room she studied her reflection in the glass, assuring herself that she looked as well as she ever had, perhaps better. Amelia had taken her to Madame Minotier for the sole purpose of having the gown designed and everything about it was perfect.

Not so the evening. Emma had not anticipated the stir her exhibition would cause, nor the number of people who would flock about her to comment—not always favorably—on having seen her paintings. By the time the second waltz arrived, her nerves were so shattered that she barely realized that Dunn was her partner, despite the gentleness with which he treated her. Long before the end of the ball her face ached with the effort of smiling and her head had begun to pound unmercifully. Though she longed for the solace of her own room, she forced herself to stay and fulfill the dances she had promised, until Dunn came to claim her. He took one look at her drawn face and snapped, "For God's sake, what are you doing to yourself? You should be in bed. Get your wrap. I'll see you and your aunt home immediately."

Even that might not have been so bad. At any other time she might have appreciated his strength, his charming presence in their carriage, but he was unaccountably tight-lipped and silent. Emma noticed several glances pass between him and her aunt but she had not the resources left to contemplate their meaning. When they stood in the hall, Emma was sternly instructed to take herself off to bed without delay, and the last thing she heard as she trudged up the stairs was her aunt's melodious voice asking, "Won't you join me for a glass of brandy, Dunn?"

Emma numbly allowed the maid to undress her and slide a nightdress over her head. Who in heaven's name wanted to be a celebrity if it meant such an intrusion into your life? She had literally not had ten minutes of peace throughout the evening except for the dance with Dunn, and then only because he had the sense to say hardly a word. There had been cranky dowagers ready to revile her for making such an exhibit of herself, stodgy old men eager to insist she knew nothing whatsoever about portrait painting, young men who thought her talent exceeded that of Reynolds (since they had not as yet been to the gallery), and young ladies who regarded her as though she had grown another head. So much for her beautiful ball gown! Besides, Lord William had caught his foot in the hem and it would have to be repaired. Despite her aching head, she refused the laudanum her maid solicitously suggested and crawled into bed as though it were a burrow in which she could hibernate for the duration of the season.

How had Lord Byron stood the attention he received when the first two cantos of *Childe Harold's Pilgrimage* were published? From all Emma had ever heard, he had absolutely lapped up the attention and idolatry. She had expected little attention, and no idolatry, but the novelty of a woman exhibiting portraits (and all of men, as had been frequently pointed out to her!) seemed to have caught the imagination of London's bored elite. She prayed fervently as her head sunk into the feather pillow that it would be a nine days' (or better yet, one-day) wonder. As she drifted off to sleep, she reminded herself that even Byron had had his problems since he woke up famous that day. It was perhaps this unconsciously nagging thought that brought her out of a restless slumber a while later.

More likely it was the dream she had just had in which Sir Nicholas had stood in a gallery exhibiting a painting he had done of her, totally nude. He was pointing out to Dunn her various feminine allures in grotesquely intimate detail, and Dunn was following the exposition with horrified fascination, asking ribald questions with a completely serious demeanor. Shaken, unsure what time it was, Emma sat up in bed and lit a candle with unsteady hands. She felt suddenly young and alone, a child once more who was not wanted anywhere but was constantly shuffled from one well-meaning relation to another. They had not known, any of them, that she was afraid of the dark, because she was too proud to tell them.

Emma slipped her feet out of bed and carried the candle across to check the clock on the mantel. Almost two thirty, but they had not come home until late. It was possible that her aunt was still awake, since she had stayed up to have a drink with Dunn. Not in all the time they had spent together had Emma gone to her aunt's room at night, but she felt desperately anxious for some human contact, and she knew her aunt would be more than willing to give it if she were awake. The memory of that one night she had seen a man enter her aunt's bedchamber had long since faded, and as she made her way down the dark hall she was more intent on how she would explain her need for comfort than on the possibility of interrupting a clandestine meeting.

There was a sudden gust of air that blew out the candle and left Emma in the dark. She felt a flicker of alarm as she heard soft footfalls on the hall carpet and stepped back into a doorway. A man passed without noticing her, obviously sure of his way without the aid of any light and so clearly not expecting anyone to be about that he didn't even look around him. This time Emma had a slightly longer glimpse of him when he opened her aunt's door, though the lighting from within was poor. His build, his features, his athletic grace . . . Emma thought her heart would stop and she pressed a hand against her lips to still the cry that threatened. No, oh, God, no, don't let it be Dunn! She began to tremble so violently that she had to lean back against the door to steady herself. No, it wasn't possible. A trick of the light, that was all. She hadn't been able to see at all clearly. There had never been the slightest sign that Amelia held any particular regard for Dunn and her aunt was not an accomplished actress. Emma felt sure she would have been able to tell if Dunn was her aunt's lover.

And yet . . . Dunn had been here in the house, tonight. In the carriage she had seen them exchange glances. Neither meant a thing, she told herself stubbornly. She had thought at the time that it was concern for her that motivated them—and it was! Any number of men might have looked like Dunn in the dim light. In any case, considering that her aunt had a visitor, Emma knew she should instantly make her way back to her room, close the door, and go to bed. She fully intended to do so, but when her legs felt strong enough to support her, she found herself in something of a trance approaching her aunt's door. There was the muted sound of a deep male voice. Could it be Dunn's? Impossible to tell. And then her aunt spoke, even more softly, totally indistinguishably except . . . Did she call him by name? No, it could not have been "Dunn" that she said. Probably "John" or even "Tom." Emma waited for some time to hear if Amelia repeated the name, waited until the murmurs of passion within drove her back to her room, so distraught that she hardly knew what she was doing.

It wasn't Dunn. It could not be Dunn. He had been so very kind to her of late. There were even signs, however faint, that he was taking particular notice of her. Had she not dared to hope only this afternoon that he was beginning to feel an attachment toward her? Had he not been eager to learn if her own affections were already engaged by Sir Nicholas? Why else would he be interested, if not that he had some partiality of his own? And then Emma realized what was most likely the truth of the matter.

Dunn *was* beginning to care for her, just as she did for him. But the thought, which had made her dress with infinite care earlier in the evening, no longer had the power to enchant her. Rather, her stomach churned so wretchedly that she rushed to the basin in the corner and held her head over it, almost wishing for the relief that vomiting would bring. Even that easing did not come to her, and she eventually climbed wearily back into her bed, pulling the covers up over her head with a groan. Yes, Dunn was beginning to care for her—which was the most logical explanation for the way her aunt had been acting for the last few weeks.

Lady Bradwell, the most generous, openhanded, amiable creature on earth, had become withdrawn, absentminded, lethargic. Attending the usual social functions of the season had become a chore rather than a pleasure. Emma had noticed, after a fashion, but she had been too busy with her painting and with dreams of Dunn to realize the import of this condition. Amelia was thirty-nine now, probably deeply in love with Dunn, and the prospect of losing him at her age could only be blighting. Gentlemen were always looking for newer, younger mistresses, not for a lady of her age, despite her innumerable fine qualities. Emma, all unconsciously, was stealing away her aunt's lover.

And that in itself was an almost unbearable thought. All very well for Lady Bessborough to see her niece married to her former lover; Emma was not of a constitution to bear the pain of such a situation. Why couldn't anything be simple? she wailed silently into her pillow. She couldn't blame Amelia for loving Dunn; she couldn't blame him for choosing such a lovely, warm woman for his mistress. *But why did she herself have to become entangled in such an awful situation? It wasn't fair!*

Emma's last thought before falling into an exhausted sleep was a fast-dying hope: Perhaps it had not been Dunn after all.

Emma paced the back writing room while Sir Nicholas watched with lamentable amusement. He had been surprised, when informed that Lady Bradwell was out, that Miss Berryman would see him, not in the drawing room or the studio, but in her writing room. Her explanation, that she wanted privacy, was the reason for his wicked grin. Miss Berryman had not previously even allowed the door of the room in which they met to be closed.

"Oh, do sit down," she admonished him, "and take that ridiculous smile from your face. This is serious business."

"I didn't know," he drawled, lowering himself onto a chair. "I assumed it would be a light dalliance."

She scowled at him but soon marched off to the window again, too agitated to seat herself. "Sir Nicholas . . . Oh, I don't know how to begin. Have you noticed that Aunt Amelia is not herself these days?"

Mildly surprised, he nodded. "Yes, she hasn't been at all in spirits."

Emma wandered about the room, picking up a book and replacing it, straightening the pens on her desk. "Do you know why?"

He sat silent for a moment, his lips pursed. "I think so."

Oh, to have this over with. Emma sat down facing him but before she could bring herself to speak was once again on her feet. He couldn't see her clearly when she stood before the sunny window, but even he could tell by the high pitch of her voice that she was greatly disturbed. "I can't ask her. You can see that, can't you? And there is no one else I can ask . . . except you. Once, a long time ago, you hinted that you knew who her . . . lover was. I must know."

"Why?"

"Because . . ." Emma turned away and laid her forehead against the windowpane. In a muffled voice she said, "Because I seem to have inadvertently . . . Nicholas, is it Dunn?"

Any trace of amusement had long since left his face. He neither moved nor spoke for what seemed a very long time. "I think so. You must understand that I can't know for sure, but I have suspected as much for several years. Amelia had never confided his identity to me, and certainly Dunn would never speak. There is no way for me to know absolutely. I could be wrong."

When she remained standing there with head bowed and shoulders slumped, he rose and went to put an arm about her waist. A comforting gesture, understood by both of them. "I'm sorry, Emma. In my awkward way I tried to warn you, or perhaps to warn him off. I'm not very good at that sort of thing. Amelia and I have been friends for twenty years, give or take a few, and I really don't want to see her hurt. Strange, she's one person I've felt rather close to. There have been times when I've actually been downright open with her, talking out some forgettable problem, and she's shared a few of her own." He grimaced at the back of her head. "Never any names, of course. The woman is undoubtedly the most discreet human being I've ever met. Do you need a handkerchief?"

"No, thank you." Emma stepped out of his encircling arm and went to sit on the chair she had formerly vacated. Her attempted smile did not noticeably affect her stricken eyes. "Well, I'm glad to know in time. It would have been easier if she'd told me, but of course she never would. I appreciate your honesty. Aunt Amelia has quite a friend in you, though I must confess I found your tactics odd in the extreme. Not until . . . recently did I have the slightest idea what you were about, and I don't think Lord Dunn did either."

"I didn't want to be obvious," he grumbled.

"You weren't," she informed him dryly.

He stood staring down at her woebegone face and sighed. "I tell you what, Emma. I'll take over your driving lessons."

"Is no sacrifice too great for you?" she asked in mock wonder.

"Don't get uppity with me, young lady. You won't want to spend a lot of time with Dunn now, and I think it's only fair that I take over where he has begun."

Emma smiled tremulously at him. "You're very kind, Nicholas, but life isn't always fair. There's no need."

With a muttered oath he strolled to the door, pausing only to say, "I'll pick you up tomorrow afternoon at three."

There seemed little likelihood of meeting Dunn at the Fulbrook card party that evening, or Emma would have cried off with a headache. Amelia enjoyed playing whist and was an exceptionally skillful and lucky cardplayer, which was why Emma had originally told her aunt that she preferred the card party to the Hunters' rout. And indeed neither of them were particularly devoted to the morose pair the Hunters made (Woeful and Wretched, Sir Nicholas disrespectfully called them), or to the Smythes, whose minuscule town house was always crammed to the walls when they had a musical evening, as they were planning that day. It seemed clear to Emma that Dunn, if he went to any of those particular entertainments, would choose the rout. She had not once during the time she had spent in London chanced to meet him at a card party and assumed, as was likely, that when he wished to play he went to White's or Watier's. Most of the gentlemen of her acquaintance did.

Tables were set up in three different rooms and Emma found herself partnering a middle-aged gentleman she had met on several occasions. His good humor did not belie the fact that he took his cards seriously, and she turned her full attention to the game. Cards had never particularly interested her; she had only learned the previous season to play the most common games. Her concentration on an appropriate play was entirely ruined by her absent glance at the doorway, where Lord Dunn stood watching her, a faint smile on his lips. She acknowledged his presence with a restrained nod, playing the first card that came to hand. Her partner regarded her with surprise, which turned to glee as the play progressed. The hand won, he beamed across the table. "A brilliant play, Miss Berryman. I would never have attempted it."

Aware of Dunn standing behind her, Emma said, "Thank you. I fear it was more luck than skill, Mr. Jackson. Perhaps Lord Dunn would care to take my place, as I feel a slight headache coming on."

Politeness required that Dunn accept, but he regarded her with a puzzled expression as she excused herself, and his eyes followed her hasty exit from the room. Unwilling to seek out her aunt and sure that Dunn would be unable to leave the card game for some time, she made her way to the dining saloon, where refreshments were set out on the table and sideboard. Neither the lobster salad nor the garnished ham appealed to Emma, nor in fact did the fruited jellies or raspberry cream. She helped herself to a small portion of charlotte russe just to have something on her plate and allowed her gaze to wander about in search of a familiar face. There were usually fewer at card parties than at any other type of entertainment. To her vast surprise she saw Maggie and her husband standing apart from the others near the window. With a teasing smile she joined them.

"Ah, I see Lord Greenwood has allowed you to escape from your cage for an evening." She laughed. "However did you manage to convince him it would do you no harm to have a little fun?" She would not have dared to such familiarity, had not Maggie just a week ago shyly confessed to her that Greenwood had "expressed his affection" for her. Trust Maggie to understate the case; Greenwood positively radiated his pride in her, his "affection," and his protectiveness.

"Couldn't see any harm in a card party," he assured her in earnest. "There's never a crush like at a ball or rout, and I could see Margaret was in need of something livelier than another evening at home. I suggested the musical evening at the Smythes, but she said she preferred this."

"I don't blame her," Emma murmured.

Maggie grinned. "I won half a crown, too, partnering Mr. Fulbrook. Greenwood won't play for such paltry stakes, so he stood muttering over my shoulder."

"I never muttered!" he protested. "Thought you played the hand just right. It was Fulbrook who nearly scotched your chances, but he's a wily old devil. I never sit at a table with him at the club."

"Would you find me a glass of champagne, Greenwood?" Maggie asked.

"Of course, my dear. Won't be a moment."

When he had left them Emma looked questioningly at her friend. "Are you feeling well?"

"Oh, yes. The doctor says it will be a few weeks yet. What I wanted to say was that I've been able to come up with no solution to curbing Sir Nicholas's wayward tongue. I've thought about it a great deal but can see no way to change his penchant for taunting you other than to sit down and talk it out with him. You might be able to do that."

Emma felt the numbness invade her body again, though she tried her best to allow no hint of it to show in her countenance. "I did, this morning. I don't think he will do so again. We . . . understand each other now."

"I'm so glad." Maggie was not wholly satisfied with Emma's strange expression but she made no mention of it. "Is Lord Dunn here this evening?"

"Yes, he's in one of the card rooms." She saw Greenwood approaching with the champagne and changed the subject. "Have you been to the gallery? I'm afraid not everyone is as complimentary of my work as you!"

"Greenwood has promised to take me tomorrow. You're not upset, are you?" Perhaps this was the explanation for her friend's odd lack of vitality.

"A little," Emma confessed, accepting with thanks the glass Greenwood handed her after his wife. "I suppose it's like someone coming up to your new baby and saying, 'By God, he's ugly.' It tends to make one a bit defensive."

Adam accepted her rueful smile at face value. "Pay no heed to 'em, Miss Berryman, is my advice. I've talked to several chaps who were most impressed, and the others . . . well, what do they know?"

"That's what I ask myself," she said, managing a laugh. "I'm almost satisfied with my portrait of you, Lord Greenwood. Why don't you bring Maggie around to see it?"

"Are you?" Maggie asked, surprised. "But I thought you said . . ."

"I did, but I have a better vision of him now, so to speak."

"We could come tomorrow morning," Adam suggested, "just after we go to the gallery. I've never understood why you had so much trouble with mine when you hadn't the slightest problem with anyone else, after the start."

"Perhaps it was because you have such a complex personality," a voice behind them remarked dryly.

"Dunn!" Adam looked guiltily at his friend's brother. "I didn't know you were here. Whatever possessed you to come to such a tame party?"

"I rather fancy my motives were similar to yours," the viscount replied with a glance in Emma's direction.

"Couldn't have been," Adam declared stoutly. "I came because Margaret wished to have an evening out. I never urged her to come! Promise you I am seeing that she gets all the rest and exercise the doctor recommends!"

"I'm sure you are," Dunn said absently. "You look in blooming health, Lady Greenwood. I wonder if you would mind my borrowing Miss Berryman for a moment."

"Not at all," Maggie agreed, assuming this was precisely what Emma might wish.

Emma reluctantly moved off with him as he helped himself to a serving of the lobster salad. With his back to her he asked, "Is your headache better?"

"It didn't develop after all. Seeing Maggie quite cheered me."

"When is her lying-in expected?"

"A few weeks yet."

"Did you find partnering Mr. Jackson particularly trying?"

Emma stiffened. "No, not really. I don't enjoy cards very much."

He lifted one dark brow. "I'm surprised that you came, then."

"Aunt Amelia is fond of a card party. I think she's tiring of the larger entertainments."

"The season has hardly begun." He surveyed her skeptically and added ham to his plate. "Can I help you to something?"

"No, thank you. I'm not hungry."

As they walked past the heaped plates he added several other items to his before directing her to some chairs in the corner. "Have people been annoying you with their comments on your portraits?"

"No, no. Hardly anyone has even mentioned them this evening. I don't think this particular group frequents art galleries." She smoothed the skirt of her lilac gown with nervous fingers.

Silence descended as he sampled the various items on his plate. Emma could think of nothing to say. When from time to time he glanced at her, she gave a perfunctory smile and looked away.

"I think probably you are in need of some fresh air and exercise," he remarked at length. "Shall I give you another driving lesson tomorrow afternoon?"

"Oh, no, I can't! Thank you. You've been very kind to take the trouble."

"You can't stay locked in your studio all day. I'm sure even Reynolds takes a break."

It was difficult to summon up a smile for his attempt at lightness. Emma tried. "He probably doesn't go out every night, though."

"Are you worn down by the season already? I was used to think you possessed of boundless energy."

"It seems to have deserted me."

"So I see. Well, perhaps I could take you driving the day after tomorrow. You'd have time to build up your resources."

"Thank you, no. That won't be possible." Emma rose abruptly. "I really must speak with Maggie before she leaves. Please don't get up."

He did rise, though, wearing a puzzled frown, and reached over to place his plate on the table. "I think they've returned to one of the card rooms. I'll help you find her."

"No, really, I'm capable of finding her by myself," she said firmly. "I insist that you stay and finish your supper."

His bow was minimal, almost mocking, but she could not explain herself. She spent the rest of her time at the Fulbrooks' avoiding him. When she and Amelia at last climbed into the carriage, she heaved a sigh of relief. But she did not rest well that night and Maggie remarked the next morning, when they came, that she looked peaked. "I'm fine," Emma insisted. Their pleasure with Adam's portrait did not noticeably lift her spirits, and an amusing review of her work in the paper did not make her smile. By the time Nicholas came to take her driving she felt absolutely cross.

"I've taken the edge off them," he told her as he handed her into the curricle, "so you may drive straightaway if you wish."

"Thank you, no. I had not progressed to the busier London streets as yet, and I'm unfamiliar with your pair. If you don't mind, I'd rather wait until we get to the park."

"As you wish." He placed a booted foot on the iron step and swung himself up beside her with all the grace of a man half his age. Emma had still not learned to think of thirty-nine as anything but "older" and she was admiring of his dexterity. Nicholas eyed her askance and muttered, "I'm not decrepit, you know, Emma."

"I never said you were—or thought it. You're remarkably active."

"For a man my age." His voice was laden with sarcasm. "You will find, my dear girl, that twenty years from now you will feel very nearly as young as you do today. Any signs of aging you will studiously ignore and press yourself the harder to do anything you could do in your youth. And frankly, there are very few things I can't do now that I could do then. I come from a long-lived family, you know. My mother is still gadding about the Continent at sixty, showing not the least inclination to slow down. My father did not die of age, but of a riding accident. My grandmother is still alive at eighty-five and I have a great-uncle who boasts of ninety-two, though my mother swears he's only ninety. I'm a comparative babe."

Emma restrained a chuckle as they swept into the park. Her mentor glared at her as he handed over the reins. "There are advantages to age, Emma, and one of them is that you command the respect of youth," he reminded her loftily.

"Oh, I have the greatest respect for you," she retorted. "I venerate the very gray hairs of your head."

"Gray hairs! Doing it too brown, my girl. Keep your eyes on the road. My pair aren't used to an unfamiliar hand on the reins. Did Dunn not teach you that you must be constantly alert?"

"Of course he did." Her voice was cool and she said nothing further until she had successfully negotiated a box that had fallen in the road. "He was an exacting teacher but he did seem to think that it was possible to carry on a conversation while driving."

"I see he has also directed you to the proper type of gauntlets for driving."

Emma flushed slightly. Although Dunn had told her on that first drive to purchase appropriate gloves, she had been surprised the next morning by a box in the hall that had contained the gauntlets she now wore. The accompanying note had explained his concern that she would not know where to shop for such an item and his hope that she would accept them in lieu of a posy. They were rather an expensive present to accept, and so she had protested when next he came, but he had shrugged off such niceness. "I could have sent you an out-of-season apricot tart that would have cost more"—he laughed—"or a bunch of lilies of the valley such as I saw in the hall on the way in." She had thanked him and kept them.

"The reins bite into your hands in riding gloves," she answered Sir Nicholas as she slowed the pair to a sedate pace to cross the Serpentine. A pink-breasted linnet flashed in the bushes ahead and she heard the first notes of his song spill out over the spring greenery. "We're having remarkably fine weather for this time of year, aren't we?"

He regarded her quizzingly. "Have we sunk to banalities, Emma?"

"You wouldn't want me to discuss something so engrossing that my attention to your pair was disturbed, would you?"

"Heaven forbid! You needn't say a word! I shall just tell you that you look remarkably fine with some color in your cheeks. And that I like the way you're wearing your hair this season. The curls over your ears are decidedly provocative. Now as to your lips . . . I know how provocative they are, but you have barely smiled since I called for you. Not that I can't appreciate the serious side of a woman, but I find it disconcerting to have it exhibited when I'm being my most charming. Or so I thought. Do you call that a Russian wrapping-cloak? How clever of you to choose one with a pelerine of such enormous size. It shows your long neck to admirable advantage."

"Really, Sir Nicholas," she protested, flustered.

"Nick, if you please. In case you haven't noticed, I've been calling you Emma all day."

"I had noticed, and I don't mind, so long as we're alone, but it would look strange for you to do so in company."

Her concentration, such as it was, was on the pair ahead, but he had noticed a rider approaching them down the path to the right. He touched her cheek familiarly with a gloved finger, saying, "You're quite as courageous as you are lovely, my dear Emma. And not a bad driver at that."

Her flush of pleasure was easily discerned by Dunn as he drew abreast of them. For a moment he could not believe his eyes. Miss Berryman handling the ribbons of Sir Nicholas's curricle. Unheard of. He, Dunn, was supposed to be the one teaching her to drive. She had refused his offer last night so that she could drive with Nick. He repeated the self-evident fact to himself, with only slightly more credulity than the first time. Naturally she would find the victory of Nick's allowing her to handle the ribbons something out of the ordinary, but did that excuse her from not mentioning it to him, allowing him to come upon them without warning? And why did she permit Nick to be so familiar with her, and look pleased by the gesture? Dunn was hardly conscious of how grim his countenance had become.

After a glance at him Emma drew the team to a halt. "Good afternoon, Lord Dunn," she said brightly. "As you see, Sir Nicholas has agreed to take over the responsibility of teaching me to drive. He's as hard a taskmaster as you are! His pair are not as well-trained but that will only add to my experience, won't it?"

"No doubt. I didn't mind teaching you to drive, Miss Berryman."

Emma wanted nothing more than to erase the hurt and perplexity she read in his eyes, but she forced herself to choke down the words that would make everything right with him. She cast a helpless glance at Sir Nicholas, who immediately thrust himself into the breach.

"Emma will progress a little faster with me, I think. For early lessons the park is all very well, but I plan to have her driving in London traffic on the way back to Bruton Street. Trial by fire, and all that. She's a bit more adventurous than you gave her credit for, Dunn . . . in many ways."

Cringing at the flare of anger in Dunn's eyes, Emma placed a pleading hand on Nicholas's arm. Don't go too far, her eyes begged, and he put a hand possessively over hers as he remarked, "We are two of a kind, you know, Emma and I. Daring enough to seek more enjoyment than most; prudent enough to stay within society's bounds. It's not often one finds a kindred spirit, is it?"

"No," Dunn replied through tight lips, "it isn't."

Emma paled. "I . . . I appreciate all the trouble you've taken with my driving lessons."

"Yes, so you said last night. I trust you will enjoy yourself." Dunn gave a brusque nod to them both, set his heels to his horse, and rode off.

Her hands clenching the reins, Emma sadly watched as he grew more distant. "Did you have to do that?"

"Yes. I'm sorry but it was necessary. You will learn, my dear, that there's never the least use in trying to extricate yourself gently from a delicate situation. The misunderstandings you save yourself by a good clean break are worth the momentary discomfort."

Momentary. Did he believe that? Emma peered up at him through moist lashes but could read nothing in his averted face. With a shaking breath she gathered up the reins and asked, "Did you really mean I could drive through the streets?"

CHAPTER TWENTY-TWO

The gallery on Bond Street was closed, as any right-minded shopkeeper would insist, on that Sunday afternoon. Nonetheless, there were several visitors, each of whom left with a large, flat parcel, wrapped in brown paper to protect it from the inclement weather. Dunn had agonized over the decision from the moment he had seen Miss Berryman with Sir Nicholas in the park. Her defection had not changed: she was not at home to him, politely refused to stand up with him at dances, avoided his company whenever possible. What distressed him most, perhaps, was that she had obviously lied to him. Only a green girl, she had said, would find any substance on which to attach her affection for Sir Nicholas.

And yet, since that day, she was to be found more and more frequently in the baronet's company, always vivacious, occasionally almost flirtatious. Her animation, which appeared to vanish entirely in Dunn's presence, peaked in Sir Nicholas's. At first Dunn had thought she meant to make him jealous and he scorned such an obvious gambit, but it became more and more clear that she really wished no part of him at all.

Through the weeks of the exhibit he continued to champion Emma's portraiture, though he refused to comment on whether he intended to have the one of himself. In the end, unable to do otherwise, he had arranged with Mr. Wigginton to purchase it anonymously. Having no desire to be seen at the gallery, he had picked it up himself Sunday morning while most people were in church, climbing into his closed carriage afterward with a sigh of relief at not having encountered anyone he knew.

Mr. Wigginton had been sympathetic to Lord Dunn's request,

despite the fact that he had agreed with the other purchasers to be in the shop on Sunday afternoon, some time after the hour Dunn wished to call. There was a new exhibit to be planned for a Tuesday opening and he found plenty to busy himself in his office. If he was amused, or surprised, by the sour look Dunn bestowed on the portrait of Sir Nicholas, he didn't show it. When Dunn had reminded him abruptly that no one was to be informed of his purchase, Mr. Wigginton had merely replied, "Of course, my lord."

Sir Nicholas had made no such clandestine appointment. He had arrived slightly later than he had promised, laughed at his tardiness, cheerfully wrote out a bank draft for the painting, tucked it under his arm, and accosted a friend in the street to describe his pleasant mission. "I shall hang it in my drawing room so that any visitors who have to await me will have my likeness to keep them company." He laughed.

There had been buyers, even, for the portraits of Mr. Hill and Mr. Bampton, and they came soon after Sir Nicholas to walk off with their prizes. The last gentleman to arrive at the Bond Street shop was Mr. Hatton, subject of "The Fencer." He was neither circumspect nor ostentatious about his purchase, and because he lived in Albemarle Street, he merely carried the painting to his lodgings, where he instantly had a servant hang it in his breakfast parlor and stood back to admire it. "She's flattered me," he said aloud to the empty room, but he was nonetheless delighted with the painting. "I must invite Persigny around to see it."

And the thought of his fencing master induced an almost irresistible urge to have a go with the foils. Persigny was used to his aberrations and would not, if he weren't otherwise occupied, take it amiss if Mr. Hatton arrived on his stoop for a bit of sport. Their acquaintance went back over a period of ten years, all told, and their skills were now so well matched that the teacher-pupil relationship had broken down into one of sporting associates, a social leveler if ever there was one. Mr. Hatton grabbed up the curly-brimmed beaver he had tossed on a chair, disposed it casually on his head, and departed for Argyll Street.

The porter who answered M. Persigny's door announced that his master was out and not expected back until late. This was a setback, of course, but Mr. Hatton was of an even disposition and was seldom cast down by any circumstance over which he had no control. When he turned from the door his eye was caught by the house across the street, and he remembered Mr. Rogers saying that his sister had painted him while sitting in their drawing room on the first floor. With opera glasses at the ready, he thought ruefully. He could see no movement in the first-floor window, but his curiosity was aroused and before the thought had barely had time to take root, he crossed and beat a tattoo with the brass knocker. "If I might just have a word with Miss Rogers," he said to the aged retainer who opened the door. Handing the man his card, he added, "She might not recognize my name. You may tell her it is the Fencer." Skeptical but polite, the servant ushered him into the hall, opening the first door on the right.

"If you will wait here, sir, I will ascertain whether Miss Rogers is available."

The room he entered was a small breakfast parlor done in shades of green and beige. On the walls were numerous watercolors so exquisite that he wandered bemused from one to the other. They bore not the slightest resemblance to the painting she had done of him, being nature studies and landscapes, but he was the more enchanted not to have to fight his own vanity in order to appreciate them.

A movement in the doorway made him swing about guiltily. "Miss Rogers?" he asked uncertainly, faced with a white-haired lady of what age—twenty? thirty? It was impossible for him to tell.

"Yes." She stepped into the room, leaving the door open behind her, and extended her hand. "Mr. Hatton. How nice of you to call. My brother told me that you had offered for my painting of you."

He gripped her hand firmly, forgetting for a moment, until he saw her wince, that his handshake was notoriously strong. He had been cautioned by more than one gentleman of his acquaintance that he should bear in mind he was pressing human flesh and not taking a life-or-death grip on a fencing foil. "I beg your pardon! Have I hurt you? Lord, I'm frightfully sorry." He could see, close up, that she was young, not much above twenty, he would guess, but the hair was stark white, naturally. No powder could have given it that clean radiance.

Helena laughed. "No, you merely startled me, Mr. Hatton. Won't you sit down?"

There were two chairs near the front window placed there for just such visitors. The house in Argyll Street was not large enough to have a special waiting room for guests, and the breakfast parlor, cozy and comfortable as it was, served a dual purpose. Harold was out and Helena didn't like to have strangers brought to the drawing room, especially if their calls were likely to be brief. She seated herself and expected Mr. Hatton to do likewise, but at the last moment his eye was caught by the watercolor that flanked the window and he stood before it, shaking his head.

"These are yours, too, aren't they?"

"Yes," she admitted. "I'm afraid I doodle in my spare time."

"Doodle?" He turned on her with a fierce frown. "How dare you call such delicate work doodling? Why wasn't it shown at the gallery along with 'The Fencer'?"

"Mr. Hatton," she said, a trifle nervous, "I haven't the courage to face criticism the way Miss Berryman has. And you may be sure they would be criticized! If not for the technique, then for the subject matter. Have you ever known a member of the ton to go into ecstasies over a watercolor of a leaf? The very medium is a schoolgirl's. I happen to like it, but it does not make for works of distinguished art."

"How old are you?" he asked suddenly.

"I can't see what my age has to say to anything. Did you have some purpose in calling, Mr. Hatton?"

"Of course I did." He sat down beside her and grinned. "I didn't mean to set up your back, Miss Rogers. Your brother may have told you that I was a bit annoyed when I learned how you came to paint me fencing. It was just the original shock. Really, I'm out of reason delighted. I bought the painting; took it home today, and had it hung in my breakfast parlor—like you do. But seeing these," he said with a grandiose gesture about the room, "I find that the room lacks quite a bit. I really am enchanted by them. Have you others? May I see them? Would you be willing to sell some?"

Helena held up a protesting hand. "You are going too fast, Mr. Hatton. No one has ever offered to buy one of my watercolors before, and I promise you any number of people have seen them. My brother has several hanging in the drawing room, so it is impossible for visitors to miss them. Not that he calls attention to them," she assured him earnestly. "I couldn't bear that. What I mean to say is that, although a few have been so kind as to praise them, no one has ever shown the least inclination to have them decorate the walls of their homes. You would be considered . . . eccentric if you were to do so."

"Nonsense. And even if I were, what difference would it make?" Mr. Hatton eyed her quizzically. "Do people consider you eccentric because you have white hair?"

Helena bit her lip. "Yes," she said coldly.

"Exactly. It's out of the ordinary. You could have it dyed, but you prefer to leave it untouched because it's yours, it's natural, it's the way you like it."

"Possibly."

"You're angry with me for mentioning it." He stood up and paced about the table, stopping before one of the watercolors of a garden in spring. "Have you a series of this garden? You know—spring, summer, autumn, winter?"

Surprised, she nodded.

"They shouldn't be separated," he informed her flatly before walking to the next one. "And this landscape. Have you done it at different times of the day—morning, noon, evening, night?"

Again she nodded.

"These were done in the country. At your home?"

"Yes."

He faced her, his countenance serious. "Let us set a time when your brother will be here for me to see what works you have available. I can see you're uncomfortable being here alone with me. You needn't be, but I don't suppose I could convince you of that. Say, Wednesday morning at eleven. I have an appointment with M. Persigny that morning and could come here afterward."

Helena was well aware that he came to M. Persigny every Wednesday morning. "I will try to arrange for my brother to be here. He often has business in the City."

Mr. Hatton was not the least daunted by a gentleman's connection with the City. "So do I," he assured her cheerfully. "If he can't be here Wednesday, we'll set another time. Now, before I go, I want to tell you how much I like 'The Fencer.' You've flattered me, of course, but the sheer movement you've captured is remarkable. I hope you'll not stop at one such effort, though from what I've seen here I wouldn't want you to abandon your watercolors, either. Does that sound patronizing? I don't mean it to. I simply want to tell you I think you have a marvelous talent. Different from Miss Berryman's. Hers has a brilliance, a flamboyancy, that yours cannot, and should not, aspire to. Your work has a shining simplicity, an enduring delicacy that she could not achieve if she tried a thousand years. But I'm sure both of you have the sense, the integrity, to stay with those things you do best. There, that's all I wished to say—except that I like your white hair!"

Too astonished to do more than rise, Helena speechlessly watched his elegant bow and graceful departure from the room before collapsing back onto her chair. So that was Mr. Hatton. A rather outspoken fellow . . . but with excellent taste, she told herself, amused. She had watched him come and go, observed his fencing, and wondered about him. More than wondered, she scolded herself. She had allowed herself girlish daydreams about him, adding to his fantasy dossier whenever nothing more pressing kept her busy on Wednesday mornings. Had she not invested him with a love of art? And a philosophical turn of mind, despite the careless good humor his very walk denoted? There were times when she had even envisioned Mr. Hatton having some business transaction with her brother in the City, and Harold bringing him home to dine with them.

One would think I hadn't a thing better to do than let my mind gather wool this way, Helena thought as she rose. Being in London is always disconcerting in a way. At Farthing Hill I would mingle the painting with the mending, but here . . . Well, if I haven't found a subject with Mr. Hatton's fascination to paint, at least I have the friendship of Anne and the stimulation of meetings of the Philosophical Society. And, she mused, her eyes dancing, the possibility that Mr. Hatton will decorate his breakfast parlor with her watercolors!

It was not necessary for Adam to go to the shop in Bond Street for his portrait, since it had never been there. Emma had had it sent over to his town house in Half Moon Street a week after he and Maggie had gone to see it there. His likeness hung, temporarily, in the hall outside his wife's room, and he sat gazing morosely at it now, seated on a chair that had been placed there for him. Eventually the portrait would be taken to Combe Lodge to be hung next to that of his wife in the gallery, but he wasn't thinking about that. He was thinking about Margaret, and for possibly the first time in his life he felt sick with anxiety. When the door opened, he jumped to his feet, attempting to peer into the room before his sister firmly shut it after herself.

"How is she?"

Cynthia smiled and pressed his hand. "She's doing very well, Adam. The first baby always takes the longest to put in its appearance. Maggie is a regular trooper."

"But the doctor thinks everything is going all right, doesn't he? There's no danger, is there?"

"Nothing whatsoever unusual, I assure you. Dr. Botley asked if you would have a glass of brandy sent up to him."

Adam frowned. "I don't want him foxed when it comes time to deliver the baby."

"Oh, Adam"—she laughed—"you remind me of James. Dr. Botley is not likely to becomed foxed on a glass of brandy. Remember, he's been here for eight hours now."

"We've fed him," Adam muttered, "and we'll feed him again, I daresay. Cynthia, I hear her cry out sometimes."

"Childbirth is not a painless activity, my dear brother, as I am sure you are aware. It won't do you the least good to sit here and worry about her. Go down to your library and try to engross yourself in a book. You may be sure we will call you if there's anything you should know. And don't forget to have a glass of brandy sent to Dr. Botley."

"Oh, very well." Adam wandered disconsolately down the stairs, feeling woefully left out of the important events transpiring in his own house. He did remember to have a footman take brandy up to the doctor but paused undecided in the entry hall. A few weeks ago, or perhaps months, he would have considered distracting himself by going out to White's, but he hadn't the slightest desire now. What he needed, he decided rather forlornly, was someone to talk to, and the idea of sending a message around to Stephen Midford occurred to him. No, that was impossible: the captain had gone off to Newmarket. The idea of writing to Dunn edged into his mind and he tried several times to dislodge it. This was no time to have the viscount berating him for something he didn't even know he'd done. But once the idea took hold, there was no denying the plan. If Dunn would come, Adam would be grateful for his companionship.

The note was penned and dispatched in a matter of minutes and Adam prowled about the downstairs receiving rooms waiting for a reply. His eye fell on the art book that he had intended to lend to Miss Berryman. The works of Sir Joshua Reynolds, Gainsborough, William Beechey, George Romney, Sir Thomas Lawrence, Sir Henry Raeburn, and John Constable were represented among others, and he felt sure Miss Berryman would be interested in the collection. Had Margaret paid her for the portrait? Would Miss Berryman have allowed it from one of her best friends? Adam carried the book into his library, absently gave his setter a quick pat on the head, and seated himself at his desk. By Jove, he would just send the book to her from the two of them, whether she had been paid for the portrait or not. Margaret would be pleased with him for doing that. If they wanted a copy of the book themselves, they would simply go out and get another one.

The footman, who was requested to bring some brown wrapping

paper and string, showed no surprise. Adam was hard at work wrapping the package, a task with which he was unfamiliar and hopelessly devoid of expertise, when Lord Dunn was shown into the library.

"Your problem," Dunn informed him with twinkling eyes, "is that you need a pair of scissors. Then you could cut the paper to size, and you wouldn't have to struggle with breaking the string. Did you send for me to help?"

"Certainly not!" Adam pushed the package away from him with a disgusted motion. "Scissors, you say? Margaret could have done it a lot better but she's started her lying-in, you know."

"I didn't know," Dunn replied, taking the seat to which Adam waved him. "This must be a very alarming time for you."

"Well, it is and all. Cynthia says she's doing just fine, but, Dunn, it must hurt like hell. I've never heard Margaret cry out like that, except when she lost the first one."

"You mustn't dwell on that. Is Dr. Botley here?"

"Oh, yes, he came eight or nine hours ago." Adam scratched his head with an unconscious nervous gesture. "Cynthia said the first one takes a long time. I don't know if I could go through this more than once."

Dunn regarded him sympathetically. "I'm sure you could if you had to. Lady Greenwood is a resolute woman. I don't think you need fear for her endurance. Is your sister with her now?"

"Hasn't left her side since she got here, and she got here before Botley did. Do you think Botley knows what he's doing? I mean, a man and all. What can he know of how a woman's body works?"

"He has a solid reputation," Dunn soothed him. "I believe he studied surgery before he became a man midwife. Your wife has confidence in him; that's the important thing."

"How do you know she has confidence in him?"

"Because she told me so, Adam, when I asked her."

Adam groaned. "I never thought to ask her that. Will I ever learn to be a proper husband?"

Although Dunn's eyes remained serious, he smiled. "Do you know, I think you have. I admit to having had my doubts at the start—but we won't go into that. These last weeks your wife has shown more than the surface calm she always projected. There's a deeper peace, a real happiness, that I don't think she could have achieved without your concurrence. I don't think she ever expected you to change, Adam. Probably all she ever wanted was your affection."

"She has it," Adam said fervently, and flushed with embarrassment. In a gruff voice he changed the subject. "Cynthia sent me away, told me to busy myself elsewhere. I thought I would just wrap this art book to send to Miss Berryman. She finished my portrait."

A guarded expression settled on Dunn's face. "Did she? It wasn't in the exhibition."

"Oh, she finished it after the show opened. We've hung it upstairs in the hall until we can take it to Combe Lodge."

"Might I see it?"

Adam was more than eager to have an excuse for being in the hall outside his wife's room. Actually, he hadn't liked being as far away as the library, so he was perfectly willing to stand and talk with Dunn, whose intense interest in the portrait did not seem out of the ordinary to him in his present distracted state.

"I understand Miss Berryman started it at Combe Lodge," Dunn remarked conversationally.

"Some months ago, yes, but she couldn't seem to get it right. I overheard her talking with Margaret one day, and Miss Berryman said the strangest thing. Well, I can't really go into that, of course, but when Margaret told her that I thanked her for . . . something, Miss Berryman said, 'How sweet! Perhaps I shall be able to finish his portrait after all.'"

Dunn stared at him in the dim hallway light. "Did Miss Berryman say anything about her other subjects? How she had come to paint them, perhaps?"

"No, she was annoyed with Sir Nicholas for something. I don't remember what . . . Oh, yes, it had to do with his teasing her. I gather he'd kissed her once and wouldn't let her forget it." Adam strove to recall the conversation. "Ah, yes, I have it! She was angry with him for always teasing her in front of you. Told Margaret she wished your good opinion. Isn't that a kicker, after the way she has pinched at you for the last year?"

"Very amusing," Dunn remarked in a strangely tense voice. "Did she say anything else?"

"Not that I recall. I had other matters on my mind."

There was the faint sound of an infant's wail from Maggie's bedroom and Dunn immediately clapped him on the shoulder. "I think the worst is over, and since there's been no chaotic activity, things must have gone well. I shan't stay. Would you like me to deliver the package to Miss Berryman?"

Adam hardly heard him. His eyes and ears were trained on the closed door. "Why doesn't someone come?"

"Someone will, in a moment," Dunn assured him. "They will have to wrap the baby and Lady Greenwood will want to see it. Ah, here is Mrs. Morton now."

Cynthia stood in the doorway, her eyes brimming with joyful tears. "Maggie's fine, Adam. It's a boy. If you will be patient just a few more minutes you may come in and see them." And she closed the door abruptly behind herself again.

Feeling as though he had been holding his breath for hours, Adam let out a long, grateful sigh. "She's fine, and it's a boy," he told Dunn, either momentarily forgetting that the viscount was not hard of hearing, or simply wishing to say the words aloud himself.

"Congratulations to you both!" Dunn shook his hand firmly. "Now I really must disappear. This is no time for me to be intruding. Shall I take the package to Miss Berryman?"

"Certainly, certainly. I'd meant to write a note, but my handwriting's so poor she probably wouldn't be able to read it, anyway. She'll want to hear the good news and you can tell her. Thanks for stopping by, Dunn."

"Anytime. Give my best to Lady Greenwood."

Dunn had the inelegantly wrapped package under his arm when he descended the front steps into Half Moon Street. He had walked from his home but now debated the wisdom of returning for his curricle, on the extremely remote possibility that Miss Berryman would agree to accompany him for a drive. More likely she would be out with Sir Nicholas at this very moment, he decided, pulling his watch from his pocket. Almost five. No, even Nick wasn't likely to have her out so late, when the traffic in the park became unnervingly heavy for a new driver. She would be in Bruton Street, perhaps preparing for the evening. His mental scan of the night's parties added no pleasure to his somber thoughts. Without intentionally deciding, he had begun to stride along Curzon Street, his pace more rapid than usual. She could be cozzened into seeing him, if she was at home. The news he brought would be of great interest. But what if her aunt was there, or Sir Nicholas?

When he handed his hat and gloves to the butler, Dunn felt a twinge of trepidation. The butler had been instructed on every recent occasion (when Lady Bradwell was out) to inform him that Miss Berryman was not receiving. Taking no chance of another rejection should she be home, Dunn asked him to convey the message that he had word from Half Moon Street. Obligingly North led him to the front drawing room, remarking blandly that he would see if Miss Berryman was available.

There were several magazines spread on the low table by the sofa and he sorted through the fashion gazettes to find the sporting journals that Lady Bradwell invariably had ready for her gentlemen friends. He had barely begun to thumb through the *Turf Remembrancer* when Emma burst through the door.

"Is she all right? Has she had the baby? Have you just come from Half Moon Street?"

"Yes, to all of your questions," he replied, rising rapidly. It moved him to see the anxiety in her face fade and be replaced by a wide smile. "Not half an hour ago. It's a boy."

"A boy." Emma appeared to give this a great deal of consideration. "Well, I'm glad it's a boy, for Lord Greenwood's sake, of course, though I think a girl might have been easier for Maggie to raise. Did you see them?"

"No, no. I was with Greenwood at the time. He was showing me his portrait, which was excellent, by the way. Mrs. Morton and Dr. Botley were with Lady Greenwood. I left before Adam went in to see them. He was wrapping this when I arrived." Dunn picked up the disreputable bundle and handed it to her. "He wished to send it to you as a token of his appreciation for the portrait, I think."

"How could he think of sending me something at such a time?"

"I gather Mrs. Morton wanted him out of the way."

His eyes were laughing and she allowed herself an answering smile. It seemed to him a long time since she'd done that. Then quickly she lowered her gaze to the package. "He's not much of a hand at wrapping, is he?" She pulled the loose string over the corners and unfolded a long sheet of brown paper, twice as much as would have been necessary. "How very thoughtful of him!" she exclaimed as she glanced through the book. "Sometimes he amazes me."

"He's progressed a long way in a year. I think your friend need not despair of him any longer."

"She never did!" Emma told him, a note of reproach creeping in. "Maggie is the most accommodating person in the world. I'm sure she never voiced a word of complaint."

"No, probably not." She hadn't offered him a seat and he picked up the brown paper she had dropped, carefully folding it in smaller and smaller squares. "Miss Berryman, have I done something to offend you?"

"Offend me? Of course not. Wherever could you have gotten such an idea?"

"It wasn't difficult," he said grimly. "You stopped allowing me to teach you to drive, you won't stand up with me at dances, you are not at home to me. I promise you I am not aware of having given you cause to treat me so cavalierly. I had thought we were . . . becoming good friends."

Emma had retrieved the string and was wrapping it round and round her fingers. "I certainly hope we are. I should hate to be at outs with any of Aunt Amelia's friends. If you think I am not grateful to her for taking me under her wing, you are mistaken. She has been the soul of kindness to me and I wouldn't do anything to hurt her."

The speaking glance she gave him did nothing to alleviate Dunn's confusion. "It never entered my mind that you weren't grateful to her or that you would do anything to hurt her. I think Lady Bradwell was pleased that we weren't forever going hammer and tongs at one another."

Emma's smile was bleak. "Yes, I think she *was*."

Again she seemed to stress this, and Dunn did not understand her. Trying to be reasonable, fighting against an intangible resistance, he said gently, "Then I think you can only be upsetting her by keeping such a cool distance from me. She will think that we are once more at odds."

"You mistake, Lord Dunn. I am not keeping you at a cool distance, as you phrase it." Emma jerked the string from her fingers and set it firmly on the table. "There is no excuse for my infringing on your time when Sir Nicholas is willing to teach me to drive. I'm sure I haven't refused to stand up with you for any other reason than that my dances were previously accounted for. And as to not being at home to you . . . Well, you better than anyone must know that my work has become important to me. Just last week I sat with you and Aunt Amelia for some time one afternoon. I am often out, and when I am here, I am frequently painting. You make it sound as though I am avoiding you!"

Dunn noted, as dispassionately as possible, that she managed to regard him with wide, innocent eyes. What was going on here? Did she really believe what she was saying? Or was she lying to him again? *Was* it a lie about Sir Nicholas? He remembered what Adam had said about Nick kissing her. Did that have something to do with this? When had he done it? Surely some time ago. Nick had been teasing her as far back as last season—about his portrait hanging in her bedchamber. Perhaps that wasn't the same thing. The questions buzzed in his mind like so many irate bees while he searched for something to say that would cut through the fog of half-truth and shed some light on the situation.

He set the brown paper on the table beside the string. "We have little opportunity for private discourse," was all he finally said.

To his surprise, she involuntarily drew back from him, forcing an insincere smile to her lips. "As I understand it, that is just as society could wish! No lady is supposed to be alone with a gentleman. Lord Dunn, I do appreciate your coming with the marvelous news of Maggie's safe delivery, and for bringing Lord Greenwood's package. I fear my paints are drying where I left them. Please excuse me."

"Wait," he pleaded, scorning himself for doing so. "Could you . . . would you save me a waltz at the Barnfield ball next week?"

Emma stiffened. "I suppose I must if I have given the appearance of neglecting you as a partner, Lord Dunn."

The acceptance was unsatisfactory: they both knew it. It was ungracious, even when spoken as lightly as she did. At most she expected a curt nod from him. She got it, with a sardonic "Thank you" as well. When he had left, she fled to the refuge of her studio.

CHAPTER TWENTY-THREE

Anne stood with her mother, father, and two brothers in the reception line, more unsettled than she had been the previous year for her coming-out ball. The marchioness gave a ball every season and was rather amused at Anne's request that this year's be given on the same date as last year's. Her assumption, that Anne was nostalgic about that important event in her life, was only partially correct, but she had agreed to the suggestion without the least hesitation. Anne greeted each dark-coated gentleman and turbaned grand dame with her usual easy grace, but her eyes constantly wandered to the hall beyond the ballroom. Her brother Will poked her playfully in the ribs and murmured, "Looking for Langham or Brackenbury?"

"Both of them, of course," she retorted, determined not to give him cause to tease her again.

Grave with the responsibility of the evening, the butler intoned, "Miss Helena Rogers, Mr. Harold Rogers."

Anne pressed Helena's hand. "I'm so glad you came."

"I didn't even have to miss a lecture on metaphysics this year." Helena laughed, passing on to greet Will.

Mr. Rogers next took her hand, surprised by the distinct light of challenge in her eyes. So, he thought, momentarily stunned, there was to be no more polite skirting of the issue. Perhaps it was time, but he hardly felt ready. "Lady Anne. Always a pleasure to see you."

"Mr. Rogers. A pleasure to see you . . . always."

A chuckle escaped him, quickly stifled as he asked, "May I beg the first cotillion with you?"

She raised quizzing eyes to his. "Did you think I would forget, Mr. Rogers? It was a week ago yesterday, at precisely three twelve (I had a timepiece hanging about my neck) when you asked me. I was in company with your sister at the time, in the Green Park, carefully studying the peeling paint on the bench and wondering whether it would be the minuet or the cotillion. I knew it would not be a waltz."

"The minuet," he said firmly, "should be reserved for someone of higher stature than myself."

"You are by far the tallest man in the room," she returned pertly.

"When precedence depends on height, you may be sure that I will solicit your first minuet of the evening."

"When precedence outweighs preference with me, you may be sure I will tell you." Anne nodded to him, graciously, as he was forced forward by the press of people behind him. With a mournful shake of his head, he left her. Decidedly, Lady Anne had thrown down the gauntlet.

Anne allowed herself to be led out for the first dance by Lord Langham, since he insisted. She could not have cared less who her partner was, and her gaze frequently wandered about the room, never resting on Mr. Rogers, but constantly aware of where he was. Helena, too, she kept an eye on as the ball progressed, checking to see that she had partners, and several times leading a gentleman over to be introduced. Maggie was still recovering from her lying-in and Emma never lacked for a partner. On the other hand, Emma was acting rather oddly tonight, Anne thought as she watched her friend being led out for a waltz by Dunn.

Emma had chosen a round dress of Urling's net over rose satin, which hung in gentle folds about her figure, a far cry from the provocative gown she had worn the previous year. When Anne saw her with Dunn, Emma had achieved a particularly bland expression, and she kept touching the garland of roses that encircled her shining blond hair. The action denoted a nervousness, a self-consciousness, totally foreign to Emma's character.

It would have been better, Emma thought unhappily, if she had not promised Dunn a waltz. His nearness was unsettling, and his attempts at lightness she found impossible to respond to in the circle of his arms. Even the way he was looking at her was disturbing, with that crooked little half-smile and his gray eyes warm with . . . No matter. It was better not to think of that.

"You look enchanting, Miss Berryman. I don't believe I've seen that gown before."

"No, it's new."

"I was wondering if you might join us on a picnic out to Richmond. My brother Stephen has tentatively set next Wednesday for an excursion with a small party, if the weather holds good. Mrs. Tremaine is coming as chaperon."

Mrs. Tremaine, mother to a young lady in her first season, was already becoming known as a remarkably lax, though wholly good-natured, chaperon. Dunn's brother, no doubt, had been the one to choose her, Emma surmised. Still, there would be no in harm in it, except that she couldn't possibly go with him. "I'm afraid that isn't a good time for me, Lord Dunn, but thank you."

"We could change the day."

"No, no, not on my account, I beg you. I have a great deal of work to do. Did I tell you I've begun a portrait of Anne?"

Dunn had noticed before now that she was becoming deft at changing the subject with him. No personal references were to be dwelled on, no plans made, where the two of them would be together. He had felt surc, that day in the garden, that the two of them were working their way toward an understanding. Carefully, but progressively, they were narrowing the gap between friendship and marriage. What had changed that so abruptly? Had he frightened her in some way? The answer, which kept putting itself forward in his mind, and kept being summarily rejected, was that she had decided against him. She didn't need to give any explanation; it was her right to make such a decision. Until now he had refused to accept the unsavory truth: She had turned him off before he reached the point of making a declaration, saved him the embarrassment of being refused. Dunn could feel little gratitude for her tact.

His mind had wandered, he had been silent too long. Emma was looking up at him inquiringly and he tried to remember what she had asked. Oh, yes, the portrait of Anne. "No, I didn't know you were doing Lady Anne. Have you finished Lady Bradwell, then?"

"Oh, yes, a few days ago."

"I should like to see it. Is it hanging in the house?"

"In the dining saloon. Next time you visit her, have her take you to see it. I would be interested in your opinion."

But not interested enough to show it to me yourself, he thought wearily.

"How is Lady Greenwood coming on?"

"Extremely well." She smiled at him, but not an intimate smile. "They had a bit of a contretemps. Maggie wished to feed the baby herself and Greenwood insisted that they use the wet nurse they had arranged for. Of course *she* thought he didn't trust his heir to her and was greatly hurt. *He* thought she was exhausted from the lying-in and shouldn't tax her strength when someone else could as easily take over the task. Apparently she is a bit weepy since the birth, not an uncommon phenomenon Cynthia tells us, but I assure you it alarmed me to walk into her room and have her burst into tears. Everything came out and Cynthia spoke to Greenwood and Maggie is feeding the baby herself, which makes Greenwood inordinately proud." Emma shook her head in wonder. "Why don't people *talk* to each other? The whole episode need not have happened."

Dunn had a mocking gleam in his eyes. Why indeed, Miss Berryman? he might have asked, and saw that his message was so clear that she looked away. Ah, well, he would not plague her. The decision was made and it behooved him to accept it with a good grace. For the remainder of the dance he spoke on impersonal topics, and when he left her with Lady Bradwell on the side of the dance floor,

Emma gave him a grateful smile that made him feel even worse than he already had.

The cotillion provided less opportunity for the discussion of weighty matters, and Anne and Mr. Rogers said very little during it. A polite compliment on her gown. A remark about his sister. He pointed out an old school friend of his. She mentioned a book she was reading. They agreed that the evening fared well to being a success and, as the dance drew to a close, that it was rather warm in the room.

"I haven't promised the next dance," Anne informed him.

Mr. Rogers regarded her ruefully. "Then perhaps we could take a breath of air on the balcony. I doubt anyone else will have adjourned there so early in the evening."

"Yes, that's what I thought." The light of challenge remained in Anne's eyes.

It was cooler on the balcony, though in truth the ballroom was not nearly so warm as it would become later in the evening. A gentle breeze stirred her curls and rippled the yellow gown as they stood silently gazing over the back garden. Only a faint glimmer of moonlight touched the scene, picking out the silvery gravel path and reflecting on the placid ornamental pond. His hand closed over hers where she had rested it on the railing.

Anne said nothing, lifting her eyes to his, the challenge gone but something far more essential remaining. Mr. Rogers had no difficulty reading her beloved face and his whole being responded to her. As usual the cautionary voice rose in his mind to warn him and he struggled to listen to it. He was a man who had trained himself to act with reason and prudence, but this emotion was too strong to be denied. He bent to kiss her. Her response was not so tentative as it had been the first time he kissed her, but warm and eager . . . and delightful. When they drew apart she kept her eyes on his face. He cleared his throat.

"Your father and mother have every right to expect you to marry someone of your own standing, my dear," he said softly.

"They have never insisted. They have never even mentioned it."

"It's something understood."

"My parents are more interested in my happiness than in my position."

He sighed and resisted the impulse to kiss the slightly trembling lips. "Financially I cannot offer you the elegancies to which you are accustomed, Anne."

"My dowry—"

"Your damned dowry is half the problem!" he retorted, exasperated.

"Papa wouldn't think you were marrying me for my dowry! Besides, half of the titled gentlemen who have offered for me are only interested in it."

He grinned. "And the other half?"

"Don't be so provoking! You may be sure *none* of them would turn it down. The others only see me as an *appropriate* wife. Not one of them is . . ." But she could not finish, and she turned back toward the railing.

"Not one of them is attached to you?" His voice was soft, persuasive. "I think you mistake, my dear. It would be impossible to know you and *not* be attached to you. Are you sure you've given them a chance? Have you had an opportunity for quiet conversation with them?"

"Several of them have been to Parkhurst and were forever trapping me into 'quiet' conversations in the arbor." She eyed him defiantly. "I even let some of them kiss me."

"Did you?" He felt momentarily shaken, but his tone was as light as ever when he asked, "And did you enjoy it?"

"No, of course not! I was just . . . curious."

"Were you curious when you let me kiss you?"

Anne bowed her head and whispered, "I was more than curious."

"Yes." Mr. Rogers moved to stand beside her, not touching her hands now, and not looking at her but gazing absently at the moonlit path in the garden. Behind them the door stood slightly ajar and the strains of music flowed out into the night. In an unusually tight voice he said, "Let us admit that there is an attraction between us. It would be foolish to deny such an obvious state of affairs. Since the day I saw you at your ball, so vivacious, so charming, so lovely . . ."

"It was a year ago today."

He glanced quickly at her, knowing she was right, but she didn't meet his gaze. "Ah, I see. And a year is quite long enough to judge of your own sentiments?"

"You mock me, sir." Just the slightest quiver marred her words and she took a firmer grip on the railing. "We have had every opportunity to get to know one another. You have even been at Parkhurst. I have not tried to disguise my failings from you. Though I am sometimes quick to anger, I do not hold grudges. And if I am at times frivolous, well, I do not believe I am often *very* frivolous. I am not, perhaps, especially devout, but I try to live by my beliefs. I—"

"That's enough, Anne! There is no question of your failings as you call them, being a deterrent to our . . . marriage." He had said it, after all those months of schooling himself to put the thought from his mind, to keep their interactions to those of friendship. Mr. Rogers was not a self-effacing man, nor did he have a small conception of his own consequence, but he was all too well aware of the gulf between them. It was not insuperable of course, but he could not fail to be aware that men of far higher rank and fortune had sought her hand—for whatever reason. And in the society in which they lived it would be counted a great pity for her to throw herself away on him.

The music coming from the ballroom ceased and he gave a "Tsk!" of annoyance. "Are you promised for the next dance?"

"Yes."

"Then we will have to go in, my dear. I'm sorry. Perhaps, if I called tomorrow to take you walking I could explain . . ."

Anne bit her lip. "Thank you, no. I *do* understand. Girls my age are accounted romantic fools, I believe. If they will but listen to the guidance of their elders, they can be relieved of such foolish notions and delivered into bleak but advantageous marriages. How consoling! Good evening, Mr. Rogers."

With head held high she stepped past him and into the crowded ballroom. Her dance was promised to Lord Brackenbury and she could see him across the room anxiously scanning the masses of people for her. Behind her the door closed softly and she knew without looking that Mr. Rogers was standing to her left. On her right was Captain Midford and she smiled at him as he turned to her.

"Lady Anne! Forgive me! I didn't see you there. May I hope you are free for the set forming?"

"Thank you, Captain Midford, but I believe my partner has spotted me." She watched Brackenbury advance in her direction with a purposeful air. His brown hair was plastered to his head in an absurd imitation of a Brutus style and his beaklike nose twitched as though he were a hound on a scent. Anne had to press her lips together to keep from smiling.

"There you are, Lady Anne," he panted as he finally reached her side. "Servant, Midford. Had the devil of a time finding you, my dear. Knew you had on a yellow dress but so do a dozen other ladies this evening." Lord Brackenbury would never admit to his shortsightedness, so he made what he considered a most useful suggestion. "You might wear something different next time, something that stands out a bit, don't you know. Like my waistcoat. I daresay no one would have the least problem spotting you if you wore a pink and purple gown."

"No, I imagine not, my lord, but I doubt that my mother would sanction such a . . . colorful costume on one of my years."

"What's that? Ah, well, the marchioness won't be concerned with what you wear once you're married, now, will she? Dresses a trifle plainly for my taste, your mother, if you don't mind my saying so."

Anne smiled sweetly. "I do mind, Lord Brackenbury. Shall we join the set?"

Profusely apologizing for offending her, he led her off, leaving Captain Midford grinning. Mr. Rogers did not share the captain's amusement. He stood watching the couple, apparently at his ease, but his countenance was grim and it was a moment before he realized his sister had joined him. To avoid the questioning look in her eyes, he said, "I'm sure you know Captain Midford, my dear." And the good captain as was expected of him, led Helena onto the dance floor.

When supper was announced the guests began to retrace a path through the white and gold music room, the two card rooms beyond (one hung with crimson and the other with blue damask), and down the magnificent staircase to the dining room, salon, and gallery. Dunn was looking about the tapestry-hung ballroom for an unpartnered lady to escort when the marchioness caught his eye. He presented himself with an obliging bow and a questioningly lifted brow. "May I assist in some way, ma'am?"

Lady Barnfield smiled. "I knew I might count on you, Dunn. Langham is going to insist on taking Anne in to supper if you don't claim a prior arrangement with her. Would you mind? Something has upset her—I'm sure I don't know what, for she started the evening in remarkable spirits!—but I think you are just the one to restore her equanimity."

"With the greatest pleasure, Lady Barnfield." He raised a quizzing glass, quickly located his new supper partner, and arrived in time to hear Langham grumbling, "Well, whoever he is, he has forgotten. You might as well accept my escort, Lady Anne."

Dunn's voice held just a trace of amusement as he offered his arm to her. "Can you forgive me, Lady Anne? In such a crush I have had the most difficult time making my way to you. Servant, Langham."

Without the least hesitation, Anne accepted his arm. "There's no need to apologize, Lord Dunn. Once the gong rings, it's almost impossible to move in any direction but toward the dining room. If you will excuse me, Lord Langham."

In an aside that Anne distinctly heard, Dunn informed her erstwhile suitor that Miss Breighton was apparently in need of an escort in to supper. Langham looked mulish, but after reflecting that it would do no harm to pique Lady Anne's jealousy, he did offer his services to Miss Breighton, who accepted with giggling alacrity. Anne smiled slightly as she fanned her flushed cheeks.

"Do you know, Lord Langham actually thought you had *forgotten* me. Imagine such impudence. *I* know it would have been impossible for you to forget."

"Would you care to tell me who you *were* supposed to have supper with?"

Her eyes dropped before his kindly regard. "No, if you don't mind. It is not that he forgot, you understand. I had saved supper for him and he did ask, but I . . . thought it wisest to change my mind. He was probably relieved."

"Did he look relieved?" Dunn asked, curious.

"Well, no," she admitted. "He said, 'Dammit, Anne, we haven't finished discussing the matter,' and he got that very stern look of his."

Hastily reviewing his acquaintance for anyone who might have a remarkable "stern" look, Dunn failed to pinpoint any particular gentleman. But he found the conversation intriguing (which is to say, distracting) and pressed on. "I hope you intend to give him the opportunity to conclude your conversation. Nothing is more frustrating than not being able to speak one's piece."

"You don't understand, Lord Dunn. He had no intention of ever broaching the subject, though I did not precisely force him to do so. I think it is a matter of different values."

"What sort of values?" Since the progress toward the supper room was appallingly slow, the viscount kept his voice as discreetly low as hers. At any time he might discover (from a stray clue) whom they were talking about.

"Some people consider that rank, and fortune, are of paramount importance."

"Aren't they?" he asked with twinkling eyes.

"Certainly not! Neither rank nor fortune can guarantee happiness. They are convenient; I do not deny that. And a total lack of rank or fortune would be most unfortunate, but that is certainly not the case."

"You relieve me."

"Well, really, I doubt there is a person here tonight totally lacking in both rank and fortune. Not that my parents are particularly top-lofty, but it is, after all, a ball, and I am sure they have made every effort to invite only the haut ton."

"With perhaps the exception of some of your brother Will's friends," he teased.

Anne frowned. "Perhaps. I fear I am boring you."

"Not at all. You were telling me that some people consider rank and fortune to be of paramount importance, but you had not told me what . . . other people believe to be of value."

"Other people," she said defiantly, "think that character, and goodness, and sensibility, and intelligence, and an ease of manners, and a lack of affectation, and honesty, and openness, and a lively wit, and dignity, and resolution, and constancy and . . . and any number of other things are of far more importance!"

"Dear God! Never tell me you have met with such a paragon!"

Anne couldn't help but laugh at his horrified expression. "Well, I am inclined, I think, to exaggerate just the tiniest bit. What I mean to say is that such virtues weigh a great deal more with some people than do rank and fortune. Fortune, after all, may be dissipated, and rank is a relative matter. Of what practical use is precedence? Do you really care if Lord Langham goes before or after you?"

Dunn appeared thoughtful. "That would depend entirely on where we were going."

Anne chuckled. "Yes, I perfectly understand, but you know what I mean. I don't intend to make light of a man's rank, but I think his character is of far more consequence."

"As to Langham's character, I would not like to make any comment. I might just say that I do think he must have some, and if he shows any, I will be more than happy to let him go before me," Dunn conceded graciously.

Impulsively, she squeezed his arm. "Mama sent you to me, didn't she. Sometimes I am in awe of her wisdom."

"Sometimes?" He raised one impressive brow. "My dear girl, you should *always* be in awe of the marchioness. I have never met anyone quite like her, myself."

The dining parlor was already filled, and the salon beyond, but there were several empty, and even more partially filled, tables in the gallery. Dunn cast an eye over the various groups. "We shall not sit at Langham's table, since he has gone before me without any ostensible exhibition of character. Shall we sit with the Fieldings?"

Anne had done a survey of her own and was glad enough to acquiesce in his choice. Mr. Rogers and Helena were seated some distance away, and though it hurt her to see the startled look in Helena's eyes when she did not accept her smile of invitation, Anne could only shrug slightly as she allowed Dunn to lead her elsewhere. But for the first time it was borne in on her how difficult her encounter with Mr. Rogers could make her friendship with Helena.

Though she had often worried what Helena would think of her if she took the idea into her head that Anne only called in hopes of seeing Mr. Rogers, Anne knew that her affection for Helena was quite apart from that for her brother. They were in the habit of having a comfortable coze every few days in Argyll Street because there were fewer visitors coming and going there. And Helena didn't always have access to the one carriage Mr. Rogers kept in town, since he frequently needed it. Once Helena had walked to Grosvenor Square, laughingly protesting that she enjoyed nothing more, but a walk in the city was not the same as one over fields and country lanes. For Anne to go now to Mr. Rogers's house to see Helena was not out of the question, but it could be very awkward for her.

Dunn, too, had surveyed the supper rooms, and remembered the table at which he and Lady Anne had sat the previous year. Emma had been with Lord William then, but her attention had been on Sir Nicholas, as it was tonight. He forced himself to look away from where the two of them were sitting with Lady Bradwell and Sir Arthur Moresby, and chose a table as far away as possible. The Fieldings were good company and there was no lack of amusing conversation during the meal. He firmly thrust his own problems from him to join in the discussion, and when he and Anne rose to return to the ballroom, he said kindly, "We have allowed ourselves to wander from our previous discussion. You were explaining to me the value of character. Though I didn't feel comfortable discussing Langham's qualities with you, I would be happy to consider someone else."

"Who?"

"The gentleman you decided not to have supper with. If you would care to divulge his name, I would count it an honor to hear your estimate of his character. I might even be persuaded to venture an opinion of my own."

Anne raised her eyes to his. "Thank you, no. It's not that I don't value your opinion. I promise you I do! But this is not something I can discuss with you, and I would appreciate it if you said nothing to Mama of our talk."

"As you wish, of course, but it might be useful for you to speak with your mother. We have already established, I believe, that she is a wise woman."

When she glanced fleetingly at him, she could see only friendly interest in his eyes. She pleated the skirt of her gown between restless fingers. "I . . . I may. I thought I was being mature, rational, and patient and it turns out I have only been childish, romantic, and forward. It would be embarrassing for me to explain that to Mama, as devoted as she is to all of us. Perhaps *because* she's so devoted. Living up to her example is difficult. Not that she expects us to be perfect, but I have come to demand it of myself—within reason."

Her voice trailed away and Dunn considered the slightly averted face. "The marchioness would be horrified, I think, to find that you consider her perfect, and distracted to hear that you compare yourself to her, and find yourself wanting. She has, after all, quite a few more years to her credit than you do, and all the experience that comes with them. I can perfectly understand why you would choose to emulate your mother, but comparing yourself to her will stunt your growth, my dear child, as surely as smoking cheroots!"

A nervous giggle rewarded this sally and Anne faced him, her countenance puzzled. "Do people often confide in you, Lord Dunn?"

"All the time," he said with a sigh. "I think it is my age."

"Why, you can't be much above thirty!"

"No, but I must *look* older. And I admit to feeling a great deal older at times." His mouth twisted in a wry grin that did not quite match his tone. "And even the old can't solve every problem."

"No one expects them to," Anne said softly, giving his arm a squeeze. "In the end, we all have to solve our own problems—or live with them."

Their eyes met in a moment of understanding before she was claimed for the next dance.

CHAPTER TWENTY-FOUR

The bustle of the previous night had receded, but there was still a certain amount of activity going forward in the Marquess of Barnfield's Grosvenor Square town house. Maids and footmen tidied rooms or stored silver from the previous evening's activity and the door knocker was beginning to sound with unnerving regularity, bringing a collection of flowers and notes of appreciation. A posy arrived for Lady Anne from Lord Dunn with the simple message: "*You are quite right, of course. Character is paramount*. Dunn."

"What does he mean?" Will asked, peering over her shoulder to read the words.

They sat in the breakfast parlor at the back of the house, *en déshabillé* due to the relatively early hour of eleven, sipping from steaming mugs of chocolate. Anne folded the note and placed it on the table beside her plate. "We were discussing the relative merits of character and rank last night, not to mention fortune. It was quite a philosophical conversation," she teased.

"At a ball! Lord, you're not supposed to consider anything more significant than whether you'll have another glass of champagne. Whatever possessed Dunn?"

Anne gazed out the window, a tiny frown creasing her brow. "He was in rather a melancholy mood, I think, but it wasn't his choice of topic. I—"

Her remarks were interrupted by a discreet knock at the door. A footman entered to inform them, "Mr. Harold Rogers has called to see Lady Anne. He mentioned that he had an appointment to take her walking."

"But he didn't!" she protested, flushing.

"Oh, Annie, you've simply forgotten," Will scolded her. "Which is really no wonder when you consider how very long an evening it was. We weren't in bed before five! How could you have told him eleven?"

"I did no such thing!"

The footman coughed discreetly. "I should tell Mr. Rogers . . . ?"

Before his sister could speak, Will intervened. "Well, you must certainly go, Annie. He's Helena's brother, after all, and I daresay he was no more pleased to be abroad at this hour after such a late night than you will be."

"I can't . . ."

"Pooh. It won't take but a few minutes to change into something decent." Will turned to the footman and declared, "You must have Mr. Rogers wait in the blue saloon, Fredericks. Tell him Lady Anne will be with him shortly."

When Anne made no further demur, the footman departed, closing the door carefully after him. Anne distractedly deposited her chocolate mug on a gateleg table and rose, but before stomping from the room she muttered, "Really, Will, you haven't the slightest idea what you've done."

Mr. Rogers was standing by the mantelpiece, gloves in hand, when Anne entered the room some time later. She had taken the time to put on her best walking dress, but had then placed over it a hooded cape of navy blue that covered her whole ensemble and made her look more an orphan than the petted daughter of the Marquess of Barnfield. The marchioness had protested her bringing it to town at all, considering it worthy only of strolls on blustery days at Parkhurst, but Anne had truthfully protested that it didn't take much space, after all.

Inside the door of the blue saloon she paused long enough to regain her composure after seeing him and then walked purposefully toward him. "You know very well we had no appointment to go walking, and I would have refused but for my brother's being so densely insistent. He even scolded me for forgetting and for setting such an early hour."

Ignoring her sparking eyes and her tirade, he lifted her hand to his lips. "Good morning, Lady Anne. I would commend you on your looks but frankly you appear the veriest waif this morning."

"Perhaps you have forgotten, Mr. Rogers, that the ball lasted until after four. I was barely up when you called."

"I am surprised that your brother would disturb your rest. You did say that it was he who insisted on your coming?"

"We often take our chocolate in the back breakfast room the very *first* thing after arising."

"I see. Shall we go?" Imperturbable, he held the door for her, and after one last defiant glare she walked past him with as much dignity as she could muster. They continued in silence out of the house and along Upper Brook Street to Hyde Park. There was but a solitary gentleman to be seen in the promenade, and a pair of riders beyond the rows of trees. Anne concentrated her attention on a patch of spring flowers and then a stray dog trotting across the path.

As though he had not a worry in the world, Mr. Rogers strolled beside her, matching his pace to hers, his hands clasped loosely behind his back. "Helena has created a delightful flower border at Farthing Hill. It seems almost a pity to be in town in the spring, when it's in full glory. The display is remarkable in summer, too, of course, but I prefer the muscari and tulips to the lupine and iris. Purely a matter of personal taste, I suppose."

Anne said nothing.

"And then there are the birds at this time of year. One sees far more pipits and buntings than in the heat of the summer. And the song of the warbler is captivating, though perhaps not as liquid as the blackcap. Have you the lesser spotted woodpecker at Parkhurst?"

"Yes."

"Helena is particularly fond of drawing them. We have an ancient pine forest along the path to Enfield where the crested tit makes its nest in holes of decayed trees. Helena will sit for hours, waiting for a sight of one. I'm sure she's shown you her sketchbooks."

"Yes."

"She won't bring them up to town with her most years, for she says there is little occasion to employ them here. Too busy with other things, and the variety of birds is limited."

Anne adjusted the hood of her cape.

Mr. Rogers proceeded as though she were showing an absorbed fascination with his commentary. "Farthing Hill is not a large house; it could fit in the east wing of Parkhurst. Originally it was simply a timber-frame hall house built by a small squire about 1480. It has been extended and renovated over the centuries, but there are any number of inconveniences remaining. Still, in all we find it a comfortable *small* house, with only three bedroom suites and three reception rooms, including the dining parlor. Enfield is the closest town of any size. When the opportunity arises I add to the farming land, but I'm cautious about over-extending my resources. And I have chosen to invest a certain amount in London itself, or rather those areas which are likely to be overrun by the city very shortly. I see no end in sight to the expansion of the city and have bought up pieces of undeveloped land on the fringes, which appear to me to be in line for building."

"Have you in mind to hold onto the land until its value increases or to pursue a building scheme of your own?" Anne could not help asking.

"That will depend on whether my first venture is successful. There are several houses being built now in the area off Grosvenor Place. I have put up the land as my share of the venture and I had the final say as to the finished design."

"Why have you never told me of this before?"

"You might better ask yourself why I am telling you now, Anne," he suggested, studying her face.

"Oh, I'm sure I know the answer to that," she returned with lofty dignity. "You are illustrating to me, in the gentlest possible manner, that you are not a wealthy man and that you have speculated on a project which could make your position even less desirable. Do you think I care?"

"You should, my dear, and your parents certainly would. Actually, I don't think there is any chance that this venture will leave me any the worse off and I've found it stimulating, if rather time-consuming." He directed her to a bench and waited as she seated herself. With an automatic movement he swept the skirts of his coat out of the way and joined her, his face mirroring his concentration.

"I have given a great deal of thought to what I wish to tell you. Not just since last night. For most of the last year I have considered the deterrents to and the possibilities of our relationship, when I was unable to thrust it from my mind altogether, as I knew I should. I have tried to weigh the advantages of rank and fortune against the intangible and possibly illusory benefits of affection." She was regarding him intently and he offered a disparaging smile. "It can't be done, Anne. Not by me, at least. I don't wish to suggest that our attraction is purely sensual; I know very well that it isn't. Which is why I have cherished the idea that we could always remain friends."

"Hogwash!" said Anne, unmoved by his reason.

Mr. Rogers grinned. "I do love your very direct outlook on life, Anne. But let us consider what is expected of you. You come from a prominent, titled, wealthy family and have every right to marry into a similar situation. It is hard at your age to realize the difference these things make to one's comfort and position. To you they are as natural as the air. Much as I would wish to, I cannot duplicate such a setting."

"Very well, Mr. Rogers. As you are intent on considering my future so carefully, I should like you to visualize me married to one of these eligible men you have in mind for me. Not Brackenbury or Langham, I think that is going too far. Even I would never contemplate accepting such fools. But someone else, say . . ."

"Lord Dunn. You seemed to thrive in his company last night." His gaze was on a squirrel scampering up a nearby tree.

"Yes, a very easy man to talk to. Do you know I had a bouquet from him today?"

Mr. Rogers said nothing.

"Now Dunn is a family friend and I consider it unlikely he would ever offer for me, but as he is the best of the crop of suitable gentlemen, we shall suppose that I marry him. I really couldn't do better, I think, from your point of view. Although he is only a viscount, he has other virtues to offset such a mediocre title. I can't think of any earls, marquesses or dukes just offhand who would do as well. We would be married in town, of course, a large, extravagant wedding with everyone invited, including you. And I suppose he would take me to Waverton Street for the night, before traveling to France. My maid would select the most luscious of my new nightdresses from my bride clothes and I would wait in my bed—or possibly his—for him to come to me."

Since he sat very still and refused to look at her, Anne swallowed painfully and continued. "Perhaps you think you know how I would feel then. You don't. It is difficult enough for a woman to contemplate sharing a bed with a man for whom she has a great deal of affection, almost impossible to judge the distress when she doesn't. But Lord Dunn is an experienced man, a considerate man. I don't doubt for a minute that he would be very patient. But eventually, Harold, he would take my body—with my mind rebelling every step of the way. For you see, Harold, I was not raised to prostitute myself for position and luxury. Ah, but you can say to yourself, 'In time she will grow to love such a man and actually welcome him in her arms.' I don't think so. With the loss of respect for myself such a course would engender in me, I would be incapable of respecting him, either, and without respect there can be no love—for me. But heaven knows that's irrelevant, isn't it? I would have an enviable position in society, an inexhaustible source of funds at my fingertips, children—oh, yes, I would bear him children, but would I have anything to give them? Does not every worthwhile virtue spring from self-respect? And that,

Mr. Rogers, is what it would be like—provided I could induce Lord Dunn to marry me. In all likelihood it would be someone a great deal less acceptable."

Anne blew her nose; Mr. Rogers looked sick. Only the twittering birds and distant hoofbeats broke the silence.

Eventually Mr. Rogers cleared his throat. "I apologize, Anne. It was I who did not understand. Please don't put me through such agony ever again. You may be mistaken in thinking that you will not eventually find another man you can go to with your heart, but I have no intention of allowing you a chance to discover him. As it is I shall never view Lord Dunn in quite the same way again!"

"How absurd you are, Harold. I told you he would never offer for me."

"He shan't have the opportunity, if I have anything to say about it. Dear Anne, are you quite sure this is what you want? I want so much more *for* you, my love."

"If you want my happiness, you will have to give yourself."

"There is nothing I would rather do." He regarded her misty-eyed smile with distinct approval and drew her into the circle of his arm. "I am not going to kiss you now. We will seal our agreement if the marquess and marchioness approve. If they don't . . ."

"Will you speak with them now?"

"As soon as we return, provided they're receiving. I don't want Dunn to have a chance to follow up his stupid flowers."

"They were quite pretty," she protested, laughing.

An hour later Anne was descending the stairs after urging her brother Will to get a move on so that they could have a glass of champagne when she encountered Lord Dunn in the hallway waiting to see if the marchioness and her daughter were receiving. She grinned impishly at him and said, "Character has won out, my lord. Would you care to join us in the library for a toast on my engagement?"

"I doubt this is a time for me to intrude, Lady Anne." He grasped her hand and pressed it. "May I offer my congratulations? And find out at last of whom we were speaking last evening?"

"I shan't tell you. You must come with me if you wish to learn his identity."

Dunn sighed woefully. "Do you know you are a very provoking young lady? I would come, of course, but this is a family celebration."

Anne linked her arm with his. "You are a family friend, sir. And I must admit that I used your name shamefully this morning to entice Ha—my fiancé to overcome his scruples. Not that I suggested you had an interest in me exactly, but, well, it would be difficult to explain. I proposed a hypothetical situation and my friend suggested your name to fill in the story. I hope you don't mind."

"Not at all. Feel free to bandy my name about at your whim. I'm sure it has never served so useful a purpose before."

Smiling at his sardonic tone, Anne continued cheerfully, "My friend may be just the least bit chilly toward you, Lord Dunn. He took my fairy tale very much to heart, as I meant him to, since in theory it was no more than the truth. I think men don't understand women as well as they believe they do."

"I'm sure of it."

The library door was open and from the hall they could see Lord and Lady Barnfield talking to Mr. Rogers and Jack. Anne turned questioning eyes to Dunn.

"I didn't guess, though I might have. Really, he fits your description extraordinarily well—from your slightly exaggerated estimate of his character to his 'stern' look. I am currently involved with him in building some houses off Grosvenor Place and have the greatest respect for his judgment. Ah, I see you are right. He does not usually bestow his 'stern' look on me, but on the builder when he does shoddy work. Whatever did you say to him?"

No answer but a grin rewarded his query. Anne led him into the room, announcing to her mother that she had found Dunn in the hall and invited him to join their celebration, "being a family friend and well known to Mr. Rogers." Her fiancé could not maintain his "stern" look in the face of Dunn's enthusiastic congratulations, but he did manage to shake his head in mock censure at Anne for her mischievous conduct.

Lady Barnfield observed the interchange with a reminiscent sigh. Meeting her husband's understanding gaze, she murmured, "I do believe our Anne has been very fortunate, John. Imagine her keeping such a secret from my watchful eye! The only disadvantage is that we don't know him as well as we might, but I think I am going to like him very well, don't you?"

"Definitely, my dear."

Not until there had been three interruptions to inform the family that there were callers did the party break up, with Viscount Dunn being the first to announce his absolute intention of leaving. Anne accompanied him to the door.

"I haven't thanked you for your flowers, Lord Dunn, or for being so gallant to me last evening."

"Was I gallant?" He accepted his hat and gloves from a footman, his gray eyes thoughtful. "Perhaps I was, but I should not like the word to get about and have to make a habit of it."

"Oh, pooh. Don't you remember our ball last year when you were so annoyed with Emma and I made you stand up with her?"

"I remember it vividly," he said, turning to go. "And *she* cozened me into teaching her to drive my curricle. The effects of gallantry are far-reaching."

"Yes, but now Sir Nicholas has taken over the instruction," she called after him, "and you needn't be bothered."

"My good fortune overwhelms me," he said dryly as he stepped out into the sunny street.

Anne stared after him with a puzzled expression but eventually shrugged and returned to the library, where Harold awaited her, alone. She felt suddenly shy, and a little fearful that she had pushed him into something he might not have wanted so very thoroughly as she did. As though he could read her mind, he held out his hands to her, murmuring, "Thank God you had the resolution to show me the error of my reasoning, Anne. Your family have been generous in their acceptance of me, but it is your own acceptance which I never even allowed myself to contemplate seriously. You aren't having second thoughts, are you?"

"Never," she assured him shakily as he drew her into his arms.

"Then I think it is high time we sealed our betrothal."

If their first kiss had been a bit of a surprise, and their second given with reluctance, their third in no way compared with either of them. Free from the torment of indecision and hopelessness, Harold displayed an ardor that would have astonished anyone who had judged him by his rather ascetic countenance or his occasional stern look. But Anne had judged him by neither, had always supected the depths of desire not only in herself but in him, and allowed herself to be crushed to his chest with a delight she had never before known. A considerable time passed before she exclaimed, "Oh, my God, we haven't told Helena yet!"

* * *

Helena was studying the chipped and bedraggled canvas with interest. "How did it get in such horrendous condition?"

With a shrug Mr. Hatton pointed to the water stains on the frame. "I suppose it was stored somewhere damp long ago. Why it was ever stored at all is the mystery. Since I was a boy it has hung in the white saloon. Not in the place of honor, of course, because of its condition, but off to the side. Do you think you could restore it? Or if not, could you duplicate it?"

"I'm afraid I know nothing about restoration, Mr. Hatton. Harold could possibly direct you to a professional." She could understand why he had brought it to her, however. There was a similarity of style between the painting and her own work. Although the purpose of the work had obviously been to portray the manor house, the unknown artist had chosen to view it along a lime walk and spring garden, both treated with a delicacy rare to such paintings. "It's a shame to see such deterioration in a fine painting, but you might best employ someone to come to your estate to attempt another. Duplication would not have quite the same effect, I think."

"You don't understand. The old manor house burned down fifty years ago. This is the only surviving picture of it, and I fear a few more years will see it in such poor condition that it will be a mockery even to hang it." He set the painting aside carefully and accepted the chair she had previously offered him, smoothing his pantaloons with an absent gesture. "The modern house sits in the grounds like a whale. My grandfather designed it himself."

Helena laughed. "I take it your grandfather's taste in architecture is not to your liking, sir. How unfortunate that the old manor should have burned. From this view of it I would assume it was a lovely old house."

He startled her by saying, "I think he burned it. That's how bad his taste in architecture was: he didn't like it. Or maybe he was just crazy. No one seems to know now, or care. But it's important to me to have a painting of the old house. It's part of the Hatton heritage, such as it is. Won't you give some thought to my suggestion of duplicating it?"

"Duplication is a mechanical task, Mr. Hatton. I would find it restrictive, lacking in challenge. Please don't misunderstand me. I think the painting is well worth being restored or copied, but that isn't the sort of work I enjoy doing. And, as you know, I haven't worked much in oils. You would do better to employ someone more familiar with the medium." They could hear the sounds of arrival downstairs and Helena said, "That is probably Harold now. If he can't give you some advice, I'm sure Mr. Wigginton could."

Disappointment was plain in Mr. Hatton's doleful gaze. "I went all the way to Suffolk to bring the painting back so that I might convince you to work on it. While I was there I showed my mother some of your watercolors and she was tremendously enthusiastic about you doing the manor house painting. I thought—"

The door to the drawing room stood open. Mr. Hatton had not only called on two occasions to look at Helena's watercolors, but had developed the habit of paying a call when he was in Argyll Street for his fencing lessons. After the second visit, when he had purchased half a dozen works under Harold's interested guidance, Helena felt she could no longer relegate him to the breakfast parlor. Mr. Hatton's eyes had danced when he was first shown into the drawing room where Helena sat alone. "Ah, I can see that I have advanced in the world," he had quizzed her. "If you *will* keep calling, I can see no reason why I shouldn't be comfortable," she had retorted.

Helena was surprised now to see her brother and Anne appear in the doorway. A barely suppressed excitement glowed in Anne's eyes, and Harold, staid, undemonstrative Harold, had an arm about her shoulders. For a moment she sat immobile, casting a hasty glance at Mr. Hatton as though he might have some explanation for this unusual occurrence.

The frozen tableau was broken up when Anne hurried across the room to grasp Helena's hands. "You're astonished, aren't you? I told Harold on the way here that you would be! He said I had been so brazen that you couldn't have missed it."

"I never said any such thing," Harold laughingly protested. "I said Helena must have been able to guess how things were with me, though she never said a word."

"You're . . . going to be . . . married?" Helena gasped.

"Isn't it wonderful?" Anne squeezed the limp hands. "My parents hadn't the slightest objection. Oh, Helena, we are going to be sisters."

"Sisters," Helena repeated blankly. "But when . . . How could I have been so blind? I had no idea. I . . . I don't know what to say, except that I am so very happy for you both. Has this . . . just happened? I mean, nothing was said last night."

"I twisted your brother's arm this morning when he came to tell me that under no circumstances would he marry me," Anne explained, her eyes dancing. "I have no patience with such snobbery."

Helena's mind whirled with the impact of the announcement. It was *good* news, she informed the panicky part of her that kept throwing up questions like: What will I do? Where do I belong in this arrangement? How will I cope with having my poor placid life so thoroughly disrupted? She forced herself to behave properly, to smile and squeeze Anne's hands in return, to salute her brother's cheek, but her stomach was suddenly in knots. Over and over she chastised herself for only thinking of how their marriage would affect *her*. Somehow she felt embarrassed to have Mr. Hatton there as a witness to this scene of her replacement in Harold's household. Oh, my God, she thought, no one has even acknowledged Mr. Hatton in the excitement. She turned to find that he was watching her curiously from the far side of the room to which he had retired.

"Anne dear, I don't know if you remember Mr. Hatton. He came by to show me an old painting he wishes to have restored. Mr. Hatton, Lady Anne Parsons."

The subsequent exchanges gave Helena an opportunity to compose herself. Mr. Hatton excused himself almost immediately, taking Helena's hand before leaving. It was the first time he had done so and she was left in no doubt as to his purpose. He dropped his voice so the others could not overhear and, green eyes merry, announced, "You are likely to have more time on your hands now, Miss Rogers. May I leave the painting and hope that you will change your mind? As a project to keep you busy I'm sure it would have its merits."

She frowned and looked away from him, but replied, "Very well. Leave it and I'll see how I feel about the work another day. I may decide against doing it, but I can check with Harold about alternatives when he is less . . . occupied."

His gaze went to the other couple who stood talking by the windows. "Every change has advantages and disadvantages. In time they sort themselves out and become new patterns, quite as easy to live with as the old ones. Good day, Miss Rogers. I shall look forward to hearing your decision about the painting."

The sound of his footsteps had receded down the stairs before she turned to her brother and Anne, smiling. "Shall I ring for some champagne to celebrate?"

CHAPTER TWENTY-FIVE

Emma watched as her aunt read the short letter from Lord Bradwell and set it aside with a sigh. "Is he well, Aunt Amelia?"

"Apparently." Amelia retrieved the embroidery frame she had put aside and set a stitch. "As usual he hasn't much to say to me. My quarterly allowance was sent to the bankers, but I already knew that. They notify me, and it was some time ago. The spring planting went well and he has hopes of a good crop. His favorite stallion is suffering from an infection. Sometimes I wonder that he bothers to write at all."

"He doesn't, very often."

"No." Amelia stared into space for a moment and then brought her attention back to her niece. "How are Lady Anne's plans progressing for the wedding?"

"Marvelously. Every time I see her she's *aux anges*. I still cannot believe that I never suspected her affection for Mr. Rogers. Helena didn't either, though. She's a bit at loose ends, I think—Helena, that is. Oh, she's helping Anne with any number of things—shopping for a trousseau, making lists of wedding guests, arranging for the move to the new house—but she's not sketching at all. I'm a little worried about her."

"New house? I hadn't heard of that. They're not going to live in Argyll Street?"

"No, Mr. Rogers is involved in building some houses off Grosvenor Place and they intend to live in one of them." Emma shifted in her chair. "I think Helena will miss the house in Argyll Street. She watches the men fence across at M. Persigny's. That's how she met Mr. Hatton, who has bought a number of her watercolors. You remember I told you he was the subject of her painting 'The Fencer,' which he bought after the exhibit."

Amelia's needle hung poised over the embroidery for a moment before she set another stitch. "It's probably all to the good that they're moving, though. Helena has been mistress of the house in Argyll Street and it will be best for Lady Anne to start fresh as mistress of a new house. You can't blame Helena for feeling unsettled. As good friends as they are, it's an awkward situation. Helena is going to be unseated from the role she's played for her brother for years now."

"Hmm. I hadn't really considered that facet of the arrangement. Do you suppose Anne has?"

"If she hasn't, she will, and I'm sure she will handle it with the greatest tact, but that won't prevent Helena from suffering some pangs of regret." With an accomplished motion she threaded and knotted a new length of gold thread.

Emma rose and walked about the room. "Nothing is as simple as it seems. Even the very best of solutions has some bitter side effect for someone." Realizing that her statement might be misinterpreted, she glanced sharply at Amelia, but her aunt was placidly setting another stitch, not even looking in her direction. Emma returned to her chair and reached out to touch her aunt's shoulder. "Dear Aunt Amelia, I never meant to be on your hands so long. Do you know, before we left school I had such conceit that I was sure I would marry long before Maggie or Anne? And now look at me, not a prospect in the offing."

Amelia set aside the embroidery and concentrated on her niece. "You've learned a lot since then, my love. And you mustn't worry for a moment about being a bother to me. I've loved having you and no sensible girl rushes into marriage." A frown puckered her brow. "I had thought for a short while that you and Dunn—"

"Oh, no!" Emma cried, stricken. "Never! He chose to make friends with me for your sake. It seemed to be so pointless to be at outs with each other when we were both so close to you."

A sigh escaped her. "Well, I'm glad that the two of you are at least friends. He's a fine man, Emma. One of the truly worthy gentlemen of my acquaintance. I can understand why you would find it difficult to choose a husband. So many of the young men are ramshackle to the last degree. And those who aren't, well, they tend to be pompous and lacking in any joie de vivre. You need someone who can share in your high spirits and yet provide a steadying influence. I cannot honestly say I know any other such gentlemen."

"No." Emma felt frozen with sadness. Not for another moment could she bear to sit here discussing Dunn, however, and she jumped to her feet, carefully placing a smile on her lips. "I shall find one, though, dear Aunt Amelia. Heavens, if I am to finish the portrait of

Anne before her wedding, I'll have to do better than sit cozing with you. If Sir Nicholas comes to take me driving, you may send him to the studio. He wasn't sure when he would be able to get here today."

The portrait was coming along very slowly. Anne sat for her twice a week, despite her busy schedule. Emma wanted to capture the radiance that Anne seemed to exude, but her own numbness refused to allow her to get it on canvas. Her very strokes seemed too controlled to portray the splendor of Anne's emotions. Far from eagerly setting out to work on it each day, Emma had to force herself to enter the studio. This was not the way she wanted to paint, and the portrait of Anne was especially important to her.

Even before she closed the door behind her, she had taken in the whole, awful scene. Just for a moment she thought someone else must be guilty of wretched carelessness, but she knew almost instantly that it was her own fault. The portrait had fallen from the easel and lay facedown on the floor in a rubble of dirt and leaves blown in through the open door to the garden. Last night, late, after the servants had locked up for the night, Emma had prowled restlessly about the house, eventually wandering into the studio for a brief, unsatisfactory glance at the portrait. Her nerves on edge, she had then unlocked the door and marched out into the blustery night, defiantly fearful of running into Dunn should he come to visit Amelia that night. The protection her dressing gown gave her was negligible, and she felt the rising wind tug at her hair and chill her straight through. She didn't care. Let them find her dead of exposure in the morning, her overly dramatic mind taunted the fates. Who would mourn her? Quite a few people, she acknowledged, but she made no move to return to the house.

Instead she sat down on The Bench, as she thought of it in her mind, and recalled that last conversation held there. Was she mistaken in thinking that it was the prelude to an offer? Had she built up a fantasy out of whole cloth? No, she had known. Just as she had known, earlier that evening, when he spoke to her, distantly polite, and did not ask her to stand up with him, that he had accepted her rejection. He would not approach her again, would not make any move to change her decision. She should have been relieved. A despair so black had settled on her that she had hurried back into the house, up to her room, without even realizing that she had left the studio door open.

And the wind had raged. She had heard it in her room, beating about the house, later dashing rain against the windows. Her studio now looked as though the storm had invaded it in force. Fortunately, there were no other works in progress, but the portrait of Anne . . . Emma went to lift it from the floor and winced. Ruined. Twigs, leaves, dirt imbedded in the fresh paint, distorting the already imperfect image. The tears Emma had not allowed herself the previous evening now would not be denied. She leaned her head on the picture frame and wept, great shuddering sobs that racked her body, made her throat ache unbearably, their intensity refusing to diminish.

"My dear girl! Whatever is the matter?"

Emma raised her tear-stained face only briefly. "Oh, Nick . . ."

The portrait was held toward him and he grimaced at the unsightly mess. He prized it gently from her shaking fingers and leaned it against the legs of the easel, turning to pull her stricken body against his. With the hand not used to support her, he awkwardly patted her head. "There now, it's not the end of the world, my dear. You have said you weren't satisfied with it, so perhaps it is all for the best. Was the door left open?" He could barely understand her reply that she had accidentally done so. "Hell of a storm, Emma. Most unfortunate. There now, it will be all right." Her efforts to bring the sobs under control were not noticeably successful. He stroked her hair and placed little kisses on her forehead, pulled out his handkerchief and dabbed at her eyes. Those large, swimming eyes, overflowing even as he blotted at them. Unaccountably he crushed her to him, rubbing his hands soothingly up and down her back. "Don't cry, my love. I can't bear it," he said with a shaky laugh.

Under his stroking hands Emma's sobs had begun to diminish slightly, edged out by new sensations. She was no longer unaware of the warmth of his body pressed against hers, of the strangely husky voice in which he murmured his comforting words. The high pitch of her emotions shifted slightly, unnervingly, into another channel. She became intensely aware of his hands on her back, of the whisper of breath in her hair. The hammering of his heart beneath her ear had quickened, and she could feel her own heartbeat speed to match it, could feel that her breath had quickened and her own arms longed to cling to him. Shaken, uncertain, she gently drew back from his embrace.

When she looked up, she found his eyes filled with tenderness, ready to comfort her aching heart . . . and with desire, willing to fan the flickering flame he had struck in her. They regarded one another silently for a moment, and then he opened his arms invitingly. Emma stepped into them, her hands going about his waist as his lips sought hers. There was an urgency to their kisses in keeping with the heightened emotional atmosphere. Desire replaced despair, blocking everything from her mind except the need for his lips, his touch. The relief of simply succumbing to this new need, of not fighting any longer, was in itself a euphoria.

His lips brushed her eyelids and her cheeks. His hands caressed her shoulders and back. Warmth flooded through her body like nourishing sunlight. And then his tongue penetrated her mouth, strangely exhilarating. One hand slid to cup her breast, the other to press against her buttocks. She could feel the hardness of his sex, frightening and yet exciting. His hand at her breast coaxed the nipple erect against her morning dress, making it so sensitive that she could feel the texture of the material. And still his tongue explored her mouth, his lips urgent against hers, until she felt so light-headed that she could barely stand.

"Oh, Lord, Emma," he whispered, cradling her more lightly against his body, dropping his hands to her waist. "It would be hypocritical for me to apologize."

"Of course it would," she murmured against his coat, "or for me to wish you to."

He ran his hands through her silky blond hair. "Frankness is one of your besetting sins, and one of your most marvelous attributes," he informed her dolefully. "I never doubted your sensuality, or your ability to admit it. But I *have* taken advantage of your lowered resistance."

"I don't mind." Emma lifted her head so she could look at him. "I feel a great deal better than I did when you came in."

"I'm not surprised. You could hardly have felt a great deal worse."

"True." She pressed his hands and stepped away from him. Though her body gradually calmed, a glow of excitement remained, apparent in her flushed cheeks. "I don't know why I should have been so upset about the portrait. As you said, I wasn't satisfied with it. But Anne hasn't the time to sit very often, and it isn't that long until her wedding."

"You don't have to finish it by then."

"I know, but I wanted to." She gazed about the littered room and shook her head. "I'll have to have someone come in and clean up this mess. It only makes me feel worse to realize it's my fault."

"We all make mistakes." He saw that she was headed to the door, acting immediately on her words. "Emma, wait. I want to talk to you for a moment."

"We would be more comfortable in the drawing room."

"Yes, but Amelia's there."

She cocked her head at him, smiling. "*More* private conversation, Nick?"

"Private conversation is not criminal conversation," he retorted.

"So I am not to be the subject of crim. con. stories." She sighed, her eyes twinkling. "We can *talk* in the back writing room. I'll meet you there in a moment."

When she joined him he noted that she had washed her face and combed her hair. All traces of tears and arousal alike were gone. By mutual assent they seated themselves on the small gold sofa.

Nick reached out to trace the oval of her face, testing her. She made no effort to avoid his touch and he grinned. "Contrary to what you may think, Emma, today is not the first time I've had a desire to ravish you. Our regular proximity has produced a growing ambition on my part, and I am prepared to act on it."

"Good heaven, Nick, you aren't going to offer me a carte blanche, are you?" she protested, indignant.

"The thought never entered my mind." His leering eyes belied such puritan sentiments but he proceeded seriously. "No, I'm offering you marriage, Emma. Please, don't say anything until I've finished. This is difficult enough for me. We would suit very well, you know. Our temperaments are similar and I think we would have the sense not to interfere in one another's lives beyond what was pleasurable. You have your painting, I have my sporting activities. I've never felt the need to marry and have an heir, but if you produced one for me, and kept him from being a nuisance, I daresay I shouldn't mind so very much. I would hate to see my cousin Herbert inherit my worldly goods when I die. And, if I've not been misinformed by common gossip, your dowry is quite sufficient to any expense you might incur. You wouldn't cost me a penny!"

"Really, Nick!"

"There are worse fates, my dear. And being a spinster is one of them." He regarded her shrewdly for a moment. "I think you're fond of me, other attachments notwithstanding. I know I've grown exceptionally fond of you. Marriage would give you more freedom, a home of your own, a chance to release Amelia from the care of you.

Call it a convenient marriage if you wish." The rakish gleam she had portrayed in his portrait was again in his eyes. "*I* would deem it wonderfully convenient to find you in my bed each night."

Despite herself, Emma flushed. "No doubt," she said dryly. "Nick, I . . . I can't argue with your reasoning; it makes a great deal of sense . . . for me. But you, well, you don't really want a wife. I would be a hindrance, a nuisance. Occasionally you would have to think of me, take me into account when you were making your plans. And I'm too young for you. People would be sure to comment on that."

"What the hell do I care if people comment on it? It's none of their business. Besides, it simply means you'll still be young enough to make another match when I'm in my grave."

Her voice became sharp. "Don't say things like that! You're not *that* old."

"I know." He took her chin gently between his fingers and gazed intently into her bewildered eyes. "Now listen carefully, my love. Marriage to me would be a great deal more comfortable for you than to one of those young gudgeons who follow you around like puppies. You would have the house in Upper Brook Street to live in here and the estate in Wiltshire when you wished to retire to the country. There is no reason you couldn't be as happy as most wives, probably much more so. There are areas in which I flatter myself I could make you very happy indeed."

His lips descended on hers then, and his hands began to stroke her sides gently. Emma intended at first to protest. Her attempts to think his proposal through were so easily distracted by other matters thrusting themselves on her attention—Dunn's distant politeness of the previous evening, Anne's ruined portrait, Maggie's disapproval of Nick, even Amelia's pointing out her need for a guiding hand in marriage. Emma hadn't thought herself in any mood for further lovemaking, but she found almost instantly that she was wrong. This time the desire rose more quickly and she almost wished that he were not being so very gentlemanly with his hands. When he drew back from her, there was no smug satisfaction at her response, merely a matter-of-fact acceptance of it.

"You really should be married, Emma," he said gently. "You have a store of sensuality that can't be expressed any other way, for a lady of your birth. As I see it, I am by far the most suitable of the gentlemen available to you. Or am I wrong about that?"

"No," she whispered.

"Then I suggest that you agree. Never mind what other people will say or think. You have only yourself to please, thank God. Will you have me?"

Emma moistened her lips and met his eyes. "Yes."

"Good." He pressed a kiss on her cheek, nothing more. "When shall it be?"

"After Anne's. I don't want anything detracting from her special occasion. And small, Nick. I don't want all the trappings she will have. Just a private ceremony with a few friends. I can't abide stately ceremonies."

He took her hand, smiling. "I told you we had a great deal in common. Not that I am especially pleased to wait for another month. I could get a special license and have us joined within a day."

"Aunt Amelia would call that unseemly haste." Emma tried to return his smile, but her emotions were in such turmoil that her lips would not behave properly. "I'm sure I can be happy with you, Nick. I only hope you aren't making a mistake."

"Don't worry your pretty head about that, love. It occurred to me some time ago that I couldn't possibly choose a better wife for myself than you."

Emma refused to listen to the nagging doubt in her head that protested that he shouldn't be choosing a wife at all, that he didn't need a wife and wouldn't know what to do with one—other than in bed. She refused, also, to ask for the reassurance of his kisses. Instead she rose and said, "Let's tell Aunt Amelia. The hardest part of the whole thing is going to be breaking the news to our various and sundry acquaintances."

He grimaced. "I know. I'm likely to be hooted out of White's."

When Amelia found that an hour's quiet conversation with Emma did nothing to shake the girl's resolve to marry Sir Nicholas, she decided to accept the inevitable and make an announcement at the soiree she was giving that evening. Fortunately it was not to be a large gathering, but it did include their closest friends and seemed a fitting occasion, provided Sir Nicholas had his wits sufficiently about him to show up with an engagement ring. Taking no chances, Emma sent a note to Upper Brook Street conveying her aunt's intention, and her own ring size, mentioning that it would be prudent for him to arrive before the other guests. "And if you can't find anything at such short notice, or don't wish to," she had written, "I shall wear my mother's engagement ring, which is quite lovely and fits perfectly."

Dressing for the evening proved more difficult than Emma had anticipated. Her plan to wear the blue satin had to be discarded: it was not glamorous enough for the announcement. Her white crepe had been worn too recently, and the primrose gauze was a little too fancy for the evening's entertainment. An emerald crepe that she had not worn as yet because of the low, square cut over the bust began to take on particular appeal for her. Somehow it seemed appropriate to wear it when announcing that she was to be married to Sir Nicholas. The sarcenet slip clung to her body, while the crepe overdress shimmered whimsically over it. In the costume plate the dress had had long sleeves, but Madame Minotier had insisted that on Emma a rouleau of crepe at either shoulder would be most becoming. Madame Minotier had also scorned the long veil, telling Emma such tricks were for demure misses who hadn't the style to carry off such a dress. Emma decided as she slipped into matching emerald shoes that Nick would appreciate her choice. It didn't matter if there were some who would frown. She allowed her abigail to arrange her hair with a part on the forehead and loose ringlets disposed over each ear, the back braided into a crown in which was settled an ornament of semiprecious stones.

The mirror reflected a most alluring image scarcely detracted from by the nervous flush that stained her cheeks. Was she really doing the right thing? Marrying Nick was at the same time sensible and hopelessly foolish. What sort of reaction would there be to the announcement? Anne would be there with Mr. Rogers. Even Maggie might come if she were feeling particularly well. Would they pretend to approve? She turned away from the glass and picked up her reticule. Emma had sorted through the acceptances for the soiree, hoping against hope that Dunn would have refused, but his bold-handed reply was there, in the affirmative. Perhaps he would change his mind. Oh, please, Nick, come early, hold me for a minute.

Emma waited alone in the drawing room. Her aunt was a casual hostess, always ready by the time her first guests arrived, but not a minute sooner. When the knocker sounded early, Emma realized she had been clasping her hands tightly in her lap, staring at the closed draperies but not listening for the sounds of carriages. She felt vaguely feverish and placed a freezing hand to her warm forehead. Decidedly she had a fever.

The sound of lone footsteps crossing the hall toward the drawing room made her jump to her feet and smooth out any creases in her skirts. Sir Nicholas opened the door for himself and stepped into the room with lazy grace. He was impeccably dressed and looked, Emma thought, impressively handsome.

"You see, my dear, your word is my command. I am here early, with ring in hand and arrow through heart, just as any young bride-to-be could wish." He laughed, clasping her hands and holding her at arm's length to have a good view of her costume. "And you . . . You must have read my mind—or your dressmaker did."

"I hoped you would like it. I've felt too modest to wear it, until now," she teased.

"Modesty is not one of the virtues I prize in maidens," he informed her, eyeing her cleavage appreciatively, "and I would positively dislike it in my wife."

"I doubt you have the slightest cause for alarm."

"No, I think not." He released her hands after a chaste kiss on her cheek. From his breast pocket he retrieved a small jeweler's box, which he opened with a deft flick of his finger, much as he might have treated a snuffbox. "Rundell and Bridges had a shockingly large assortment of rings to go through. I swear I was there for over an hour. The old man pointed out the advantages of a whole case of stones. I should have taken you with me, for I hadn't the slightest interest myself. In the end I chose the diamond set round with emeralds; it will go well with your gown. Seemed to me a bigger diamond would have been vulgar, but you should have seen the size of some of the stones he showed me. Costly, of course, but I won't have you thinking I balked at the price. Do you like it?"

Emma watched as he slipped it on her finger, a stupid great lump in her throat. "It's beautiful, Nick. Thank you."

"Is it nicer than your mother's?"

"Much," she assured him, suddenly grasping his hand for courage. "It's much nicer than anything I own."

"Really?" His voice was quizzing but he put a comforting arm about her waist. "We'll have to remedy that by adding a few pieces to your stock. A necklace, say, and some earrings, and maybe one of those things women wear in their hair. What do you call them?"

"Tiaras?"

"Right. We'll have them all match your ring." He was studying her face and now laid a hand on her forehead. "You have a fever, don't you?"

"Perhaps a little. It's the excitement."

They could hear Lady Bradwell issuing some last-minute instructions to a footman. Before she entered the room Nick said, "Have courage, my girl. After tonight the worst will be over. I put a notice in tomorrow's paper and you can lie low all day if you wish. No one is likely to make a fuss."

Far from making a fuss, the guests, when Amelia made the announcement early in the evening, stood in stunned silence. It was a reaction Emma had never before seen in a similar situation, and she bit her lip to restrain a nervous giggle. Nick made not the least attempt to hide *his* amusement. He turned to her, laughing, and said, "You see, my love, they are positively overwhelmed by the *fitness* of our union."

Anne was the first to reach them, holding out her hands to Emma and smiling at Sir Nicholas. "Congratulations! I am not the one to scold you for keeping such a secret, am I? You know I wish you every happiness. You are not even to think of working on my portrait, Emma."

"It got ruined in the storm last night," Emma told her sadly. "Marrying Nick seemed to be the only way to avoid having to finish it by your wedding."

Her jest shocked Anne, though she tried hard not to show it. Mr. Rogers was later to point out to her that Sir Nicholas had been vastly amused by the joke, and that he and Emma had shared a disturbingly speaking glance when she made it. After Anne and Mr. Rogers came Maggie, a puzzled quirk to her brow, but a warm smile on her lips, and Adam at her elbow.

"Congratulations, my dear. I hope you will both be very happy."

The words were repeated continuously as each member of the party approached them. If they were curious or surprised or even disapproving, no one so much as hinted, at least not to the couple involved or to Lady Bradwell. Out of the corner of her eye Emma could see them standing in small groups discussing the unexpected development, considering its cause and its ramifications. Lord Dunn was the last to approach them. He made no attempt to smile, his dark eyes cold, almost angry.

The formal bow was no less chilling than his eyes. "Miss Berryman, Sir Nicholas. I see the driving lessons have promoted more than Miss Berryman's skill with the ribbons." His lips were a tight line, through which he murmured, "My best wishes, of course."

His tone, Emma thought, more precisely conveyed the message "drop dead," encompassing them both. If he has the bad taste to mention Nick's portrait now really hanging in my bedchamber, I'll kick him in the shins, Emma decided furiously. But of course he would never do such a thing. Instead he stood with them a moment conjecturing on who might be employed to do Emma's portrait—or whether she might consider doing her own. Emma told him she had not so much as given the matter a moment's thought and he soon moved away.

The evening was a wretched strain on her. The ring on her finger twinkled in the candlelight and Nick was frequently at her side, but it was difficult to appear joyous when her head ached and her fever kept rising. She lost track of how many times she explained that they would be married quietly in a month or so, that no, she had never expected Nick actually to come to the sticking point, that they had not as yet discussed any plans for a wedding trip. The heat of the rooms became unbearable and she wandered alone out into the hall and back toward the coolness of the studio, where everything was once again in order, the unfinished, ruined portrait of Anne turned to the wall.

Dunn saw her leave and was tempted to follow her. He had no idea what he would say, but he would have liked to upbraid her for her lies to him. Good manners prevented him from doing any such thing, of course, and he returned his attention to Lady Anne's comments on the play she had been to the previous evening. Having seen the production some nights previously, however, his mind soon drifted away again. What he really should do, he mused, was have a serious talk with Miss Berryman before this engagement became widely known. It was folly for her to consider marrying Nicholas. The man hadn't the first qualification for being a decent husband, even if he did care for her. His life was a model of self-indulgence that could not easily adapt to a wife, no matter how independent. At an appropriate moment Dunn excused himself from the small group and headed directly out into the hall. She would have gone to her studio, he decided, to have a respite from the prying questions and curious stares.

It didn't surprise him that the studio was in darkness. In fact he rather welcomed the lack of illumination so that she might not read any untoward emotion in his eyes. He found the door slightly ajar and pushed it farther, preparatory to speaking her name. But the sound of voices within froze him, and his eyes quickly adjusted to the studio's dimness.

"Oh, Nick, I wish it *could* be tomorrow. I don't know if I can stand a month of this."

"Just say the word, my little love, and I'll get a special license first thing in the morning. I'd far prefer it."

There was the whisper of a sigh. "I can't do that to Aunt Amelia. Hold me, Nick."

"Dear Lord, Emma, you're burning up. You should be in bed."

"I know, I know. As soon as the guests leave, I promise you. Maybe I shouldn't let you get close to me; you might catch whatever it is."

"Damned if I care," he retorted jovially. "Talk about hot lips!"

"You're impossible!"

Dunn was ashamed of himself for continuing to observe them, but he had no more power to remove himself than to fly. Not that they did anything totally outrageous, nothing more than an engaged couple passionately in love might do. But he could hear the quickening of her breathing, the murmur of pleasure. Somehow it surprised him that Nicholas was as gentle as he was, as restrained in his demands. Emma's ardor did not surprise him at all. Hadn't he always realized that sensuality floated close to the surface of her polished veneer?

Her gown was cut too low for any sane man in Nicholas's position not simply to push it down a little lower, an expedient he shortly resorted to. Dunn caught a glimpse of the proud white breasts and turned away, pulling the door almost closed. But he was unable to move, leaning against the door frame for several minutes until his sluggish brain bore it in on him that it would be totally unforgivable for him to be found there either by the participants or anyone else. He walked numbly back to the drawing room. He, too, was a sane man, he told himself fiercely, and he knew there would be no talk with Emma. A woman who was sexually attracted to a man would never listen to reason. Emma would marry Nick, and from the looks of it, he thought, the pulse in his neck throbbing, the sooner the better.

CHAPTER TWENTY-SIX

The carriage had slowed to a crawl along Bond Street because of the press of other vehicles. Emma and Amelia, exhausted from shopping, said little as the coachman guided them into Piccadilly to deliver Emma to Maggie's. The expedition had not been successful; Emma had not decided on a gown for her wedding.

As though continuing a conversation, Amelia finally said, "I don't think you should be concerned that Sir Nicholas has missed escorting us the last two evenings, Emma. Undoubtedly he has any number of things to arrange for your marriage and he will never be one to sit in your pocket. You told me you knew that from the start."

"I do know it, and I'm not overly concerned at his defection. Frankly, I've been astonished at how regularly he *does* escort us." Emma gazed unseeing out the window. "I wouldn't marry him if I thought he wouldn't be able to maintain his freedom. It's more important to him than I am."

Amelia looked positively stricken. "Don't be absurd, Emma! He's head over heels in love with you. Anyone can see it."

Turning from the window to meet her aunt's eyes, Emma said softly, "I think he does love me, yes, in his way, and certainly he wants me. But he doesn't *need* anyone, and he only felt it possible to marry me because I wouldn't need him, either. We understand each other."

Amelia shivered in the warm carriage. "That's . . . awful, Emma. You're either terribly mistaken or you are making a terrible mistake."

"No, I don't think so," Emma replied, her voice gentle. "I'm very fond of Nick, and . . . attracted to him. I shall like being married, you know. Every young lady wastes a great deal of time searching for a suitable husband, attending parties, setting up flirtations, worrying about whether she will be left on the shelf. I have other things I want to do. Well, one thing, really. I want to have time to paint, to concentrate on it. When your mind is continually skipping about, wondering who you will dance with one night, and if you will receive a posy the next day, continually assessing the gentlemen you meet for their potential as husbands instead of simply enjoying their company—oh, the whole lot of it distracts and absorbs unnecessary energy. I want to get on with my life. I want to let you get on with *your* life. I'm not saying there is no affection in this marriage. There is. We're simply not talking of the great passion of the century, my dear, and you must know as well as I that such passion is rarely sustained."

The carriage had drawn to a halt in Half Moon Street and Emma pressed her aunt's hand. "Can you understand that?"

"I don't know," Amelia whispered. "I thought there was more. There should be more."

"Perhaps neither of us is capable of more," Emma replied lightly as she allowed the footman to hand her down from the carriage. "Anne will drop me off later. You needn't send for me."

As the carriage drew away, Emma felt sure she saw the gleam of tears in her aunt's eyes and bit her lip. Why had she felt it necessary to tell Amelia the truth? She hadn't told anyone else; she wouldn't tell anyone else. The strain of trying to live up to other people's expectations was taking its toll. Everyone assumed that Emma Berryman—pretty, sought after, well dowered—would marry precisely whom she chose. And she was going to do just that, wasn't she? She had suddenly felt an urge to speak of her true feelings because she was about to face Anne and Maggie, and somehow with them she could not be so honest. For a variety of reasons the three of them had not been together in some time, and probably wouldn't again for heaven knew how long. Anne was getting married, Maggie would go off to the country with her husband and her baby. They had both achieved a very special relationship in their lives and they wanted to believe that she had as well. Emma felt she had to perpetuate the illusion so as not to diminish their happiness.

Anne had already arrived and Emma sensed that they had been discussing her, which, under the circumstances, was only natural. Their smiles of greeting were warm and real, but there was an undercurrent of curiosity, of speculation. Emma regarded them with a rueful smile, instinctively knowing that any forced gaiety on her part would be suspect.

"Just look at the three of us," she opined, seating herself. "Sent out into the glittering world of society from Mrs. Childswick's haven of peace over a year ago. Who would have suspected that Maggie would be pushed into a marriage with a rattle, Anne would throw herself away on an untitled gentleman, and I would become engaged to an aging rake? Do you suppose the girls at Windrush House whisper amongst themselves of our folly? For how can they know that Maggie has steadied her carefree spouse, and Anne has discovered that character, wherever it may be found, is more important than position, and I . . ." She hesitated, to add to the suspense, offering a wicked, leering grin in imitation of Nick's. "I have succumbed to the lure of the flesh?"

Anne's irrepressible chuckle escaped her. "Oh, Emma, how can you? Surely you see more in Sir Nicholas than that."

"Well, I do, of course, but I won't admit it to him. He's vain about his sexual prowess, you know, and not the least interested in hearing that it is his mind which intrigues me. Ever since I painted his portrait, displaying his true colors to the world, he has felt he had to live up to his image. Far be it from me to discourage him! If he's willing to see me as a portrait painter, I'm willing to see him as a rake. There is, I hope, a little more to each of us than that."

"He *is* rather attractive," Maggie said doubtfully. "Ever since you became engaged he has been utterly charming to me, and I confess I'm not immune to that rakish grin of his. But, Emma, I don't think he would tolerate even a shadow of interference."

"Interference? Merciful heavens! He couldn't want it any less than I do. Now don't tell me I need a guiding hand, either of you. Even if I did, you know I would chafe under any restraint whatsoever. I've learned how to behave myself, I hope, and Nick has always known how to get away with his outrageous conduct." Now, though, Emma wore a soft, misty-eyed smile. "He really is a love, you know."

Her companions seemed somewhat mystified but her apparent frankness was disarming. Maggie rang for tea and the talk turned to Anne's wedding and Maggie's baby, who was brought in for them to see. Nothing is quite so distracting as admiring an infant or guzzling tea, Emma mused, satisfied with her performance. But just when she thought she had lulled any faint fears, Maggie asked, "Do you remember our discussing Sir Nicholas last year toward the end of the season? You said then that he didn't care about other people, and he didn't care about himself, that he didn't take anything seriously. I should think it would be difficult to live with such a person."

Emma sat very still for a moment and then said softly, "He cares about me."

There was such quiet conviction in her voice that neither of them thought to question the statement. In fact, they were both aware that what she said was true. His method of showing his affection was not perhaps just what society was accustomed to: teasing his prospective bride and puffing off her talent as a portrait painter. Both Maggie and Anne had observed him carefully, had heard the surprised comments of others that he had been snagged at last, well and truly. Decidedly, Sir Nicholas cared for Emma.

Anne hesitated as she set down her cup and asked without looking at Emma, "And do you care about him, my love?"

"Yes." Why did it make her heart ache to say that? She did care about Nick, very much.

Anne decided to press just once more. "Well, yes, actually I can see that you care about him, Emma, but is that why you agreed to marry him? I mean—please don't be offended—you didn't accept him just because he was such an elusive fellow did you? I know it would be a challenge having everyone say that he would never marry, you said so yourself last year. No, of course you wouldn't accept him for such a stupid reason," Anne hastened to add, disgusted with herself.

Emma sighed, smiling. "I see the two of you know me too well, and I actually might have done something so simpleminded last year, but not now. Have no fear that I accepted him as some sort of conquest. I wouldn't do that to Nick."

All their unacknowledged resistance seemed to melt. Maggie was suddenly saying that they *did* suit awfully well, and Anne remarked that Sir Nicholas was only seven years older than Mr. Rogers, after all. By the time Anne and Emma took their leave, there was a general agreement that Emma was doing quite the right thing, and they hugged one another in real accord. On the ride to Bruton Street, however, Emma kept the conversation strictly to Anne's wedding and her role as bridesmaid in it. When she reached her room, Emma lay down on the bed, allowing the tension to drain from her. Everything was going to be all right.

Sir Nicholas arrived to escort them to the theater that evening in less than jubilant spirits. His scrutiny of Emma's new gown was cursory and his compliment on it lacked its usual enthusiasm. She had ordered it a few days after their engagement, and had chosen it specially for his approval. Though she felt a twinge of disappointment at his indifference, she allowed none of it to show. Nick in a dark mood was something alien to her, and she was wise enough to respect this, toning down her own revived spirits to match his more reserved demeanor. They sat together on the seat opposite Amelia in the carriage and Emma allowed her aunt to carry the conversation. Eventually Nick took her hand and squeezed it.

"You're a clever girl, my dear," he murmured into her hair, but his disposition did not vastly improve.

From her seat in Lady Bradwell's box Emma could see that the house was filling rapidly. The candlelight was bright enough for her to distinguish familiar faces even in boxes across the way. She almost wished it weren't, for she saw Dunn take a seat with Lady Rowland and her daughter Caroline, saw him bending to catch the girl's words when she spoke. Emma forced her attention back to her aunt and Nick.

"Did you decide on a wedding dress today?" he asked when informed by Amelia that they had shopped.

"No, I'm torn between two very different designs," Emma replied.

A trace of impatience tinged his voice. "You haven't much time, Emma. The dressmaker will need several fittings, which could take weeks. I want you to make a decision tomorrow."

Emma stared at him for a moment before lowering her eyes. "Very well, first thing in the morning, Nick."

Amelia watched the interchange with trepidation, knowing that Emma was not one to take an order lightly. She could not put a finger on the undercurrents and was not even sure from which of the two they issued. Most likely it was just two strong-willed people sparring for advantage, seeking limits or asking for reassurance. Her philosophy, however, was not to interfere, and she turned aside from them to concentrate on her program.

"It seems to me," Nick was saying, "that you aren't taking our wedding very seriously, Emma. It's not another rout party, you know. We've decided to have a very private ceremony but that does not relieve you of a few duties. Have you sent the invitations?"

"Several days ago." Emma tried hard to keep her tone level while her fingers picked unconsciously at her beaded purse. "I've set myself a schedule for making arrangements, for shopping and such. The only thing I'm behindhand on is the gown. I wanted it to be something you would especially appreciate."

"I'm not likely to disapprove of your choice."

"No," she said frankly, "but I can't decide whether you would prefer me to look virginal or seductive."

His brow became thunderous and he glanced to see if Amelia had overheard. Well, he knew she had, but she gave no indication, continuing to concentrate on the uninformative program. In a low voice he growled at Emma, "You don't say things like that in a box at the theater, my girl."

"Yes, I do," she retorted. "For God's sake, Nick, what's put your nose out of joint? Since when have you become so concerned with propriety?"

"Since I decided to take on the responsibility of a wife."

Emma leaned toward him; a demure look settled over an impish grin, and she whispered in his ear, "If you're going to behave that way when we're married, I'd as soon forget the whole thing. I'd rather be your mistress."

Hard as he tried, Nick was unable to suppress the grin that twitched at his lips. Emma thought for a moment he had so forgotten himself that he was going to kiss her on the lips, right there in public, but instead he kissed her hand. She had already pulled three beads off the purse and they fell from her hand when he lifted it. Nick cocked his head sympathetically and took the mistreated reticule from her nervous fingers. For the entire first act of the play Emma's reticule rested on his elegantly clad knee in plain view of anyone who cared to look.

At the first intermission they were visited in their box by several acquaintances; at the second they wandered out into the corridor, speaking briefly with friends. When they were just opposite the box in which Dunn was sitting, the door opened and he came out with Caroline Rowland on his arm. Emma assured herself that it was her imagination that he stiffened, though Miss Rowland looked up at him questioningly.

"Miss Berryman, Nick. I'm sure you know Miss Rowland."

"Yes, of course." Emma smiled at the young lady. "Are you enjoying the play?"

Miss Rowland wrinkled her aristocratic nose. "It's not really to my taste. I prefer something a little more elevating to the mind." At Dunn's startled look, she waved an airy hand. "But that is neither here nor there. I don't believe I've had the occasion to congratulate you on your engagement, Miss Berryman. My felicitations to you and Sir Nicholas."

"Thank you."

"I understand that you are to be wed fairly soon."

"In about two weeks," Emma said, "shortly after my friend Anne. I had no wish to be off on a wedding trip and miss her celebration."

"Then she will miss yours," Miss Rowland pointed out, as though the knowledge would come as a surprise to Emma.

"Yes, but we are having a private ceremony with only a few friends."

There had been some debate in Emma's mind as to whether she should include Dunn amongst that number for the wedding. Certainly she didn't want him there, but possibly he should have been included. When she made the brief list, she had left off his name, and Nick had perused it, nodding. Dunn had not received an invitation.

"Are you being married at St. George's?" he asked now.

"No, St. James's. Aunt Amelia was married there." Emma met his polite gaze steadily.

Miss Rowland nodded her approval. "I think it is always appropriate to promote such a tradition. Not for the sake of sentimentality, mind you, but for the substance that custom gives. Is your aunt with you this evening?"

"She stayed in the box to speak with Mr. and Mrs. Whitechapel. I suppose we should be getting back."

"There's plenty of time." Nick turned to Dunn. "Have you heard whether Ashby has decided to sell his grays?"

"He mentioned it again at the club today. If you're interested, you'd best see him before he puts them with Tattersall's. That will only raise the figure higher. I didn't know you were looking for another pair."

"I might be." Sir Nicholas was strangely noncommittal, casting a hasty glance at Emma to see if she was listening, but she was responding to a question from Miss Rowland. "Last time I saw the grays they look spirited but not mettlesome. Ashby likes a controllable pair. That's what I had in mind."

Dunn, too, looked at Emma. So Nick intended to give her a carriage and pair as a surprise wedding present, did he? It was precisely what Dunn had planned to do if she had agreed to marry him. The thought was oppressive and he addressed the ladies with a slight edge to his voice. "If we are to stop in at your aunt's box, Miss Rowland, we had best excuse ourselves."

The remainder of the play and the farce that followed it made little impression on Emma's mind. It was better, she knew, to keep running into Dunn. Only with regular casual contact would she learn to control the sad ache she rarely acknowledged in herself. In time a pattern of a sort of friendship would be established. Emma could not help but experience a prick of alarm, however, at his being with Miss Rowland. Not because of her aunt; Amelia would realize as well as she did that Miss Rowland was entirely too haughty and humorless to be a threat to Amelia's position in his life. But Emma disliked his being with her because she was such a total contrast to Emma herself, as though he were flaunting the difference between them, to Emma's disadvantage.

In the hall, back in Bruton Street, Amelia surveyed her companions with a knowledgeable eye. "You have some matters to discuss about the wedding I daresay. Why don't you offer Sir Nicholas a glass of brandy, Emma? If you don't mind, I won't stay up with you. It's been a long day."

His mood had lightened during the evening, and when he sat holding his glass of brandy, he smiled at her. "Did I tell you how charming you look this evening?"

"No. You mumbled something about never having seen the gown before."

"I haven't, have I?"

"No, it's new."

He ran his hand along her uncovered arm. "Your gowns seem to be getting more seductive since we became engaged. I'm not complaining; I like them."

"And the wedding dress? Which shall it be?"

Running a finger along the low scoop of the neckline, he said, "Virginal. Does that surprise you?"

"Not at all. I rather prefer it myself." She allowed him to draw her closer. "I'm sorry I've waited so long to choose it. Somehow the decision was paralyzing."

"I wonder why." If he was really curious, Emma could not tell, as he started to kiss her then. After a while he said, "You would probably make an excellent mistress, Emma."

Her eyes were too close to his to focus properly and she drew back a bit. "Would you prefer that, Nick? To be relieved of all this responsibility you seem to think marriage entails?"

"Well, it is a responsibility, dammit," he grumbled. "I'll have to keep track of where you are and you'll want to know where I am."

"I can't see why," she said, eyes dancing.

"For one thing, so I'll know when you'll be in my bed. I'm likely to come home earlier on those evenings." He slipped her gown off one shoulder and stroked the satin skin he had uncovered. "I'd hate to come home early and find you'd gone off into the country."

"I promise to let you know at least a day ahead of time. There's no necessity for you to do the same if you don't wish." There were a dozen questions she wanted to ask him: Do you have a mistress now? Will you keep her? Will you be more discreet when we are married? But any one of them she felt sure he would consider an infringement on his personal life, an invasion he would resent. And there were probably things he wanted to tell her: how he expected her to conduct herself, whether he cared if she had liaisons, what he envisioned as her role in his life. But he said nothing, allowing his hands and lips to do the only talking he was willing to do.

His touch, and the sensations it stirred, were their common ground. Perhaps not their only common ground, but the one on which doubts and fears were banished. The rising tide of desire in Emma's body effectively blotted all thoughts from her mind. She never protested the gradual slipping of her gown to her waist. The need for his hands and his lips on her bare breasts was too great. Always she was surprised that he did not demand more. She was willing to give everything when her body ached with urgency, but he murmured, "Soon, my love, very soon." And she would lie against him, feeling the gradual diminishing of the tension, which would not entirely disappear even when he rearranged her clothing, kissed her good night, and left. Where did he go then? To his mistress? Emma would not have blamed him, in fact could quite understand such a course of action.

But why didn't he satisfy himself with her? Surely he must know she was willing. Emma lay in bed after each of these encounters trying to understand, desire still clinging about her like an elusive mist. They were going to be married. What difference would it make? Even if she conceived, who would notice a baby born two weeks early? But he wanted her gown to be virginal, he wanted her to be virginal. As a sop to convention? She wouldn't have expected that of Nick. Much more likely that he wished to see the desire build and build in her so that on their wedding night . . . Yes, Emma decided drowsily just before she fell asleep, that must be the reason.

In the days that followed she found support for her theory, though she became more and more confused by Nick's behavior. He always treated her gently, politely, even lovingly once they were together, but he invariably arrived moody and uncommunicative. It was as though he forgot in between meetings how much he liked her. And it wasn't only the passionate moments at the end of an evening. Half an hour after they had been together he would grin at her, touch her nose with a playful finger, or whisper in her ear some delighted word of self-congratulation at having won her hand.

"If I had known you fifteen years ago, Emma, I would probably this moment be surrounded by a parcel of brats unexceeded by the old king himself."

"Fifteen years ago I was four," she laughed, "and I have no intention of being so prolific as the queen. For your sake, you understand. *She* is all right. It was the poor beleaguered king who was mad."

The night before Anne's wedding he was especially low-spirited. During the whole course of the evening he rarely smiled, though he was sweetly solicitous of her welfare, insisting that she not stay out late because of her bridesmaid's duties the next day. Emma thought it was merely a ploy to have her alone in the drawing room in Bruton Street, and she was not averse, but when they arrived at Amelia's house, he merely kissed her forehead and wished her a good night's sleep. Emma gazed after his retreating figure, stunned and more than a little disappointed.

CHAPTER TWENTY-SEVEN

Maggie watched Anne walk toward Mr. Rogers with a sense of complete happiness. Not only was the occasion joyful, but her own remembrance of that last time she had been in St. George's, frightened, miserable, was now totally overlaid by her own contentment. At her side sat Greenwood, the same man she had married, and yet not quite the same. For one thing, ever since little Charles had been born, her husband, flirting with jealousy over the child, had insisted that she call him by his Christian name, too. They had agreed to stay in town through Anne's wedding, and Emma's, before settling into the country for a long rustication. Adam would have friends to stay and Maggie would have both him and the baby to care for. She couldn't think of any arrangement more in keeping with her desires.

And Anne was a beautiful bride, blushingly ecstatic in her white lace gown. Maggie had been invited, even coaxed, to be a bridesmaid, but she had gently refused. It would be enough, she had said, just to be there. As Anne spoke her words of commitment Maggie remembered her own silent promise to Adam at that altar. He *had* given her a chance, and she had kept her vow to make him an acceptable wife. Her eyes misted as Mr. Rogers, his voice resonant with affection, took Anne to be his lawfully wedded wife. Maggie felt Adam's hand steal into hers and she turned to see his beloved smile beaming down on her. How very lucky she was!

Strangely enough, Anne was experiencing much the same thought. So many things might have prevented this moment. Harold might not have been brought to see the wisdom of their marriage. Her parents might have objected that his position was not equal to her own. Someone else might have won his affections. She might not have become friends with Helena and had the chance to get to know him. Oh, yes, things might have been far otherwise than they were that day.

Instead, here they stood being pronounced man and wife with Emma and Dunn, Helena and Jack attending them, with her parents and Will and Maggie and Adam watching. No one else really mattered. In fact, Anne admitted to herself, a dimple peeping out in her cheek, even her family and friends did not matter all that much, right now as she stood beside Harold. For today that was surely permissible. He caught the buoyant light in her eyes and responded in the only way he could, considering the solemnity of the ceremony: he pressed the fingers next to his. He, too, found the occasion one of joy.

Emma was close enough to observe this silent sharing of their delight, and she tried very hard to let their happiness rule her own emotional temperature. But her eyes glanced beyond them to Dunn, who was staring at her, his face frozen in an aspect of bewilderment. Was he seeing her four days hence, at another altar, exchanging vows with Nick? Or was he comparing her own strange choice with Anne's? Was he thinking of her at all, or merely absentmindedly looking in her direction? Emma returned her gaze to the newly wedded couple. How could she think of anything else in the face of their marvelous union?

As she followed Anne and Harold out of the church at Dunn's side, she searched the faces in the congregation for Nick. Surely he had not missed the wedding! He had said he would be there, but her hasty glance over the multitude of faces failed to pick him out. Finally she spotted him, in the last row, as though he could barely bring himself to be there. The hollows of his cheeks looked prominent in his drawn face. When her eyes met his, she suffered an almost electric shock of knowledge. It seemed hardly credible that she could have deluded herself for the last month. Out of sight of him, she stumbled in the vestibule and Dunn automatically reached out a firm hand to steady her.

"Thank you."

Dunn regarded her with cool gray eyes. "Are you all right?"

"Oh, yes. I'm afraid I wasn't paying attention." But she knew her face had paled perceptibly and she hastened forward to hug Anne. "Everything was perfect, absolutely perfect. You looked positively radiant and Mr. Rogers the most proud and handsome fellow in the world. Oh, how happy I wish you both!"

Fortunately Anne was too engrossed in her own concerns to notice Emma's paleness. She was soon surrounded by her family and hustled into the waiting carriage. Emma found herself with Helena, Dunn, and Lord Maplegate in another being driven to the house in Grosvenor Square where a wedding feast was to be held. Helena looked teary-eyed and Emma pressed her arm in an encouraging gesture, but the sympathy was more than Helena could bear and she burst into real tears, much to Dunn's astonishment and Jack's horror.

"My dear, whatever is the matter?" Emma begged, putting an arm about her shoulders. "You could not possibly have acquired a more wonderful sister, and your brother is the happiest man on earth."

"I know, I know." Helena struggled for control. "Please forgive me. How senseless to shed my tears on such a happy occasion. Don't tell them I cried."

"Well, of course not." Emma laughed. She accepted the handkerchief Dunn passed across to her and wiped away the other woman's tears, but the look in Helena's eyes arrested her. "Something is the matter, isn't it?"

"She's not coming," Helena tried to explain, though her words were totally incomprehensible to the others.

"Who's not coming, my dear?" Emma asked, mystified.

"My aunt. She was to come and stay with me in Argyll Street until they returned from their wedding trip. I couldn't tell Harold. It would have spoiled everything at such a late date. I told him her carriage had broken down and that she had sent a note saying she would be here this evening. Oh, Emma, they mustn't know, but there wasn't time for me to make other arrangements. Harold would be so upset to think of me staying alone in Argyll Street."

"Well, of course you shan't. You shall stay with me, goose."

"But you are to be married in only four days."

"I . . ." Emma saw Dunn's intense gaze on her and looked away. Jack was staring out the carriage window. "Yes, but you shall stay with me until then. It will give us time to make other plans for you. And if that should prove impossible, I am sure Aunt Amelia would not mind in the least your simply staying on with her."

Before Helena could respond, Dunn interrupted to ask, "Why is your aunt not coming, Miss Rogers?"

"She's ill. Her daughter is there to nurse her, and I really could not impose on them at such a time."

Emma handed the damp handkerchief back to Dunn. "There is no reason whatsoever why Helena shouldn't stay with me for a few days. Aunt Amelia has tons of room. That is all we need decide for the present. Please say you will, Helena. You would be of great . . . assistance to me."

The carriage drew to a halt in front of the Barnfield's town house as Helena nodded mutely. Emma smiled and said, "We won't mention a word of this until Anne and your brother are safely departed for their trip."

Maplegate and Dunn agreed, though Dunn eyed Emma speculatively. She returned his gaze with unwavering eyes and he shrugged, climbing down to hand her out. His touch was the second shock she received that day, but in the bustle she was sure he failed to notice the tremor of her hand. She found that she was to be seated next to him at the table and made a casual excuse for changing places with Helena. No one seemed to notice the difference, especially as Sir Nicholas was still on one side of her. His drawn look was somewhat alleviated by a glass of champagne, though Emma could still detect the haunted look in his eyes. This was not the time to discuss what they had to settle, with toasts on every side to the smiling bride and groom.

If Amelia was surprised to learn that they were going to shelter

Helena for a few days, she showed nothing but pleasure. "Another sane head at such a time is precisely what we need," she assured the girl. "And you are not to think of hiring a companion for such a brief period as a month. With Emma gone off on her wedding trip, I shall enjoy nothing so much as your company." While Amelia proceeded to enumerate the benefits Helena's stay would bring her, all manufactured from her generous heart, Emma and Nick sat side by side saying nothing. This did not appear to surprise her aunt, but Emma's request to speak privately with him on their arrival in Bruton Street did. Amelia was about to protest that Emma now had company, but the distraught light in her niece's eyes restrained her.

"Of course, my dear," she said, taking Helena's arm. "I'll just show Helena to a room. She'll wish to send a note round to her maid to bring her clothes."

Emma did not take Nick to the drawing room where they might be interrupted, but to the back writing room, which seemed appropriate. All of her really important conferences seemed to have happened there—or almost all of them. He eyed her warily as they took seats on the sofa.

"You can't go through with it, can you?" she asked gently.

"Go through with what? The wedding? Don't be absurd, Emma."

"Nick, this is the time to be honest with me. It's driving you crazy, the thought of being married, isn't it?"

He ran a hand distractedly through his hair and gave a hollow laugh. "It makes me nervous. I never thought I'd marry."

"And you never wanted to."

"That was before I met you," he protested. "I'm dashed fond of you."

Her lips trembled. "And I am fond of you, Nick, but that is not quite what we're discussing. I don't doubt your affection. I doubt your ability to remain the sort of man you are under the bonds of matrimony. You have had too long and too strong an aversion to marriage to adjust your mind to it. I tried to tell myself otherwise, but . . . you would feel like a caged beast."

"Emma," he said stubbornly, "I'm just a little tense about how it will be. I couldn't possibly marry anyone who would be more understanding than you. I know you're not going to tie me down with a lot of unnecessary demands."

"Oh, my dear heart, if we were bound with threads of gossamer you would feel them. Don't you understand, Nick? I didn't—until I saw you in church today."

"Churches make me nervous, too."

Emma gave a sad chuckle. "Anything that reminds you of marriage makes you nervous, my dear. I can't say that I completely understand your doubts, but I respect them. And so should you. It is not reason that will make a marriage work. I didn't realize until now that over these last weeks you've been struggling to come to terms with your fears. Do you know, it doesn't matter how unreasonable the fear is, if you have it, you must acknowledge it."

His glare was real. "I'm not afraid of marriage, Emma. I'm not afraid of anything!"

"Perhaps the word fear is wrong. Shall we say—distrust?"

He seemed to mull over the new term, considering it from various angles. "Very well, I distrust marriage. But I don't distrust you, my love."

With a sigh she rose to walk to the windows. "No, and I could not have placed my trust in a better man than you, Nick. How I wondered why you didn't finalize our lovemaking! How I stewed and rationalized! He wants me to be a virgin, I told myself. He is trying to behave conventionally, I told myself. He is building my desire to a crescendo for our wedding night, I told myself." She smiled at him, a crooked, helpless smile. "He was saving my virginity, just in case—on that statistically minute chance—that we did not marry. Thank you, Nick."

He was on his feet, striding to crush her in his arms. "We *are* going to marry, Emma!"

"No." Her head was buried against his shoulder. "I won't do that to you. I'm far too fond of you to ruin your life. All the benefits to be derived from our marriage would have been mine. Oh, you could have slept with me, but there are any number of women you could sleep with, and when all is said and done, women aren't all that different, are they?"

"You are, to me. Emma, it's too late to change our plans."

"Thanks to you, Nick, it's not." She raised her head to meet his gaze. "What a sense of self-preservation you have! Imagine your showing such restraint on the off chance that I would call it all off. I never meant to, you know. You offered me too much, my dear, and at just the right moment. If you will remember, it was my tears that pushed you over the brink. You felt sorry for me."

"That was far from the whole of it." But already some of that vitality that had seemed dissipated since their engagement was coursing through him again. "Are you sure this is what you want, Emma? It's no pleasure to be the butt of the gossipmongers and any broken engagement, especially one so close to its fruition, is subject for the most rank speculation. I'm perfectly willing to go through with the ceremony. I'd quite convinced myself that it wouldn't be half as bad as I've always thought."

"It wouldn't be, you know," she teased him, before standing on tiptoe to kiss his cheek. "I won't change my mind, and I won't regret my decision. What I *will* do is get out of town. The season is almost over anyway. Aunt Amelia had suggested that we go on to Brighton for a month or two, but that would be almost as bad as London. If she's willing, I'd rather go to Lord Bradwell."

"What do you want me to do?"

"Three things. Put an announcement in the paper. Tell anyone who asks that it was my decision. And, Nick . . ." Emma flung her arms about his waist and hugged him tightly. "Most of all, my dear, please, please stay my friend. I couldn't bear it if this silly interlude were to estrange us forever."

His eyes shone with wonder. "Dear Lord, I really do think we could have made it, Emma. But let's not chance it!"

She laughed. "No, we won't chance it. Can we still be friends?"

"I could ask for nothing more. Tell you what I'll do. I'll come to visit you at Bradwell's, in August."

"Just in time for the shooting season. I might have known."

"Well, a fellow has to have something to occupy himself besides doing the pretty, my love." He gave her a lingering kiss. "*That* I shall most certainly regret."

"Not for long, I daresay," she remarked dryly. "But I fear you've made life a lot more difficult for me."

"I shall be happy to accommodate you at any time. You have only to say the word."

His eyes were gleaming, his grin wide. Emma sighed. "How easy it was to restore your spirits, Nick. I wish I had been clever enough to realize what the problem was some weeks ago. I dislike thinking what a difficult time I've put you through."

"It had its compensations." He made a move to touch her breast, but withdrew his hand. "Truly, Emma, I'm sorry it has to end this way, but it may be for the best. Do you want me to speak to Amelia?"

She shook her head, leading the way to the door. "I'd prefer to do it myself. I was more honest with her than with the others. In some ways she'll be relieved." When he eyed her questioningly, she continued, "I tried to explain that we didn't need each other. That we were good for one another, but not necessary. She thought there should be more."

"She's probably right." He cupped her chin, his countenance serious. "You deserve more, Emma. I hope one day you'll find it."

"Thank you. Good night, Nick. Don't forget the announcement in the paper."

"I won't!"

Both Amelia and Helena were in the drawing room when she entered some minutes later. They looked up expectantly and seemed surprised that Sir Nicholas was not with her. Emma closed the door and leaned against it.

"Did Sir Nicholas leave already?" Amelia asked.

"Yes. I said I would make his apologies." Emma found that doing the right thing was even more exhausting than she had expected. She moved wearily to a chair beside her aunt. "We're not going to be married."

Two stunned faces turned toward her, speechless. Emma felt a lump rise in her throat. "I called it off, Aunt Amelia. I regret all the bother that it will cause, but it was necessary. Do you remember the day I told you I wouldn't marry him if I thought he wouldn't be able to maintain his freedom?"

Amelia nodded mutely.

"Well, I suddenly realized today, at Anne's wedding, that he couldn't. Or at least that he had come to believe that he couldn't. You can't have missed how moody he's been the last few weeks. I allowed myself to be deceived by his happier moments. And, really, I don't think it would have been at all as bad as he feared, but there it is. I'll write notes to everyone and he'll put an announcement in the paper."

"My poor, dear child." Amelia came to put an arm around her. "How very upsetting for you. In a way, of course, I can't help but feel you have both done the right thing, but it doesn't make the present any easier, does it?"

"No, not much." Emma stared at the ceiling a moment to keep any stray, foolish tears at bay. "He was too old for me, you know, and too set in his ways. I have always thought it impudent for a woman to think she can change a man, or vice versa. But just look what Maggie has accomplished."

"Greenwood was younger and, whether he knew it or not, wanted a little peace in his life."

"Mmm, I suppose," Emma replied, dispirited. "Oh, Aunt Amelia, I've worked my way through another season without removing myself from your care. And what is worse, I don't at all want to stay in London another day. Could we . . . could I go to Lord Bradwell's?"

Amelia cast a hasty glance at Helena, who felt quite forgotten and desperately wished to remain so. "Why, of course you can go. I'm sure he'd be delighted to see you. I . . . I have some engagements in town myself, but will follow in due course."

The urgency of her excuse made Emma smile. "I haven't forgotten Helena for a moment." She turned a pleading gaze on her new friend. "I knew I was going to call off the wedding when I spoke to you in the carriage, and it is my fondest wish that you will come with me. Somerset will provide you with a whole new vista to sketch and Thorpe Arch has the loveliest gardens. Please say you will. We can arrange for your return to London or Farthing Hill whenever you wish."

Helena looked back and forth between the two welcoming faces, and smiled. "I'd love to come."

"Good. And let's leave soon. I don't want to hear all the old crows whispering about me. Nick said he'd come to visit us in August, for the shooting, of course." Emma caught her aunt's surprised eyes and laughed. "We're to remain the best of friends. So much for convention."

THIRD SEASON

CHAPTER TWENTY-EIGHT

Everything had seemed so simple then. Emma perused the last invitation, wistfully remembering how orderly she and Anne and Maggie had thought life would be when they left school and burst on the London season. They had expected the stacks of pasteboard invitation cards, including them in masquerades and rout parties, balls and soirees. Wasn't life to be a whirl of carriage drives, picnics, strolls in the park, visits to the theater?

For three young ladies with the proper backgrounds, the best schooling, adequate dowries, life in London's exhilarating social clime, was to be the greatest adventure thus far embarked upon. They had spent hours discussing fashion plates and members of the ton, most of whom they would not have recognized had they come face to face. But their visions were peopled with handsome gentlemen of rank, ballrooms bedecked with spring flowers, sparkling sunlight pouring down on them as they walked in the parks. For who could escape their own shining freshness: Emma's exotic coloring, Maggie's fine eyes, Anne's glorious hair? Girls fresh from the schoolroom, eager for what life had to offer them. What gentleman could be so insensitive as to pass them by?

But they *were* girls, when all was said and done: girls with more eagerness than knowledge, more enthusiasm than prudence. Emma could look back and see that now. Their dreams of how their lives would progress when they walked out the doors of Windrush House had not a shred of practicality. Things had, in fact, started to go wrong even before they left school. Reality had intruded on their make-believe world and they had been powerless to handle even that first crisis. Emma had thought herself stronger than the others, but she had found herself no more effective then than she had been later in solving her own dilemmas.

As she placed the last invitation with the others in the stack, Emma sighed. Another season, and she was not at all sure she could face it. She smoothed out the skirt of the gray Circassian cloth dress, amused at its lutestring roses and modest bodice. Not exactly the sort of dress she had expected to be wearing! Though, come to think of it, probably it was more in keeping with the school dresses they had all worn that day two years ago.

Not that she hadn't worn some rather sensational gowns in between, but in returning to London once again it seemed prudent to dress as modestly as possible. Even the better part of a year was not always enough time to still the wayward tongues that delighted over nothing so much as speculating on a broken engagement, especially one where on the very day the announcement appeared the erstwhile husband-to-be arrived at his former fiancée's residence with a pair and phaeton that she was known to accept. Weren't the horses kept in Lady Bradwell's stables and seen to make up a part of the procession that left town that very day for Lord Bradwell's estate in Somerset? Just what had Miss Berryman done to receive such largesse from her not-to-be husband?

Emma smiled even now in remembering her protestations. She had been quite blunt in telling Nick what people would say, and he had given her a superbly haughty stare in return. "My dear girl, who cares what they say? I bought the grays for you and I want you to have them. It's as simple as that. Tell people anything you wish, but my advice is to tell them nothing at all." She had followed his advice, since there was really no other course when they left town the same day.

Thorpe Arch had seemed a welcome refuge after the turmoils of that second season. Emma and Helena had hiked on the moors, had gone driving in Emma's new phaeton, had painted and sketched, had talked for hours at a stretch. Even when Harold and Anne returned to town, Helena had chosen to give them privacy in their new London house for the rest of the summer, staying on with Emma until September. As promised, Nick had come in August, entertaining them all with his restored good humor. He teased Emma, laughed with Amelia, chatted with Helena—and went shooting with Lord Bradwell. When September came he escorted Helena back to town, suitably accompanied (he remarked ruefully) by *two* maids to protect her virtue. But Emma and Amelia did not form a part of the party. They never actually discussed the matter, never outlined reasons for wishing to stay in the country, they simply never made any plans to leave. Perhaps it seemed too soon to return to town, perhaps the country setting was inspiring. For whatever reason, they stayed and Emma painted Lord Bradwell's portrait. They went amongst the neighbors and had company; Lord Bradwell grumbled and appeared to enjoy himself.

The idyll could not last forever, for it, too, was a make-believe world. Emma had begun to hear raised voices behind closed doors as the spring season approached. Lord Bradwell, who had been the soul of hospitality and amiability, now withdrew to his study or to the field, and Amelia wandered endlessly about the rambling house. But when Emma tried to assure her aunt that she really didn't care if they went to London, Amelia had regarded her with astonishment. "Well, of course we're going to London!" And they had.

But it was a different London for Emma. The invitations no longer held the same magic, her aunt was not particularly happy, her friends weren't there. Both Maggie and Anne had recently borne children, another boy for Maggie and a girl for Anne, and they both stayed on at their country homes. Helena, finding herself useful at such a time, had also stayed at Farthing Hill, but Emma had reason to believe that she might wish to be in town. Helena's letters in the autumn had mentioned, ever so casually, that even in her new home off Grosvenor Place, Mr. Hatton occasionally called. Twice he had taken her walking and once he had taken her for a drive in the park. Not an especially impressive record for three months in town, but Emma sensed that it was important to Helena.

Looking up from the invitation cards, she asked, "Aunt Amelia, would you mind if I invited Helena to stay for a spell? Anne's baby is over a month old now and I'm sure Anne can manage without her."

"Why, certainly, dear. We have more than enough room, and she's such a lovely girl. I've asked Felix to send some of her drawings up to town for me. I miss having them on the walls. How I could have managed to forget them in Somerset is quite a mystery to me."

It was not so great a mystery to Emma. The tension at Thorpe Arch preceding their departure was quite thick enough to slice with a knife. Emma considered it a wonder that her aunt had remembered to bring her *clothes*, what with Lord Bradwell stomping about the place and slamming doors with unnerving frequency. Amelia had been tight-lipped and silent. What had happened to upset their customary domestic arrangement was the mystery to Emma. After all, Amelia had come to town for every season the last twenty years without this sort of bother, if one took her word on the matter. She had, in fact, spent most of her time in London, only secluding herself in Somerset for a few months a year. Well, she had made it to London again, Emma thought uncomfortably, and she didn't seem the least pleased with her victory.

"Then I think I shall write to Helena immediately," Emma finally said. But as she rose to leave a footman appeared to announce a visitor, Sir Nicholas Dyrham. When he entered, Emma held out her hands to him. "Nick. It's so good to see you again."

He ran a critical eye over her costume. "What's this, Emma? Planning to surprise all the old harpies with your modesty?"

"Especially when I drive out in my phaeton," she said laughingly.

"We'd have made a great pair," he pronounced with mock gravity. "Too bad she turned me off, eh, Amelia?"

"The wisest move she ever made," Amelia informed him as she watched him raise her hand to his lips. "You would have forgotten you were married half the time."

"Ah, but the other half!" He seated himself and accorded Emma a speaking glance.

Emma folded her hands demurely in her lap. "Now don't start that, I beg you. The quizzes will have quite a wonderful time without your assistance. If you intend to make sport of me every time I go out in public, I shall sit in my room and read."

Amelia looked upset at this exchange and turned an adorably stern gaze on Sir Nicholas. "You are not to roast her that way in public, Nick. Do remember that she hasn't the freedom you have as a gentleman. When around Emma you should be particularly gallant and perhaps act just the least bit wounded. And it wouldn't hurt for you to treat her as an unattainable lady rather than a favorite mistress."

Emma giggled; Nick stared at Amelia. "You're serious!" he declared, shocked. "I've never treated anyone as an unattainable lady in my life!"

"You may start now, with Emma."

He bent his head toward the "unattainable lady." "Shall you mind dreadfully?" he asked.

"Not at all. No one has ever viewed me as unattainable."

The ludicrousness of the situation set them both to laughing as a footman appeared to announce, "Lord Dunn."

Dunn's first view of the occupants of the room was rather unsettling. Emma was laughing so hard she had pressed a square of lace to her eyes while Sir Nicholas hooted with merriment. Amelia regarded them both as recalcitrant children, and since they did not seem to have noticed Dunn's arrival, she crossed the room to offer her hand.

"Never mind them. Some people *will* see a joke where none was intended."

Nick was on his feet, holding out a hand to Emma and saying in a stage whisper, "Come, my girl. It's time for our first performance."

The sight of Dunn after such a long absence might at any other time have shaken Emma out of her customary poise, but she allowed herself to play-act with Nick, and to be seen to be play-acting. Nick gave her a long-suffering look and she responded by pointing her nose toward the ceiling.

Nick said, "Lord Dunn has called, fair one," and she replied, "How nice." When Dunn shook her hand, Nick winced and said, "Carefully. She's as delicate as china."

"Gossamer," she retorted.

"No, china," he insisted. "You know, breakable."

"Gossamer sounds more sylphlike."

"Then it's not appropriate!"

And the two of them eyed each other with feigned hostility, Emma graciously motioning Dunn to a seat, explaining, "Sir Nicholas does not have a metaphorical mind, as you can see. Plus which, of course, he is still suffering under the blow of our broken engagement."

Amelia spluttered, "Emma!"

"I'm not, either," Nick announced. "I always knew Emma was too good for me . . . ah, unattainable."

Dunn sat back and draped one long leg over the other, watching the two with interest.

"He was always jealous of my portrait painting," she said.

"She was always jealous of my mis—my independence."

Amelia put her head in her hands and Emma took pity on her. Addressing Dunn, she asked, "Did you have good hunting this winter, sir?"

"Better than some years. My brother Stephen was out every day, but I'm getting a little old for that. I enjoy the crackling fire afterward almost as much as the run itself." His eyes were not the least serious and he turned to smile at Amelia. "I trust your Somerset winter was not too harsh."

"Actually it was beautiful. I haven't spent so much time in the country since I was a child. I had practically forgotten how peaceful it could be."

Nick could not resist the opening. "There, you see, Emma? Not everyone objects to spending time in the country. You could have found a thousand things to do while I was out with the hounds."

"Oh, certainly, I could have sat with my tatting! I expected you at least to offer to have a studio set up for me at your estate, if not the London house. But no, all you could think about was those poor, innocent little foxes. Well, it's a good thing we got it all out in the open before it was too late!"

"I take it," Dunn remarked to Amelia, "that your niece found a dozen reasons for changing her mind about marrying Nick."

"They're incorrigible," she groaned. "All I wanted them to do was behave with some sort of reserve in public. Not everyone can understand how two people can part on such totally amicable terms. And the carriage! She really should not have accepted the phaeton and pair."

"I'd already bought them for her," Nick said, casting a baleful eye on Emma. "She told me she wouldn't marry me unless I did, and then she told me she wouldn't break our engagement unless I gave them to her!"

"Despicable man! I said a curricle, but your hearing must be going with your advanced age. You're lucky I agreed to accept them!"

"Lucky! The whole cost me four hundred guineas. And don't forget the ring! You never gave it back either! That was another hundred."

"Only a hundred! Is that all you paid for it? I shall give it to my maid," Emma cried.

"I *told* you I was going to make it a whole set with earrings and a necklace and a tiara. Besides, I had to pay for *two* newspaper announcements, and you would be surprised at how dear they have become."

Dunn's lips had begun to twitch, and Amelia, reconciling herself, rang for tea.

"Tightwad!"

"Designing hussy!"

"And it wasn't fair of you to agree to a wedding trip only if you could bring your . . . your friend."

"Well, she'd never been to Paris. After all, Emma, you have to be reasonable."

"No, I don't. It is a woman's prerogative to be unreasonable. I've *always* been unreasonable."

"Don't I know it! That's what makes you so . . . so unattainable."

Having come full circle, they smiled at one another peacefully, as Amelia asked the goggle-eyed footman to bring them tea.

"Perfectly suited," Dunn murmured.

"Yes, well, they do get on extraordinarily well," Amelia agreed, and added cryptically, "but I have always said that is not all there is to marriage."

A gleam in Nick's eye warned Emma that he was more than willing to get started again with such a perfect opportunity. She lifted a protesting hand, laughing. "Enough. You have exhausted my store of vituperation and inventiveness for a week!"

What perhaps surprised Dunn most about the whole scene was that Nick acquiesced to Emma's wishes without so much as a further jab, settling into the ordinary social intercourse with perfect ease. He spoke of the entertainments that were offered for the next week, proposed himself to escort the ladies to one or two of them and, after finishing a cup of tea and three tarts, took his unhurried leave. Dunn sat on with Emma and her aunt.

"I understand Nick visited you in Somerset last summer," he remarked as he refused another biscuit.

"He spent almost a month at Thorpe Arch with us," Emma said, "mostly out shooting with Lord Bradwell."

"The ton held their breath when he returned to see if another announcement would appear to proclaim a renewed engagement." His eyes rested on her with thoughtful intensity.

Emma seemed surprised. "Oh, there was never any possibility of *that*. He came because we are friends and was a delightful addition to our little house party, wasn't he, Aunt Amelia?"

"Oh, yes. We had Helena Rogers with us as well. I do wish I had brought some of her drawings so that you could have seen them, Dunn. Felix is to send them to me."

"She does excellent work. Did you paint as well, Miss Berryman?"

"A portrait of Lord Bradwell, one of Helena, and two others of neighbors. I gave them away."

"No exhibition this year?"

Unable to tell whether he was teasing her, Emma hesitated. She thought of saying that she was to be the exhibit herself this year, but refrained. "I have nothing to show."

"You'll never make a fortune giving all your work away." This time it was obvious that he was teasing, because he smiled.

"The whole line of work is wrong for making a fortune. I only like to paint subjects who interest me, and unfortunately they are not the ones who approach me to paint them."

His gaze sharpened. "You've had people ask you to paint them? People who wanted to commission you?"

"Of course I have. A dozen or more after the exhibition last spring. I thought you had more faith in my abilities."

"I do have faith in your abilities. It's just that I never heard anyone speak of your potential clients. Would you be interested in painting Stephen?"

"Captain Midford?" Emma tried to call his face to mind and sat for a moment staring at the fire screen. Then she rose, excusing herself as she went over to the Pembroke table to extract a pencil and paper from the drawer. Amelia and Dunn exchanged bewildered glances, but Emma stood thinking and then started to sketch rapidly. When she returned, she asked, "Would he sit for me?"

The idea had just occurred to Dunn but he answered without the slightest pause. "Yes. May I see what you've drawn?"

Emma handed him the quick sketch she had made of Stephen from memory. He glanced at it and then studied it more carefully. There was something akin to amazement in his eyes when he looked across at her. "You have an incredible memory for faces. This is a remarkable likeness."

"Thank you. It's much better, of course, if a subject will sit for me, but as you recall, I did both your portrait and Nick's from sketches."

Dunn set his teacup carefully on the table as he said, "I bought your portrait of me."

"I'm glad. Mr. Wigginton never said who had purchased it."

Amelia, who had not said anything for some time, added, "I think that was wise of you, Dunn. Emma really did capture a certain something about you."

His gray eyes never left Emma's face. "She did, didn't she?"

Emma felt a tremor run through her under his searching gaze. She moistened her lips and said, "I will paint Captain Midford's portrait if you wish. He would make a good subject, provided he would sit. I don't think I could paint him unless he did."

"He'll sit for you."

"Very well. If you will have him call, we can arrange a time to begin."

"I'll bring him around myself tomorrow. Would two o'clock be suitable?"

"Certainly . . . but there is no need for you to come. That is, you may have something more pressing to do."

"I doubt it."

Really, what more could she have said, Emma wondered, without being rude? She drummed a quill against her desk in the writing room, trying to bring her concentration to bear on the letter she was writing jointly to Anne and Helena. If Helena would come there would be a better chance of maintaining the status quo with Dunn. Was it possible that her aunt's long absence from town had cooled his interest? She chided herself for clutching at straws. Even if Dunn were to terminate his affair with Amelia, or vice versa, Emma could not possibly bring herself to consider a closer understanding with him—could she? Dipping her quill in the inkpot, she forced herself to continue the letter. Her urgency to have Helena with her must surely strike a chord at Farthing Hill. She hoped they would send Helena up to town within the week. And in the meantime, she decided as she dripped sealing wax on the sheet, she would, no matter how despicable of her, listen in the nights to hear if her aunt had a visitor.

CHAPTER TWENTY-NINE

Emma lost several hours of sleep that night, and the next, and the next. When nothing happened, she began to feel tired . . . and hopeful. But on the fourth night she heard a stirring in the hall, and though she wanted desperately to believe it was nothing, she raced across her dark room and peered out the door. Definitely a figure disappearing into her aunt's room, unrecognizable but very tangible indeed. Emma could have wept with frustration.

By the following day she had convinced herself that it was possible Dunn had only called the previous evening to take permanent leave of Amelia. After all, one needed a certain amount of privacy for such an ordeal. So she sat up for several more nights, not allowing herself to become hopeful again, but patient. Helena arrived during this ritual and was welcomed by aunt and niece with equal enthusiasm. Also during this period Emma began the portrait of Stephen Midford, who was not a particularly good sitter, as he found it difficult to remain in one spot for more than a few minutes at a time. Her nerves were so on edge, and he seemed so young to her, that she almost snapped at him that she was going to tell his brother if he didn't just *sit still*. Despite her edginess, the portrait was coming along well.

Daytimes were enjoyable, since she could keep busy with her painting or with Helena, shopping, visiting, going to art galleries and libraries, and evenings were bearable because they went off to the theater or to a rout, but nights had become exquisitely painful, sitting in her room listening for footsteps in the hall. Eventually, as she had tried to prepare herself that she would, she heard them again. She did not even bother to open the door this time but crawled under her covers and beat a helpless tattoo against her unfortunate pillow. After that she forced herself to go straight to bed when they returned home in the evenings, and to pay a little attention to the gentlemen who showed some interest in her at social gatherings.

If Helena had some ulterior motive in the frequency with which they visited art galleries, Emma could feel nothing but sympathy for her. About a week after she arrived they had the good fortune to meet Mr. Hatton outside an art gallery. His pleasure at seeing Helena was obvious.

"I had no idea you were in town, Miss Rogers! When I called round at the new house I was told that the family was still in the country. I hope your sister and brother are well."

"Oh, yes," Helena admitted, "they are all doing well, the baby included. You . . . you called in Montrose Place?"

"To be sure, a good two weeks ago. They said the family wasn't expected. The knocker wasn't up, of course, but I beat on the door until someone came."

How very promising, Emma thought, delighted. She was not quite sure what caused the exchange to go wrong, for Mr. Hatton then said, "But you are obviously here now and with your permission I shall call on you."

"I'm not staying in Montrose Place. Harold and Anne are still in the country so I'm staying with Emma and her aunt, Lady Bradwell."

There was no denying this news caused him a certain amount of agitation. He absently put his hat back on, and then hastily removed it, tucking it under his arm. Next he passed his cane from one hand to the other, accidentally dropping it on the return trip, and in bending over to retrieve it, lost the hat as well. A gust of wind blew the hat into the street, where it was trampled by a passing horse and rider. By the time he returned to them from rescuing it, his face was red and his pantaloons dusty from trying unsuccessfully to reshape the hat against his leg.

As Helena handed him his cane, he mumbled, with absolutely no conviction, his intention of calling on her shortly at Lady Bradwell's. "It's in Bruton Place," Helena told him hopelessly, "number Twenty-three."

"Is it? Yes, well, that's not hard to find, is it? Everyone knows where Bruton Place is. Daresay half of London could direct you to Bruton Place. Not far from Bond Street, and everything. Well, I must be off. I'm a little late for an appointment." And he strode away at a pace indicative of the truth of his mumbled words, not that either of his auditors believed him.

"Oh, dear," Helena sighed. "Did I say something wrong?"

"I cannot for the life of me understand what got into the man," Emma said. "One minute he is eagerness itself and the next he is scuttling off like a frightened crab. I would say that he disapproves of your staying with my aunt, but I very clearly recall his standing up with her at an assembly a year or two ago. Of course, men are truly incomprehensible, if you wish my opinion, which I am sure you don't. My aunt's reputation is not altogether . . . unquestionable."

Helena rose instantly to Lady Bradwell's defense. "You aunt is a charming woman and no one in his right mind could take the slightest objection to my staying with her. Such generosity in her even to have me! Really, I am most distressed at Mr. Hatton's unaccountable behavior. I had thought him a gentleman. I do beg your pardon, Emma. Please don't say a word of this to your aunt."

"I shan't." Emma took Helena's arm and guided her across the street. "It may be simply that Mr. Hatton was suddenly taken ill and did not wish us to realize it, you know. Stranger things have happened. And if that is the case, his behavior may be excused, I suppose. He really was delighted to see you."

"If you shouldn't mind so very much, Emma, I'd rather not discuss it. My head has begun to ache abominably."

"Why, of course, my dear. Not another word."

Mr. Hatton did not call. Days passed when Emma watched Helena stiffen as the footman came to announce visitors, and then relax when they were informed that it was Sir Nicholas, or Lord Higham, or Mr. Stutton, or Lord Dunn. And then Dunn stopped calling.

At first Emma attempted to find some consolation in this. The signs he was showing of renewed interest in her were more discreet this time, but still her aunt seemed most unhappy. Emma began to speak to her aunt of the attentions paid her by Lord Higham, the only one of her followers whom she had any cause to believe her aunt would take seriously. But Amelia only showed an absent sort of attention, saying, "That's nice, dear." It was frustrating to make the effort to no avail, especially since Emma considered Higham, for all his good nature and acceptable looks, only slightly more intelligent than a turtle, which was not at all true, but suited her own irritable mood. What was more, her aunt's disposition did not improve in the slightest when Dunn stopped calling. And then she found out *why* Dunn had stopped calling.

Amelia arrived home one afternoon with two volumes of a marble-covered book under her arm, her eyes snapping with anger. Emma happened to be in the hall at the time and gasped, "Whatever is the matter?"

Without a word Amelia took her arm and hustled her into the drawing room, removing her pelisse as she went, but not letting go of the books. "You won't believe it, Emma. The impertinence! The gall! The sheer unmitigated cheek of the woman!"

Alarmed that someone had snubbed her aunt, Emma prepared herself to dismiss the episode as a mere nothing, unimportant in the least degree. She grabbed the pelisse before it had time to fall to the floor and tried to relieve her aunt of the burden of her books, but Amelia vigorously shook her head.

"No, you have to see what she's written. How anyone could publish such stuff is beyond me. He should sue them for every last penny they own!"

Bewildered, Emma asked, "Who wrote these scurrilous lies, my dear?"

"That Livingstone woman. Eliza Livingstone. Mistress to the great and near-great. Lord, Emma, from what I've heard she has as good as named three dozen men in her wretched memoirs. You know how they do it, giving an initial at the first and last of a dash, and any letters they happen to feel necessary in the middle just in case you're not clever enough to guess from the description and situation. I started to hear a buzz about it last night at the Dinsmores' but I wouldn't credit it until I had the volumes before my very eyes."

Emma was beginning to experience a sort of nervous shock. "Who did this Livingstone woman name?" she breathed.

"Everyone!" Amelia made a dramatic, comprehensive gesture with her hands. "I thumbed through it at the bookstore. Sir Nicholas early on, when she was much younger, though he wasn't her first. Melson was, if you will credit her story, at fifteen! Fifteen, for heaven's sake. And the worst of it is that most of it, *most* of it, is quite believable. Beresford and Fyfield and Sir Nicholas you cannot have the least doubt of. Even Harstrow and Rusholme and Stutton. Oh, really, you can believe every one of them, except . . . Here, read this. Just read it," she commanded, rapidly turning pages until she came to the appropriate place. "I read it in the carriage."

The entry she referred to was not a short one; in fact it went on for more than twenty pages. The subject of the commentary was referred to as Viscount D—n, described as the owner of a vast estate in Herefordshire and a handsome town house in Waverton Street, London, amongst other holdings. For all the hoopla there always was when a courtesan such as Eliza Livingstone took to penning her memoirs, there was nothing particularly explicit about the entry. D—n was described as a tall, fine figure of a man, three and twenty when Miss Livingstone knew him, and the gentlest, most ardent of her lovers. There was a nostalgia about the interlude that clung to every word, every enamored phrase. Miss Livingstone, incredibly perhaps but truly, fell in love with this man. She could not so much as recount some clever thing that he had said to her without describing her own heart-palpitating response.

Over a period of months Miss Livingstone recalled their various encounters: her waiting for him to come to her after late sessions of Parliament; his thoughtful, expensive gifts to her; his consideration in matters financial, sexual, and emotional. How many times she quoted him as calling her his "sweet delight," Emma lost count. There was the suggestion that not only did Miss Livingstone love D—n, but that he was growing to love her as well. She had begun to speculate on the time when he would shun society's conventions, ignore the censorious gazes of his fellow man, and take her for his wife. She put words in his mouth that indicated this to be so. She showed him restless with the restrictions that prevented him from joining with her in holy matrimony. And then . . .

"Oh, God," Emma moaned.

Then she revealed that she had become pregnant by him. Miss Livingstone described her delicious secret joy over this event, and her fears of telling D—n of her condition. She did not want him to think, she said, that she was pressuring him into a marriage that would ruin his standing in the world. She was entirely self-effacing over the whole matter, a martyr to society's hypocritical rules. But what was she to do? When the truth could scarcely longer be concealed, she threw herself on his mercy, sure that he would love her and the child, that he would provide for them, perhaps even marry her.

Her story became quite a tearjerker here. This gentle, perfect lover spurned her from the moment of revelation. He denied any responsibility for either mother or child. He went away, never to return, refusing to answer her letters, her pleas for assistance. Nightly she haunted the environs of Waverton Street to catch a glimpse of him or to beg for his compassion. Needless to say, she went into a decline. None of her friends could get her to eat a morsel of food or drink a drop of water. And she lost the child in a painful, life-sapping miscarriage. It was a wonder that she had not died. Miss Livingstone told in great detail of her struggle against death. Her will to live had been greatly reduced by the cruel fate Lord D—n had meted out to her, but her indomitable spirit had won over all. Was she not a child of God, sinner that she was? Had she not suffered enough to redeem herself at least to a life of sorrow? Miss Livingstone lived, to take (from the size of the second volume) quite a substantial number of further lovers.

"Poppycock!" Emma snapped, slamming the first volume closed.

"Yes, I daresay it is," Amelia retorted, "but there are those who will believe it, Emma. Some people love to have a good scandal to mull over. There is something in them which loves to see the mighty laid low. She could not have chosen a better target than Dunn. And why did she choose him? I tell you there seems little else in the book which is not accurate at least to some degree."

"Oh, I'm not denying that he was probably her lover. It's the histrionics of the pregnancy and rejection which don't have a word of truth in them. She loved him and he ended their affair. But you can't make good copy out of that. Our heroine cannot merely suffer unrequited love, shining example of womanhood that she is. She must be the victim of treachery, of unscrupulous villainy. Otherwise her readers would see how improbable it was that she could ever have believed Dunn would marry her."

"Do you suppose he really called her his 'sweet delight'?" Amelia asked, irrelevantly.

"How should I know? Frankly, I don't see why not. Nick was given to using terms of endearment such as that when he was . . . Well, anyway, I should think a man who was making up to Miss Livingstone would offer her some verbal honey. It doesn't cost him anything, after all. I'd like to ring her neck!"

Amelia studied her glowering face with satisfaction. "So would I. He'll have to sue, of course, but the harm is done. I got the last copy at Hamlin's after going to three other bookstores that were already sold out. Poor Dunn! How very uncomfortable for him. No wonder he hasn't been to call."

Emma lifted eyes that sparked. "Does he think we're only fair-weather friends? I should like to ring his neck, too, for having such a low opinion of us!"

"Now, dear, I'm sure that's not the case at all. His consideration for us would make him think it prudent to remain absent for a time."

"Prudent! I can just see him now sitting in his library refusing callers because he doesn't wish to contaminate them with his unsavory reputation. The truly honorable man! Making his friends helpless to see him through a difficult time because he has too much respect for them to drag them into the mud with him. Ha! It is his pride, my dear aunt, his insufferable pride which would prevent his accepting their assistance. The Great Dunn can extract himself from any quagmire without asking a hand from his friends. I should like to tear his hair out."

"Emma!" Amelia protested, laughing. "How very fierce you are. I had no idea you felt so strongly about him."

"I *don't* feel strongly about him! Do you know how kind he has been to Maggie and Anne? Do you know how patient he has been with Greenwood? But would he let any of them return the favor now? You may be sure he wouldn't. Doesn't he know that it is a privilege to be allowed to stand by a friend in trouble?"

"Emma, you don't even know that he isn't allowing his friends to help," Amelia pointed out patiently.

"Then why hasn't he come to call? Aren't we his friends? You may be sure he would be the first one to know about this wretched book."

"As to why he hasn't come, my love, I can only suppose your pointed avoidance of him has something to do with it. Even a man with a very thick skin could not have missed your intention."

"But . . . but he comes to see you. I've been busy. Not too busy to help in this crisis, you understand, but busy enough with Captain Midford's portrait and going about with Helena." A horrible thought struck her and she gasped. "You don't think he believes I'd already read the book and have been abrupt with him because of *that,* do you?"

"Nonsense! The book has only just come out. I'm sure he has reached entirely different conclusions as to why you are abrupt with him."

Amelia's gaze was strangely searching and Emma felt herself flush. "I daresay he hasn't given a thought to it one way or the other. He—"

A footman entered to announce a caller and was closely followed by a harried Captain Midford. Stephen's eyes went immediately to the two volumes lying on the table and he ran a distracted hand through his hair. "I see you've heard about it. Have you read the part on Dunn?"

"Yes," Amelia returned, "and we don't believe a word of it."

"Well, I wouldn't go so far as to say not a word. I think she *was* his mistress for a while, when I was away at school. Dash it, everyone's asking me about it. I haven't the first idea what to say. I wish to hell he weren't away right now."

"A-away?" Emma asked, looking slightly embarrassed.

"He went to Knowle Park a few days ago. Some problem with spring flooding, I think. I sent an express off to him yesterday but I haven't heard a word as yet. Of course, there's hardly been time, and maybe it would be all for the best if he stayed there for a while. He's going to be mad as fire to be the on dit of London."

Amelia urged him to a chair, her brow wrinkled in concentration. "We must think of precisely how you should answer anyone impertinent enough to ask you questions, Captain Midford. You could say they must apply to Dunn for any information. That would send them off in a hurry. Can you imagine anyone asking Dunn to his face if he behaved like a heel? Lord, I should like to see the look he would give them! Or you could ask the questioner when he had begun to have the bad taste to believe Eliza Livingstone's trumped-up tales. But you mustn't on any account act as though you take this matter the least seriously. Dunn will have to sue, of course, which is a great nuisance, but there it is."

"I wonder if he will," Emma mused. "I would be surprised if he took the least notice of the affair, when I come to consider. The whole messy business will be beneath him. And you know, Captain Midford, he is likely to set up people's backs that way. I do hope he has the sense to stay in Herefordshire until some of the worst has blown over. Did you send him a copy of the book?"

"Oh, yes, though I had the devil of a time laying my hands on one."

"Is his Christian name really Oliver?" she asked, intrigued.

Stephen grinned. "I think he will be almost as annoyed about that as anything. Imagine the woman saying she called him Ollie! He wouldn't have stood it for a minute! Hates the name Oliver; hasn't used it since he was a child. Even I don't call him anything but Dunn."

Nor does my aunt, Emma thought, remembering the murmured name in the night. Giving herself a mental shake, she stood and addressed the captain. "Come and sit for me for a while, sir. I daresay you will be an even worse subject than usual, but it will keep you away from the curious throngs for a while. And your unaccustomed gravity will provide me an opportunity to give your portrait some sadly needed depth," she added with an impish smile to offset her mocking words.

CHAPTER THIRTY

Ordinarily Helena only attended an occasional evening function with Emma and her aunt. Her taste was for quieter dinner parties and lectures on topics of philosophical interest, but when Emma explained the problem that had arisen from Eliza Livingstone's book she instantly took up the cudgels in Dunn's defense.

"What an infamous libel! I have known Lord Dunn for years, through Harold, and I am sure both he and Anne would want me to stand by him at such a time. You go to the Heathermore ball tonight? I must have something with me which is adequate to such an occasion. I know just how it will be! The old snips will stand around in corners whispering about him and the young blades will wear those cynical, knowing smirks. I won't have him be made a laughingstock for their flimsy, gossiping pleasure."

Her description of the situation was not far off. It seemed that everyone in town had either read the book or had heard of it from a friend. Dunn and Eliza Livingstone were the overwhelming topic of choice that evening, with starchy matrons breathing trite sentiments such as "There can be no smoke without fire," and pretty young girls protesting that they had never heard anything in their lives that shocked their sensibilities so. Emma was disgusted with the lot of them. She refused to let her dancing partners so much as mention the book, and when she found herself near anyone who dared breathe an insinuating syllable about Dunn, she would fix the offender with a glowering eye and ask, "How can you credit such a base untruth? Have you no self-respect that you would accept the word of a notorious courtesan over that of an honorable gentleman?" If it was pointed out to her that the honorable gentleman had not as yet seen fit to comment on his former mistress's colorful account of their affair, Emma would reply coldly that Lord Dunn was in Herefordshire attending to his responsibilities as a landlord.

Not until she was cornered by Lady Redwick (the ancient dame who was once apostrophized by Dunn as being able to reduce a seasoned matron to tears in three minutes), did Emma finally lose her temper. Lady Redwick's sole pleasure in life was such displays of power as her caustic tongue produced, and she went out into society at her advanced age only to pick quarrels that would provide her with that reward. From the moment she had heard of Eliza Livingstone's memoirs, and she had heard of them very early on, she had been searching an opportunity to put her unusual talent into practice. Emma, she decided with real satisfaction, provided the perfect target.

"So you are convinced Miss Livingstone lied, are you, Miss Berryman?" she asked, her cold birdlike eyes glittering. "What purpose would she have in doing so?"

"Any number of purposes, ma'am. She would gain the sympathy of her reader, she would sell more copies of her book, she would have a chance to exercise a little revenge on Lord Dunn for not marrying her."

"Ah, but he could sue her if it wasn't true. She wouldn't have dared to put into print something which could lose her all her profits."

"Balderdash. Lord Dunn could sue her if it *was* true. There is only her word against his, after all."

"Precisely. Which is only to say that the truth will never be known, will it?"

Emma narrowed her eyes to furious slits. "The truth *is* known, my lady. No one who knows Lord Dunn could fail to recognize it. He would not be capable of acting in the base way Miss Livingstone says he did. There is not a dishonorable bone in his body."

A hush had fallen on the assembly about them, but Lady Redwick was too engrossed, and Emma too infuriated, by their discussion to notice. The old woman jabbed a gnarled finger at Emma's arm. "Do you think you know Lord Dunn so well, then? You seem to know all the men well, like your aunt. And yet I notice you could not hold onto Sir Nicholas long enough to get the ring on your finger, my girl."

Emma was stunned by the turn the conversation had taken. She could hear the rapid intake of breath behind her, but refused to be distracted from the odious woman's innuendos. "If you knew men a little better, Lady Redwick, perhaps you would not make such a mistake. Is it so difficult for you to discern character in those about you? I do not have to know Lord Dunn 'so well' to find him incapable of villainy. How sad your life must be with nothing better to do than destroy the reputations and comfort of others. You have my most sincere pity!"

When she swung blindly away from the old lady's shocked countenance, she found herself facing Lord Dunn himself. There was a smattering of applause from some of the braver souls who had been listening, and Dunn was smiling. "I believe this is our dance," he said smoothly.

Emma was sure she had promised it to Nick, but she caught his eye and he shrugged in resignation. Her trials were not over, however, for she and Dunn were the only ones to take the floor. Sweeping the watching guests with irate eyes, she found that they were not censorious, as she had expected, but amused and perhaps a little fascinated. It was supposed to have been a country dance; the musicians played a waltz. Dunn took her in his arms as though there were nothing unusual about the empty ballroom floor and proceeded to talk as he danced.

"Did you think you had to defend me? My dear Emma, no one who matters will believe such heart-wrenching tales of my callousness."

"Your opinion of your contemporaries is slightly higher than mine, Lord Dunn. Aunt Amelia and Helena and I didn't think it would hurt to dampen some of the gossip."

"When I said no one who matters, I meant no one who matters to me. Such as you."

Emma turned her head away, only to be reminded of the watching crowd, and looked back at him. "I didn't believe it for a minute—about the way you treated her, I mean."

He grinned and held her a little closer. "To be sure. The way I treated her. That's what I meant, too."

His eyes were dancing but she maintained a stiff formality. "It seemed to me that you might be too . . . too unbending to take the least note of her book, and people would think you deserving of a bit of a set-down. No one likes someone who is holier than thou."

"Just so," he agreed after judicious thought. "Do you know, I think it would be best if you were to make a regular habit of instructing me on such points, Emma. I am likely to go astray without your guidance."

Her eyes snapped at him. "You are unkind to mock me when I have only your best interests at heart."

"Ah, we have come to the kernel of the matter now. Your heart. I'm glad that my best interests are there, but I am tempted to ask for just a little more. Rash, no doubt, but still a matter of the most pressing concern to me. Emma, Emma, why do you persist in fobbing me off with lame excuses of how busy you are? What is it that you fear in me? You weren't afraid of Nick."

He hadn't meant to let that last slip out. She could tell by the way his lips tightened, almost as though he would have bitten off the words if he could. Her mind raced back over her engagement with Nick, settling numbingly on the night of their engagement. In the studio, after the announcement, she had sought comfort from Dunn's cold congratulations in Nick's arms. Color rose violently into her cheeks. Her attempt to speak was no more than a moan.

Momentarily at a loss for words himself, Dunn surveyed the intrigued company. As the object of every eye, it was no wonder that they perceived her blush. What did they think of Emma Berryman blushing? More important, he decided, was whether she was going to faint on him. Slowly, carefully, he began to speak. "Emma, I've been intolerably envious of the striking rapport you have with Nick. With me you are aloof, unapproachable. Every time I hear the two of you teasing, I want to banish him to India. I want it to be me! Last spring . . . there seemed a possibility of that. I don't know what happened. I wish you would tell me."

Was that all he had really meant? Emma couldn't be sure, but his smile was tender. The color in her cheeks began to recede, but her throat still felt constricted. "I saw you," she whispered.

"Saw me? Where?"

"In the hall."

His puzzled frown remained, unenlightened by the words she obviously thought would explain the whole. The music stopped and they stood facing one another. "But I don't understand."

"You must," she said firmly. "I could never do that to Amelia."

And then they were surrounded by dozens of people who wished to take the opportunity to speak with Dunn. No one mentioned the Livingstone book at all: they remarked that he had been out of town, that he had missed the running of a race between Norwood and Thresham, that he would surely want to know what had happened in Parliament the previous day. Emma returned to her aunt with a bright smile.

"Well, everything seems to be in order after all. Would you mind if we had an early night? I'm a trifle exhausted by all the excitement."

With her back turned, she did not see Dunn's frustration at being unable to get away from his well-meaning friends.

An hour later the house in Bruton Street was quiet, though Emma found it impossible to sleep. It would be better if she could simply stop going to parties where she was sure to meet Dunn, but that was next to impossible. No, she would have to sit down and talk with him, make him understand that she could never accept his attentions, even if he were willing to stop seeing Amelia. The whole situation was fraught with pain, no matter how one looked at it.

Emma turned restlessly in bed, seeking a comfortable position. And then she heard the footsteps. Surely not! Not tonight of all nights! How could he be so heartless! True, he didn't know she would hear him—the footsteps were as stealthy as ever—but really, it was too much. In a blinding flash it occurred to her that he was coming to end the affair because of what she had said at the ball! He mustn't do that! Before he made any final step she must warn him that she would have none of him even after the affair was ended. Emma quickly struck a flint, lit a candle, and ran to the door, pulling it open with an urgency bred by her fear that he would already have reached her aunt's room.

"Wait!" she called softly to the shadow in the hall. He paused, turning in her direction. "I must talk to you first. Wait there just a moment while I get my dressing gown." And she vanished into the room again.

The shadow retraced his footsteps to her open door, watching mystified as she, unaware, wrapped the concealing robe about her with hasty fingers. When she considered herself suitably clothed, she picked up the candle and headed for the door. Even before the light was close enough to fall perfectly on his features, Emma sensed that there was something wrong. He was not quite the right height, wasn't wearing quite the clothes in which Dunn had been dressed that evening. Alarmed now, she raised the candle higher. "Oh, my God. Mr. Hatton."

He looked very uncomfortable and mumbled, "Servant, Miss Berryman."

"You . . . You're . . . Oh, for the love of pity! I don't believe it. Yes, I do. No wonder you acted so strangely when Helena told you she was staying here."

"I couldn't very well call. I say, you won't tell her, will you? I promise you I am on my way to Lady Bradwell now for no other reason than to tell her about Helena . . . Miss Rogers. It's been the devil of a tangle. I haven't known which way to turn. And don't think I would have left your aunt even now but that she's not happy. We went on very well for years but something has changed. I'm sure I don't know what it is. She won't say a word. I think she'll understand about Helena."

"Mr. Hatton, what's your Christian name?"

Startled by the question, he nevertheless answered. "John."

Emma put a hand to her forehead, pressing as though to clear her thoughts. "But Sir Nicholas thought it was Dunn, too."

" 'Done?' Oh, 'Lord Dunn.' " His brow furrowed. "You thought it was Dunn who was . . . Oh, I see. Some years ago, when I was letting myself into the house, Sir Nicholas was passing by. I thought I had managed to look away in time. There weren't any lights about."

"Obviously you did look away in time," she said dryly. "Up close you don't look so much like him, but at a distance . . . Even on my first glance at Helena's painting, 'The Fencer,' I thought for a moment that it was Dunn. I'm sorry to have surprised your secret. Well, no, I'm not, really. A year! A whole year! And I might have married Nick! The thought makes me positively quake."

Mr. Hatton, not comprehending half of what she said, shifted restlessly. "Mmm, would you mind if I were just to go along to Amelia's room now?"

Poor Amelia, Emma thought with a sigh. "Yes, of course, Mr. Hatton. I am sorry to have delayed you. If . . . if she should be upset, please tell her that I am still awake."

Mr. Hatton offered a solemn nod and strode down the hall once more. He hadn't come again to Bruton Street since he had known that Helena was there, but today he had sent a note around to Amelia to ask if he might come to discuss a matter of importance with her. In the ordinary way of things Mr. Hatton was a self-possessed man, but his conflicting emotions for the last year had made him a bit jumpy. When Emma had hailed him in the hall, he had been terrified that it might be Helena herself and had frozen with alarm. He was no less anxious in facing Amelia. Their liaison had continued happily for more than half a dozen years, providing them both with a great deal of pleasure. But when she had returned to London after her stay in the country a year before, there had been a subtle difference in their relationship. She had only stayed in town for a few months before again bolting to Somerset, and had not returned until April.

Amelia sat at her dressing table fully clothed when he entered. A sad smile, one he was becoming familiar with, was on her lips. "Hello, John. I'm glad you came tonight."

He placed a chaste kiss on her forehead and took the gold velvet chair nearby. "You look tired, Amelia. I'm not saying you aren't as beautiful as ever! But perhaps tonight is not the night we should choose for our discussion."

"I am tired, John, but I would as soon talk to you." She smiled faintly. "We've been very close over the years, and I hope you will understand that my decision is not because of you. I know I've been contrary for some time and I never meant to be. I certainly never wished to hurt you. It's entirely my fault, and very silly of me besides, but I simply cannot sustain our affair any longer."

Astonished eyes met hers. "You can't?"

"No, I'm sorry. I hope you can forgive me."

The thought occurred to Mr. Hatton that he had been spared a great deal of trouble, but no sooner did it enter his mind than he realized it wasn't possible for him to evade his own responsibilities. He would wish to call on Helena while she resided here, and Amelia would have to know how things stood. "There's nothing to forgive, my dear. I had come tonight to explain the dilemma in which I find myself. You know how deeply I care for you, but I have, all against my own desires, begun to feel a growing attachment for Miss Rogers. It's a little difficult to understand how it could happen, but it has. She is such a unique woman—so talented and intelligent—and her brother's marriage has placed her in a rather awkward position. Don't think I would offer for her because I felt sorry for her! I never would! It's a great deal more than that. I need a wife. I want the companionship that being with someone day and night can bring." He made an expressive gesture with his hands. "The long and short of it is, Amelia, that I've grown to love the girl, with her beautiful white hair and her exquisite drawings and her sheer determination to make the best of whatever life brings her."

Amelia's lips trembled and a touch of moisture glazed her eyes. "Oh, John, I'm so glad for you. She's a lovely girl. I hope she will have you."

"Well, I thought she might if . . . if she didn't know about us. There's nothing unusual in such an arrangement for an unattached gentleman like myself, of course, but I think it would be asking a great deal of her to accept what we've been to each other. If you take my meaning . . ."

Before Amelia could express her agreement, the sounds of commotion began. There was a long, continuous banging on the front door, as of the head of a cane repeatedly struck against that unyielding portal. Amelia jumped to her feet and ran to the window overlooking the front steps. "Oh, my God, it's Felix. He didn't let me know he was coming to town. Oh, dear, you'll not be able to make a retreat, for the servants are even now letting him in. Drat! Would you mind so very much, dear John, hiding in one of the rooms down the hall?"

Mr. Hatton was more than willing to hide anywhere he could find. Never having met Lord Bradwell, he had no wish to do so in his present position. He pressed Amelia's hand before darting out of her room, but already Lord Bradwell's heavy tread could be heard on the stairs and the only thought he could keep in his mind was to slip into one of the rooms along the hall before he was seen. Remembering not to choose Emma's, he pulled open the next door beyond, only to find himself staring at Miss Rogers's fascinated eyes. He cast a panic-stricken glance out into the hall and made as if to leave, but Helena motioned him into the room.

Trapped, he closed the door quietly behind himself as they listened to the sounds of startled greeting down the hall. The voices could be heard for a few minutes before there were sounds of Lord Bradwell and his lady going into her room, closing themselves off from the curious household. Mr. Hatton eyed Helena warily in the wavering light of the candle she had lit when the disturbance began.

"Do sit down, Mr. Hatton," she said quietly, indicating a straight-backed chair near the bed. "I take it you have been with Lady Bradwell."

Seating himself, he gave what might have been considered a nod, if one were watching closely. Helena was. "I see why it would have been impossible for you to call on me here."

"Yes." He searched her face for any sign of anger. "Helena, may I explain?"

She bit her lip, pulled the covers a little higher, and then smiled, if rather shakily. "Please do, Mr. Hatton."

CHAPTER THIRTY-ONE

Since Emma's room did not overlook the front steps, she was not aware of who was causing the terrible commotion that jarred the household. Like Helena, she had lit a candle; in addition, she had risen from her bed to peer out into the hall, just as Mr. Hatton unerringly chose the worst possible door in the whole house. There was no way she could warn him, since her uncle had already reached the head of the stairs. Amelia met him there with fluttering exclamations of her surprise, her pleasure, and her confusion. Before withdrawing into her room, Emma heard her Uncle Felix grumble, "Well, I brought the drawings you wanted. They were far too valuable to send by the post or even with a messenger, so I brought them myself."

Exhausted, she lay down on the bed thinking herself too highly strung ever to get to sleep, but the next thing she knew her maid was shaking her shoulder with more vigor than Emma considered necessary. She opened one sleepy eye, saw that it was still early morning, and muttered, "Go away."

"I can't, miss. He says you're to be in the writing room in fifteen minutes or he's coming up to get you."

Her head still whirling with the previous night's events, Emma frowned. "Who? My uncle? I'm surprised he's even out of bed yet."

"No, miss, Lord Dunn."

The wonderful sense of release that had descended on her the previous evening returned. She grinned at the maid, her eyes sparkling. "Tell him he'll have to come and get me."

"Oh, no, miss, I couldn't do that. Whatever would Lady Bradwell say?"

"Likely she'll never know, Susan. There's a good girl, do what I tell you."

Obviously willing to expostulate further, Susan stayed by the bed until Emma dove under the pillow. When she heard the door close after the girl, she darted to her dressing table to run a comb quickly through her hair before hastily snatching up a shawl and returning to bed. She settled herself against the headboard with the shawl draped carefully over her shoulders to conceal anything the nightdress might leave exposed, and waited.

Not three minutes passed before the door was rudely thrust open and Dunn stalked into the room. He was not the least taken aback that she was still in bed; he probably wouldn't have been alarmed if she had been in the midst of disrobing.

He wore a hastily tied cravat and a prodigious frown. "How the *devil* did you get the idea I was your aunt's lover?" he roared.

"Hush! For God's sake, Dunn, Lord Bradwell arrived during the night and I won't have you bleating your protestations to the world."

"Bleating? Now you listen to me, my girl—" He stopped, arrested by what he had just absorbed. "Lord Bradwell? Here? I don't believe it."

"Nonetheless, it's the truth. He arrived quite unexpectedly late last night. Do you know, he hasn't even a key to the door, or at least he couldn't be bothered to use it. He brought Aunt Amelia the drawings she had requested from Somerset."

"Your bamming me. The man hasn't been in town for twenty years."

"He is now, and I do wish you would keep your voice down. He may not approve of my having a gentleman in my room at this hour of the morning."

"He shouldn't approve of your having a gentleman in your room at any hour," Dunn grunted, looking about him for a chair. When he found none to his liking, he sat down gingerly on the edge of the bed. "It took me hours—hours, Emma—to figure out what you were talking about last night. At first I thought you meant that Amelia would not approve of me as a suitor for you, but that seemed utter nonsense. She has encouraged me all along. And then I thought that perhaps you didn't want to leave her alone, since she has seemed anything but happy recently. The talk of seeing me in the hall was what was so damnably confusing. I could not for the life of me think what hall you referred to, or why it should have made the least difference what hall you saw me in."

"The hall was quite dark at the time," Emma confessed.

"I should hope so, for you never saw me in any hall in this house—

except for the entry hall." He was completely baffled by her lack of interest in his denials. She sat there smiling quite angelically at him. "The reason it took me so long to understand what you meant was because it was such a ludicrous idea. Emma, I am not now and have never been your aunt's lover."

"I know."

"Then what *did* you mean by that piece of flummery last night?"

Emma clasped her hands together in her lap. "Last night I thought you were my aunt's lover and this morning I know you aren't. I happened to see the gentleman in question a little better this time. He does bear a resemblance to you."

Dunn pursed his lips. "Hatton."

She smiled at him as though he were a very bright pupil but said, "I'm afraid I'm not at liberty to disclose his identity."

"Did Lord Bradwell happen to arrive at a particularly inauspicious moment?" he asked doubtfully.

"It could have been worse. The gentleman was forced to take refuge in Miss Rogers's room, which in this particular instance must have been rather awkward for him, since he had just told me he intended to offer for her."

Dunn shook his head in amazement. "I should have loved to be here."

"I wish you had been."

The teasing tone was nicely calculated to return his mind to more important matters. "Do you?" He lifted her clasped hands to his lips. "I still find it difficult to believe you thought I was involved with your aunt."

"Nick did, too. He had seen . . . the other gentleman entering the house one night some years ago. That was why Nick was making such a nuisance of himself when you were . . . paying a little attention to me."

Exasperated, Dunn asked, "And was it why he offered to marry you?"

Emma laughed. "Heaven forbid. He offered to marry me because I am such a desirable catch . . . and because he found me crying one day. I think he's a little vulnerable to tears, but I shouldn't want to have to cry all the time."

"I promise you won't have to," he told her as he drew her to him.

But she put a hand against his chest, suddenly serious. "I . . . I don't know how much you saw. I was very lonely, Dunn. We never . . ."

He placed a finger against her lips. "I can't say I don't care, but I don't want you to tell me. Have you forgotten you are speaking to a man who is written up in a courtesan's memoirs?"

"Her most passionate, gentlest lover." Emma sighed as she received one of his most passionate, gentle kisses. And she could understand the difference Miss Eliza Livingstone had obviously sought to describe. Where there was love, there was more than the simple "lure of the flesh" she had experienced with Nick. There was a wholeness, a rightness, a blending far beyond what she had dared hope. "Oh, Dunn, what a lot of time I've wasted for us."

"We'll make it up, my love."

Emma drew away from him when a discreet tap sounded on the door. "Who is it?"

"Amelia, dear."

"Come in."

If Emma had expected her aunt to look haggard, she was enormously surprised. Amelia entered, cast a curious glance at Dunn, and smiled. She was positively radiant. "I see Susan did not misstate the case. She was worried for your virtue, dear."

"Susan will go far," Emma retorted.

Dunn rose to take Amelia's hand. "I hope you have no objection to my marrying your niece."

"He's a much better catch than Sir Nicholas," Emma interjected.

Her aunt ignored her and kissed Dunn's cheek. "I had begun to think the two of you would never manage on your own. To think of all the times I made such a point of letting you know just which entertainments we were to attend, for all the good it did. Of course, you have my blessing. Did Emma tell you that Felix has come?"

"Yes." He eyed her with interest. "You seem quite pleased about it."

"Pleased? I had nearly despaired of him. When he kicked up such a fuss about my going to London this spring, I was sure everything would be all right, but he's a stubborn man. Look how many weeks it has taken him to follow. Now I ask you, is two months in town so dreadful a fate? He knew I had to see Emma settled. Heavens, now that it's done he will probably expect me to go back with him tomorrow." She gave a little moue of disappointment.

"Surely he will have to stay for the wedding. We'll plan it for the very end of the season," Dunn promised her.

"Excellent. Now I don't wish to sound prudish, Dunn, but I do think you should give Emma a chance to dress." And she floated out of the room without waiting for a response.

"Do you want to get dressed?" he asked her as he resumed his seat on the bed and drew her to him.

It was impossible to answer with his lips on hers, she decided. And she had no wish to answer when his touch made her body warm with desire. His strong, capable hands stroked her hair, her shawl-covered shoulders, her skin. What was it he had asked her? Oh, yes, did she want to get dressed. His lips were now caressing the rapid pulse in her throat and she murmured, "Soon."